A Snake Under
A Thatch

A Snake Under A Thatch

Chike Momah

To order additional copies of this book, contact:
Xlibris Corporation
1-888-795-4274
www.Xlibris.com
Orders@Xlibris.com
46310

Dedication

This book is affectionately dedicated to my grandchildren:
Kyana and Brit;
Ose, Abi, Akhere, and Odion;
and Ama;
and to their parents and grandmother Ethy.

BOOK ONE

CYRIL and ROSEMARY

Chapter I

I LOOKED AT the young man who stood nervously by my daughter's side, and saw myself. The scene could not be more alike, though some twenty-five years had passed since the day I stood in front of Mr. Akamelu.

The memory came flooding back: me, standing uncertainly just behind Rosemary, struggling to find the right words to tell her father that I loved her. I had lost all control over my arms and feet, which seemed to have taken on a life of their own. I could not stand still for longer than a second. And my hands twiddled with the hem of my shirt.

Like Chizube now, Rosemary had been the more courageous of us two, as she declared to her father that I was her boyfriend. I do not recall her exact words, but she left her old man in no doubt that we were serious. If memory serves, I was on the point of explaining just how serious we were, when the old man cut me short, and refused to hear any more. That was the day before I left Nigeria, in April 1974, for my undergraduate studies in the United States of America.

Twenty-five years! But it seemed like only yesterday, as I looked my daughter over. Chizube stood very close to her nervous young man, allowing almost no daylight between them. Her resemblance to her mother is so striking, my Igbo friends say Rosemary practically vomited her. Her face has the same triangular shape as her mother's; and the tone of her skin, her mother's light coffee color. Some people, eager to caress my ego, say she has lips like mine, and her mother affirms that Chizube's smile, which has a certain tremulous, timid quality, always reminds her of mine. That smile, and our daughter's adorableness, had helped keep Rosemary's spirit up during my long, unavoidable absence from them, when I was an unwilling guest of the United States government.

Chizube, now turned nineteen, was about two years younger than her mother was, when, in 1974, we confronted Rosemary's unsmiling father. Like Rosemary and me then, Chizube and her handsome young beau stood before us, arms linked.

"His name is Jacob," Chizube said. "Jacob Bola Akande."

"Oh, my God! Yoruba!" my wife's expression said, as clearly as if she had spoken the words.

Clearly too, Chizube saw what I saw, because she immediately reacted. "Mum, please . . ."

"Chizube," I quickly called out to her, but very softly, and then spoke to her in Igbo. "Easy now. It's okay."

I spoke to her in Igbo, though I did not expect a response from her in our language. I did so because it had become a central policy between her mother and me to always endeavor to speak Igbo at home. But, as so often happens with the children of our Diaspora, they understand the language, but mostly respond in English. Which can sometimes be extremely awkward.

Fortunately now, she knew not to respond verbally to my appeal. It might have been purely instinctive, or perhaps just a good daughterly desire not to needlessly contradict me. More than likely, however, she was, from long habit, familiar with situations such as this, when silence – hers, not mine – is golden, and an unguarded reply in English could give the game away. Or so I thought.

But this was no game. Chizube looked as serious as I had ever seen her. Jacob continued to twiddle with the hem of his *danshiki*, though he still linked arms with my daughter. I watched him for a moment or two, and was struck by the way his eyes roved around the living room. He seemed much taken by the African masks, eight in all, four of which were hugely grotesque if not downright scary, and which hung in matching pairs on the four walls of the room. Two of the more monstrous masks were placed on either side of a large framed photograph of Rosemary and me. I saw Jacob's face break into a smile as his eyes lighted on that odd arrangement. And watching him, I could guess what thoughts went through his mind.

I am not sure why it took me so long. But as I watched my daughter, arm in arm with a young man on whom I had never before set eyes, it struck me for perhaps the first time that Chizube was a grown-up girl. And with that came the frightening realization that she was now old enough to fall in love; and yes, old enough for her heart to be rent by those unfeeling young men whose interest in her might be other than honorable.

She was beautiful, though I say it myself who perhaps shouldn't. At nineteen, going for twenty, she stood almost a head taller than her mother, and was strong and athletic. She did track and field, with some success in the quarter mile. She also loved basketball, though no scouts ever came knocking at our door, which may have been because she was only a sophomore at Rutgers University.

My mind again went back twenty-five years. It had seemed to me crucially important then to more or less declare myself to Rosemary's parents before I traveled to America for who knew how many years. In the upshot, I did not think I scored many points with the old man. And had it not been for Rosemary's courage and aplomb, I would undoubtedly have retreated from his presence with my tail between my legs.

"Jacob Akande," I declared firmly, with half an eye on my wife, "you're welcome to our home."

I could not read the expression on Rosemary's face. There was a light in her eyes that hinted at hostility to the young man who stood meekly before us; hostility, it seemed to me, she was trying valiantly, but with little success, to mask.

"You're in Rutgers too?" she asked plaintively.

"No ma," he answered.

"He's actually in Columbia," chipped in Chizube.

"Chizube, why don't you let him speak for himself?" I heard myself ask.

At that instant, as if drawn by a magnet, Rosemary and I looked at each other, and the half-smile we exchanged was a knowing smile, born of the memory of things long past. Same question, but a different location! But her father's reprimand, though similarly couched, had not doused Rosemary's spirit on that occasion.

Our daughter, who caught our smile but had no clue from whence it came, also smiled – at Jacob, and with what seemed to me deep satisfaction.

"Sorry, Dad."

"And what are you reading at Columbia, young man?"

"I'm in my final premed year, ma."

"Oh!" I said. "You look rather young for someone who's been in college for almost four years. I could have sworn you were still in high school."

He took that as a compliment, and smiled. "That's what people keep telling me, but sir, I'll be twenty-three in about three months."

"That's good."

"Dad, can we sit down?" Chizube asked, fixing me with imploring eyes, head inclined respectfully to one side, and the ghost of a smile playing at the corners of her lips. It was her patented smile, against which I had little or no defense.

"Yes, yes. I'm sorry. Jacob, please make yourself comfortable."

Chizube had not forewarned us that she was bringing a young man to meet us. From Rosemary's reactions to him, I was sure that, like me, she too had been taken by surprise. I did not know that Chizube was dating anybody, though with her looks, it should not really have been a surprise to me.

There was an awkward pause, during which a thousand questions assailed my mind. Where did they meet? And, though God forbid, were they already sexually involved? What did my daughter know about him? Or perhaps more to the point, what did he know about us, *me* in particular?

Out of the corner of my eye I watched as Jacob went quite out of his way to pull up a straight-backed chair from the dining area, adjacent to the sitting room, and placed it, for himself, next to the love seat, behind which he and Chizube had been standing. Momentarily nonplussed by this move, my daughter shrugged her shoulders and went and sat by herself on the love seat, but on the half of it closest to him. Rosemary, who had evidently also observed all this, looked at me and pursed her lips, as if to say: "Well, well!"

The Igbo say that hot soup is best eaten slowly. Clearly Jacob, who chose to sit all by himself, at this first meeting with Rosemary and me, seemed not to want to rush things. And just as clearly, Chizube was raring to get on with it. My interest piqued, I studied the nervous young man as he sat rather modestly, hands clasped tightly and resting on his lap. I think it was at that moment that my heart began to go out to him.

He was tall; a strapping six feet four inches or so, drop-dead handsome as some might say and, for a person of Yoruba ethnicity, rather light complexioned. He was dressed very casually, sporting a light blue cotton *danshiki*, and dark blue jeans that looked like they had seen better days, but probably cost more than their faded, frayed condition might have suggested. He wore his hair very close-cropped, and sprouted a minuscule goatee that I did not much care for. When he smiled, which was not something he did often at that first meeting, his cheeks dimpled. His feet were shod in sandals that looked larger than life, at least size fourteen or fifteen, which was a size I could not recall ever seeing in a shoe store. It occurred to me, as I gazed at them in wonder, that they were probably custom-made.

He looked like a young man of fairly comfortable circumstances. Oddly, that impression was created, not so much by his physical appearance or his clothes – the latter in fact looked quite pedestrian – as by a certain air of graceful ease, and a little *je ne sais quoi* that seemed to envelop him like a cloak, and which his nervousness did not altogether erase.

"Last year premed, you said?" I asked, more to break the awkward pause than because I needed to hear him repeat himself. "And your parents, do they also live here in New Jersey?"

"Er – New York actually, sir," the young man replied, even as he half turned to Chizube, with whom he exchanged a long sustained look.

Rosemary and I also exchanged glances, and I could tell, from the way she fleetingly arched her brows, that she too had noticed that hesitant answer, and the way he had looked at our daughter. But I let that pass, and was forming my next question, when he added:

"I mean my mother, sir. She lives in Queens."

His mother? It was on the tip of my tongue to ask about his dad, when I saw the way my daughter was looking at me. I hesitated, but not only because of that look. I was suddenly mindful of a seemingly nonsensical but aphoristic Igbo question: "If, in answer to your persistent questions, you receive the head of a goat, what will you do with its jaws?" So I desisted, and the moment passed. But I made a mental note to ask Chizube, at a more opportune time, the question her imploring eyes had not allowed me to ask Jacob.

All of a sudden, Chizube got up and turned to Jacob. But before she could get a word out, Rosemary held up an arm to stop her.

"Chizube," she said, and then asked her, in Igbo, "is this visit just a friendly visit, or is there some purpose to it? You did not tell us you were bringing a boy . . ."

"It's my fault actually, ma," said Jacob Akande. "I persuaded her to bring me here so I could meet her parents. She talks so much about you two, I just had to find a way to get to know you . . ."

I forget what else he said, because I was staring at him open-mouthed. So was Rosemary, except that her eyes looked likely to pop out of their sockets any moment. Our daughter was struggling to hide an impish smile that had suffused her face.

Jacob had replied, in English, to Rosemary's question; a question that had been posed to Chizube in *Igbo;* a question he was not supposed to understand, since he is Yoruba. I know I would not have asked Chizube such a question because it is the type of question she would have felt compelled to answer, inevitably in English, and almost certainly to Jacob's hearing. If I absolutely had to ask the question, I think I would have taken Chizube aside, and spoken softly. But Rosemary is not so careful. Women!

"I was born and raised in Enugu," said young Jacob, mindful of our discomfiture. "I also did my elementary and secondary schools in the Enugu area."

He spoke so matter-of-factly, and with such a disarming smile, that my wife visibly relaxed. I remember thinking that the least Chizube could have done was to let us in on the fact that Jacob understood Igbo. She could have done so right from the outset, when she made the introductions. Instead, she stood there, still smiling impishly, as if she was enjoying the spectacle of our embarrassment. "Serves you right!" her expression seemed to be saying.

Rosemary never learns. No matter how frequently she suffers this type of embarrassment, she never learns. I know I have told her, times without number, to be more guarded in using our language when she thinks the object of her comments does not understand Igbo. But does she ever listen? Not if her life depends on it! I never give up trying. But she never learns. She and I, and some of our friends, have swapped stories of similar scenarios. There was the case of an Englishman that I ran into in a part of Nigeria where few people spoke Igbo. This English gentlemen had done nothing to arouse my hostility other than that he was pink-skinned, and belonged to a race that had colonized my country. As he walked by, I ripped into him with a nice choice of the most inelegant Igbo words that sprang to my mind, and mouth. The fellow stopped, turned to me and, speaking in accented but precise Igbo, told me he had heard what I said. *"Dalu,"* he ended, and turned and walked away. And as he did so, to my mortification, he seemed to walk with added buoyancy in his stride. That day, I learnt my lesson.

"You went to a secondary school in Enugu?" I asked Jacob. "Which one?"

"College of the Immaculate Conception, sir."

"The famous C.I.C.," I said unnecessarily. Embarrassment sometimes makes me garrulous.

"Oh, so you're a Catholic?" Rosemary asked evenly.

Rosemary has this maddening gift of recovering fast from her embarrassments, certainly much faster than I. It never seems to matter that the awkwardness may have been caused by *her* faux pas, not mine. Her embarrassment is only fleeting and, very quickly, all's well again with the world. I have often found myself bearing the burden of her guilt, just as the Igbo maxim has it, that the relatives of a thief suffer more mortification on his account than the miscreant himself.

"Chizube, you've offered our guest nothing," I suddenly asked.

"I know, dad. I was about to do just that when mum . . ."

"So ask him," I quickly interrupted, eager to lay the ghost of her mother's faux pas.

"I know what he likes. Bola, a shandy as usual?"

"Please," said the young man, exchanging sweet smiles with my daughter.

She went to the kitchen and soon reappeared with a bottle of beer, two cans of ginger ale and two glasses, on a round tray. She did not ask her mother or me if we, too, could use a drink, which was something she usually did, if we had guests. Why she overlooked us this time, I could not imagine. But then again, we had never before played hosts to a young man she brought to our home to introduce to us. Besides, it was early afternoon, on an April Saturday of glorious sunshine, but with the temperature only in the low 60's. Not exactly conditions to make one thirsty. She may also have noticed, though she had as yet done nothing about it, that the kitchen sink was cluttered with evidence of a recent midday meal.

"What about something to snack on?" Rosemary asked.

"Oh ma, not to bother," said Jacob very softly.

Because he had spoken softly, I pretended I had not heard him. I happened to be sitting, in my king's chair, in front of a big commode, and within easy reach of the compartment in which we had an assortment of snacks. I half-turned, reached for and opened the compartment door, and produced a packet of shortbread cookies (the more tasty British, not the American, variety), and a can of mixed nuts. I suspected young Jacob would not be able to resist these delicacies. He could not, and was soon tucked in.

"You're a Catholic?" my wife asked again, but this time in Igbo, and with a smile that acknowledged her previous gaffe.

We were not prepared for the manner of his reply, which he spoke in Igbo that was so good – intonation, accent and all – that a native speaker of the language would have been hard put to it to improve on it. Sure, he said a word here and there in English. But that was all right. Even those for whom Igbo is the mother tongue often and unashamedly lapse into that kind of linguistic heresy.

"I'm not really a Catholic, though I often went with my mother to the Catholic Church. Looking back now, I think she was – how to put it – rather confused. Her own mother was an Anglican, but her father was a Catholic. I myself went to an Anglican primary school."

The conversation drifted somewhat after this, and soon, my mind began to wander. As I contemplated young Bola Akande and my daughter, I suppose my mind went back to the days of my youth in Enugu, especially to my first meeting with Rosemary, in the parlor of my father's house. And from that contemplation, and those memories, my mind was filled with remembrances of my first years in America, when I was a student at Rutgers University, and the world seemed so innocent and my future so rosy. Then dark clouds descended on those halcyon days, and the next I knew, I was embroiled in a mind-bending situation that I had not seen coming and certainly had no clue whatsoever how to confront or deflect.

I went into a daydream, as a myriad of thoughts chased one another fleetingly across my mind. This was a habit I had picked up when time weighed heavily on me, during the many years of my incarceration. An incarceration for a crime I did not commit. Through the eight years of that confinement, I had seized every opportunity that came my way to protest my innocence. Unfortunately for my credibility, more than half of my fellow inmates were just as insistent on their innocence as I was.

I threw my head back, and stretched out my legs the farthest they could go, as I struggled to relax my mind and body. Some thirteen years had passed since my release from captivity. A captivity that had stretched out like a never-ending nightmare! If you have not walked in my shoes, you probably will never understand what it feels like to be incarcerated. I was like a caged animal whose every activity – sleeping, waking, eating, working out, and even moments of idleness, when one could just sit in the open air and stare "as long as sheep and cows" – was controlled by jailers whose powers over me were so absolute they were almost omnipotent. And as if that was not bad enough, I literally had to walk the finest of lines to avoid being badly used by other inmates. There were, indeed, moments when the terror engendered by a handful of inmates was worse than anything the jailers did, or threatened to do.

They were years I am not likely ever to forget, even if I live to be as old as Methuselah, the patriarch of patriarchs who, in biblical mythology, lived for 969 years. How could I? How does one forget a total eclipse of some of the best years of one's life, a nightmarish darkness into which one had been pushed by the chicanery and perfidy of one's best friend?

He really was my best friend, was Bernard Ekwekwe, unless I do not understand what best friend means. Bernard was the one person with whom I enjoyed – or thought I did – a mutual affection that might have rivaled the legendary friendship between the biblical David and Jonathan. We were like brothers.

Someone touched me lightly on the shoulder. I must have been in a trance because, when I looked up, I thought I was looking into the eyes of a goddess of surpassing beauty. Coming instantly fully awake, I saw that it was my daughter. The expression in Chizube's eyes was so loving and tender that my face broke in a smile.

"Dad," she said softly, "you're wandering off again."

"I was, wasn't I?" I said, and then noticed that Jacob too was on his feet. "What's going on? Don't tell me you're leaving."

"Sorry, dad. We must."

"But it's only six o'clock. What about supper?"

"Which supper, dad? Is that the one we eat at 8 or even 9?"

"Of course it's early," said Rosemary, and then turned to Jacob. "We haven't yet learnt to eat like the Americans."

"I know, ma," said Jacob. "They have their supper at 5 o'clock, latest 6. But that's all right really. In any case, I have a lot of catching up to do for my exams. It's crunch time now."

Chizube suddenly knelt by my side, flung her arms round my neck, and rubbed her cheek against mine. She does that sometimes, but always unpredictably, knowing what joy and solace it gives me. Especially, as now, when my heart was heavy with remembrance of things best forgotten.

"I love you, dad," she said. "Bola will come again. That's if it's all right with you guys."

That is what she often calls us: you guys. I never enjoyed the easy familiarity with my parents that would have emboldened me to call them guys. Come to think of it, I do not believe I knew such a word – in English or Igbo – when I was growing up. But the young today are a different generation, and I suppose Chizube gets away with it because we let her. Of course we objected, firmly at first. Latterly, however, our objection has been mostly muted. Mine especially. Indeed there are times when I think I give the impression that I enjoy it. But, in the final analysis, Chizube is a loving daughter, and nearly always very respectful.

"He's welcome," I said, glancing at my wife. Rosemary smiled in agreement.

Chizube put her mouth next to my ear. "Remember, dad," she whispered, "mum and I are here for you when you get into these moods. You're always telling me that mum is your angel."

"You too," I whispered back.

"Thanks, but I'm talking about mum. She'll take good care of you. You know she always does. And everything will be all right."

"What are you two whispering about?" Rosemary asked, feeling, I supposed, left out.

Chizube quickly stood up. "Nothing, mum. Come Bola, let's go."

At the door, she stopped, turned, and looked around her as if she was missing something. "It's been unusually quiet around here. Where's he?"

"Where else?" her mother asked. "It's warm, and there's still plenty of daylight. Why do you look for the living among the dead?"

"The village park, of course!" said Chizube. "Come Bola. Don't mind my mum. She says things like that sometimes. Let's go look for him there. I want you to meet the little devil."

The 'little devil' was my daughter's affectionate name – one of a few actually – for her brother Ndubisi, as irrepressible a seven-year old as I have seen. I know she loves him to death, and seems unable to let him be. Apropos of which, I had no doubt that her eagerness to introduce Bola to Ndubisi had a major purpose. Not to put too fine a point upon it, she wanted her brother's approval of her boy friend. Whenever Chizube has been home from her college dormitory, at weekends and vacations, and suchlike, I have watched, with a mixture of wonder and enchantment, the interactions between them. Of all the things we might have done for Chizube, I believe that the greatest was giving her a brother, just when she was beginning to think that her mother and I had decided to leave her without a sibling.

Chapter II

THE OPTIMISM OF youth! Everything was *not* all right. But Chizube was right on one point: Rosemary was – still is – my angel. Through my darkest moments, when it seemed as if nothing was going right for me, she was there for me, always comforting, hardly ever complaining, a bulwark against the forces that threatened from time to time to overwhelm me. But she had her moments of doubt. Who wouldn't?

There were times I wallowed in self-pity, which was the one thing she would not stand for. But for the most part, when she told me to snap out of it, she did so in a manner that let me hang on to *some* self-respect. And did she not carry our child – conceived in an unguarded moment of delirium while I was on bail prior to my incarceration – to full term? She might well have terminated the pregnancy. And who would have blamed her, considering how things were with me? If Rosemary came to the prison for perhaps a hundred visits, she must have come with Chizube at least two out of every three visits. Which helped me bond with my daughter to a degree I had not imagined possible.

And she married me! Against all odds, and in the teeth of strong opposition by her father, she married me. I never got to know how her mother felt about it all. Some women of her generation tend to keep a low profile in such matters, particularly if their husbands loudly carry the fight to the 'enemy'. The old man lashed out at me, and I could scarcely blame him. What father wants his daughter to marry an ex-convict?

Perhaps my sister Adaku had a little something to do with Rosemary marrying me. They had been friends from their high school years in Queens School, in Enugu, and had maintained a steady stream of correspondence with each other through the two or so years of their separation. Enugu was my city, the town in which I grew up and lived my life as a boy and a young man. That is, until my cousin Aloysius Jideofo, M.D., invited me to the United States for my college studies. Enugu was also my friend Bernard Ekwekwe's city. But Bernard's is another story.

Adaku came to America in mid-1982, about two years into my incarceration. That was definitely not the way I had envisaged her coming to this country. It had been my intention to bring her over, as Aloysius had brought me, and as Rosemary's uncle Frank Akamelu had brought her; but only after I would have become financially able to do so. In the event, destiny stepped in, and two things happened: Bernard's treachery blighted my life; and a young Igbo doctor, a slight acquaintance during my college years in Rutgers University, went home to Nigeria in search of a wife, and found my sister Adaku.

Adaku arrived in America as Mrs. Theophilus Agu. Perhaps my sister's buxom beauty was her main attraction in Theo's eyes. But I doubt she was attracted to him by any consideration of *his* physical attributes. If you had no reason to look closely at him, he was the type of person you could easily miss in a crowd. And I have seen more prepossessing faces. But if you took a second look, you would have to admit that he had some kind of a presence. Barely an inch taller than Adaku, who was herself only marginally taller than average for a girl, Theo nevertheless carried himself with quiet assurance. And he was fast becoming one of the better known and admired doctors in the Nigerian communities of the Eastern seaboard of the United States.

Although I became aware, through Rosemary, of what was afoot between Adaku and Theo during their very brief courtship, Adaku did not ask me what I thought, though Rosemary informed her that I knew Theo in college. I found myself wondering if perhaps she did not want to ask me about him because she was concerned I might remind her of her strong predilection for men of a certain height. That was what she often told me, in the days of our innocence: that tall and imposing men had an allure that was denied to shorter men.

She had an opportunity to put that matter to rest when, within days of her arrival in the country, she came to the prison with Rosemary, but without her husband. I seized the moment, but without malice, to make some disparaging remarks about Theo's physiognomy and his lack of height.

"Don't our people say," Adaku countered, "that men are never ugly? I've learnt that quite a while ago. Theo's a good man. And that's all that matters to me."

That, I said to myself, plus the fact that Theo is a doctor, and lives in America. America! God's own country! The country whose roads are paved with gold! The land flowing with milk and honey! I really could not blame my sister even if her sole reason for accepting his proposal was the opportunity it offered her to escape from the hellhole that Nigeria had become. And anyway, I thought wretchedly, who was I to judge? Was I not desperately clinging to the hope that, after my incarceration, Rosemary would still find it in her heart to marry me, notwithstanding everything that had happened to me, not to talk of my almost ugly face, and much besides?

Rosemary and I talked endlessly about the child forming in her womb. She told me about pressures on her to abort it, but would not reveal from whence the pressures came. When I speculated that it might be her dad, she replied proudly that her parents' religious convictions would never let them think such thoughts. It was then that she said something that astonished me, and that sent me into such paroxysms of delight I temporarily forgot where I was.

"I'm glad," she said, "that what happened between us happened. Now I have a piece of you in my womb, and nothing will happen to it until it comes to full term."

"So help us God!" I added, crossing myself in supplication.

I will not likely ever forget the first moment I took Chizube into my arms. I forget how old she was then, perhaps three months. I was surprised I could wait that long before seeing my baby girl. It was not easy. But I think I came to terms with the wait because, of course, it seemed like a blink of an eye compared to the eight long years of my incarceration.

She was an absolutely gorgeous baby, though then she was a little inclined to cry at the slightest provocation. Perhaps her baby instincts told her she was in an environment of misery and sorrow. But on that first day of such pure joy as I had never before known, I clasped Chizube to my bosom, and would not let her mother take her from me until the wrenching moment of their departure. Or when she needed to have her nappies changed.

There were times, perhaps inevitably, when it seemed to me that Rosemary was hesitant. About me, and what the future portended for us. They were not happy times for me. Her uncertainty was like hell to me. I can tell of nights when I lay awake on my bunk, not sleeping a wink, worried to the core of my soul that Rosemary was wavering in her steadfastness to me. There were days when I was so caught up in the dread of a miserable future without her that I walked about like a zombie, scarcely acknowledging my fellow convicts, even those who went out of their way to be friendly. At such times, when I was able to snatch some sleep, I had dreams – nightmares actually – in which I would see my Rosemary coupled with some dashing young man or the other, dancing and smooching. I could go on and tell of other miseries that my tortured mind inflicted on me. But what would be the use? It is not everything that the palm-wine tapper sees from the top of the palm tree that he recounts to the world.

My sister Adaku, fortunately for me, arrived in the United States during one of the worst periods of my despondency. She really picked me up, from her very first visit to the jailhouse. For the first several years of my incarceration, that was what it was to me: a jailhouse. During those years, I found it difficult to come to terms with the – to me – mockery of a trial to which I was subjected. I preferred to think of myself as a suspect still awaiting a real trial. In the event, the villain got away, and I was put away for *his* crime, and served the term imposed on me. But I know that on the Day of Judgment, at the bar of the Almighty, if not at the overrated bar of public opinion, I will be cleared. And then my friend will answer fully for what he did to me. I believe in God.

Adaku wept when she first set eyes on me. But she wept so quietly that if you were not watching her, you would not, for a while, have noticed. I watched her helplessly, knowing I could do, or say, nothing to console her. After a while, Rosemary put an arm round her shoulders, and drew her close.

A jailer stood hard by, but he did not exist for me. Not then, at any rate. Adaku did. Her sibling love and concern for me shone so brightly, even in her tear-stained face, it lit up the miserable room in which we were.

I was amazed at the effect of her tears. They flowed so freely, that I felt as if I bathed in them, and they washed me free – of my guilt, which was really no guilt; only my stupidity in being so naïve and trusting that I misread all the signs that should have put me on the alert against the machinations of the devil. I paid the price. Now, too late, I have learnt my lesson.

Looking at the two friends, one my sister, the other my girl friend and mother of my daughter, I learnt something else. They both loved me. But there was a difference in their love. Rosemary's was at once passionate and all consuming but variable, depending on the swings of her mood. Adaku's was as simple as nature, and contingent on nothing, being – as the Bard might have put it – as constant as the Northern Star.

I knew I could tell Adaku anything, and that if I needed her help, she would do her utmost for me. Which was why, when Rosemary excused herself and went to the women's room, I seized the opportunity with both hands, and poured out my soul to my sister.

"Rosemary and I are going through a difficult patch now," I said, very softly. "It seems her parents –"

"I know," she said.

"You do?"

"Of course," said Adaku. "Rose hides nothing from me. She's told me her parents are pressing her to – well – sort of – leave you. And when I asked about the child, she said her father didn't seem to care. You know how it is with our people. Parents usually do everything possible to ensure that the man who does to their daughter – er – what you did to Rose, must do the right thing, and marry her. But not this time, it appears."

"Can't say I blame them," I said reflectively. "Look what I got myself into. What parent wants that kind of permanent stain to the family name? I'm afraid Rosemary will sooner or later give up on me. You know, she hasn't been to see me for quite some time, and it's only because of you that she's here today. She didn't even bring Chizube. Instead someone's baby-sitting her now, and that costs good money."

Adaku looked keenly at me for a long moment, and then took and pressed my hand. "Don't worry," she said. "There's nothing new in any of this. You know what our people say, that it is only an animal that one has never before killed, that one doesn't know how to cut up for the soup. Let me talk with my friend, and we'll see how it goes. You remember I was with her that first day you two met in Enugu, and you went kind of crazy over her. And she's told me so many wonderful things about you two since she came to America –"

I think she might have seen the expression on my face, and stopped and smiled.

"Yes, I know what you're thinking. But where you are now doesn't make any difference to her. I cannot believe she'll just go and leave you. I know how she feels about you."

"You mean, felt."

"Did I say you shouldn't tell others what I said?" Adaku asked rhetorically. "I know what I said: how she *feels* about you."

Our conversation ended abruptly because just then I sensed, rather than saw, Rosemary reenter the room. Adaku and I had been sitting with our backs to the door leading to the restrooms. But the moment Rosemary passed through that door, I knew it. It was as if I had somehow sprouted eyes at the back of my head. Which, I suppose, is what prison life can sometimes do to you.

I was lucky I did not have to receive my visitors across a wire mesh, or a glass pane, using a telephone for communication. I was never sure why I was accorded this privilege, which was denied to several of my fellow inmates. But of course God works in mysterious ways and, who knows, might have led the prison authorities into *some* awareness of my innocence.

Adaku might also have sensed Rosemary's reentry because, wordlessly, she again reached for and held my hand, which I had let lie idle on the square table by which we were sitting. She gave the hand a reassuring squeeze for a moment or two, and then let go, and the sparkle and smile in her eyes, as she squeezed my hand, said it all. I knew I had nothing to worry about.

But of course I worried. It may have been illogical, but I worried. It was not easy for me to sit in my prison cell and not worry. The days, the years, stretched out endlessly, nightmarishly, before my eyes. I was full of horrendous thoughts. About everything. About what might be my fate, with each passing day, within the unscalable walls of my prison. There were inmates who looked as if they could as easily slice my throat as cut the wretched piece of meat on their dinner plate. Several of the jailers looked as hard as nails; and were. They needed to be, or some of the inmates would probably have tried to take advantage of them.

I worried about what real prospects I would have, when released, to land a meaningful job in accounting, which had been my major when I graduated *cum laude* from Rutgers University in May 1978. How could I satisfactorily answer the probing questions I would be asked by a prospective pot-bellied, fat-arsed employer, eyes bulging with suspicion, and more than likely a white American? How explain away the eight years of my peculiar and utter darkness, a lacuna in a resume that I could never really hope to paper over? And if I dared to tell the truth, the whole truth, and nothing but . . . , about the time I did in a Federal joint, what employer would want to employ me?

A lawyer friend, no doubt eager to lift my spirits, once told me about a law against discrimination in hiring. And when I asked him if that law extended to ex-convicts, I think his answer was an emphatic yes. If I sound unsure of this, it is perhaps because the conversation took place soon after my release, when my head was still in the clouds, so to say, and a lot of what people said to me went into one ear and exited from the other. So, perhaps I could sue an employer who would not give me a job? But is that any way to seek employment? In these United States? For an African, worse still a Nigerian who, in the eyes of the public, belongs to what a noted American General once undiscriminatingly branded a nation of scammers? A Nigerian that, at the point of incarceration, did not have any enabling papers for residency, not to talk of citizenship!

Apropos of which, the same good lawyer also told me that the Immigration and Naturalization Service, that most potent arm of the United States Department of Justice, deports persons like me just as soon as we are released from prison. No questions asked. And no appeals. No doubt, in my case, American justice has been tempered with mercy. For the moment, at any rate.

All that aside, I kept asking myself, over and over again, how reasonable it was for me to hope that my Rosemary would put her life aside on my account, and wait, and wait, for my release, so we could pick up the shreds of our battered, mangled lives. There were moments I thought the only manly thing to do was to release her from her promise, made to me on the day of her first visit to the prison. But I lacked the courage to do so. The searing thought of losing her, out of some outmoded sense of chivalry, was more than I could bear.

On that first visit, I could barely look her in the eye. I was overwhelmed by my sense of guilt. Guilt that I had let her, and myself, down. And not only the two of us, but my benefactors, cousin Aloysius Jideofo and his good wife Obiamaka. My parents, and hers too, in Nigeria. Her father had struggled to tolerate my immature, bumbling efforts to give advance notice of my budding relationship with his daughter. I had no doubt whatsoever, as I mulled my situation in my prison cell, that for Mr. Akamelu, I had blotted my copybook. Permanently! Could anything be worse than to be jailed for drug trafficking, except murder? Perhaps not even murder.

We sat opposite each other, across a small rectangular table, on which she placed her black imitation leather handbag, and her bunch of keys. That was not how I wanted us to sit. She could have sat by my side. I had wanted her to sit by my side. But she elected not to.

"That guard frightens me," she said, pointing surreptitiously to a superbly built jailer who stood by the door of the visitors' room, stiffly erect, eyes roving from corner to corner, seeing all, but saying nothing. He frightened me too. "I think he'll be less suspicious if he sees us like this."

Rosemary initially spoke little, other than to tell me that her uncle, Mr. Frank Akamelu, Civil Engineer, sent his greetings and best wishes. Rosemary lived with his family in Washington, D.C., where she did her undergraduate studies in Howard

University. I could not blame her for her taciturnity. What was there to talk about? I myself was tongue-tied too because, at that early stage of my incarceration, all I could think about was how unjust life was, and what the hell did I do to deserve being where I found myself? Those were not the happiest topics of conversation between my girl and me. Or anybody else for that matter.

Rosemary seemed content to just gaze at me. She was pensive, which was all right with me because I too was pensive. From time to time we held each other's hands. Once or twice, doing so, I caught her peeking at the ramrod guard, as if she feared he might raise objections to our innocent petting.

It was towards the end of that first visit that she spoke the words that have remained carved indelibly on my mind and memory.

"You should not be here," she said, waving an arm around her to take in the entire room where we were, and much else beyond it. "They had no right to put you here. You know it, and I know it. Your friend Bernard knows it too. That's why I'm asking you to never give up on yourself. Are you listening? You can't reject yourself just because society seems to have rejected you. You can't give up on us – you and me. There'll be dark days. That's almost inevitable. But I want you to know this. We'll see it through together, you and me."

At her words, my head jerked up. She noticed it; noticed too the way I was gazing at her as if her words were utterly incomprehensible to me.

"Yes, Cyril, you and me. You will be physically alone here. I know that. But I also know that I will always feel as if I am here with you, suffering what you suffer, feeling the pain you feel, crying when you cry, and sometimes even when you are not crying. You see, unlike you, I'll not be ashamed to cry when I feel like it."

She gave an extra squeeze to my hand. She spoke mostly in our Igbo language, though sometimes she lapsed into English. As she spoke, she looked steadily at me, and with an intensity that caused me to waver and to look away from her.

"Cyril, please look at me when I speak," she begged in a voice that sounded like a command. So I raised my eyes to hers. "Good, because I want to make you this promise, and I don't want you to be in any doubt that I mean every word I say. You may –"

I put up an arm and stopped her, because I had a sense of what she was about to say. "Rosemary," I said quickly, "you know you don't have to make me any promises. This is your first visit here, and I'm afraid I'm going to be here a long, long time. No one knows what God plans –"

"If there's a God," she cut in, "He should not have let this happen to us. And if there's a God, perhaps you may be let out after a short while –"

"Or perhaps not," I said. "Please don't blame God for what I'm suffering now. And don't talk as if you've lost faith in Him."

Rosemary smiled sadly, making a guttural sound that came from deep in her throat and belly. "I still believe in God," she said slowly. "And as He's my witness, I promise you I'll never leave you. It doesn't matter how long you stay here, one year or eight years. I'll wait."

"Rosemary," I said, struggling to articulate my thoughts, as a big lump lodged itself in my throat. "You don't have to say things you may be unable to do. Why should you? You are only human. Why do you think you need to tell me this now? Let's wait for some time, and see how –"

"Cyril, shut up! Can't you see why I'm telling you all this? Don't you know it's because, well, there's nobody else I'd rather spend my life with than you?"

Our eyes held, steady, for some moments, and then she looked down. In those few seconds, as I gazed into her eyes, I saw something I had never before seen in them. I saw fire. Her eyes sparkled with quite unusual intensity. There was defiance and, for her, some kind of dare-devilry. There must have been fire in her belly as she spoke the words that, I think, surprised even her. When she looked down, it seemed to signal that her force was spent.

I reached out and put a finger under her chin, and lifted up her head so that, once more, we were looking into each other's eyes. "I love you, Rosemary," I said. "I'm really sorry to have to put you through all this."

"Don't worry too much," she replied. "I love you too."

I cannot explain what happened next, but my head fell forward, involuntarily, and came to rest on my arms on top of the table. I stayed like that for a long moment, as my emotions cartwheeled uncontrollably. When finally I raised my head and looked at Rosemary across the table, her face and her eyes were smiling at me.

I was surprised she could smile, given the solemnity of the occasion. But I knew why she did so. And, to judge by the twinkle in her eyes, she too knew it. The simple fact was that, in the close to seven or eight years of our friendship, this was the first time she had spoken the words.

"I love you."

She said it so simply, so naturally, I was amazed at the effect the words had on me. There was a sweet sound to it, and I knew the sweetness had nothing to do with any artfulness. She certainly chose the best, and the worst, moment to tell me she loved me. But she knew, she must have known, the impact those words would have. She must have known, or guessed, that the words would lift my spirits up wonderfully, would chase away – temporarily at least – the lowering clouds that were blighting my life, and would give me something to forever hope for, at the very beginning of my incarceration.

The problem for me, of course, was that the very words that brought sweet solace to my tortured mind, as I began my confinement, were sure to keep me on tenterhooks thereafter, wondering, always wondering, if Rosemary would be able to remain steadfast in her love through my many years behind bars.

As any mere mortal would, she wavered now and again. I knew, because I could tell from those subtle changes of demeanor that might have been unobserved by a mere acquaintance, and from even the way she sometimes looked at me as we talked, that she was under strong emotional distress. She would become a little distant, and easily distracted. But in the final analysis, thank God, she remained constant in her love for me. And through it all, from the moment she reappeared in my life, my sister Adaku would not let me lose hope. I did my best to hide my fears from Rosemary. But on the rare occasions when I was alone with Adaku, I let it all – as Americans say – hang out. And she was always ready with an encouraging word or two, assuring me that Rosemary would never let me down.

"How d'you know?"

"I just know."

I lost count of how many times I asked that question, and got her unchanging answer, on which she would not elaborate further. "You're my brother," she would say. "There's no way I can sit by and let bad things happen to you."

To this day, I do not know exactly what my sister did to encourage Rosemary to stay on course with me. I know she did not wave a magic wand, or waste her breath unduly singing my praises to her friend. The former would have been inutile; and the latter would have worn thin in very short order. But this I know: Adaku stayed close to Rosemary.

That was not difficult for her. She and her husband Theo lived in the state of Maryland, in a little town called Laurel, about a half hour drive to Washington, D.C., where Rosemary was entering her junior year in Howard University, at the time of Adaku's arrival. In the Laurel Regional Hospital, Theo worked as a Pediatrician, and Adaku as a Registered Nurse. She got a job there easily, with her Bachelor of Science (Nursing) degree from the University of Ibadan, in Nigeria, and her Maryland board certification, which she obtained within a half-year of her coming to America.

Adaku baby-sat one-year old Chizube as often as her work schedule allowed her. On occasion, she even took Chizube to her Laurel home, a semi-detached house in Cottonwood Terrace, which both Adaku and Rosemary described as an elegant estate of the affluent middle class.

The two friends reconnected, and stayed connected, as best friends often do. And they did so more intensely than might otherwise have been the case, because circumstances took them out of their homeland and brought them together in a foreign land. It is in a foreign land, as the saying goes, that we are most our brother's (and sister's) keepers.

I reaped the benefit of their strong connectedness, even if Adaku had not deliberately planned it so. She told me she put in a good word for me now and then, though I am convinced that was only a very small part of it. What mattered most was the tightness of their friendship, which, in a manner I cannot explain, was extremely salutary for Rosemary and me.

Perhaps I am over rationalizing things, but that was the way it looked to me. But no matter! On the day I stood before the Registrar of marriages, and joined my life to Rosemary's till death, the only witnesses we had were Adaku and Theophilus. Not my benefactors Obiamaka and Aloysius Jideofo; and decidedly not Rosemary's uncle, Frank Akamelu and his wife Nwamaka.

The truth was that we could not, for the best of all possible reasons, let any one of them know what we were up to. We did not elope, but it was as if we did. Rosemary's father's intransigence, in his refusal to give me the hand of his daughter in marriage, settled the matter. If I was ever going to marry the girl of my dreams, I had no other option than to do so in secret. Happily for me, Rosemary said: "Let's do it!"

And we did. On a Wednesday of mild sunshine, in the middle of June 1992, with twelve-year old Chizube happily sandwiched between us, we did it. I remember that the Judge, who married us, recited some of the same words of advice that I had regularly heard from priests at church weddings. It made me feel good, though I would have much preferred that we had wedded in church.

Perhaps, who knows, we might yet do so: on our tenth anniversary, which is just around the corner, or our twenty-fifth. That seems to be the developing trend in our Igbo communities, here in the United States, for couples who, for whatever reasons, did not wed *in church*. They celebrate the anniversary as a church wedding, presumably so they can at last feel *properly* married, and the wife gets to wear her white bridal gown, with all the trimmings. And so that some of their friends will desist thenceforth from accusing them of living in sin.

Chapter III

I SUPPOSE ONE could say that Rosemary and I lived in sin, up to the moment of our registry wedding. Within a month of my release from the penitentiary, I had moved in with Rosemary and Chizube. Chizube was seven years old then, or as close to it as makes no difference.

Cousin Aloysius and his wife gave me shelter during that month. But it quickly became clear to them, and to me, that I could not live with them. They did the best they could to dissuade me from moving out, particularly seeing I had not as yet found a job. But through it all, I had a strong suspicion that they were merely going through the motions. Their concern, however, became less perfunctory when I disclosed to them that I was moving in with Rosemary.

"Her father," Aloysius warned, "will be mad with you, that's both of you, when he hears this. Are you sure you're prepared for his anger?"

"Tell you the truth," I confessed, "I'm not sure. I suppose it depends on Rosemary herself."

"But that's not fair to her," Obiamaka protested.

Fair? Mrs Jideofo evidently forgot she was talking to me. She knew, but perhaps forgot, that she was talking to a person who had, for eight long years, lived out the utter hollowness and meaninglessness of that over-abused word. For eight nightmare years, I had fought an endless battle with myself to be on my guard, and not to over-react, when words like *fair* were hurled at me. It was a word I had frankly heard only infrequently in the often tense and raw environment of my prison, where many worked the system for what they could get out of it, and few worried about the ethics of what they were doing.

I immediately brought my emotion under control, and even smiled at Mrs. Jideofo. I had little choice, anyway, than to bring my emotion under control.

"You're probably right," I said to her. "Perhaps it isn't fair to leave everything to Rosemary. But what else can I do? It isn't as if, at this stage, I would dare go – ."

"And speak to her parents?" asked Aloysius. "No, I don't think it would be a good idea. And you know of course you dare not leave these shores, or you'll never be able to get back here. I guess what I'm trying to say is, lie low for the moment, and let's see how this thing works itself out. If you expose yourself by setting up a family unit with your daughter and her mother, it may be the worst move you can make at this juncture."

But what else was there to do? I knew I had to be careful, at least until I had a clearer idea of what the I.N.S. would do to me. I was well aware that persons who had no legal papers to reside in this country often played a cat-and-mouse game with the authorities. But I did not want to do that. All my instincts rebelled against the idea. I had a feeling, born of my recent past, that my luck would run out just as soon as I got into that game. I had done nothing involving moral turpitude, or that was legally wrong, and I still wound up in prison for an unconscionably long time. So why would I think that, as a fugitive on the run, my luck would change?

I thought long and deeply about my situation, and decided that, NO! I would not hide. I had to assume that the INS, vigilant as ever, knew that I had been released from prison. So, if that agency wanted to forcibly repatriate me to Nigeria, there was precious little I could do to stop them. Except that perhaps, in this most democratic of countries, where human rights have their loudest and profoundest expression, I might be able to find a court that would be willing to hear my appeal against the INS, and a lawyer that would handle my case for a bag of peanuts.

But I also strongly believed, with my people, that the gods chase away the flies that harass a tailless cow. And that whatever destinies put this skunk into my hands would provide the water with which to wash them clean of the stench. I decided to try to live as normal a life as my circumstances allowed me.

My resume was skimpy in the extreme because my world had turned on its head even before I was able to take up my first accounting job, after my college graduation. And it had that gaping eight-year hole that was sure to catch the eye of even the most incurious employer. I could not, realistically, believe that I would get anything from the accounting firm that had offered me a job in Washington, D.C. a few months after I got my degree. That firm was Gable, Kline and Stevens, Inc.

The memory of their job offer now flooded my mind. It would have been a groundbreaking job for me. In the solitude of my prison cell, I had often spoken their name, letting the words roll off my tongue easily, but with a poignant regret that what they had held out to me had turned out to be beyond my reach.

Rosemary was, at the time of our wedding, a social worker in Washington, DC. She had graduated from Howard University, Bachelor of Science in Sociology, in 1984.

Two years later, she took her Masters Degree. That was the year before my release from jail in 1987. Her uncle, Frank Akamelu, had insisted that she not interrupt her studies, after her first degree. So she had worked straight through to her Masters. He had even wanted her to go on to her Doctorate, but she had declined.

"That's almost criminal," I told her. "If I'd had such an opportunity, I would have grasped it with both hands. Why the hell didn't you – ?"

"Do what, C.Y.?" She had latterly begun to call me C.Y. It sounded affectionate, so I let her. "What will I do with it? Have I ever told you or anybody that I want to teach in a university? We have more important things to look forward to – ."

"Such as?" I asked, smiling.

My smile told her it was not a serious question, and that I only wanted to hear her say what I knew she would say. Her return smile told me she knew, but she said it anyway.

"In another what – ten or so months, you will be a free man," she said. "Now, that's something really worth looking forward to. Not a Ph.D." Then she added seriously: "You'd better look out then."

"Why? You think something bad might happen to me, or what? Perhaps the INS?"

"None of the above," she said calmly. "It's me you have to worry about. I just might eat you up, or something."

"Which just goes to show that great minds think alike," I said seriously.

Those were the very same thoughts that had begun to crowd other thoughts out of my mind, for quite some time, as my V-day approached. I had become somewhat prone to exaggerated flights of fancy about what might happen between Rosemary and me after my release. It had gotten so bad that I knew I was in some danger of losing the self-control I desperately needed to see me through the remaining year of my agony.

I do not know about other prisoners. But as my freedom neared, Rosemary's visits became less comforting, and more tantalizing. I was near her. Near enough to touch her, which I often did. But I was not with her; certainly not in the sense of being alone with my girl. I sat next to her, or opposite her. But we were separated by more than the infinitesimal space, or the table, between us. We were separated by the invisible chains that shackled my feet, and would not let me walk towards, or away from, her as I jolly well pleased, and by unseen handcuffs that would not let me touch and hold her any way I fancied. And there was always that stiff ramrod jailer, with searchlight eyes that, in all probability, could see even in the dark. When I smiled, it seemed to mirror the torture in my soul. And when I laughed, it might have sounded like the baying of a caged animal. I was caged, wasn't I?

On the day of my release, she did not eat me up, nor I her. With freedom ringing like a joyous bell in my ears, I had no need to. I knew, and so did she, that we had all eternity to do, as we wanted, to and with each other.

I have watched the movie, *The Ten Commandments*, a dozen or more times. And seen the euphoria and jubilation with which the Children of Israel trooped out of the land of their captivity. Then they came up against the Red Sea. Fortunately for them, they had their deliverer Moses, who just happened to be a man who walked and talked with God. In the movie, if not perhaps in historical reality, Moses struck the Red Sea with his staff, and the waters parted, making a way for the Israelites. Egypt had been their prison, their place of enslavement.

I too had my prison where, for a quarter or so of my life up to the time of my release, I had been worse than a slave. I too walked out of my prison with my heart full of exultation, my head held high, my seven-year old daughter Chizube in my arms, and Rosemary's arm around my waist. I did not immediately encounter anything I could call my 'Red Sea'. Only later did it dawn on me that my Red Sea was not a visible and physical obstacle, but that I was carrying it around with me, like a constant companion, my shadow in fact. Prison or, to put it another way, my imprisonment, was my Red Sea; a sea that ran so deep I was never ever going to be able to ford it, and leave it behind me.

I had no Moses, but I had Rosemary. She may not be a consort for any god, unless that god be me. But her love for me was her staff. And that staff has worked, and to this day still works, wonders for me.

That love saw me through my darkest days, when prospective employers, one after another, turned me down on account of that gaping eight-year hole in my resume. When I moved in with her and our daughter, one month after my release, I brought nothing with me that would help us sustain our lives together. One month, I had quickly found out, was too soon, after a lengthy term in jail, for me to find a meaningful job. That month, during which I was virtually a parasite in the home of cousin Aloysius, was like a whole year to me. But I had learnt, through my prison experience, to be patient.

Neither my cousin Aloysius, nor her uncle Frank approved of my moving in with Rosemary. She had lived with her uncle until about a year after her Master's degree. Then she had moved out with our daughter, in mid-1987, three months before my release from prison, into an apartment with two bedrooms and one and a half baths.

That move very seriously upset her uncle, she told me. "I'm not sure if he lost his voice too," she recounted. "But, for two or three days, he almost wouldn't speak to me, and just barely acknowledged my presence. If he spoke to me at all, it was on account of Chizube whom he doted on as if she was his granddaughter."

"Can't say I blame him," I said. "You're like a daughter to him, no?"

"I suppose I am. I know I love him like my dad, and of course I'm so grateful to him. Which is why I don't understand why he seems to be offended whenever I try to thank him."

"That's just like our people. He obviously believes he's done for you exactly what was natural for him to do. Look what cousin Aloysius did for me, and he's only a cousin. I don't know what our blessed country's coming to, but I hope this is something we'll never lose. What about your uncle's wife?"

"Oh, I don't know," said Rosemary reflectively. "I think she saw, earlier than him, that it was all right for me to move out. With you due to be released within, what, two, three months, and Chizube growing, what other choice was there?"

"Not to forget you are already earning good money in your Social Welfare office," I added.

"That too. But auntie asked me what I would do about Chizube."

"Meaning what exactly?" I asked. "Chizube is what, seven years, and no longer a baby."

Rosemary looked balefully at me. "Well," she said, "it's not really as simple as it may look to you. You see, auntie has been wonderful with her, and goes and picks her up from school and all that, which has been just super for me. She's been more practical and realistic than my uncle about the whole thing. She was the one that suggested that I not move too far from them, so she can continue to do what she's been doing. She even insists on bringing Chizube to our apartment when I return from work, and call her. She says she needs the short walk to our place."

Rosemary and I had this conversation when she came visiting, two or so weeks after she had moved into an apartment located, she told me, five blocks from her uncle's house. I was surprised at the location of the apartment, because I was quite unaware that there were any apartment buildings that close to where her uncle Frank lived in a suburb of Washington, D.C.

"They moved back into the city," she said, "about three months ago. I must have forgotten to tell you about it."

"Back? Did they ever – ?"

"Yes," said Rosemary. "They used to live in the city. Their new place is not far from his present office. That's why they decided to move back."

Normally she came to the prison once every month, on the third Saturday of the month, and most times she came with Chizube. I was privy to all her plans, and gave my unstinting approval to the move into an apartment.

It felt wonderful, indeed absolutely heavenly, to talk about things ordinary people talked about routinely outside of prisons. And as we talked, I began to have visions of life in freedom. *My* freedom, at long last! A feeling of elation coursed through my body, like an electric ripple, from time to time.

A song arose in my head, and in my heart, and soon, I gave it voice, softly but audibly enough for Rosemary to look sharply at me, as if in disapproval. I knew she worried on account of the guard, but I was heedless of any potential consequences.

"Eternal Father strong to save
Whose arms hath bound the restless wave
Who bid the mighty ocean deep
Its own appointed limits keep
Oh hear us when we cry to thee
For those in peril on the sea."

It was my favorite church song, sung to a hauntingly beautiful tune. Why that song sprang to my lips, I did not know. I only knew that, in some way, it was a cry from deep down in my heart, though I was nowhere near a sea. Perhaps I worried that on my release, I would face certain peril in my efforts to find my feet as a free man who could never totally be free in a world that would always look askance at me. I think I knew that I would need God's saving grace as I never before needed it, to survive in a world made turbulent for folks like me. It was sure to be a rocky sea.

I lived on tenterhooks because I did not know what the Immigration and Naturalization Service would do with me. That I did not mentally cave in was almost entirely due to Rosemary, whose love for me was like a lightning rod that absorbed and diverted the slings and arrows hurled at me. And of course my daughter, little Chizube, whose cherubic face and delicate beauty gave me the most solid reason of all to stand firm when I was being constantly buffeted by the conscious and unwitting cruelties of an unforgiving world.

At first, I worked at odd jobs, where my employers asked few questions, but made me work the longest hours they could inflict on me without being in breach of the laws. Perhaps they thought I knew the law, because it was pretty evident to me that I commanded some respect from these employers, no doubt on account of the quietly dignified manner with which I always tried to carry myself. Looking back now, I think it was an act on my part, a defensive mechanism and mode of behavior calculated to ward off suspicion that might otherwise have been directed at me. That was something I constantly worried about: suspicion. I worried about the way my fellow employees looked at me, and the way they sometimes fluttered their eyes. If a girl winked at me, as some did, I could never be sure if it was a come-hither look, or a conspiratorial, your-secret-is-safe-with-me, signal. My boss had only to say to me, "I want to see you in my office" for my heart to go pounding wildly, and for visions of the hated pink slips to torment my already harassed mind.

Throughout this tense period of my life after prison, a span of about two years, Rosemary stood by me. She would not let me lose hope, or denigrate myself, or curse my fate. She constantly exhorted me to "stay positive" which, unfortunately, is not one of my favorite American expressions. But of course I knew she spoke from the heart.

She had latterly been attracted to Pentecostalism, whose form of worship is loudly participatory, but whose central doctrine appears to be that God's revelation of Himself to man is not a phenomenon of the past, but continues to this day. Rosemary says she is 'born-again'. I have my private laugh about that, though I have never once challenged her claim. I cannot seriously challenge her because, in fact, I suspect I do not fully understand what that term really means. If they are such fundamentalists that every wrong step is a sin, how come she was willing to shack up with me before we were married? A born-again Christian would not do that, or would she?

I have been to several of her Pentecostal church services and, to this day, am still fascinated by the way the congregation sometimes works itself into a frenzy. Rosemary may not see it that way, but that is how it looks to me. As the pastor leads the ritual, preaching or praying, the worshippers lift up their arms to God in supplication, and sometimes in exultation. Many sway their bodies from side to side. Several throw their heads back, eyes shut tightly as if in fear that God's incandescence or effulgence might be too bright for them. Shouts of "Amen! Praise the Lord" rend the air even when the pastor has not yet come to the end of the particular prayer he is reading. Reading? Most times, their prayers are not actually read, but declaimed vociferously, and almost vehemently, gushing out in sustained and oratorical torrents from their seemingly overcharged hearts. Indeed the passion and fervor generated by their total immersion in the rituals can sometimes be so thick you could almost slice it with the proverbial knife.

But though often fascinating, it can also seem somewhat unreal. I was a staunch Episcopalian, and very partial to our calm, quietly sedate form of worship. I probably still lean the Episcopal way, but something in me changed the day a woman, who had whipped herself into a kind of ecstatic delirium turned to me, and placed an arm on my head, as I sat quietly by her side. It was my third or fourth Sunday at The Church of the Blessed African Martyrs, located at the intersection of Revolution Avenue and N Street in a quite respectable neighborhood in the District of Columbia, about a mile from our apartment.

With Rosemary to my right, and Chizube seated between us, this woman turned to me and, for a full minute or more, jabbered away in a tongue that did not sound like anything I had ever heard. By then, of course, I knew about the Pentecostal proclivity for what they call "speaking in tongues", though my Rosemary was never once – to my knowledge – caught up in that act.

The woman, when she had somewhat calmed down, placed her right hand on my head and spoke to or, more correctly, at me in English, interspersed by unintelligible words that must have come from that other tongue that only she and her God understood.

"My son," she said, "do you know Psalm 113? You should read it when you get home. If you do, you will see where it says: 'Who is like the Lord our God, who sits enthroned on high but stoops to behold the heavens and the earth? He takes up the weak out of the dust and lifts up the poor from the ashes. He sets them with the princes, with the princes of his people.' "

She paused for a moment or two, and then said: "Your quest for justice will be answered. And you will see God's judgment flow like a strong stream coming down from His place of abode on Mount Zion."

That was all she said. I had no chance to ask her if she knew me, or what her words might portend because, in the very next instant, she turned away from me, and was gone. No, she did not leave her seat beside me. But she was gone to that other world that I could not share with her, where she communed perhaps with the angels, in their unearthly tongue.

I looked at Rosemary, and she looked at me. Then she smiled, and made a hand and mouth gesture that told me to hold my curiosity and wonder in check, and that she would, later, offer some explanations.

For the rest of the service, I kept my eyes on the hallucinating woman, though I tried not to let on that I was much interested in her. She, for her part, seemed scarcely to pay attention, for much of the time, to what the pastor was saying or doing. She remained, as it were, in her own world of supernal beings, and now and again smiled or scowled depending, I imagined, on what they revealed to her about the future.

She was large, this woman. But there were others larger than she, in this overwhelmingly black church. And that's another thing. I have something against churches that are defined by race or color, which is how it seems to be in this, God's own, country. The Episcopalian church, my predominantly white American church, is just as guilty. But at least, it is, for me, the Anglicanism in which I was nurtured back home in Nigeria, and there is nothing I can do about that. American history, in particular the slave trade and slavery, may have a lot to do with all this, and I cannot undo history. But I still think it is a crying shame. So, though Rosemary often makes me go with her to the Church of the African Martyrs, and I have begun to see that church in a new light, I know where my heart truly belongs.

As soon as we stepped outside the church, I stopped Rosemary, and demanded to know what the large prophetess was all about.

"You won't believe this," she said, "but I've never spoken to her about you."

"You mean you know her?" I asked, my suspicion rising.

"Of course, I do. Who doesn't?"

"I don't," I said emphatically. "Who's she? And what, in heaven's name, was she talking about?"

Rosemary looked anxiously around her, and would not respond to my question until she had pulled me out of earshot of everybody else. And even then, she lowered her voice.

"The woman's a little – how do they say it – a little gaga," she confided, gesturing with a finger to the side of her head, close to the ear. "But when she talks, people listen."

"What's her name?" I asked, and quickly added, "not that that has anything to do with anything."

"Evangeline. But I don't know her father's name."

"Or her *married* name," I suggested.

"Oh, no!" said Rosemary. "She's not married. Which is just as well, because I doubt any man can live with her."

"That's neat," I said.

"What?"

"I mean her name. You said Evangeline, didn't you? Isn't that something to do with bearing good news?"

"Aha!" shouted Rosemary, but in a subdued tone. "This explains it."

"Explains what? What are you talking about?"

Just then Chizube, who had been playing with several other kids, came running back to us. She was talking excitedly, and pointing to the door of the church.

"It's Evangeline! It's Evangeline! She's coming out, see?"

"So even little kids know her?" I asked Rosemary.

But Rosemary was not listening to me. She seemed transfixed where she was, her head turned at an uncomfortable angle, staring at the large woman called Evangeline as the latter wended her way through throngs of worshippers, trailing a crush of obvious admirers, and dispensing smiles all around.

I gazed in wonderment at Rosemary, and recalled that only moments earlier, she had described Evangeline as a little gaga. Then it occurred to me that she might have used that word only in an off-handedly derogatory manner. There was respect, bordering on awe, in Rosemary's eyes as they stayed fixed on the wonder woman till she turned a corner of the church building, and disappeared from our view. Rosemary was still gazing after her when she began to speak. It took a moment or two for me to realize she was talking to me, and that she was in fact responding to my question.

"People say Evangeline was not her name," Rosemary said, "when she first joined this church. That was years ago. At least ten or fifteen years."

"So what happened?"

"I'm not sure," said Rosemary. "But from what you said –"

"What did I say now?" I asked, when she hesitated.

"I mean," she said, "about her name. It must have been a name the pastor or the people gave her. No, not the people, but the pastor, because I don't believe the ordinary members of the church would know much about the meaning of names and such things."

"So she's some kind of a prophetess?"

"That's what she believes," said Rosemary, "and the people believe that too."

"Including you?"

Before she could answer my question, little Chizube said, with glee: "She told us you would come out of prison, daddy. Didn't she, mummy?"

Rosemary looked reproachfully at our daughter, and then her face broke in a smile. "I suppose you could say she did."

"And what's that supposed to mean?" I asked. "She did, or she didn't. Which is it?"

"Well, she said something about my agony being over soon, or words to that effect."

"And no doubt you understood what she said to refer to my approaching release, and told Chizube so?"

Rosemary looked down at her feet, and muttered something to herself. I put a finger under her chin, and lifted her head so she was forced to look at me.

"I couldn't hear you," I said encouragingly.

For a moment or two, she stared wildly at me, not saying a word. And then: "I'm a little ashamed to confess, yes, that was how I understood Evangeline's words. What else could she have meant?"

"Had you been talking to her much before she said what she said?"

"Meaning did I tell her about you?" Rosemary asked, looking at me this time with pain in her eyes. "You think I'm in the habit of –"

I did not let her finish her question because, all of a sudden, I was overwhelmed by shame. Shame that I was putting the girl who meant the world to me through some kind of an inquisition. What did it matter, I asked myself, if, now and again, she spoke to her pastor, or to a sympathetic prophetess, about her worries and troubles, and my name happened to be mentioned? Her pastor was Christ's representative here on earth, or is that not what apostolic succession is supposed to mean? Pastor or prophetess, they were both God's interlocutors trained or, as in the case of the prophetess, endowed with the unique ability to dispense spiritual authority. And did not our Lord himself say: "Come unto me all ye that travail and are heavy laden, and I will give you rest"? Spiritual rest was what Rosemary sought, because her world was in a shambles.

Whatever tribulations I suffered, I knew I brought on myself. Like, by being a simpleton, and trusting too much. And thereby letting a friend, who did not know the true meaning of friendship, play me for the sucker that I was. I was still angry with a legal system that did not see through the shenanigans, the skullduggery, and the downright perfidy of the real villain of the piece, my one-time friend, Bernard Ekwekwe. In other words, I felt like the cow or other animal, in the Igbo aphorism, that went to the house of a meat-loving king, and never returned to his home because it got eaten up. Rosemary did not do that to me; I did it all by myself.

"I'm sorry, Rosemary," I said. "Please forget I asked the question. It really doesn't matter. You knew I was coming out soon anyway."

Chapter IV

I LIVE MY life in perpetual fear that the INS could come calling any day. If I am permitted an analogy, it is rather like waiting for the second coming of the Lord, except that, in one important respect, it is worse. The second coming is an event that even the most devout Christian sometimes blithely assumes is unlikely to happen in his lifetime, and the unbeliever totally disregards. The INS inspires mind-bending, unholy fear, especially if they have written to inform you that they have begun a judicial process that you know could ultimately lead to your forcible repatriation to your homeland. And at this point in my life, returning to Nigeria is the last thing I need. Not to put too fine a point upon it, it would be distinctly unhealthy for my body and my spirit. Repatriation would mean, for a convicted felon like me, a spell in a Nigerian prison. Enough said!

A lawyer friend, Cornelius Okwu, one of only a handful of persons who knew my story in its entirety, advised me to get on with my life, and not worry too much about the ways of the INS. That was easy for him to say, and I knew he meant well. But there seems no way to not worry about an agency that has my fate in its cold hands. The INS is, for a person like me, the most chillingly un-empathetic agency that there is. That has been my view of that body for a long time now, and I have had no concrete reason to see it any other way. Except, of course, that I am still here in the country. A dozen years or so have passed since my release from prison in 1987. In that time, I have watched my daughter grow from a seven-year old child to a beautiful young lady of America. And I am still struggling to understand what has happened, indeed what is happening, to me.

The INS has left me in virtual limbo all of those dozen years; and no lawyer has even come close to giving me totally satisfactory explanations of why I am still here.

As time rolls by, one stealthy week after another, I sometimes dream that I could grow wings, literally, and fly. Nothing seems to be in my way. Except, of course, myself! And the gnawing fear, if not certainty that, with my kind of luck, the moment I sprouted those wings, a chill wind, or that most uncongenial agency, the INS, would shrivel them up.

In the upshot, I sprouted no wings. But I did something, perhaps infinitely more mundane, but that did wonders for my self-esteem. I got my MBA degree.

I had begun to prepare myself, while still incarcerated, for a course leading to a Masters in Business Administration. Of course I would much rather have studied for the accountant's certification. My original ambition, which had become an unattainable obsession, was to be a Certified Public Accountant. But now I knew the count. I was painfully aware that the tin-gods, the cabal, whoever they were, that controlled the profession in America, and made the rules determining who can, or cannot, aspire to be a CPA, had no room in their hearts, or in their charter, for ex-convicts like me. I am sorry if I sound just a little bitter about this, but what would be the point of pretending otherwise?

In the fall of 1987, the year of my release from prison, I enrolled in Howard University's School of Business, in Washington, D.C. I chose Accounting and Taxation as my areas of concentration – no surprise here! I did the course part-time, attending classes in the evenings. Even so, I needed some financial assistance and, once again, cousin Aloysius and his good wife Obiamaka came through massively for me. It took me all of six semesters to do so, but finally, in 1990, I got my MBA.

I was proud of my MBA degree. So proud indeed I wished I could have made a trip to Nigeria, to personally recount my American experience to my parents, and my friends, and to show off my degree certificates. Besides, I had not been home in sixteen years! But it would have been suicidal, I knew for sure, to do so. There would have been no return from such a trip. My air ticket would have been a one-way exit ticket out of the United States of America. For a variety of reasons, not the least of which were Rosemary and my daughter Chizube, I knew I had to hang on, with every fiber of my being, to my toe-hold in America. And there was the near certainty that the moment I reached Nigeria, some over-zealous government functionary, citing laws that have no basis in equity or morality, might have clamped handcuffs on me, and led me directly to a *Nigerian* jail. For bringing the good name of Nigeria into disrepute in the United States of America!

I did not want to do that to myself. I wanted nothing to do with my country – for the next several years, decades possibly. Nigeria might be my home, even my sweet home. But it is a country where nothing seems to go right, where one's growth is stunted, hope withers, and ambition wilts, for no logical reasons that I am aware of. Except that a country blessed munificently by nature has somehow found ways to curse itself and to stall its manifest destiny.

I wrote to my father and asked him to undertake a task that I knew I could not, in my situation, do for myself: to go knock on the door of Rosemary's father's home.

And, if the atmosphere was congenial enough, to begin the process that would lead to my betrothal and marriage to Rosemary.

The answer came back in double-quick time, but not in the form of a letter from my dad. It was not the answer I had hoped for, but had feared nevertheless. In un-camouflaged language, long on rhetoric but short on warmth, Rosemary's father's letter wrecked my hopes. At least that was his clear intent: to push me as far away from him, and his, as he could. But the man knew his daughter, and how stubborn she could be; knew too that his six thousand miles of separation from us effectively paralyzed him, and there was precious little he could do to stop us if Rosemary and I were of one mind on the subject. Our people say that the jaw has to be near enough for the hand to administer a really stinging slap. That, I believe, was the reason he copied the letter to his brother, Engineer Frank Akamelu.

The letter was addressed to Rosemary, not to me, which was as it should be. The surprise was that, by the date on the letter, 15 October 1990, he had written it just one day after my father, accompanied by the usual entourage of relatives, had called on him to begin the traditional opening of the negotiations.

I could not understand his haste. Perhaps he thought it best to strike while the iron was still hot. But my iron with Rosemary was no longer malleable metal. It had become steel. We had been on our love trip for over ten years and, in that time, had given life to our beautiful daughter, Chizube. We could also claim that our love had endured more than our fair share of woes and tribulations, and grown stronger for the test. We were now coasting along almost serenely, and knew that it would take much more than a hastily written letter, by an angry and unwilling parent, to sever that relationship.

My prospective father-in-law chose not to mince words, which was his right. Indeed few fathers would willingly give away their daughters to convicted felons like me. That said, I had desperately hoped that in my case, his judgement would have been tempered by a consideration of my probable innocence. I knew that Uncle Frank, who has never seemed to waver in his belief in my total innocence, had discretely put in a good word or two for me to his older brother, in that regard. But evidently he had not been persuasive enough. And perhaps the old man has never forgiven me for my bumbling temerity in coming to his home in Enugu, on the day before I left Nigeria for the United States, to declare my interest in his daughter.

I still tingle all over, at the thought of my boldness on that day. But it was an experience I would not now exchange for anything else in this world. And the vision stays with me to this day: Rosemary and me, standing so close to each other that there could not have been any chink of daylight between us, from head to toe, as we took on her father, and made declarations about our love. At least Rosemary did; I merely nodded my affirmation. It must have seemed like immature love to her dad, who thereupon upbraided us for our audacity, and then bade me farewell, and Godspeed.

"If he is innocent of the charge of drug-trafficking, as he claims," Mr. Akamelu wrote to his daughter, "let him get his conviction overturned. Is he not in America?

Or perhaps he can try to obtain a pardon from the President. Otherwise, as a person convicted of that crime, he cannot expect our family to accommodate him. If I allow that, how can I look our relatives in the eye? Can you imagine what they will be saying behind my back? And, of course, people will believe that anything of value that I buy is with money from his drug trade."

In another part of his letter, he admonished his daughter, and reminded her that her uncle spent good money on her American education, "so that you will eventually return to Nigeria and help build the country. Frank did not intend that, after your graduation, you would be living the way I hear you are living, with someone who will surely bring shame on our family, unless he can prove his total innocence.

"I hope you will listen to me, and not go and do something we will all regret. However, I am not too worried about this, though I know you can sometimes be a strong-headed girl. Your uncle knows how I feel about what you are doing, and I am sure he will do the right thing by the family.

"You may tell your boyfriend Cyril that I have no problems with his parents, who are good upstanding persons. And tell him that his father says he thinks his friend Bernard is here in Enugu, though he has not seen him. I myself have heard the rumour that Bernard is back in the country"

Then Mr. Akamelu added, as a postscript: "Please tell him I have not forgotten the day he came to see me and your mother before he left for America so many years ago. Since then I have kept wondering what was in his head that day. Someone should have told him that is not the way we do things. The trouble is that you young people think you know everything, like people who can see with the backs of their heads, as they say. But don't they also say that what an old man can see, *sitting down*, the young cannot see, *standing up*? Go and think about it."

I do not know why, but Uncle Frank told Rosemary and me that his brother sent him a copy of the letter. I am sure the elder Akamelu had not intended that he should reveal this fact to us – especially to me. It is, however, possible that, in telling us about his copy of the letter, Uncle Frank had merely intended to let us know he would be watching us, on behalf of his brother. But there had been a kindly light in his eyes as he spoke to us; a light that seemed to say he understood how Rosemary and I felt about each other.

Perhaps illogically, when we wedded in court, we did not tell Uncle Frank what we were up to. Rosemary was certain that he would have tried to stop us, if only because of a sense of loyalty to his elder brother.

"I agree," I said. "He must not know, until it is too late for him, or anybody else, to stop us. If he knows, and doesn't stop us, your dad might hold him responsible for doing nothing, which would be unfair to him. So he must not know."

"And your daughter, will you tell her?"

"Chizube?"

"Who else?" Rosemary asked. "Or do you have another daughter I don't know about?"

"Who knows?" I asked. "You know what they say: ask me no questions, and I'll tell you no lies. But seriously, no."

"No? Meaning you don't have – ?"

"Oh, shut up," I said with a laugh. "I mean we must not tell Chizube. She'll know on that day, when we dress her up, and take her to the court-house. Children talk."

"And we don't want that," agreed Rosemary. "Still and all, I hate to do this to her. It would have been nice for her – you know – the anticipation and all that."

"She's much too young," I said dismissively, "to understand all that stuff."

"No, she's not. She's what – almost twelve – certainly old enough to be aware her dad and mum are not married. Trouble with you is you don't know what goes on in a little girl's head. You're just her dad."

I looked sharply at Rosemary, and saw that she was not smiling. Clearly her last remark had been meant seriously. For just a second or two, I thought to protest, to defend the male honor. But I desisted, because it suddenly hit me that she might be right. What did I really know about my little girl and her world-view? Her mother was much closer to her; had been, for every blessed day of her eleven plus years, while I mostly wasted in prison.

The upshot of all this was that we kept our secret from everybody, except my sister Adaku and her husband Theo. And of course we set an early date for our marriage, knowing that a long delay might be hazardous for our little secret.

Our little party of five, after the formal tying of the knot, repaired to a Japanese restaurant, and dined on *sushi* and *daikon*, both well cooked. That was Rosemary's idea, though Japanese was not her favorite oriental menu.

"You know I prefer Chinese to Japanese," she said. "But I don't want, on my wedding day, to go and stuff myself on *Mi-fun* or *General Tso's chicken* or, worse still, my absolute favorite, shrimp fried rice."

We had no cause to regret her choice. The astonishing dexterity of the Japanese chef, twirling and tossing his long-bladed kitchen knives and forks, as he cooked our food right there on our table in front of us, quite took our breath away. Chizube, in particular, alternately roaring with excited laughter, or taking quick cover whenever the chef's long knife went flying in the air, had a marvelous time, and was difficult to restrain.

Uncle Frank was extremely upset with us when, two or so weeks after the event, we unwrapped our secret to him. He did not rant and rave, as he might, with reason, have done. That was not his way. Rather, he conveyed his displeasure by the manner in which he quietly and repeatedly shook his head, as if words failed him altogether. And all the while, he stared long and hard at Rosemary and me, especially Rosemary, with eyes that held our anxious attention, and that let us know how terribly, very terribly, we had let him down. When he found the words to admonish us, he spoke in a soft tone that actually cut us more to the quick than harsh words might have done.

"I don't know if I'll ever forgive either of you for this."

He spoke, carrying his head in both his hands, now gazing piercingly at us, now staring down at the top of his dining table, around which we sat, though we had long finished dinner. His wife, Aunt Nwamaka, said or did absolutely nothing except keep her eyes on her husband as he spoke. I could not read her face. Like her husband, she too must have felt badly let down. But her expression was tight. Her eyes looked dead – to us, that is. Her lips were partially open, perhaps in shock at our behavior. When her eyes shifted from a contemplation of her husband, they rested on Rosemary. She just would not look at me.

"I'll tell you something you obviously don't know," Uncle Frank said, after a long pause. "Of course I don't need to tell you that what you did was wrong. We simply don't do things like that. But I suppose you young persons of nowadays, you copy everything Americans do, and call it civilization. I'm surprised you didn't run to Las Vegas to get married. They call it eloping, don't they? Why didn't you? It would have been better, had you done so, than to marry here in Washington, under our very noses. It's adding insult to injury."

He paused, and regarded Rosemary briefly. "What do you want me to tell your father in Enugu? D'you think he will believe me when I tell him you got married here in my city, in a court not quite a mile from my house, and I did not know about it?"

Rosemary somehow found her voice. "Uncle, we just couldn't have told you anything. You remember you told me about a month ago –"

"I know what I told you," Uncle Frank interrupted. "I told you your dad had written two more letters to me. Looking back now, I believe he must have had some kind of premonition about all this. And he pleaded with me not to let anything like that happen."

Again he paused and, for a long moment, looked steadily at his wife, eyebrows raised, as if in consultation about something. As I watched both of them, I saw Mrs. Akamelu nod imperceptibly to him. Then he shifted his gaze on me. His piercing eyes held me in thrall.

"There's something I must tell you now. You of course know I had absolutely no knowledge of what you two were plotting. But, had I known, had you chosen to take me into your confidence, I WOULD NOT HAVE OPPOSED IT."

It seemed to my suddenly dull senses that his last statement had been spoken in capitals! My head jerked up in total surprise, and I stared at the man as if his words, though said loud and clear, were incomprehensible. I was not the only one in shock. Rosemary, who was in the act of lifting her coffee cup to her mouth, dropped it back in its saucer with a clatter.

"Uncle!" she said in a hoarse whisper. "What did you say?"

"You heard me," said her uncle. And for the first time, there was the ghost of a smile on his face. "You heard me all right. The reason your dad wrote two or three frantic letters to me was because I had written him and, in effect, pleaded with him to accept the inevitable."

"You did?" I heard myself ask.

"Yes. And the reason I did, was my unshaken conviction that you were never a drug trafficker, no matter what the U.S. courts said or did to you, and that you are a decent and hard-working young man. But evidently my brother has remained to this day unconvinced about your innocence."

This was not the first time he had let me know he believed in my innocence. During the dark days of my trial, when it had seemed to me that the whole world was against me, Uncle Frank had sent word to me about this, and urged me to keep the chin up. And I had kept the old chin up, right up to the day of the guilty verdict, and the even more catastrophic day of my sentence. And then I had collapsed, mentally and physically.

Uncle Frank came to the prison to visit me about once a year, which was more often than I had any reason to hope for. He always came with Rosemary, often bearing such innocent gifts as prison regulations allowed, mostly cookies and candies, and a ballpoint pen now and again. This last he would bring (or would give to Rosemary to pass on to me) whenever I expressed the need for one. I had told him I was writing the story of my American experience while I rotted in prison. He heartily approved of that endeavor and, in consequence, also brought me writing paper, to supplement the paper the prison guards so unexpectedly made available to me.

"Why were you so convinced about my innocence," I somehow found the courage to ask him, "when nobody else believed me?"

"Excuse me?" Rosemary asked, looking at me with a very hurt expression.

"Except you, of course," I quickly added. "I didn't think I needed to say that, surely."

She relented, and smiled. But our hosts were not smiling, and this time it was Aunt Nwamaka who spoke.

"Whatever we thought about you at the time," she said, "was because of your cousin Aloysius and my namesake Amaka. They knew you much better than anybody else in this country did. And they swore to us that there was no way you could have been involved in this kind of thing. My namesake said she would have somehow known if you were mixed up with your friend."

She was namesakes with my cousin Aloysius Jideofo's wife, Obiamaka, only because they shared the same shortened form of both their names: *Amaka*.

"And they told us," added Uncle Frank, "how, during your interrogation by the police, and even during your trial, you actually refused to tell on your friend, when it might have helped your case. You even went so far as to deny knowing Bernard was in the country, when only a day or so earlier, you had met him in a mutual friend's house."

The 'friend' was Obi Udozo, who lived in East Orange with his wife Joy, and their daughter, and who had been one of the dramatis personae in the chain of events that ultimately blighted my life, and put me in prison. Obi was Bernard's friend, not mine. I met him because Bernard, when he visited New Jersey, stayed in his house. A friendship might well have developed between us. But it just was not in the cards. He

A SNAKE UNDER A THATCH

colluded with Bernard to thwart my defence in court, when he would not produce, or give evidence about a letter, written to him by Bernard, that would assuredly have set me free.

"Aloysius told you all that?" I asked.

"They told us everything," said Uncle Frank. "And when I had the opportunity to visit Bound Brook, I took Aloysius with me and we went and saw your East Orange friend –"

"Obi Udozo was not my friend," I said emphatically.

"I know," said Uncle Frank in a soft and gentle voice. "I know. It's just a manner of speaking. I met him and we talked, and he told me about Bernard's letter –"

"And did he confirm – ?"

"He did not. He maintained the story that there was no such letter. He used the words 'Bernard's letter' because he knew that I knew you had raised the issue in court. But, though I could not shake his story, I knew he was lying. He could not look me in the eye, though I challenged him on that, and his eyes were – how does one say it – extremely shifty."

"You never told Rosemary all this. I'm sure she would have told me about it."

"What would have been the use telling her? But I did tell her that Aloysius and I did the best we could to find a lawyer – I mean a really good lawyer – that would take an interest in your case. But it did not work out. I'm not really sure why? Aloysius suggested we find one of our bright Nigerian lawyers – there are quite a few of them – but there's this thing about taking a case like this to one of our own; the fear being that – well – the story might get around in the community. You know what I mean?"

"I do," I said. "Rosemary told me about your efforts. I don't even know how to begin to thank you for taking so much trouble on my account – ."

"Don't thank me, Cyril," Uncle Frank said. "Thank my niece. If you must know the whole truth, what little I tried to do I did mainly for her. I only became really convinced about your innocence because your cousin was prepared to swear on the Bible that you were not a part of this awful trade. He even showed me your bank account statements – ."

"My bank statements?" I asked, surprised.

Then I remembered that the police had searched my room in my cousin's house looking for damning evidence of my complicity in my friend Bernard's drug trafficking. They had impounded some of my papers, and later returned them to Aloysius. My bank statements must have been among those documents and papers.

"Yes, your bank statements," said Uncle Frank after some pause. "And they showed the normal deposits one would expect from the kinds of jobs you did – unless, of course, you never paid any monies from your supposed drug trade into your account, but spent them as fast as they rolled in. And even in that case, according to Aloysius and Amaka, there was absolutely nothing they noticed that might have made them wonder where the money was coming from.

"But, to return to what you two did two weeks ago, you have embarrassed me and your auntie here." He looked across at his wife, who nodded in agreement. "But I suppose there's no more to be said about it. What's done is done, as far as I'm concerned. You only have to worry about my elder brother, and on that, you are pretty much on your own."

Rosemary rose from her chair, and went and stood behind her uncle and, before any one knew what she had in mind, leaned towards him and encircled him with her arms, resting her head on his left shoulder.

"Uncle," she said very softly, "I've always known you'd do anything for me; well, almost anything. But what you are now telling Cyril and me today, is completely beyond my wildest dreams. I never imagined that someone like you would – what I mean is – accept what we did."

"You mean, don't you, what you did behind my back, not so?" asked her uncle seriously. "Please Rose, let go a little, or you'll choke me. You're stronger than I thought. That's better, thank you. Hey! I didn't mean let go altogether. It isn't everyday that I have a young person like you holding me like this."

His wife looked at me and gestured with the slightest movement of her head towards her husband and my wife.

"Look at them," she said, doing her utmost to look the part of the jealous wife. "They've been doing this, it seems, for ever."

I laughed, wishing it was me that my Rosemary held in her arms, however tightly – indeed, especially tightly. But this was not an evening for jealousy.

"So, what was I saying?" said Uncle Frank, now smiling radiantly. "Ah, yes! What you two went and did, like thieves in the night. You're surprised I can accept it? Your dad, Rose, when I tell him about this, will probably have a fit. I think, if I was in his shoes, I might be – how to say – pissed off. I'll talk to him as soon as I can get him on the phone – ."

"Which could take several days," I dared to interject.

"I know," said Uncle Frank. "We all know how it is with our Nigerian telephone system. It's a real shame, but what can one do? So I'll try and reach him, and then I'll tell him what you did. My poor brother! What he probably doesn't understand is that his younger brother who left home almost three decades ago – I was what, twenty-eight or twenty-nine then – is not the same Frank who, as we talk now, is fifty-seven years old. How time flies! Take my little boy now, Chukwuma. He's close to thirty, and married – a little too soon, if you ask me – and expecting his second child. He couldn't find a girl from the Nigerian, not to talk of our Igbo community, and he went and married an *Akata* girl. What could his mother and I do, but grow up fast, and learn to accept that times have changed, and that we can no longer control where our kids choose their wives or husbands from? I'm not sure if Chukwuma's marriage to an African-American girl is the reason I think the way I do now. I suspect not, but it doesn't matter.

"There's nothing more to be said. Cyril, look to it that my niece is well cared for. I know she'll take good care of you, and my little angel, Chizube. Where's she? She disappeared as soon as dinner was done."

"As if you don't know!" said Aunt Nwamaka. "She's in the den, of course, watching T.V."

"You have a good job now, Cyril," said Uncle Frank. "And the INS has probably forgotten about you. Don't look back now, or I'll want to know why."

He stopped, and looked back and up at Rosemary who was still standing behind him, but now only with one hand on his shoulder. He gently pushed the hand away, and got up. He made a signal to his wife and walked away from the dining room, and upstairs to their bedroom. Aunt Nwamaka dutifully followed him.

They were gone perhaps five or six minutes. Time enough for Rosemary and I to breathe a joint sigh of relief. Relief that what we had most feared did not happen, and that our news was received, if not exactly with joy, at least without bitterness. I had always known that Uncle Frank was a large-hearted and very accommodating modern man. But he and his wife had gone well beyond all reasonable expectations, and given Rosemary and me a wonderful fillip to start our married life.

It turned out that that was only a half of it. When our hosts came down from their bedroom, they handed Rosemary a cheque for one thousand U.S. dollars. When I saw what it was, my knees almost buckled from under me. I think my mouth also dropped open in stupefaction, but no words came from it.

Rosemary, as always, recovered more quickly than I from the shock. "What's this?" she found the voice to ask.

"Your wedding gift," said Aunt Nwamaka. "You took us completely by surprise, so this was what we came up with, to wish you everything you wish for yourselves, and God's blessings."

Uncle Frank stood by her side, and beamed his approval of his wife's wishes for us. "There's just one other thing," he said, "and then I'm done. In spite of that cheque, I cannot truly recognize this marriage unless and until you do everything you're supposed to do. My brother has no alternative now but to accept what has happened – ."

"I know dad," said Rosemary despairingly, now by my side, and holding tightly to my right hand. "He may never – ."

"He will," Uncle Frank asserted. "As I said, he has no choice now. I'll explain that I have given you my reluctant blessing, and that he cannot expect, as they say, that I will give you a bag of salt and then invoke the rain to drench you and the salt. In due course, when tempers cool, tradition will have to be fulfilled, and you will do the wine-carrying ceremony, and pay some bride-price, and even present your child or children – I hope Chizube will not be an only child – to her mother's people, our family, at home."

"I hope and pray," I said, finally finding my voice, and crossing myself. "Come Rosemary, it is time for us to leave. Uncle and Auntie, we thank you so very much."

"Good things happen to those who believe, and pray, and are patient," said Uncle Frank. "Where's that child of yours? It must be well past her bed time."

Chapter V

IN LATE 1992, on the last day of November, I relocated to New Jersey, arguably the most beautiful of the American States, with its luxuriant flora and many parks. I believe that is why it is called the Garden State. New Jersey was the State where I went to college in Rutgers University, and where I did most of my jail time.

But my relocation to New Jersey had as little to do with my attraction for the flora of the state, as my eight-year sojourn in a penitentiary had to do with a predilection for prison architecture. The move was forced on me because Washington, D.C. suddenly became uninhabitable for me. And when my wife and I cast about for a new place of abode, we settled on a little known town, called West Brook, just off Route 1, and quite close to Newark, N.J.

We took our time about our search, because we needed to be sure that the move, though dictated by a sudden ill wind, would be for the long haul. It was important to us that the town was close to Newark, where I had already secured a job with the firm of Onyeama and Ani, Certified Public Accountants. The way it looked to me, with my MBA, and specializing in accounting and taxation, the firm was sure to get the most out of me, at a salary lower than they would have paid a CPA. Which was fine with me.

We rented a two-bedroom apartment, in an estate with the rather fancy name of Mount Of Olives Gardens. The land on which the estate stood was certainly undulating, but it was not hilly. And if there had ever been olive trees in the area, there were none now. They should have called it the Maple Tree Apartments, because that was the predominant tree. However, there were gardens, several of them in fact, with chrysanthemums of various colors still in bloom, though it was late fall. The lawns in front of the apartment buildings were resplendently green, and as smooth as carpets.

I lost my Washington job the day after I was forced into an altercation with a colleague who had taken too long over his lunch break, and I had dared to point it out to him. I could have done so a hundred times before that day, but chose not to. This was not out of the generosity of my heart. I think I held back because I was still feeling my way through the complexities of my new accounting responsibilities; and the maze of interpersonal relationships in an office manned by a staff of four subordinates and a boss, of whom the boss had his CPA, I my MBA, and the others could not muster up a bachelor degree between them, though I knew that one, at least, of the three, was working at it.

It had been my first real opportunity to hold down a job that was professional in much of its content. I did not enjoy the status, or earn the stipend that matched my qualifications. But of course I was very happy to have had the opportunity, and determined to let my light so shine in whatever I did, that the boss would know my worth and recognize my near professionalism. And I believe I was well on my way to making my mark, when suddenly things turned topsy-turvy.

I cannot easily explain what happened. Mr. Peter Stanley, as mellow an employer as I could have wished for at that juncture of my life, was a rotund and jovial white man, perhaps in his mid-fifties. He did not ask me too many questions when I went to see him for the job opening, and seemed satisfied with the short answers I gave him. It was Uncle Frank who drew my attention to the vacancy, which had come to his attention in his Health and Fitness Club, to which – I later discovered – Mr. Stanley also belonged, and where he pretended to work out.

Mr. Stanley now called me to his office and, unusually, offered me a chair; which immediately told me there was something of moment he wished to discuss with me. When he called us into his office, there was usually little time to sit down and chat. We stood, alertly, to answer his questions, or to explain what we needed to explain to him, to get the work in hand moving at a brisk pace. He was much given to laughter, and at the slightest provocation. But we knew his conviviality did not mean that he tolerated slovenliness, or a lackadaisical approach to our work.

"Sit down, my boy," Mr. Stanley said rather light-heartedly, though he was not smiling. "Sit down and make yourself comfortable."

I preferred to stand, and did, because that was normalcy for me and because, in my skewed world at the time, any deviation from the normal tended usually to give me the shivers. Mr. Stanley noticed my hesitation, and my nervousness, and insisted that I take a chair. So, reluctantly, I took the chair to which he was pointing peremptorily, and sat down.

"It's really a little matter," he said, and this time essayed a smile, which he probably meant to set me at ease, but did not. "It's about you and young Martin – oops! I mean Ralph Luther."

This obviously deliberate slip of the tongue was accompanied by a guffaw that, in spite of myself, evoked a sympathetic smile from me.

"It's a little matter," he said a second time, and it was then that I noticed that he, too, was a little nervous. "But the young man is a loud mouth. You know what I mean? He's been saying things – ."

"About me, sir?" I asked, when he seemed to hesitate.

"I've told you not to 'sir' me. Call me Peter, okay? Now, what was I saying? Oh yes, about Ralph. He really is a loud-mouthed son of a gun. How he got on to you, I've no idea. You get my drift? He's been saying nasty things, calling you names, that sort of thing."

"Like what?" I asked. I think I immediately had a sense of where the conversation was headed and, suddenly, anger boiled up in me. But I kept a tight hold on my emotion, and repeated my question. "What did he call me?"

"You know, names," said my boss, with a straight face. "Ex-convict, that sort of thing."

"But I thought you knew this," I said.

After a little pause, he looked away, and lay back deep in his swivel chair. "Yes, I knew," he said simply, bringing his big paws together in front of him, fingers intertwined.

"My uncle said he told you."

"Yes. Frank told me. Said he felt obliged to tell me up-front, so I would know."

"And you still employed me?"

He spread his arms wide. "Truth is, I had a long talk with Frank, and I liked what he told me about you, of course other than – you know – ."

"I know," I said. "I understand."

"Good. I'm glad you do. I decided I'd give you a chance, and I can see you're a good worker."

He stopped, and stared so long and hard at me, and so quizzically, I knew there was a downside to his faint praise. He would not, however, immediately say what was on his mind.

"But – ?" I asked, letting the question hang in the air.

"You know how it is," he finally said. "With a blabbermouth like Ralph around, the story will quickly spread – ."

I got reckless. "And I imagine," I said, "that it will not be good for the reputation of the firm."

His eyebrows rose fractionally in what I can only describe as mock surprise. "I didn't say that," he said, looking down and away from me.

"I know you didn't, but I understand," I said, bending the truth somewhat. "Thank you anyway for taking a chance on me."

I got up, and was almost out the door of his office, when he called me back.

"If you leave," he said, "Ralph goes too. It's about time I did something about him. His conduct in this matter is totally unacceptable to me. You know what I'm saying?"

For just a fraction of a second, I thought to plead on behalf of young Ralph Luther, to ask Mr. Stanley not to fire him on my account. Then I thought better of it, and simply nodded, and walked out, closing the door for the last time on my erstwhile boss. I walked out on Mr. Stanley and his office with my head held high, and of course some bitterness in my heart. But that heart burned with a renewed determination to live out the words of the immortal lines of William Henley:

> It matters not how strait the gate,
> How charged with punishments the scroll,
> I am the master of my fate,
> I am the captain of my soul.

I went straight to Ralph Luther's corner of the office, with nothing in particular on my mind. Except that I knew I had to speak to him before I left. He was much younger than I, in his late twenties, and handsome in a rough-hewn sort of way.

"I just came from the boss's office," I told him.

"I saw you go in," he said. I think he saw that my face was clouded over, and added: "Hope nothing's wrong?"

"Everything," I said. "I just lost my job, and no small thanks to you."

"Boy oh boy! What did I do now?"

I looked at him for a moment or two, and was convinced he had no idea what I was talking about. "You really don't know what you did? Well, actually, it's not so much what you did, as what you've been saying,"

"But I didn't say anything to the boss," he protested. And then perhaps he saw the light. "Oh my God, that!"

"Yes, *that*," I said, with appropriate emphasis. "And all because I drew your attention to something you keep doing, even though I'm sure you know it's not fair to the rest of us."

"I'm sorry, Cyril," he said. "I shouldn't have did it. You know I've always looked up to you as an older soul brother. I swear I never dreamt a little thing like that – ."

"A little thing, Ralph? You go around calling me an ex-convict, and you think that's a *little* thing?"

I spoke unrestrainedly, unmindful that our two other colleagues, Sam Abbott and Erica Ward, had dropped everything and were watching Ralph and me. The way I saw it, even if they had both been ignorant of my story, they were no longer so, thanks to Ralph, and his vindictive, running mouth.

"I don't know what came into my head."

"What came into your head?" I asked him. "It's your heart, Ralph. Anger came into your heart, and you lost it. You know what my people say?"

"What?" he asked, looking resigned.

"Anger is a terrible thing. My people say that if you murder someone in anger, the murder endures even after the anger has faded."

"But I didn't murder anybody," he countered.

This was just the kind of reaction I would have expected from a nitwit. But Ralph was not stupid, only a little slow. Which perhaps explained why it was taking him ages to get his Bachelor degree, even allowing for the fact that he was only a part-time student. It probably also explained why he usually took longer than anyone else over a given assignment. It certainly explained why he often seemed to lose count of time on his coffee and lunch breaks. Not that we got much of either: a miserly five minutes to go fetch one's coffee, and an even more niggardly thirty minutes for lunch.

"No, Ralph, you didn't murder anyone. You only killed the chance Mr. Stanley gave me for a really meaningful job."

"I said I was sorry," Ralph said. "And in any case he shouldn't have fired you – ."

"Perhaps you would like to go into his office," I suggested, "and tell him that. And while you're at it, quote him the law on the subject. Anyway, he really didn't fire me."

"But you said – ?" asked my three colleagues all at once. Erica and Sam, hitherto silent listeners, could no longer hold back from joining in my conversation with Ralph.

"I know what I said," I said, turning to Erica and Sam with a smile. I was surprised I could smile even after the light at the end of my tunnel had been so cruelly snuffed out. "I lost my job."

"Same difference," observed Erica, coolly examining her dainty little fingers, with their inch-long artificial nails, painted the same blood-red hue as her thin Caucasian lips.

"So what happened?" asked Sam, the worrywart, with a sad brow. The tallest of us four, and the most robust, Sam was affectionately called 'the man-mountain'. Middling in age, he was of an indeterminate status in the office, but seemed – in the short time I knew him – to be the right-hand man of the boss, whom he had served for more than a decade. He was frequently called to Mr. Stanley's office, where they caucused endlessly.

"Nothing much," I replied. "The boss and I reached an understanding, so to say, that it would be bad for the firm for people around here to be talking about me, and all that."

I said my goodbyes there and then. Erica allowed me the unusual privilege of hugging her warmly, and then I shook hands with Sam.

"If I were you," I said to Ralph, "I would go right now to the boss, and talk to him candidly about you and me. I think he's angry with you. And please feel free to tell him that's what I told you. And then perhaps mend your fences with him. Good luck."

I extended my hand to him, and he took it, and held it, and seemed unwilling to let go of it. His expression was sad and regretful, as he struggled for something to say to me.

"I'm sorry," he finally said. "So very sorry. I'll understand if you're bitter against me."

"I leave," I told him with a straight face, "without bitterness."

I think I knew I was not being wholly truthful about that, but I was determined to walk away from my colleagues with as much dignity as my tattered reputation allowed me. I told myself that I had to learn, quickly too, to take scenarios such as this in my stride. And that it would do me little good to huff and puff whenever an accusing finger is pointed in my direction.

In the month or so that I remained in Washington, D.C., when I was looking around, and considering my next move, I did not contact Mr. Stanley or my erstwhile colleagues. They were a part of my past. My time with them undoubtedly added a little something to my life experience. And the manner of my parting from them was a lesson in the harsh realities of our regular, workaday life. Once again I was reminded, if I had been tempted to forget, that I carried my Red Sea with me, as my constant shadow, and there was precious little I could do about it. I had no Moses to help me ford it, though, sure, I had Rosemary and my daughter Chizube, and their enduring love, to sustain me.

As soon as Rosemary walked into our apartment, and saw me reclining on the sofa in the living room, she knew there was trouble. For, in the six months that I worked for Mr. Peter Stanley, she nearly always returned from her work about an hour, sometimes even two, before I did. Her hours, in her District of Columbia Social Welfare office, were regular, eight a.m. to four p.m. Mine were not, except that I never ended my day's work earlier than five o'clock, and my commute, by bus, was about half-an-hour longer than hers.

"What happened?" she asked, plunking herself wearily into the sofa, very close to me, and leaning over to rub her cheek against mine.

I recounted the events of the day to her. She listened attentively, interjecting a question here and there. At the end of my story, she exhaled deeply, sat back in the chair, and was silent for a long moment, deep in thought.

"You shouldn't have walked out of the job," she said at last.

A little taken aback at her words, I turned to look at her. Our gaze held for a moment or two, and then she shook her head repeatedly.

"No, C.Y., you shouldn't have."

"But the man practically fired me," I protested.

"He did not. From your story, he never once said the words. You more or less took yourself out – ."

"So why didn't he stop me?"

"After you did the dirty job for him? It's quite clear to me he did not like that one of his staff was exposed as – er – ."

"A jailbird! An ex-convict! Say it Rosemary. The words won't bite you."

Rosemary looked at me with such sadness that I felt shame at my inconsiderateness. "I'm sorry," I said. "I shouldn't have said what I said."

She put out a hand and clasped mine, and held it firmly. "It's all right, C.Y. It's a natural reaction, but it will pass."

There was a long awkward pause, during which she squeezed my hand several times, as she muttered, over and over again: "It's okay, C.Y."

"You were saying – ?" I finally prompted her.

"What I was trying to say, about your Mr. Stanley not calling you back, is that he might have been thankful you decided to leave his firm, because he clearly was not comfortable that the word got out about you. He would have had no right, I think, to fire you himself."

"Why not?" I asked, remembering that the blabbermouth, Ralph himself, had said practically the same thing.

"Because, don't you see, he knew your story even before he hired you. I don't know the law, obviously. But he can never claim that you hid your past from him when he employed you. And that would have been his only moral basis for firing you when the story came out."

"I'm glad you used the word *moral*," I said, "not *legal*."

"That's what I think," said Rosemary.

Weary to the core, I got up, and excused myself. "Do you mind if I took a little stroll?" I asked Rosemary. "Alone."

She looked at me steadily for a moment, and then said: "You'll be all right, won't you? I hate to see you like this."

"I'll be all right," I said.

Outside, on that late afternoon in the middle of October, the air was distinctly nippy, though fall was not quite a month old. Fall is a beautiful and an agreeable season, particularly following a sultry summer. The temperature moderates gradually until, regrettably, it chills into the winter freeze. And though the trees begin to shed their crown of leaves, the rainbow colors of those leaves that still sit atop the trees are most pleasing to the eyes. But as I walked along the tree-lined avenues and streets, my harried mind would not let me see any of this beauty. All I could see, because I suppose I mostly kept my eyes down, was the accumulating mass of fallen leaves, dirt-brown in color, and trodden upon by the pitter-patter of a thousand undiscriminating feet.

There was nothing to be cheery about. The Toronto Blue Jays, not at all my favorite baseball team had, only days earlier, won the World Series. I was a fan of the Baltimore Orioles who had, for the umpteenth time, been left biting the dust, and had not even made it to the Divisional Play-Offs. If my team did not win, I rooted for the New York Yankees, America's quintessential team, and her favorite boys of summer. But the Yankees disappointed.

The clouds glowered for a while, and soon it began to drizzle. I bared my head to the inclement weather, but I had taken the precaution to bring along a light winter coat, perfect for the conditions. I walked through the drizzle for perhaps a half hour, and then decided to turn back, and go home. I should not have walked as long as I did. The drizzle soon changed to a light rain, which, progressively, became heavier. The last fifteen minutes, before I reached home, were unrelentingly miserable. The rain had intensified, and the temperature must have dropped another ten degrees or more.

Aunt Nwamaka had brought my daughter back from school. The old arrangement still held. Aunty picked up Chizube from school, took her home, and cared for her until about five o'clock, when Rosemary was due back from work. Then she would either drive Chizube to our apartment or, on days of glorious sunshine, they walked the five blocks from the Akamelu home to ours. Aunt Nwamaka, not us, absolutely insisted on this procedure.

They had chosen the wrong day to walk. As I was inserting my key into the front door lock, the door opened, and Aunt Nwamaka's large frame entirely filled the doorway. She was as wet as I was and, by the look of things, even more wretchedly cold. I did not think she was on the point of walking home in that foul weather, but I took no chances on that.

"Please aunty," I said promptly, "wait a second, and let me get the key to Rosemary's car."

"No need," said Rosemary, just then emerging from our bedroom, the bunch of keys jingling in her hand. "I was just about to drive her home."

"I'll save you the trouble," I said, taking the bunch from her. "Just give me a minute to change into something dry. Auntie, you are wet too. Is there something we can do – ?"

"Nothing," she said. "It's not so bad. I'll be home soon anyway."

When I came back to the living room, Chizube was standing by her mum, holding her hand.

"I'm coming along, and so is Chizube," Rosemary said, picking out one of her many coats from the closet adjacent to the apartment door.

"In this weather?"

"Doesn't matter," said my wife sweetly.

"Whatever you say, Rosemary. It's your car."

"Come on, Cyril!" said Aunt Nwamaka. "You must be the only person who doesn't call her Rose. And what's this about the car being her car?"

I shrugged my shoulders in hesitant reply, lacking the words to express my feelings adequately on either score. How could I describe the peculiar effect the very sound of the full name had on me when I said it? If there is a more mellifluent name, I have yet to hear it. Whoever coined the name, or first used it, might have experienced a spark of divine inspiration. Roses and the Madonna! Nature's most beautiful flower juxtaposed to the name of the Mother of Christ! What other sound could compare with that?

As to the other, the car – a Toyota Corolla – was bought and paid for by Rosemary, and there was nothing more to it. I had no car of my own, bought with *my* money. I do not know how it came about. But I developed the habit of always referring to the Corolla as Rosemary's car, which tended to irritate her no end. The way she saw it, her car was my car, man and wife being one flesh. But I suppose I had a sense – perhaps a warped sense – of my dignity. I would call no car *my* car unless I bought it with my money, earned with my toil and sweat.

It was fortuitous that it had rained, or we would not have needed to take Aunt Nwamaka home in our car. Uncle Frank was home, and very casually asked how my day had gone. He was always solicitous about me.

"Bad," said my wife, before I could get a word out.

Uncle Frank looked at me, and I nodded my confirmation.

"What happened?" he asked, looking from Rosemary to me.

So I told him my story. As I spoke, he nodded reflectively from time to time. At the end, like Rosemary when I had recounted the same story to her, he remained silent, deep in thought for several moments, as his eyes bored into mine. Then, for some reason turning to Rosemary, he uttered the words I had dreaded to hear from him, and that Rosemary had first spoken to me.

"He shouldn't have quit the job," he said to her, with a slight gesture of his head towards me.

"That's exactly what I told him," said my wife. "But it is too late now to do anything about it, no?"

"I suppose so," said her uncle. "I don't believe that even old Peter, great guy that he is, can change things back to what they were. I hope, at least, they paid you some good separation money?"

Silently, I nodded, as regret tore at my heart. Regret at what now seemed an unduly precipitate action on my part in quitting my job. Mr. Stanley certainly paid me off, more generously than I had expected; two months severance pay, to be exact. The boss had handed me the cheque, in the open office, as I gathered my papers for the last time, with a wish that better things happen to me in the future, and that I find another job soon. His parting shot, clearly for my consumption, was a summons to young Ralph Luther to "report pronto" to his office. Then I left, truly wishing that nothing untoward would befall the misguided youth on account of me. He was, after all, a soul brother.

There was a long awkward pause, broken by a sudden cacophony of sounds from the twenty-three inch television box in the living room where we sat. Chizube held the remote control a little away in front of her, pressing one button after another, in an impatient search for a program that had something for her twelve-year old mind. She smiled a sheepish little-girl smile when we all turned toward her. But then, as if by telepathy, we let her be, and she went on, happily now, searching for her program.

"Do you want me to speak to Peter about this?" offered Uncle Frank.

"No, sir!" I replied without hesitation.

Three pairs of eyes turned in my direction, and there was accusation in every one of them. "There you go again," they seemed to be saying to me. "Acting hastily, without reflection."

But I had no doubt at all, no qualms, about my stand. None of them had walked in my shoes; not even Rosemary who had clearly suffered vicariously with me during my long spell in jail. None could truly feel what I felt to be exposed as an ex-convict in my work place, where I had desperately hoped my secret would remain exactly that: a secret. None could feel the same compulsion I felt, to run, as far as I could run, from an environment where I could no longer hold my head high. Where I would be assailed by a constant temptation to misread an odd look or a wink. Where I might suffer palpitations just because a relative stranger asks innocently: "Haven't I seen you somewhere?" Somewhere? Like where? I knew I was running away from my shadow, carrying my Red Sea with me. But what else could I do?

Uncle Frank smiled sympathetically, and asked: "So what happens now?"

"I have to look for another job," I said, shrugging, fully aware I was saying the obvious.

"Here in D.C.?" asked Aunt Nwamaka.

As she asked the question, she got up from the two-seater she was sharing with Chizube, and made for the kitchen. At the kitchen door, she stopped and looked over her shoulder.

"How about supper?" she asked. "There's plenty of food in the fridge, and all I need to do is warm something up."

Chizube perked up. "Do you have pizza too?" she asked, with the uncaring innocence of a child.

"Chizube!" cried her mother. "You mustn't-."

"What?" asked auntie, walking back to the middle of the living room. "If she wants a pizza, she'll get a pizza. We'll just order one. This is her home; so let her be. Tell me, Chizube, how do you want it? Cheese or what?"

Chizube was familiar with the pizza vocabulary, and promptly said: "The whole works." And then she turned to her mother and me, as we sat on separate chairs to her left, and beamed at us.

"And what about you two?" asked Aunt Nwamaka. "I know you both love pizza. How about it?"

She had me there, and I could not hide the truth from her by any manner of dissembling. Rosemary, who had been on the point of properly rebuking our daughter for a lack of consideration, now smiled helplessly, and nodded in answer.

"We'll all have pizza," said Aunt Nwamaka. "We'll order two large ones, one with extra cheese, which he likes."

'He' was her husband. She had not bothered to ask him what he would like for supper, but she did not need to, and we knew it. Uncle Frank was certainly not a great lover of Italian food, but he was one of those men who do not much argue with their wives about their meals unless, of course, the wife asks the question, and absolutely insists on an answer. Or she has the idea of serving up dog – or horsemeat, which are taboo among some Igbo peoples.

The pizzas were ordered from Dominos. And while we waited, Aunt Nwamaka proceeded, with help from Rosemary and a delighted Chizube, to serve us drinks and snacks: a beer for Uncle Frank, and a variety of soft drinks for the rest of us. But her question hung in the air. "Here in D.C.?"

I had not much thought about it, since I had not foreseen the events of the day. But, as I quickly thought about my answer to her question, it seemed that my course was set.

"I'll not look for a job here in Washington," I said. "All things considered, I think it would be best for me to return to New Jersey."

"New Jersey?" my three companions, but not Chizube, cried as with one voice.

Then Aunt Nwamaka quickly added: "What about Rose?"

"And me?" chimed in Chizube, who clearly must not have been giving her whole attention to the animated cartoon movie on which she had seemed to be concentrating.

"Of course, my little girl," I said, in my best honeyed voice. "You'll go with us." I reached over and stroked her finely plaited hair.

"Who's us?" asked Rosemary.

"Us?" I asked, turning to her in some alarm. Probably because I had not had the chance to talk with her about the consequences for me – for us – of the loss of my job, I had not been mentally prepared for her reaction.

"Aren't you forgetting something?" she asked me.

Before I could get a word out in answer, Uncle Frank clucked several times, seemingly in distress at the turn of events. "What exactly do you have in mind?" he asked.

"I was thinking we could move to New Jersey. I believe that would be my best hunting ground for a new job."

"That's not going to be easy, you know," said Uncle Frank. "If Rose and Chizube go with you, things might get a little rough before they begin to get better. And in the meantime, you'll look like the proverbial hen, with her brood of chickens, trying to run for shelter during a rainstorm. Especially with Rose in her condition."

I looked sharply at him, and then at Rosemary. Uncle Frank was looking slantingly at his wife as he spoke and, momentarily at least, with as impassive a face as he could contrive. Then his face broke into an impish smile. I think he threw out that last remark with a deliberate intent to startle Rosemary and me. And he succeeded hugely. Our little secret was out: Rosemary was with child. But her pregnancy was barely three months old, and not obvious to the unpracticed eye.

'How ever did you know?' Rosemary asked, recovering faster than I from the shock. I saw her glance nervously at Chizube who, happily, seemed not to be paying us any more attention. She did not need to know about this, yet.

"You just confirmed our suspicion," said Uncle Frank. "Thank you. If you really want to know how we – er – how your auntie knew, you'll have to ask her."

"Now's not the time to talk about it," said Aunt Nwamaka, head tilted towards Chizube. "We'll talk later, if it's okay with you. Right now, I'm concerned about your immediate plans."

I looked sideways at Rosemary, and our eyes held for a moment or two. Then, simultaneously, we both shrugged, and turned to the matter in hand.

"I was saying that perhaps C.Y. has forgotten about my current job," said Rosemary. "My government job. What am I supposed to do about that?"

Her voice was not bitter, but there was an edge to it that cut me to the quick. And then I realized that I was perhaps being selfish. And thoughtless to boot! She did not need to say it in so many words – she was much too genial a spirit to do so – but the world, that is, hers and Chigozie's, did not revolve around only me. Indeed, in our particular situation, she was the heart and soul of the family. I had just lost my job, and the income that went with it. Worse still, at least from the unrehearsed and spontaneous reactions of my wife and her uncle, I had, more than likely, lost that job through my own precipitateness.

"You could get a transfer from D.C. to New Jersey," I suggested. "Couldn't you?"

Uncle Frank waved his arm in a sweeping gesture of dismissal. "Is that what you think?" he asked. "Unless I don't know this country, there's no transfer from one state or municipal government to another. Rose will have to resign her D.C. job and apply to New Jersey. And, if she's extremely lucky, she might find something as good as what she has here. But I am honestly a little doubtful about that."

"So what should we do?" I asked rather lamely.

"Simple. You go ahead and start looking for something in your New Jersey. And I believe you'll quite likely find a job. We say that a person groping in the dark will eventually find a place on which to rest his hands, even if it is on his own knees. But, and this is very important, Rosemary should also begin to apply to the New Jersey Department of Social Welfare. But she should – she must – remain in D.C. until the New Jersey job materializes. Her health insurance cannot be put at risk. Don't you ever forget that it covers you and Chizube, whether you have a job or not. Especially if you do not have a job!"

"What you're saying is very true," I said. "Uncle, as always, only words of wisdom come out of your mouth. We'll do as you say, and I hope we're lucky."

"There's something else," said Uncle Frank. "I'm thinking that you should perhaps try our own community in New Jersey, or anywhere else for that matter. There must be Nigerian, better still, Igbo accounting firms in New Jersey. I believe I know one or two here in D.C. and Maryland. Spread your net wide in your search. Talk to your cousin, Aloysius. He should know how it is with our people in New Jersey, and might make useful contacts for you."

I chewed on that for a moment or two, and felt a stab of unease gnaw at my innards. Unease, because I had this thing in me that would not let me readily bare my shame to my own people. Relative strangers were one thing. My own Igbo people were another. I could just see them passing the story from one person to the next, until the entire community knew about my humiliation. I did not want fingers pointed at me, at parties, or other social gatherings of the community. I would simply not be able to endure the mortification.

Uncle Frank must have read my mind. He leaned forward in his king's chair, a one-seater, with leather upholstery, and a long multi-colored, specially woven fabric that covered the seat and backrest. And he spoke even more earnestly than earlier.

"Here's one piece of advice, and you will do with it what you choose. New Jersey is where what happened to you happened. You have to assume that at least a handful of those who knew you there must have been aware of what happened. And if a handful knew, it is a safe bet that twice that number, even ten times that number, subsequently knew. You were a member of that community, and suddenly you disappeared from the scene for several years. You may not have been one of the leading lights there, but when something like that happens to even the smallest person in the community, the story gets around.

"Think about it. How did your colleague – what did you call him – Ralph? How did he know about you? Could it be that my friend Peter Stanley, with whom I was up-front about you, might have spoken a careless word at the wrong time and place? The story always starts from the inside, and then spreads out. As we say, it is the mouse in the house that tells the one in the bush that there's dried fish in the kitchen basket.

"So, this is how I see things. Try and get a job with our own people, and perhaps you will stop running whenever an ill wind blows. Assume that the Igbo accountant, who has a job to offer you, probably knows about you, and tell him your story – especially if the interview looks promising. Do you hear what I am telling you, Cyril Jideofo? You've got to stop running. And maybe, just maybe, an Igbo accounting firm, or a Nigerian firm, might be able to help you, in time, get your green card, who knows?"

"But Rosemary has one," I said. "And we've been thinking she might sponsor me."

"She might, yes," said Uncle Frank patiently. "But, with your present what-you-might-call-it with the I.N.S., that could prove difficult. That's why I think you should be patient in that regard, and let time, a secure employment and, in due course, your wife's sponsorship, if not your employer's, do the rest. It wasn't easy getting the green card for Rose, I can tell you. I had to pull some strings, in quarters not normally available to our people. Even so, I'm still amazed she got it so quickly. Some people are just luckier than others."

We enjoyed our pizzas, but left Uncle Frank's place no wiser than we were how in the world Aunt Nwamaka knew that Rosemary was pregnant. All she did was remind us that she had, years earlier, trained as a nurse and midwife, though she had had no compelling reason to practise her profession since coming to America.

"My eyes are trained to see what the rest of you might not see," she said. "I'm glad for both of you. There's one thing, though. Rose will need the care of a good obstetrician. She had her one child twelve years ago. And, she's – well, you know – ."

"I know, auntie," said Rosemary good-humoredly. "I'm getting too old for these things, no? But we pray, and hope."

Chapter VI

M Y SISTER ADAKU liked to fuss over me, and I loved it. Which was why I seized every opportunity to visit her, in Laurel, Maryland, where she lived with her husband Theo, and their three lovely daughters. But this was a very brief visit, a mere stopover for one night, on my way to Bound Brook, New Jersey. Indeed, if she and Theo had not been absolutely insistent that I stopped at theirs, I would not have done so.

I was in a bit of a hurry, for one thing. And for another, I could barely afford the three-day car rental from Hertz that my need for mobility forced on me, without the extra cost of an additional day. I needed to reach Bound Brook, and my cousin Aloysius, with the utmost haste. He had sent word to me about a Nigerian accounting firm that had a job opening. I already liked the sound of the name of the firm: ONYEAMA & ANI, CPAs. Cousin Aloysius also hinted at one or two other possibilities, but nothing as definite as Onyeama & Ani, CPAs.

Adaku and Theo knew how things were with me, because I had kept them constantly updated. They were not a little miffed with me, because I could not be persuaded to seriously include Maryland, their state of residence, in my area of job search. I did not *totally* rule out seeking a job in the D.C. area or in Maryland. Uncle Frank had hinted at the possibilities. But my heart and my hopes were set on New Jersey. And Uncle Frank had latterly decided to let me follow my own lead, though my wife remained largely unconvinced about the matter.

I could not find it in my heart to blame her. She had practically only known the District of Columbia and Maryland since she arrived in the country. And no doubt she thought she would be more comfortable there than she might be in New Jersey.

"Is it not the same New Jersey where your *chi* killed you?" she asked me.

I had no answer for her question; only hopes and dreams for the future. I could offer her no assurances that my *chi*, that personal and guardian spirit in whom my people so religiously believe, would not, once again, desert me, and give calamity a field day against me. But I had a strong aversion to remaining in the Washington area where a powerful gust of ill wind did to me what it did to the chicken in the proverb: it blew asunder its tail feathers, and thereby exposed its naked butt.

Adaku and Theo had three adorable daughters, aged nine, five and two. They gave their first daughter her mother's name, Adaku ('Daughter of wealth'). Their second daughter, they named Obianuju ('A child born into plenty'). Adaku told Rosemary that these names, at the time, had no special significance. She simply liked her own name, and thought it appropriate to pass it on. But when the third child turned out to be a third daughter, they chose a name for her, Chikodili ('It is in God's hands') which was an undisguised cry to God to give them a son, next time.

She was pregnant again, notwithstanding her and Theo's earlier intentions to have only three children. Desperate for a son, my sister vowed to go for a fifth child, if the one she was carrying turned out to be yet another girl.

"And if Theo doesn't go along with you?" I asked her.

She laughed shortly. "I can't believe you would ask that question," she said seriously. "Is he not an Igbo man? What Igbo man doesn't want a son?"

"You may be right, but – ."

"Maybe?" Adaku asked, snorting disdainfully.

"Surely not if it means five children."

"I'll go for a sixth, so help me God, if it becomes necessary," she declared with conviction. "When we named our second girl Obianuju, we were not really thinking about the meaning of the name. But it is okay. Theo is a doctor, and I am an R.N. We have good jobs, which pay us quite well. And we thank God for that. Listen C.Y. I know that things can change. But I am hopeful we will always be able to manage, even if we have six children. Who's counting anyway? As God is my helper, I hope to give Theo a son, even if it kills me."

"Don't say that!" I cried out, "or you might be tempting fate."

"You're right," she said. "Let it be as if I had not spoken the words."

On the evidence before my eyes, Theo and Adaku were comfortable. Cottonwood Terrace was an elegant estate of semi-detached houses, and lots of greenery, especially in the spring and the summer. They had a condominium with four bedrooms and three toilets, a large living room that was tastefully furnished, and with the paneling in highly polished brown wood, waxed and gleaming. When they were able to do so, usually at weekends, they breakfasted in their kitchen, which had a table that could sit six persons comfortably. They used their dining room mostly for more formal meals, especially when they had guests for dinner.

I honked as I maneuvered the car into their second parking allotment and, right away, Adaku and her daughters poured out of their house and were by my side before I had properly opened the car door. Obianuju, swift as a gazelle, leapt into my arms, fractionally ahead of her younger sister, Chikodili, who managed nevertheless to claim my right leg, to which she clung fiercely. Their big sister Ada, all of nine years, and tall for her age, hung slightly back, stiff with childlike dignity, determined to stay above the fray. By common consent, and in order to differentiate between mother and daughter, we had shortened the latter's name to Ada.

"What took you so long?" Ada asked, easing herself into my embrace when her sisters gave her an opening.

Adaku laughed shortly. "For the last hour and more," she said, "they've been standing by the kitchen window, watching as cars pulled into the parking area. We did not know in what kind of car you were coming. But, of course, you have your special way of sounding your car horn. And they were waiting for it."

She was right. Three quick short blasts, and then a longer one – that was my signature honk. I hugged my sister, and was letting myself be led by my nieces into the house, when I remembered my suitcase. But they would not let go of me.

"Daddy will bring it in when he comes back," said the bright-eyed, quick-thinking Obianuju.

"Can't do that, I'm afraid," I said, glancing at my watch. It was a quarter to five. "I'm not letting my suitcase stay exposed in the car for God knows how many hours before your dad returns from work. Some evil person might be tempted to break into the car."

"Oh, I don't know," said Adaku. "Theo might be back any minute now, though I'm not saying you should leave the suitcase for him to bring in."

"I didn't think you would," I said, laughing.

"But he always looks forward to your visits. And since we knew you were coming, he said he'd try and make sure he returns early today."

I went and retrieved the suitcase from the back seat of the car. I always travel light, except when my family accompanies me. And then, Rosemary packs a hefty suitcase full of the clothes she might need, and lots more that even she knows she would not need. "Just in case," she would say, her eyes pleading for my understanding. But no matter! We have learnt to buy only suitcases equipped with rollers.

My sister, with her daughters in tow, led me to the guest bedroom, which was at ground level. The bed was already made, with spotlessly clean light-blue sheets (she knew my favorite color for sheets), and a comforter so thick it could have withstood an Arctic cold. There was only that one bedroom at ground level; the other three were on the upper floor. The family room adjoined the guest bedroom, and had its own television set, which was normally monopolized by the kids. At a sign by their mother, Ada and her sisters, with varying degrees of reluctance, left us, and went to the family room and their T.V.

I looked around the bedroom, and inhaled. There was a sweetness of smell in the air that was most agreeable to the senses. I went to the window and ran my finger over the sill. Not a speck of dust. It was my routine – our routine, in fact – whenever I visited. And always the result was the same.

"Spotless," I said.

"As usual?" Adaku asked, with a wide and contented smile.

"Of course." I quickly shed my shoes, and threw myself full length on the bed, letting my eyes feast on the enigmatic smile of the Mona Lisa, which hung on the wall opposite my bed. "Sometimes I don't know why you bother. After all, it's only me."

"Only you!" she said. "You're my big brother, don't forget. And talking of brothers, did you hear recently from Emma?"

"No. Did you?"

"He called the other day," said Adaku. "They might be coming to visit some time in the spring, probably mid-May. Wouldn't that be simply wonderful? I can't wait."

"Don't hold your breath, sis. I don't think he'll come in May, because that means he'll miss the early part of the cricket season in England. I have not spoken with him in a while. But I have learnt not to worry too much about him. In Emma's case, silence means everything is as it should be. It's our kid-sister I'm more concerned about."

"Janet's all right, I think," said Adaku. "You worry too much about her, and that's beginning to affect me too."

"You actually think it's all right for our flesh and blood to be still trapped in that our blessed country?"

"Aren't Dad and Mum our flesh and blood? So tell me, C.Y., should they too come and live here in America?"

"Oh, come on! You know their case is different."

"Because of their age?"

"Yes, Adaku. And I know you're only joking."

We laughed, but I was serious about our sister Janet, and Chibuzo, her husband of six or so years. Chibuzo Nnamdi was a barrister struggling, like most professionals in Nigeria, to build a comfortable life for his wife and two sons, in the uncertain and often hazardous environment of Lagos, the country's bubbling, very cosmopolitan, commercial capital, where no one is his brother's keeper. After repeated but fruitless attempts to obtain visas from the American Embassy, Janet and Chibuzo were close to despair. They even tried the immigration lottery, but have had no luck, as yet.

"Not everyone," Adaku said, "can run away from home. Janet's turn will probably come. It just sometimes takes a little while for things to work out as we all wish. You'll see. As for Emma, *he* doesn't seem all that eager to come here."

I laughed. "Why should he? He lives in England, where he can indulge his passion for cricket to his fill, playing and watching. That's why I can't seem to believe he's talking about coming here in May. If you ask me, I think October sounds more like it. By then, the cricket season over there is pretty much over. "

Emma had developed his taste for cricket in his secondary school, the Government College, Umuahia. He became quite adept at it, and played for the school's first team in his two final years. He was indeed so good that he narrowly missed selection for the Nigerian national team by, he claims, a whisker. I believed him, though I knew he sometimes exaggerated. He was then doing his clinicals in the medical school, in the University of Nigeria, Enugu, Eastern Nigeria, where he played with the Enugu

Sports Club. He got his medical degree, and did his housemanship (what Americans know as internship) in the same hospital where he trained.

Then his miracle happened. How he managed to get a visa from the stiff necks at the British High Commission in Lagos remains, to this day, a mystery. But he got it, raised the money he needed, and then flew to London. Our dad scraped the barrel, and came up with a not altogether negligible sum of money, which helped Emma buy his ticket. The year was 1983. Shortly after arriving in London, and through the good offices of one of his old professors who had the right connections, and with whom he had maintained contact through the years, he found himself in Guy's Hospital, one of the most renowned in England. In time, he got his Membership of the Royal College of Surgeons. So he is now, after the manner of the British, *Mr.* Emmanuel Jideofo, M.R.C.S. – a well-regarded surgeon in Brixton, London.

He decided to settle in England, but it was not easy. He had considerable help from the girl he married, a legal resident, one Irene Wokoma, a *salt-water* girl from the Niger Delta of Nigeria. Our mother was not at all happy with his choice of a spouse. Her preference was that her daughter-in-law should be Igbo, no ifs, ands or buts. Irene Wokoma's people, from time immemorial, were considered true-blood Igbo, even though their group of villages was located at the periphery of Igboland. But, eager to distance their clan from the Igbo of Biafra, against whom the Federal government of Nigeria fought a bloody civil war for thirty months from 1967, they chose to deny their heritage, and their Igboness.

Then, in 1990, Emma took his family on a vacation visit to Nigeria. Mother and daughter-in-law finally met. And they connected, and did so beautifully. It probably did not hurt that Irene presented our mother with a grandson, Nwakozo, then just over one year old.

Emma called me now and again, mostly to talk about our Dad and Mum, and how we could help make their lives more comfortable in their advancing years. An excellent idea obviously, except that it was much easier for him, from his comfortable income as a successful surgeon in England, to send loads of money home. But he was very gracious about it, telling me to take my time and find my feet, after my recent less than happy experiences.

My brother-in-law, Theo, kept his word, and was back home within a half-hour of my arrival. We greeted each other as we had done since the day of my release from prison. I raised my right arm, and he raised his. Then we touched the backs of our hands three times, and at each touch, he greeted me by calling out "C.Y.!" and I returned the compliment by intoning his praise-name: "*Nwata-kwochal'aka!*" (A young person who has washed his hands well.) After the third touch, we clasped hands in a more or less standard handshake, with just a little bit of flourish. The Igbo say that, to dine with the wealthy, a young person must thoroughly wash his or her hands. With his medical degree, which, arguably, is accorded the highest professional status among Nigerians, Theo had done more than just wash his hands; he had rubbed fragrant ointment into them. I had nothing against praise-names. But I had as yet taken none for myself, nor had anyone in the community conferred one on me. Indeed I did not think I had done anything to merit one.

"As we say," Theo said, "one's in-law is one's *chi*. So, I had to treat your visit as a special honor, and my work has to take second place today."

"Don't let your employers hear you say that," I cautioned him.

Theo sometimes exaggerates. But I do not mind. Besides, he is a good and very considerate in-law. If I am his *chi*, I suppose he is also my *chi*, though I am sometimes out of my depth in these matters. He seems to be a good husband, too. My sister, in their many years of marriage, has never had cause, to my knowledge, to reproach him for any serious breach of his duties and obligations to her as her husband. He is always attentive to my needs, whenever I visit. Indeed I sometimes worry that I visit them too frequently. But it is an urge I can seldom resist, whenever I have the littlest window of opportunity, or excuse. Who can blame me? They treat me – and my family – almost like royalty.

I had expected the usual: total relaxation and chitchatting in the living room after we had dined. The television would always be on, though no one paid it the least attention. My three nieces – and my daughter Chizube, if my family were with me – would withdraw to the den, without prompting, to watch whatever gave them pleasure on the television, without interference from us old fogies. Chizube would be in her element, playing the big cousin, though they are really more like four sisters.

But my good hosts had other ideas. As soon as dinner was done, around eight-thirty, I caught Theo as he made some sort of an eye-and-hand signal to Adaku, who nodded imperceptibly (or so she thought). Then Theo asked me to come with him to my bedroom.

He did not prevaricate, or engage in useless doublespeak. In a measured tone that went perfectly with his expressionless face, he set my head in a whirl, and my heart beating wildly.

"We have reason," he announced, "to believe that your friend is in this country."

I think that for the briefest moment, my head drained of its life-sustaining blood. I am sure I instantly knew to whom he referred, but I was too stupefied by the news to think straight.

"Who's my – ?" I began to ask, and then stopped myself from completing a question to which I already knew the horrendous answer. "But that's quite impossible."

"No, it's not," said Theo calmly. "This is the United States. Nothing, absolutely nothing, can be said to be impossible here."

"But he went back to Nigeria," I said stubbornly.

"He was put on a plane and sent back to Nigeria," said Theo. "So?"

"So, my in-law, there's no way he can ever again return to America. Which American Embassy or Consulate will give him a visa? You forget we are talking about a Nigerian. Already very respectable Nigerians are refused U.S. visas daily in Lagos."

"I know. Americans think we Nigerians are all criminals," said Theo. "Someone called us a nation of scammers."

"Not just someone. It was a noted American General."

"Who happens to be an African American," said Theo, shaking his head sadly. "And that fact makes it worse for us."

"I know what you mean. And, as you know, even a junior embassy official can refuse you a visa on his or her whim."

"Yes, yes," said Theo, a little impatiently. "But what has all this to do with your friend?"

"Everything!" I said explosively. "Bernard cannot be back in this country. No way!"

"There you go again," said Theo resignedly. "Saying it, you know, doesn't necessarily make it so? You forget we are a very resourceful people, when it comes to things like this. I suspect your friend is one of those people who can find a way to deceive even the devil."

I looked at my brother-in-law and, suddenly, my heart was filled with suspicion. "Are you sure you are telling me everything you know? Is there something else? And, for God's sake, stop calling him my friend. What is it, Theo?"

His eyes now looked a little shifty. Then, unable to stand my intense gaze, he stood up, and walked to the window, and stood in front of it, looking out into the enfolding darkness. He stood like that, silently, for a long moment, hands buried deep in his trouser pockets, eyes staring vacantly ahead, rigidly pensive. Then he turned to me.

"C.Y.," he said, his eyes boring into mine, "what I told you, we have on fairly good authority. I cannot go beyond that to add the rumors one has heard, or to inject my own speculations on the matter. Like the frog in a stream, I don't know what I will say, and water will fill my mouth."

"You're my brother-in-law, Theo. You've got to tell me, at least, who told you about Bernard. And, by the way, does my sister know?"

I asked that question because I had caught them exchanging signals just before Theo brought me to my bedroom, to hurl his thunderclap at me. It was the worst piece of news I had heard in more than a decade, and was right up there, almost on a par with the words of my hanging judge, when he pronounced the sentence that blighted my life, in stonehearted disregard of my pleas of innocence.

With great deliberateness, but without answering my question, Theo left the window, and went back to the easy chair on which he had been sitting, one of only two chairs in the bedroom. I let him take his time, though my heart was beating uncontrollably. And, in the silence of the moment, the two famous Watergate questions tormented my mind: *What* did Theo and Adaku know, and *when* did they know it?

Theo leaned forward in his chair. "Listen to me," he said with great earnestness, "I know how hard this must be for you. But you must take it easy."

"That's easy for you to say," I said, but without bitterness.

"C.Y., my brother. You really need to think very clearly, and calmly, about the situation, what it all means, and how you might want to respond to it."

I had been sitting upright on the bed. Now, I threw myself back on it, and lay prostrate and unmoving for a long moment. I think the only part of my body that could not stay still was my mouth, which twitched with suppressed anger. And, I must confess, not a little excitement and wonder. Anger at Bernard Ekwekwe, who had been such a close friend he was like a brother, but who had not hesitated long before hurling me down to bottomless perdition – to save his own miserable skin. And wonder that, slick as ever, he had somehow found a way to outmaneuver the two agencies of the United States government – the Embassy in Nigeria, and the I.N.S. – that should have been on a perpetual alert for scoundrels like him. Who knew but that he might have reshaped his nose! Or grown a beard, or worn a false one! I have heard talk of contact lenses that can alter the hue of even a Black man's irises. Or had he come into the country with a false passport?

My excitement had nothing to do with joy at the coming reunion with a long-lost friend. That emotion is best left to television talk shows. But I must admit that I began immediately to look forward to that reunion, and with that, came an overpowering urge to kill him on sight. Or at least to wring his neck! Or something! A strong sensation coursed through my body, as I lay prostrate on my guest bed, in the home of my sister, Adaku. And I could already taste, in my mouth, the feel of my hands around his neck, their grip tightening, and his eyes dilating with wonder at the savage strength that my years of incarceration had infused into them.

Then I laughed. I laughed because I remembered that Bernard, the Bernard I knew, was like a lion when challenged to a fight; and that the fierceness of my righteous anger would likely avail me little against his dominating strength. If I had a gun, I might perhaps just shoot him.

My sister entered the room, and sat on the arm of Theo's chair. Her mien was serious, and haunted. She looked at Theo, her eyes asking him a question. He replied with a faint nod. I observed all this without seeming to, and then raised myself to a sitting position.

"You knew about this," I said to her.

"Are you asking me, or telling me?" Adaku replied.

She was not smiling. But she had not asked to what I alluded, which seemed to suggest that she knew.

"When did you know?" I asked, looking at Theo.

"Know what?" he threw back at me.

"Come on, you two! Can't you see what this news is doing to me?"

"Didn't Theo tell you," asked my sister, "that we're not really sure about all this?"

"You just answered my previous question. Anyway, Theo said it's from a reliable source. If, by not being sure, you mean you have not, yourselves, set eyes on Bernard, please say so. And then, tell me who told you, and where the person saw him, and how long ago. You can't hold back now, please."

Adaku came and sat by my side on the bed. Then she took and held my hand.

"C.Y.," she said softly, "the trouble is that no one has told us they themselves saw Bernard with their own eyes."

"And you know what they say," said Theo. "If you raise a corner of a thatch lying on the ground, and see a snake under it, you had best quickly lower the thatch. We don't know what all this will lead to, especially if it turns out to be only a rumor."

"You mean," I said, "if it turns out to be true. Because it is then that things might begin to happen that none of us can foresee at this moment. I know I would give anything to see the S.O.B. just one more time. There's going to be some serious reckoning between us when we meet again."

"That's exactly what has been bothering us," said Adaku.

"If you ask me," said her husband, "I would advise that you avoid him."

I could not believe my ears. "Avoid him! I don't understand you two. This man put me in jail for a crime *he* committed, and wasted some seven or eight good years of my life. Somehow, unbelievably, he has once again beaten the system, and sneaked into the U.S. I don't know how he did it, but I hope it is true. And if the only way I'll be able to see him is to crawl on all fours to the ends of the earth, I'll do so."

A little grandiloquent, perhaps! But at that moment, I meant every word I said. This was the scoundrel who had put me in jail for a long stretch. How many years did he, himself, serve for his own admitted malfeasance? He had, at the trial, owned up to running a drug-trafficking gang, but had lied when he informed the court that I was one of his lieutenants. The best information I had was that he had been given an extremely light sentence, because of his plea-bargaining. Something about one year!

I put a finger under Adaku's chin, and turned her head so she faced me, and we looked into each other's eyes.

"Adaku, my sister," I pleaded with her, "it's no good hiding anything from me. You must tell me who told you about Bernard. Or did you or Theo run into him? What did he look like? Was he as handsome – ?"

"A friend of Obi Udozo's," said Adaku simply.

"Obi's friend? He told you?"

"Yes. He said Obi told him."

She looked helplessly at her husband as she spoke. Theo, unable to look her in the eye, instead looked down, miserably.

"Who's this friend?" I asked no one in particular, casting my mind back more than a decade, desperately trying to recall Obi Udozo's circle of friends. I drew a blank, which was no surprise really, seeing I barely knew the fellow. Bernard had been the connection between us, and had brought us together on one of his trips to the United States, during his drug-trafficking days.

What was Bernard up to now? Evidently, the man could do the impossible. I could not get past my wonder at his presence in the United States. How had he pulled that one off? I was familiar with his assets: he was impossibly handsome, and had the charm of the devil. If he turned on his extraordinary allure, and had only women to deal with at the U.S. visa office in Nigeria, and at the J.F. Kennedy Airport in New York, it was odds-on he could have had them eating out of his hands in no time at all. But I had myself seen some of these women in action, and every single one of them seems to have her heart set at her back. They are almost unearthly, and tough as nails. Tougher, even, than their male colleagues!

I did not sleep well that night. Visions of Bernard, in his multiple disguises as my friend, floated before my mind's eye. I saw him once again at the genesis of our friendship, on the day he ejected a monstrous toffee from his mouth, and then bit off a piece, which he offered to me. That had been the first significant interaction between us. We were, if memory serves, in our third year in primary school, in the coal city of Enugu, in Eastern Nigeria. I was ten years old then.

I saw us as we sat down, years later, and swapped stories of our experiences in the Nigeria-Biafra civil war, which had erupted in 1967, our senior year in high school. My experiences had been as nothing compared to his. I was merely a batman to an officer of the Biafran Military Intelligence, and barely saw a shot fired in the fratricidal conflict. He, on the other hand, as a frontline Biafran soldier, recounted some hair-raising stories of his many encounters with the 'vandals' – our fond name for the Nigerian enemy. We had both joined the army, impelled by our enthusiasm for the Biafran cause, which seemed – and to this day still seems – so utterly just, we were willing, at that tender age, to fight and die for her. I believed every word of Bernard's many stories of his heroism in the face of overwhelming odds, against an enemy so much better armed that the war should really have been no contest. In retrospect, his stories seemed like tall tales, but I was naïve and trusting.

I saw us in Enugu, as we studied hard in the two years immediately following the debacle of Biafra in 1970, in preparation for two very important examinations. We were both successful in the West African School Certificate (a high school diploma) examination. But the entrance examination to the University College, Ibadan, was a different story. Bernard passed; I failed. Bernard was quite tearful at our parting, when I saw him off at the Enugu railroad station, where he boarded the train for the long journey to Ibadan, for his undergraduate studies. For a person as unemotional as I knew him to be, Bernard's tears were an eloquent testimony to the warmth of our friendship.

The vision shifted to the day I introduced Bernard to Rosemary, on his second long vacation from the university, in June 1973. He watched her steadily with his eagle eyes, as we sat and chatted in the Enugu Recreation Club, and Rosemary sipped her coca-cola, and he drank his warm beer, which he thoroughly detested. And then, after she left us to return to her father's house, Bernard had pronounced her "perfect". I recalled his exact words, as he marveled at my coup: "How in the world did you do it?"

Then my mind conjured up the scene of my first meeting with Bernard in the United States, on the day he so unexpectedly showed up at the gala organized by the Enyimba Union of New Jersey, then the main cultural organization of the Igbos resident in the state. It had been a surprise, but not shockingly so, because I had heard through the grapevine, days earlier, that he was visiting, though I had no clue in what part of the country he was. He had set me up, he later confessed, with his surprise appearance at the gala, and his donation of three hundred dollars to the Enyimba Union. I think I began then to smell a rat, three hundred dollars being a quite substantial amount of money for someone like him who earned his income in *naira*, Nigeria's currency. But I could not totally think straight because, I suppose, his mere presence mesmerized me. Indeed he knew it would, because I recalled vividly the wide smile that lit up his face, as he looked me over and over, while we held hands on the empty dance floor, unmindful of a thousand other persons in the hall.

The scene now changed to the day I saw someone who, he told me, was "just a friend", pass him two brown envelopes, stuffed full of dollars. "Ten thousand dollars" Bernard cheerfully told me when I pressed him on the matter. "The fruits of my labor", he had added. I did not know to what kind of labor he referred, but I had a tinge of doubt about the nature of his business. Which was the reason I had asked him, on the day of our first meeting in America, if his business was "a good business", by which I meant a reputable one. He never gave me complete satisfaction on that matter, then or later, but I still could not bring myself to put some serious distance between us.

All of this set the scene for the next segment in the kaleidoscope that was excruciatingly difficult to relive. That was the day Obi Udozo called on me, at the home of my cousin Aloysius Jideofo, to hand me a black plastic sack, and a white envelope. The sack contained eight thousand dollars, mercifully in hundred dollar bills; and the envelope, a letter to Obi, in my friend's quite atrocious calligraphy, which Bernard asked him to let me read.

The letter pleaded with me to personally deliver the eight thousand dollars to one Sam Anolue, an old primary school mate of Bernard's and mine, who was also Bernard's business associate, and was due to arrive in the United States shortly. I recalled vividly two very important statements in that letter. "Tell Cyril I am awfully sorry to drag him into this matter," Bernard wrote. And later: "I . . . promise never again to bother him with any request like this in future."

These were the two statements that would assuredly have cleared me of the charge that I was involved with Bernard in his nefarious drug trafficking, a charge that landed me in prison for eight blighted years. But, at my trial, Bernard calmly denied he ever wrote such a letter to anyone. And his friend, Obi Udozo, who was not my friend, but could have turned the scales of justice in my favor, also denied, when questioned by the police, that the letter ever existed.

Just the memory of those two devastating denials sent the blood rushing to my head, even as anger boiled in my heart. But neither the rush of blood nor my overly charged heart could save me from the worst scene of all: the day, the very moment, of my sentencing. "Eight years!" pronounced the judge, as he brought his gavel down, with a resounding thud, on his oaken desk. Eight years!

I must have finally fallen asleep with those two words reverberating in my ears and in my head, and remembering how they had sounded, at that god-awful moment, like time without end.

CHAPTER VII

COUSIN ALOYSIUS DROVE me to my interview at the offices of ONYEAMA & ANI, CPAs, on Somerset Street, off Broad Street, in downtown Newark, New Jersey. As we drove past the imposing, high-rise office building of the Immigration and Naturalization Services, on Broad Street, and turned into a public parking not quite three blocks away, I felt my heartbeat fractionally quicken. I think I was not at all sure, if I got the job, that I would be comfortable with that degree of daily and physical proximity to an agency that held my fate in its cold hands.

But I quickly overcame the shivers that temporarily overwhelmed me because I reminded myself that distance, in these matters, was not of the essence. The long arms of the INS, when it chooses to extend them, reach north, south, east and west, to the farthest corners of these United States. And I knew that against its near-omnipotence, a little fellow like me is totally powerless to offer meaningful resistance – if the agency finally got to my case!

It was an off day for Aloysius though, when I lived with him in my years as an undergraduate at Rutgers, I seldom knew him to take one. Especially on a regular workday! But he knew how to arrange his life around his needs. And, as he told me, he needed, today, to go with me.

"For encouragement, right?" I asked.

"I'm not sure I'll call it that," he said reflectively. "But, you never know, it might be useful. You look all right to me, and probably don't need my encouragement."

I did not know what I looked like, externally. Inside of me, I was a bundle of nerves. Nor did I know what to expect at the hands of the two Certified Public Accountants who would be interviewing me later. I only knew that I needed the job badly. Would they have an attitude? I kept telling myself that they probably knew everything there was to know about me. And straightaway I imagined them looking at me with a knowing smile, and eyes that would do their utmost to hide that knowledge from me.

Aunt Obiamaka, who may have seen me in somewhat clearer light than her husband did, was a tad more worried and anxious than he was, or seemed to be.

"Look, C.Y.," she said from the front door of the house, as she gently waved good-bye, "you'd better not show them you need the job desperately."

That was all she said, and I knew she was right. So, after I shut the car door and fixed my seat belt, I smiled and waved to her. And I stiffened my resolve to do the interview as if it was nothing at all – whatever that meant. Aloysius spoke little during the thirty-minute drive to Newark, except for the occasional comment, mostly uncomplimentary, about how everybody else on the road was driving. That was always his way, and the years had not changed him in that regard. I could not tell him what his wife routinely told him: that he should mind his own driving, and not worry about others. But even if I did, he had a standard response. "It shows, doesn't it, that I'm awake, and alert to what is going on around me." I could not argue with that.

Okechukwu Ani, C.P.A., received us as we stepped into the anteroom of the office. He was particularly deferential to Aloysius, which reminded me how highly my cousin was esteemed in our community. Mr. Ani bowed reverentially to him, intoning his praise-name, *Onwa-n'etili-ora* (meaning the moon that shines for the benefit of the people), and would not straighten himself until Aloysius gently patted him on the shoulder in acknowledgement of his obeisance. That degree of obeisance, most unusual for your typical Igboman, was in reality only half-serious. I knew it was so because of the hilarity it engendered between the two of them. But it was a marked and significant demonstration of respect nevertheless.

"*Onwa-n'etili-ora!*" Mr. Ani said two or three times. "You're welcome to our office."

"Thank you," said my cousin, "thank you. Now what did I do with that your praise-name?"

"Me?" asked Mr. Ani, laughing, "I'm just plain Okechukwu Ani. No praise-name for me yet."

"You're too modest, my friend," said Aloysius. "You should have taken one by now. In fact, I think I'm going to change that situation right away. Your trouble is you don't know how well you are regarded in the community. Someone like you, a C.P.A., and one that uses his expertise to help others, should not go without a good name. I know several people who say they owe you for doing their tax forms and not charging them – how do Americans say it – an arm and a foot – "

"Leg," I said, laughing.

"Yes," said Aloysius. "Leg! Whatever. Stop interrupting me. Let me see now – how about something like – yes, *Ochiora!*"

"*Ochiora?*"

"You're the President of your professional association, aren't you?"

"The local chapter of the Nigerian CPAs, yes. But –"

"So you're a leader," said Aloysius. "Or isn't that what the name means?"

Just then, Mr. Ani's partner walked into the anteroom. Chikezie Onyeama, C.P.A., stiffer in his show of respect, walked up to Aloysius and offered his hand in greeting.

"*Onwa-n'etili-ora*!" he said.

"*Ugonna*!" Aloysius responded, shaking hands. (*Ugonna* literally means Father's eagle. The eagle is known for its elegance and soaring flight.)

"And this is your brother?" Mr. Onyeama asked, turning to me.

"My cousin," said Aloysius. "Cyril Jideofo. Cyril, meet Okey Ani and Chikezie Onyeama."

"*Ugonna*!" I greeted the latter, as we shook hands.

"*Ochiora*!" I said to Mr. Ani, smiling, as we also shook hands.

"Not so fast!" said he. "I didn't say I had accepted the name yet."

"What's going on?" asked his partner, surprised. "Am I the last to know this? *Ochiora*! I must say I like the name. Suits you too."

"*Ugonna*, please!" objected Mr. Ani. But I think he sensed that the name would stick, because it had been conferred on him by one of the most respected members of the Igbo community in New Jersey. And he knew it would be futile to try to reject it.

"*Ochiora*!" Mr. Onyeama repeated, more loudly. "I like it. But why are we standing here? Please come into my office. And – where's that woman? Edith! Edith!"

A short, bespectacled woman, fortyish and plump, whom I had not seen when we first entered the office, appeared from a side-room.

"*Ugonna*," she said.

Mr. Onyeama looked at his watch. "You're not just coming in, are you? It's a quarter-past-nine."

"Who? Me?" asked the bespectacled woman. "I've been here since eight-thirty."

Then she saw cousin Aloysius. "*Onwa-n'etili-ora*!. You came to our office today? How's your wife, *Obidiya*? Hope she's well. And the little ones? Who's your companion? I don't think we've met."

"Obiamaka is well," said Aloysius. "As for the little ones, Tobenna and Ebele can hardly be described as little any more. They have so much energy I don't seem to be able to cope with them any more when they get into their playing mode. That's why I regret we waited so long before adopting them. At my age now, I don't know where I'll find the energy to deal with them."

Despairing of begetting any children from his loins, Aloysius had prevailed on his wife Obiamaka that they adopt two kids. This had not been easy. Obiamaka had stoutly resisted such a move, which, she pointed out, was a most unusual one for an Igbo couple. "We don't adopt," she had said simply. But she finally succumbed to pressure from close friends. I know that my other aunt, her 'namesake', Mrs. Amaka Akamelu had been among the most persistent. So they had adopted a boy and a girl, now aged five and three. Roy and Melissa, siblings and unbaptized at the time of their adoption, were aged three and one. Obiamaka and Aloysius retained the kids' names but, at their christening, gave them the Igbo names Tobenna (Praise God) and Ebelechukwu (God's mercies), by which they were now more commonly known.

"Better late than never," said Mr. Ani. "As in every thing, including adoption, God's time is the best." Then turning to Edith, he said: "You sure you never met this gentleman before? If so, he must really be a Johnny-Just-Come."

"Okechukwu, you've come with your taunts," said Edith, slapping him playfully on the shoulder. "You are just fishing for me to say something – ."

"That's okay, Edith," said Aloysius. "Meet my cousin Cyril Jideofo."

"Oh, Jideofo! You're here for the interview." She looked at her watch. "Aren't you early?"

"That's okay," said Mr. Onyeama.

"I'm sorry," said cousin Aloysius. "It's my fault. But I thought – ."

"*Onwa-n'etili-ora*," said Mr. Onyeama, "please not to worry. It actually suits us better that way. In any case, as far as I'm concerned, *you* can come in here any time you like, and bring whoever you want."

"And it isn't everyday," added Mr. Ani, "that the distinguished patron of our Enyimba Union comes to our office."

"Easy, fellows," said my cousin, laughing. "This is serious business. But I'm afraid I can't take the chair you're offering me. I have to run to do some errands for my wife."

"Errands?" asked Edith. "You mean to tell me *Obidiya* sends *you* on errands? What's the world coming to?"

"Hey!" said Aloysius, laughing. "This is America. And the Igbo woman is learning fast."

"Igbo? It's not just the Igbo woman, but the Naija woman."

I turned to Edith. "What's that, the Naija woman?"

Edith laughed at me. "Look at this one! You really must be new here. Naija means Nigerian. That's all."

There was general laughter, but neither cousin Aloysius nor I joined in the merriment. I could only wonder why Aloysius was not amused. But, in my warped and over-sensitized world, the twice-repeated remark about my newness in the area, though probably without malice aforethought, sounded just a trifle loaded to me. Perhaps Mr. Ani, who had earlier called me a Johnny-Just-Come, really knew nothing else about me than that I was Aloysius's cousin. But it was odds-on that Edith, plump in figure and no doubt heavy with the community's tittle-tattle, had heard something. Or, if she had not heard, chances were she would, and soon, perhaps just as soon as I got back into circulation. A woman like her was sure to be a magnet for rumors.

"Edith, please get us some coffee," said Mr. Onyeama, "and some cookies too. *Onwa-n'etili-ora*, you can't be in such a hurry that you cannot stop long enough for a cup of something? What's keeping you back, Edith?"

"Do I look like someone who'll just rush off and get a cup of coffee for someone who I know doesn't like coffee? He likes his tea, not coffee."

"So get him a cup of tea, then," said Mr. Ani, smiling tolerantly. It was plain to see that though she was their secretary, Edith had an easy, relaxed relationship with her employers. Clearly also, they respected her age.

"I know how you like your tea," she said to cousin Aloysius. "Nothing too strong, no? Just a quick dip of the tea bag in the hot water."

Cousin Aloysius, unable to resist the pressure from all sides, succumbed genially. "You certainly know how I like it, but make it decaf please, if that's no trouble."

"No trouble at all," she said, and then peered at me. "How about you?"

"Anything," I said.

"We don't have '*anything*'," she countered with a straight face, though I knew there was an impish smile lurking underneath her expressionless eyes. "Tea or coffee. You should choose one. Or perhaps you'd prefer a juice or soda?"

"Well, coffee then," I said. "Thank you, Edith."

"And Edith, the usual for us, please," said Mr. Ani.

"Two more coffees, okay," said Edith.

At the door, she stopped. "Cyril Jideofo," she said, coming up to me where I sat, and putting a hand on my shoulder. "Those two don't seem to want to call me by my praise-name. But that's all right. If you'd like to know, I'm called *Akwaa-okwulu*." She paused, and then added: "Like I said, just in case you'd like to know." And with that, she turned and walked away.

We looked at one another, and I could see that, for Mr. Ani and Mr. Onyeama, the scene I had just witnessed was what a famous baseball player, lacking the necessities for good French, would have described as "*deja vu*, all over again". Whoever bestowed her praise-name on her, knew her well. *Akwaa-okwulu* literally means 'resistant to a shove'. Edith was clearly a woman who, in a manner of speaking, could not be pushed around.

We were all seated by now, in an office notable for its neat but unpretentious furnishings. Mr. Onyeama's desk, made of highly polished oak, was positioned just about three feet from the partition wall that separated his office from Mr. Ani's. With the latter's desk also similarly positioned, the two partners, in effect, sat back to back when they were at their desks. There was a connecting door between the two offices. Both offices, I soon discovered, were furnished in an almost identical way. Each had a table, wide enough to carry a small P.C. and a printer, set close to the desk. A file cabinet, silver-gray in color and four drawers high, stood in the corner directly opposite the desk, and close to a two-door metal cabinet, with shelves for stationery and other office equipment. A small refrigerator stood by itself in another corner. There were, for the partners, navy blue swivel chairs; and for visitors, two dark leather-upholstered chairs, free moving on ball bearings, in each office. As we entered the room, Mr. Ani quickly went into his office through the connecting door, and brought in his two visitors' chairs. All four chairs were then arranged, for us, around a low central table in the middle of the room.

The thought that was uppermost in my mind, as I studied the two partners, was that this was not going to be your usual job interview. But I knew that I had to be on my guard against any assumption that the interview would be a breeze. With my cousin Aloysius almost venerated by the two gentlemen, certainly by Mr. Ani, it was very tempting for me to make such an assumption. "As man know man" is a common Nigerian expression. It is an expression that captures succinctly the universal wisdom that if you want something, and know a person who has the right connections, or can influence the outcome in your favor, your chances of success are rosier. Cousin Aloysius filled the bill, for me, perfectly.

Edith brought in the cups of coffee and Aloysius's tea. Some snacks too: honey-roasted peanuts, salted cashew nuts, as well as sweet tea biscuits, on separate paper plates. Eager to show that I was no glutton, I picked at my nuts in a most leisurely manner, and spent the time appraising the two CPAs.

Mr. Onyeama, much more than his colleague, caught and held my attention. He certainly had a presence. At first sight, his bearing seemed aristocratic, though I kept asking myself if that might not be a front, so to say, for arrogance or haughtiness. He was the tallest of us four, a good inch-and-a-half, or two, taller than my six feet. A carefully trimmed mustache, thick, and pointed at each end, evidently gave him much pleasure, judging by the way he frequently stroked and pulled at it. His well-cut dark brown suit merely served to enhance his strikingly good looks, of which – it was easy to see – he was not unaware. When our eyes met, he seemed to be looking at me with a certain degree of detachment. But I was not fooled. I could tell that he, in turn, was seriously appraising me.

His partner, Okechukwu Ani, was of average height. For a person as heavily built as he was, he looked quite athletic – an impression heightened by the way his powerful chest and upper body tapered to a surprisingly narrow waist. This was easy to see because, for the entire duration of my visit and interview, he was jacketless.

After a few minutes of light-hearted conversation, cousin Aloysius got up. "I really must go," he said. "Thank you for everything."

This time, neither of our two hosts tried to stop him. So he shook hands all around, and moved towards the door. At the door, he stopped, turned round and asked, looking at his watch: "When will the interview be over – you know – approximately?"

"I would say," said Mr. Ani, "about an hour, give or take – ."

"Thank you," said Aloysius. "And good luck, Cyril." His eyes also said he hoped I remembered what he and I had discussed about the interview.

As if I would – or could! Though we had been most cordially received, I could think of nothing else than that I had to be at my best. I came to the interview mentally prepared, fortified by advice from cousin Aloysius and his wife and, before I left Washington, D.C., by uncle Frank Akamelu. The consensus was that I should be truthful, but not gushingly so. Rosemary was the only one who thought I should bare my soul to my interviewers, whether or not they asked me pointed questions.

I was surprised at her counsel, but she remained firm in her opinion. "You remember what uncle Frank said a few days ago about all this," she said, as I cuddled her in the crook of my arm, in our bed, on the night before I left for New Jersey. "He said you should assume that the Igbo accountant interviewing you probably has heard about your misfortune. He may not tell you so directly, but you must have it at the back of your mind that he knows. Now, if you offer the information without being pushed, I'm sure he'll score one for you. And if in fact he did not know before you told him about it, it is a safe bet he would have found out anyway in due course. So I say, don't hide your mouth when replying to their questions. My father is fond of saying that *truth is life*. I really believe so."

Mr. Ani's first remarks immediately put me on the spot. We were sitting exactly as cousin Aloysius had left us, in the middle of Mr. Onyeama's office, with our empty and half-empty cups, and paper plates with crumbs and uneaten cookies, still on the low rectangular table around which we sat. I was surprised that neither he nor his partner had any papers before them as they began the interview.

"We've looked through your resume and things," Mr. Ani said, intertwining his fingers in front of his mouth, and peering at me intently for a few moments. "You graduated, cum laude, in 1978. That's very good. But we see nothing to show that you made any progress professionally since then."

"That is," added Mr. Onyeama, "other than your M.B.A."

I stared at my interlocutors for several moments, as I fought a battle with myself. Whatever cousin Aloysius had told them about me, and I believed he must have said something to them, I was pretty sure about one thing: he had not told them about my incarceration for eight years. If he had done so, he would have told me he did. It was, it occurred to me, exactly like him to let me do my own thing.

It was the moment of truth. I quickly thought about my wife, in far away Washington, D.C., and what she had told me her father liked to say. And I crossed my finger for luck, in the desperate hope that the truth I was about to tell would bring new life to me, and really set me free.

"For seven or so years," I said, "I was an unwilling guest of the U.S. government."

My two interviewers exchanged rapid glances, but otherwise said nothing. In the awkward pause that followed, it flashed through my mind that I was once again on a slippery slope. I recalled that the last time I had had any serious job-related discussion, other than in family circles, I had seemed to react with unwarranted impetuosity to a remark by Mr. Peter Stanley, my last employer and boss. And, as a result, I had walked away from a good job from which my boss had not explicitly fired me. I had thought, at the time, that I had done the right thing. But my wife and her uncle had taken issue with me on that score.

Idly, Mr. Ani picked up a cashew nut and flipped it into his mouth. Mr. Onyeama, stiffly dignified, and pulling thoughtfully at his mustache, watched his partner for a moment or two, and then turned his attention to me.

"I'm afraid," he said, "you'll have to explain what you just said."

But before I could get another word out, Edith walked into the office. She brought with her two boards, with clasps, and a foolscap-sized pad of ruled yellow paper. A long pencil that had clearly not seen much use, nicely sharpened, and eraser-ended, was attached to each board.

She stopped abruptly as she entered the office, looked around for a moment, and shook her head. "Don't tell me you've started the interview?"

"Of course," said Mr. Ani.

"Without anything to write on?" she asked, holding out the boards.

She did not wait for their answer. Instead, she put the boards down on the table, counted out four sheets from the yellow pad, and attached two sheets to each board. Then she handed one board to each of her bosses.

"There!" she said. "You look more businesslike now. And, by the way, don't you need me to sit and take notes too?"

I nearly died inside of me. I know that my heart cartwheeled in alarm at the thought that there might be a third listener to my tale of woe. Perhaps Mr. Onyeama saw the fright in my eyes, or perhaps his sixth sense was suddenly awoken. Whatever it was, he quickly shook his head, and even managed a smile.

"Not today, Edith. We'll call you when we need you. Thanks anyway."

"Okay," said she, looking anything but pleased at the seeming brush-off. "Do you want anything else? But why am I asking? Someone has to clean up this table."

And with that, unbidden, she picked up the empty paper plates and used cups, and deposited them in a wastebasket. Next, she collected the uneaten nuts and sweet biscuits in one paper plate, and placed the plate, with meticulous care, in the approximate geometric center of the table. Then she straightened herself with a mild but quite deliberate groan and, shrugging her massive shoulders in resignation, walked out of the office.

My eyes followed her until she disappeared behind the door, and then I heaved a long sigh of relief. I am not sure that either of my two interlocutors noticed my behavior. But I did not care. If I must tell the truth, I would have to admit that the fact of Edith being a woman alarmed me more than the mere presence of a third person. It was possible, I reflected, that Edith already knew, or had heard, something. If so, I could not change that fact. I was also well aware that if she did not already know, there was no way I could prevent her knowing eventually. Particularly if I got the job for which I was being interviewed. But, I told myself, the later she knew, the better.

"By the way," I asked, "is she married?"

"Not as far as I know," said Mr. Ani, turning to his partner questioningly.

Mr. Onyeama shook his head. "Unless she has somebody hidden away in Nigeria, she is just plain Ms Edith Tagbo. But let's get back to what you were saying. You were a guest of the U.S. government?"

"An unwilling one," added Mr. Ani. "Exactly what's that supposed to mean? Were you working for the government? In fact, do you have residency papers – I mean the green card, that sort of thing?"

I could have let him go on with his questions endlessly, because I was now full of regret at having perhaps spoken too much, too soon. But what would have been the use? An inner voice recalled Rosemary's words, spoken so softly, and yet so persuasively, only a few days earlier, as she quoted her father: TRUTH IS LIFE!

So I braced myself and, avoiding the two pairs of eyes staring intently at me, even as I gazed at the top of the table between us, I spoke the truth that I saw no way to avoid.

"The truth," I said, measuring my words carefully, "the honest-to-God truth is that, for eight years or so, I was in prison."

"What!" said Mr. Ani.

"Ex – cuse – me?" said Mr. Onyeama, with deliberate slowness. "Did you say prison?"

Silently, I nodded, looking from the one to the other, but in reality seeing neither. How could I, when my eyes and my mind were focused on an idea, and not on anything substantial? The idea was my obsessive fear of the unknown, a fear that suddenly gripped my heart as in a vise. I was sure I had not only lost the respect of the two accountants, but that I had also bungled my chances of landing the job.

"Why? Where? What happened?" Mr. Ani asked, staring at me as if this was the first time he ever saw an ex-convict at such close quarters. Which might well have been the case.

"It's a long story." I said, my eyes now on Mr. Onyeama. "But I can say one thing truthfully, though half the prison population, where I was, will doubtless make the same claim. I was imprisoned for a crime I did not commit. Believe me, it *is* a long story."

"That's all right," said Mr. Onyeama. "Perhaps you can give us a gist of it. Let's start from your graduation. You graduated in – er – 1978?"

"Yes."

"Take it from there," said Mr. Onyeama.

"Well," I said. "Let's see. I did odd jobs – you know how it is with our people here – while I waited for something good. My break came when I was offered a job by the accounting firm of Gable, Kline & Stevens, in D.C."

"I don't think I've ever heard that name," said Mr. Ani. "But go on."

"Just about then, a very close friend and classmate from my primary and secondary school years in Enugu, who had visited The States earlier, sent me some money to deliver to a business associate of his, also coming from Nigeria."

"But he could have given the money directly to the business associate right there in Nigeria," said Mr. Ani. "Why didn't he?"

"Simple. Bernard – that's his name – he obviously didn't have the dollars in Nigeria. So he sent a check, drawn on his U.S. bank, to another friend of his here in New Jersey. Now, and I'm not at all sure of this, but this New Jersey friend, Obi Udozo, may have been a business associate also. At least they had been in some touch with each other before I ever became aware that my friend Bernard had visited the United States a few times and had not bothered to contact me. Obi cashed the check and brought the money to me, with a request that I deliver the money to the fellow from home, one Sam Anolue, who was a classmate of ours – that is, Bernard's and mine – in primary school. When Sam arrived in the U.S. – ."

"Hold it!" shouted Mr. Ani. "And I'm going to ask the same kind of question I asked earlier. Why didn't your New Jersey friend, the fellow that cashed the check – you called him Obi, I think – why didn't he give the cash himself to Sam?"

"First, Obi is not my friend. Secondly, he had never before set eyes on Sam, and might have run the risk of giving the money to the wrong person. As I said, Sam was a classmate. We used to call him *Short man bogey*, and we teased him unmercifully because of his height. Anyway, when Sam arrived in America, he called me from his Newark hotel, and I went there to deliver the money to him. That was where I walked into a trap the F.B.I. set for me – meaning, whoever showed up with the money about which Sam had already informed them. The F.B.I. had arrested him at JFK, with some stuff on him."

"Stuff? What stuff?" asked Mr. Onyeama.

"Do you need to ask?" asked Mr. Ani.

Mr. Onyeama laughed, but without mirth. "Well, you're right. I suppose I don't need to ask. But wait just a minute! I think I heard something about this. Years and years ago! Early eighties, I think. *You* were the person in the story? I don't remember much about the details. And in any case I never did get to know the names of the persons involved. Plus, I didn't know there was any connection to *Onwa-n'etili-ora*."

"Your brother – I mean cousin – he never mentioned anything about this," said Mr. Ani, "and we must have spoken with him about three times."

"About me?"

"Yes, after he approached us on your behalf."

He turned to Mr. Onyeama, probably to confirm what he had just said. But his partner seemed totally wrapped up in his own thoughts, frowning with the intensity of someone struggling to recall an incident or a story from an elusive past. He stared hard and long at me, and then, perhaps giving up the effort, shook his head.

"This fellow, Obi, does he still live here, in New Jersey?" he asked. "I should have heard about him."

"I'm not really sure," I said. "But I intend to find out. My cousin should know. To tell you the truth, as far as I knew, he wasn't one of those people who like to come out. You know what I mean? I don't think he was a member of the Union, that sort of thing."

"Sorry, what did you say?" Mr. Onyeama asked his partner. "Oh, yes, about Dr. Jideofo. No, he didn't mention any of this when we talked with him. But that's not surprising. The places where we met and talked with him – a meeting of the Union, a wedding reception, and suchlike – I know, if I were him, I wouldn't want to talk about this kind of thing in such places. Too many ears, if you ask me."

I did not know in what direction the interview was headed. But, in the brief, very awkward pause that followed, I kept telling myself to stay positive, to remember that truth is life, and that whatever the outcome – whether I got the job or not – I did what

I had to do, what I needed to do, to avoid any future accusations of deceitfulness. I had, I thought, at least partially forded my Red Sea, and my dark secret was now out in the open.

Mr. Onyeama suddenly excused himself and went and fetched a sheet that had been lying at the top of an office file on his desk.

"This," he said, waving it to and fro, "is the only reference we have from any of your former employers. We now understand, of course, why you do not have more such references."

He looked at the sheet for a moment, and then said: "Mr. Stanley says here you were his best worker, and that you pretty much handled half the tax jobs his firm had to do. And he says he was sorry to see you go." He stopped, and looked at me. "Why did you?"

"Why did I go? That's a hard one to answer. Let's just say there was a slight misunderstanding, and I left. It had nothing, however, to do with my work."

"A misunderstanding?" asked Mr. Ani. "That seems to suggest you left abruptly. Why?"

I sensed right away that I would not be able to shake them off that trail. They needed to know. They had every right to know. Besides, I was already embarked on the path of truth, and this was no time to prevaricate.

So I told my interviewers the sordid story. In full. No punches pulled. I watched them as I talked, wondering, always wondering, if their opinion of me would change for the better or the worse. I had noted that, other than to express a natural curiosity about the whys and wherefores of it, they had not jumped all over me when I revealed that I had been in prison. Perhaps they were merely playing their cards close to their chests. But, for a mind as tortured as mine, desperately seeking any positive signs, their overall attitude was not discouragingly negative.

When my story was done, neither gentleman spoke for what seemed an eternity. They exchanged brief glances. Then Mr. Onyeama spoke.

"Hmm, I see," he said, nodding reflectively. "I think I understand why you are being so – how shall I put it – so honest with us, so upfront about your – er – ."

"Imprisonment?"

"Yes, thank you. I think you did the right thing."

"I think so too," said Mr. Ani.

He turned to his partner. "Ugonna," he said, using Mr. Onyeama's praise-name, "do you remember what the good doctor told us about his cousin?"

"Good doctor? Oh! You mean Dr. Jideofo?"

"Who else? Do you remember he said something about his cousin being someone who tells it as he sees it?"

"Actually what he said was that his cousin will tell the truth even if it hurts him." Mr. Onyeama turned to me, and added: "It is clear he thinks highly of you. And he always referred to you as 'my cousin'. He probably only mentioned your name Cyril a couple of times. By the way, can we call you Cyril? Or have you taken a praise-name?"

"What kind of praise-name would I take after what I've been through?" I asked. "My life has barely started, though I've clocked forty-two already, and have a twelve-year old daughter. No, I'm Cyril Jideofo; nothing more."

"Oh yes!" said Mr. Onyeama. "You have a daughter. I almost forgot. I believe you mentioned it in your resume. What's her name?"

"Chizube."

"From the glow on your face," said Mr. Ani, "I wager she's the apple –"

"The apple of my eyes? No sir. She's my life. She's the principal reason my life has any meaning now. She, and her mother Rosemary, my wife! I robbed them both of eight good years of our lives together, by my incredible stupidity. My stupidity in not recognizing when a friend is no longer a friend, and has become the worst type of even an enemy! An enemy that can smile, and smile, and then plunge a dagger into your heart."

I saw my two interviewers smile as, for the umpteenth time, they exchanged glances. But this time, they were both nodding as if in agreement with something I had said. What that was, I had no clue. But, from where I sat, it seemed like a good sign.

"Well, Cyril," said Mr. Ani, after the pause, "tell me something. When you were coming for this interview, what were you expecting?"

"I don't understand," I said, buying some time.

"You know," Mr. Ani explained, spreading his arms wide in a vague gesture. "As we say, the head of the he-goat is in the bag of the he-goat; meaning, you and us, we are the same; we are Igbo. I bet you've never been interviewed for a job – at least since coming to this country – by one of our people."

"Well," I said, "when you put it that way, I was not sure what to expect, except that I had a notion it would be different."

"How different?" persisted Mr. Ani.

I looked at Mr. Onyeama, and found him gazing at me with what seemed a twinkle in his eyes, and a trace of a roguish grin playing at the corners of his mouth.

"Just different," I said. "I think my principal thought – or rather, I should say, hope – was that the fact of my imprisonment would not damn me quite as completely as it might have, if I was being interviewed by an American employer."

Mr. Onyeama nodded two or three times, his face reflective, his eyes boring into mine. "That's good," he said. "But let me ask you something else. If – and I mean IF – we offer you this job, what kind of salary would you expect? As you can see, we run a very small office here. We have only one employee –"

I dared to interrupt him. "Our people say that the fact that a corpse fills a coffin doesn't mean it is a person of consequence that has died. You may be small now. But the fact that you are even considering employing one more person means you are growing – or at least, you see the possibility of growth. If you employ me, I think I can help you achieve that growth. My salary? That's a tough one to answer. I think I'll leave that to you to make an offer. I have my Bachelor degree, majoring in Accounting, and my MBA, with concentration on Taxation and Accounting."

Mr. Ani looked at his watch. "We'll get back to you in the next twenty-four hours. Your cousin should be here in the next ten or twenty minutes to pick you up. I know he's a stickler for time, one of the very few in our community like that."

"Do I have the job?"

The two partners looked at each other unhurriedly. Mr. Onyeama's eyes asked a question. Mr. Ani slightly inclined his head, and puckered his lips. I watched them anxiously, hoping they did not see me doing so.

Mr. Onyeama said: "As my partner said, we'll get back to you in the next twenty-four hours."

"There's just one little problem," said Mr. Ani. "Something we almost forgot. What's your visa status?"

"Oh yes!" said Mr. Onyeama. "I did forget."

"I don't understand," I said. But, in truth, I did. The fact was that I had not come to the interview prepared to deal with any question like that. Mr. Peter Stanley, my last employer, had certainly not asked me anything like that.

"Sure you do, Cyril," said Mr. Ani. "Uncle Sam has rules about these things. I believe you can see we want to help you all we can, if for no other reason, at least because in this foreign land we are all brothers. You need a work permit."

"I don't have one," I said. "But – ."

"But what?" asked Mr. Onyeama, when he noticed my pause.

"I don't know what good it'll do, but I have my social security number."

"That might help," said Mr. Onyeama, "provided the card is not marked: NOT VALID FOR EMPLOYMENT."

"It isn't. And, another thing, my wife has her green card, and in another year or so, will be applying for her citizenship."

"Now you're talking!" said Mr. Ani.

"Getting the social security number was, luckily for me, the last, and best, thing I did for myself before my troubles began."

"Good." Mr. Onyeama paused briefly, staring at me intently. "Talking about your – you know – troubles, have you ever thought about doing something to clear your name? I'm thinking that if, as you say – and I think I believe you – if you are totally innocent of the crime for which you went to jail, there must be something you can do to change things. That your friend, what did you call him – ?"

"Bernard? Bernard Ekwekwe."

"Yah, Bernard. Where's he? Here, or at home?"

"Who knows? He might well be here in the U.S., as we talk. But he could be in Nigeria. I believe he went back home after his one-year imprisonment."

I did not want to reveal that I had heard Bernard might be in the country. I did not know either gentleman well enough – as yet – to share such confidences with them. But what Mr. Onyeama was proposing that I attempt was something that, as far as I knew, had never been done. Having done my time, how in the world could I now prove to the United States courts that I had been innocent all along? The same courts that had condemned me! And the same United States attorneys, notorious for never accepting that they could have been wrong, and had prosecuted the wrong man! I had had my fill of courts. Of course, I knew about DNA tests that had conclusively proved the innocence of condemned persons, decades after the crimes were committed for which they had been incarcerated, or put on death row. But there was nothing, in my case, on which a DNA test could be done. Bernard's crime had been bloodless and sperm-less. There had been no hairs, no finger – or toenails, no body parts that could be tested. He had, indeed, admitted to his crime of drug trafficking. But he had plea-bargained, and then turned state witness against his best friend in the world, me. The sentencing judge had thrown the book at me, and Bernard had gotten off with a mere slap on the wrist.

"Well, Cyril," said Mr. Onyeama, "you can at least explore the possibilities. Who knows what could happen?"

"I think I know what might be worrying him," said Mr. Ani. "Are you not thinking, Cyril, that if you were to start something, you might be needlessly drawing attention to yourself, and the visa problems you might have?"

I had no answer to the question, and shrugged in silence. After a few moments, first Mr. Onyeama and then his partner came to me and shook my hand, to mark the end of the interview.

"Think about it," urged Mr. Ani. "Talk to your family. Talk to one or two lawyers from the community, at least for advice that should cost you nothing. I think I hear footsteps, and that must be your cousin. Consult him especially. He knows who's who, and what goes. He could be extremely helpful. We say that if you have easy and ready access to an ocean, you should not be washing your hands with your spittle."

"And if your friend – sorry, Bernard – is in the country somewhere," added Mr. Onyeama, "you could do worse than track him down, even if it's only to see what he's up to, this time."

There was a knock on the partition door between the offices of the partners. Then it opened, and cousin Aloysius walked in, closely followed by Edith.

"Am I interrupting?" he asked.

"Not at all," said Mr. Onyeama. "We're done."

"And?"

"Cyril will tell you everything. He'll hear from us in the next day or two."

Chapter VIII

I REPORTED FOR work in the firm of ONYEAMA & ANI on the last Monday of October 1992, a week after my interview. I needed the week because I had to return to Washington, D.C. to discuss the situation with Rosemary. And with our daughter Chizube too, who would have to change schools, and in consequence lose old friendships and start new ones. I suspected that, of us three, the relocation would be hardest on her. It turned out, indeed, that it was a bit of a wrench for her, and she cried a little. But she was a good and loving daughter, and was beginning to understand that life sometimes throws us a curve ball.

Rosemary was quite satisfied with the starting annual salary of just under thirty thousand dollars I had been offered.

"However small it may seem," she philosophized, "it didn't come to you on its own steam, or fall out of the sky like manna. Someone offered it to you. That someone could, one day, increase it. It works out at a little over twenty-four hundred dollars a month. And if you add that to what I make, we aren't too far from six thousand a month. That's not at all bad. It will put three meals on our table every day, and pay the rent for the apartment we are taking in West Brook, and so much more. Let's be thankful. By the way, C.Y., you did well to take me to see the place before you settled the deal. It's a great place."

As if I would have dared to do it any other way! The husband who commits himself to renting – or buying – an apartment, or a house, without his wife's approval, needs to have his head examined. That was cousin Aloysius's emphatic counsel, born of some experience in such matters. It was him that drew my attention to West Brook, and to the Mount of Olives Gardens – an elegant estate of tree-lined streets, well manicured lawns, gardens that gave promise of rich spring colors, and a little stream that washes its western border, its soft waters kissing the edge of the lawns as it ripples and winds it's way southward to a distant mouth, in gentle ceaseless motion.

A New Jersey Transit bus that runs by the estate – along the highway that brushes its eastern edge – takes one into downtown Newark, to a stop just two minutes walk from the offices of ONYEAMA & ANI. I bought a car, a Honda Civic, a week or so after I assumed duties in the office. But I knew the bus would come in handy on such days as I might chose not to drive my car, or the car would be at the servicing garage.

I knew the pecking order in the office from the moment I started work. I was given a desk in Mr. Ani's room. He could accommodate me because his office was quite large, fractionally larger than Mr. Onyeama's. It had in fact been the latter's office, but the partners had exchanged rooms when they decided to hire an additional staff, who would then share one of the offices. To give Mr. Ani the best shot at maintaining a semblance of privacy appropriate for a certified accountant in a two-partner firm, a moveable screen, a little over six feet high, had been so placed as to cut the room into two unequal halves. I had the smaller half. But the space I enjoyed was larger by far than the little corner in which I was tucked away, in the open office at my last working place, at Peter Stanley's, in Washington, D.C.

So, right away, I knew that Mr. Onyeama was the senior partner. And I discovered, after a quick research into their backgrounds, that he had graduated, magna-cum-laude, in 1976, at the University of Pennsylvania (a prestigious, so-called Ivy League University), from where he also obtained his MBA two years later. In fact the two partners had met in the university, in Mr. Onyeama's senior year, and Mr. Ani's freshman year. The senior became the freshman's mentor and role model. They became friends and, as Mr. Ani told me, frequently talked about their possible future as accounting partners, and dreamed dreams about what they could, together, do. They were well aware, he told me, that they would first need to break the jinx that so often afflicts Nigerian joint ventures, whose history is littered with broken partnerships, for reasons, principally, of a systemic lack of mutual trust and confidence.

They took it as a positive sign that they were both Ivy Leaguers, and hoped to tap into whatever advantages went with that fact. They noted that in the world of business, from which they hoped to attract their more profitable clientele, not a few of the CEOs and Board chairmen were also Ivy Leaguers, even if not necessarily fellow alumni of Pennsylvania. In the event, the partnership had endured for close on eight years at the time of my recruitment, though not without stresses and strains. But though their corporate clientele was not negligible, the real plums of the business world were still largely an elusive dream.

"But we're doing quite well, thank you," said the senior partner. "At least, well enough to move into our phase two."

"Hiring me?"

"You could put it that way, yes. We were lucky we found someone like you just when we most needed you."

I knew what he meant, even if he did not say so expressly. They were lucky, in the nick of time, to find someone like me who, because I had spent eight years in the nick – no pun intended – could never be a certified accountant, and could not therefore command an accountant's salary. My MBA, in accounting and taxation, meant that I could function with a high degree of expertise in those two areas, plus auditing, that are truly at the heart of the certified accountant's job.

But I felt quite good about where I was, all things considered. The future stretched out promisingly in front of me. I did not have to be a sage to know that the road could be long and winding. And no doubt treacherous! I knew I had to have my wits about me, and that I needed to tread warily for fear of springing one or more of the many mines that might lie in wait for me.

Our senior partner, Mr. Onyeama, though a little stiff in his interactions with people was, nevertheless, not overbearing. I was happy to share an office with Mr. Ani, notwithstanding the screen separating us, because I soon saw that he was a very down-to-earth colleague. And he scaled artificial barriers with the ease of an Olympic hurdler. Edith was, well, quite simply Edith.

"As you see me," she told me on my first day, "that's it. There's nothing more to look for."

Probably because I played up to her in the matter of her praise-name, she often came waddling out of her small room, adjoining ours, to ask me if there was anything she could do for me. What she did do for me, and which helped me tremendously in those early weeks, was that she typed all my documents. "But don't count on my doing so forever," she warned, smiling. I did not need the warning. I knew that her principal task was to serve the two partners, especially the senior partner, as the office secretary. And she was very good at what she did.

On the day my family and I bade our tearful good-bye to Washington, D.C., uncle Frank prayed over us. The tears were Rosemary's and Chizube's, not mine. Poor Chizube! She had made many friends in her school, and did not want to leave them. Rosemary held on to aunt Nwamaka, though her arms barely reached halfway around her aunt's considerable girth. They cried on each other's shoulders, while uncle Frank and I looked on with calm detachment; in my case, pretended calm detachment. It was not easy.

The occasion was more solemn than I would have wished. But uncle Frank said it was very important to him that the parting was done properly.

"I know," he said, "that you are moving only a couple of hundred miles away from Washington. So it's not really anything like a final good-bye. You'll be just three or so hours drive away, on a good day, from us. What is significant is that we'll no longer be seeing you on an almost daily basis."

We were at table, for dinner, in his home. But before food was served, aunt Nwamaka, clearly by prior arrangement, handed him a bowl containing one big kola nut. She had discretely kept the nut from our view, somewhere under the table, or her chair, or perhaps in the folds of her voluminous dress.

Uncle Frank cleared his throat noisily, picked up the kola nut, and held it up for us to see. It was quite large, the size perhaps of a golf ball, nicely smooth and yellow, its lobes clearly demarcated.

"This is an Igbo kola nut," he proudly announced, "and not your common Hausa *gworo*. I insisted that your aunty bought the right one for tonight. I hope, when you get to New Jersey, that you'll find a market or store where you can buy our African stuff."

He paused, and looked around the table. "I know you're all hungry," he said, his eyes focusing on Chizube, who stared back at him with her wide, open, innocent eyes. Then he smiled at her briefly. "Especially you, my little one. But everything in due time."

He raised the kola nut again. "As I break and share this kola nut with you all, I do so with a prayer to God, and our ancestors, to guide you as you try to find your way in this our uncertain world. When you are walking forward, may the devil and his henchmen be behind you. When you walk backwards, may they be in front of you. May God bless your efforts to make a good life for yourselves wherever you go, or set up home.

"There is an Igbo singer – I forget his name – who, in one of his songs, gives advice that we should all do well to remember. Always! As you struggle through life, he sings, always keep your arms straight. If you try to put yourself ahead of your *chi*, it is like beating on a metal that is not red-hot and malleable. Hold yourself firmly. Let your actions be clean. And the reason? Everything comes from God. He blesses those who walk the straight and narrow way. If you believe that all things come from Him, your burden, as you walk through life, will be immeasurably lightened. And when you reach your destination, you will find his blessings in abundance.

"Cyril," he said, turning his eyes on me, "you are a good person. In spite of what happened to you, you have not turned sour. Hold on to that quality but, at the same time, keep your wits sharp. It is good to be simple, but not too simple. And, for Christ's sake, keep your eyes open because, as we say, a rat cannot steal the food of a person who is awake. You understand what I am saying to you?"

I nodded, lacking the words immediately to thank him for his expressions of good wishes. But he was not done.

"And you, my niece, child of my elder brother, what can I say to you? Your husband likes to say you are his angel. He's not alone in that feeling. You are my angel too. And your aunt Nwamaka's! And Chizube's especially! Hold fast to what God has given you, and He'll give you more. If there's one thing I must say to you, it is this: sometimes – but only sometimes – you become aggressive. Which is not at all bad. You certainly need, occasionally, to be assertive, if only because there are persons out there who would want to pounce on you if you are too meek. But please remember what the he-goat does. When it has knocked horns with his adversary in a fight, he steps back for moment or two and watches the enemy. Do likewise. We expect to hear only good things about you all. Do you hear me, Cyril? And you too, Rose? So long as you keep your arms straight, I'm sure all will be well with you. That's our prayer for you."

I knew, when he admonished us to 'keep our arms straight', that he did not mean it literally, and that it was merely a way to say we should be honest in our dealings with others.

Uncle Frank then broke the kola nut with the solemnity of a priest at Eucharist. As is customary at the end of an invocation, we shouted his praise-name: UTA-CHUKWU (God's arrow)! This was a name he had richly earned in the Igbo community of the District of Columbia and Maryland, on account, I was told, of his habit of shooting straight, telling it as he sees it, without prevarication, or a forked tongue. We each took a piece of the kola nut, except of course Chizube who, at twelve, was too young for the honor. Rosemary seemed to eat her piece with relish, which was a surprise to me. Usually, she wrinkled her nose in disgust whenever I pressed her to try one. Too bitter, she would say. But this occasion was very special, she told me later that day, seeing it was her uncle that did the invocation.

"Plus, we had more than one reason to be thankful to God," she said. "Look at all the wonderful things He has done for us: your new job, and new car, our beautiful apartment in West Brook and, not least, the letter from the New Jersey Department of Social Services offering me a position there. I don't know about you, C.Y., but if you ask me, I'll say our cup is full, and running over. Praise the Lord!"

"Hallelujah!" I said reverently.

My car was actually not new, except in the sense that I had purchased it only a few days earlier. But a used Honda Civic, whose only previous owner had put just under thirty thousand miles on the odometer, in three years, could be considered almost new. It was, besides, in impeccable condition. I made no down payment on it, and the annual percentage rate was a modest 4.9%. I bought it with my credit card. Oh yes! I had a Visa credit card, though I wondered, and to this day still wonder, if a person like me can legally own one. I know I really should quit worrying about the potential pitfalls in my path in life. Rosemary constantly exhorts me to. But I fear I will just keep on worrying.

The next day, in early January 1993, I finally took my family away from Washington, D.C., and into our West Brook apartment in the Mount of Olives Gardens. The relocation was timed principally to let Chizube complete the last semester in her school, so she could make a fresh start in her new school in West Brook, at the beginning of a new semester.

In the two months or so that I had lived by myself in West Brook, I ran back to Washington, DC, every weekend. The truth, I must confess, was that I could just barely tolerate living far from my wife and daughter. I felt empty without them, and as if I merely existed. Uncle Frank said the distance was a *mere* two hundred miles. The same distance seemed endless when *I* was on the road. I have no doubt that my cruel separation from them, during the eight long years of my incarceration, explains my longing to be always close to them.

Okechukwu Ani and his wife Charity, Chikezie Onyeama and his wife Obiageli, and Edith Tagbo came to our apartment within two hours of our arrival. This was by prior arrangement, suggested by Mr. Ani. The senior partner liked the suggestion. So did Edith, who thereupon offered to bring a small variety of cooked foods with her.

Gradually, I had gotten into the habit of addressing the two partners by their praise-names, though Mr. Ani struggled to accept the name, *Ochiora*, which cousin Aloysius had bestowed on him. So, with him in particular, I either called him his praise-name, or I called him Okey (the short form of his given name). From the very first day I reported for work in the office, I addressed Edith as *Akwa-Okwulu*. And did she ever love it! She began in fact to harass the two partners about their reluctance to use the name, a reluctance that, she confided to me, seemed stupid to her. They laughed quite a bit about the matter. She occasionally joined in the laughter, but I could tell she was not the least bit amused. I laughed with them, but I went on using the praise-name.

Perhaps that was why Edith went somewhat overboard in the quantity of food she brought with her to my apartment. I think it helped that she – as well as the partners – had met my wife a week or so after I began work. Rosemary had taken a Friday off from her D.C. office, and so I was able to take her and Chizube to the office, where I did the introductions. Edith and Rosemary clicked right off the bat. Rosemary, having been well tutored by me, began immediately to address her as *Akwa-Okwulu*. Edith's contented smile split her face from ear to ear. And thereafter, for the entire duration of the visit, she would not be separated from Rosemary. At the end of the visit, the partners called me aside. And Mr. Ani told me he had suggested that a welcome party be arranged for my family on the day we would finally relocate to West Brook.

"A wonderful idea," said Mr. Onyeama, nodding vigorously. Which was exactly what Rosemary thought, when I told her about it.

The next day, Saturday, Edith called my apartment and asked to speak to Rosemary. "Don't worry about the food for the occasion," she told my wife, when she came on the line. "I'll cook whatever will be necessary. Just have some snacks ready, that's all."

"*Akwa-okwulu!*" I exclaimed, before I could stop myself. "God bless you."

"Who's this?" asked Edith, as if she thought it might be Chizube.

"Don't mind him," my wife said, turning to me with a dirty, but amused look. "He's listening on the extension. But he's right, *Akwa-okwulu*. God bless you. Our move to West Brook won't be for perhaps another six to eight weeks, but I'll remember your offer. It is very kind of you, and I'm not going to say you shouldn't bother to take all that trouble for us. So I'm accepting quickly before you change your mind."

"As if I would," said Edith, laughing, "even if you asked me to."

"Your kind offer," said Rosemary, "is the reason our people say that a person who enjoys the support of others is the greater and stronger for it. I won't ever forget your gesture."

The welcoming party was a small one, as Igbo parties go. But the people who really mattered to us were almost all there: cousin Aloysius and his wife Obiamaka, with their children Tobenna and Ebelechukwu; my sister Adaku and her husband Theo, with their three daughters Adaku junior, Uju and Chikodili, all the way from Laurel, MD, notwithstanding that my sister was about six months pregnant. Uncle Frank and aunty Nwamaka might have completed the roll call, but it would really have been too much to expect that they, too, could have been there.

Chizube played the big 'sister' to her five cousins. That was always the way it seemed to me. They were like brother and sisters, the Igbo language having no word for some of those other relationships that fine-tune the differences in parentage. As soon as the extended family assembled, Chizube marshaled the younger ones to the family room, where we had installed a television set, to watch their favorite cartoon shows without interruptions by the adults. That was the general idea. But, every now and again, one or more of the kids would come running into the sitting-room, to complain to a parent about what so-and-so had done, or to invite us to come share their excitement.

As a general rule our people – men as well as women – take *Igbo* praise-names. I have actually never met an Igbo man who did otherwise. But, for reasons of which I am totally innocent, the odd Igbo woman in a hundred takes an *English* praise-name. Mrs. Charity Ani was one such. Her praise-name, *Sunshine,* Edith privately informed me, had as much to do with the sunniness of her personality, as it had to do with her yellow-brown complexion. I can attest to the fact that her personality certainly shone as bright as the sun at high noon. I asked Edith if perhaps some other woman bestowed the name on her. But she shook her head, and said no. "It was her choice, and hers only." There was the faintest hint of criticism in that answer, but it was delivered with an intriguing smile.

No matter! Charity was an engaging woman, a little showy perhaps, but there was no doubt that when she walked into a room she brought something special with her. In a subdued kind of way, she seemed to electrify the atmosphere and the persons present. All eyes focus on her. I do not know about the women, but most men, in my experience from that day on, were charmed by her – with apparently little or no effort on her part. She had IT, what some people call pizzazz. Perhaps it was her smile – enchanting and sparkling – that did it.

I liked her immediately, as one likes and admires the bright and beautiful qualities that shine from a friend's personality. It was the first time I had met and chatted with her, but she struck me immediately as an outgoing and friendly person. Rosemary, too, seemed affected by her. Indeed, in little or no time at all, I observed that the two of them, with Edith, formed a small circle of their own, as they somewhat separated themselves from the other women, and engaged in long conversations, laughing and giggling as women are wont to do.

"Especially when they're peddling rumors and tittle-tattle," Okey Ani said in an aside to me.

He should know, I thought, seeing that Charity was his wife, and he knew Edith just about as well, it seemed to me, as anybody did. But, though I did not think my wife could be branded a gossipmonger, I shook my head and mumbled: "You know how women talk."

Okey and I were sitting next to each other. We did not talk much, but were mostly engrossed in watching others as they flitted around the room. And we would exchange sarcastic but light-hearted remarks about who was doing what, and to whom.

The sitting room was of moderate dimensions but, with Rosemary showing the way, we had furnished it with what cousin Aloysius described as "a nice blend of the aesthetic and the utilitarian". I remember thinking, when he spoke those words that, for a medical doctor, he certainly had a way with English words. The color of the upholstery matched the predominating color of the walls. The sofa, the love seat and the so-called king's chair (usually reserved for the head of the family, especially when there was company) were covered in a strong fabric, with floral designs, their brown color in tune with the mahogany paneling of the walls.

Two large framed scenic paintings, purchased from a small-time art dealer, hung on opposite walls. A commode, in light brown wood, with drawers that had brass handles, stood against the wall on the far side of the living room as one entered from the front door. Proudly displayed, on its top shelf, were two trophies won by Chizube in track and field. Our daughter was, even then, something of a sprinter, and had done us proud in several competitions.

Artifacts, mostly African, which we had collected over the five years of our residence in Washington, D.C., hung singly or in pairs from the walls, or shared the top shelf of the commode with Chizube's track trophies.

Unbeknownst to me, Rosemary had ordered eight African masks through Theo and Adaku, who had traveled to Nigeria in mid-December, 1992, on what was becoming, for them, an annual Christmas season pilgrimage. I suspected that that was the reason they accepted, with alacrity, to come all the way from Laurel, MD to West Brook, NJ, for what was frankly a very small house-warming party. They brought the masks, all wrapped up in protective paper. Rosemary and Adaku soon took these off, to display the masks in all their glory. Or hideousness!

"They look fearsome," I commented, holding one up, the better to appraise it.

"That's their beauty," Rosemary said, with the superior air of a connoisseur of antique art.

"You didn't tell me you ordered any such thing."

"What would have been the use? If I did, you would have opposed the idea. I know you."

"And so do I," chipped in her fellow conspirator, my sister, Adaku. "You remember how you used to react, back in Enugu, whenever you saw one of these things? Papa used to laugh at you."

I remembered well enough. My father used to more than just laugh at me; he mocked me pitilessly, calling me something of a coward. But I knew I had outgrown such childishness. I could now calmly recognize the fierceness of the masks without, in any way, sliding inevitably into the old fear mode. When our other guests arrived, they were drawn, almost without exception, to the masks, which we had immediately placed on the walls of the sitting room and the dining area.

"Where did you get these?" asked Mr. Onyeama.

"Of course from home," said Rosemary.

"He's not been home in so many years I have lost count," said Edith derisively. "I think he has forgotten his country."

Mr. Onyeama laughed. "Exactly what I expected you to say. You never disappoint me; you know that? But what you say is not really true."

"What do you mean, *really*?" Edith challenged him. "When last did you go home? Tell the truth and shame the devil."

Mr. Onyeama shrugged. "What does it matter how many years I've not been home? It's not the number that matters."

Edith gestured towards her boss. "Look at him. He'll soon tell us it's the *quality* of the visit that counts."

"And you're right," declared Mr. Onyeama. "You can go to Nigeria every year, and spend six or more weeks every time, and still come away with little or no understanding about what makes that country tick."

"So why did you ask about the masks?" persisted Edith. "You should have known these kinds of things come from home."

"Exactly my point," retorted Mr. Onyeama, his wide smile at once gracious and condescending. "You may not be aware, but you can buy the same exact masks from any number of West African countries. And not just West Africa, but Black Africa in general."

"Of course I knew that," said Edith, clearly not wishing to be upstaged.

"You can even buy them here," said Charity Ani.

"You can," said Mr. Onyeama. "But – how do Americans say it – it will cost you an arm and a leg."

"Which was why we ordered these from home," said Rosemary. "Whatever their asking price there, once you translate it into dollars, it seems usually affordable."

"There was a store in Jersey City," said Charity, "where you could have bought them for a price that's reasonable."

"Where's this store?" asked a chorus of voices.

"They called it, if I remember correctly, the Overseas African something – yes! I remember now. The Overseas United Africa Store! We used to call it the OAU store."

"Surely you mean OUA," said her husband, Okey.

"I know. But it just seemed easier to remember it as OAU."

"That's terrible," said Okey. "If I owned a store, I don't think I would like it named after an organization that's been a total failure."

"Isn't that judgement a little harsh?" asked cousin Aloysius.

"*Onwa-n'etili-ora*, I don't know about harsh," said Okey. "What earthly good has the Organization of African Unity done for Africa? They declared as sacrosanct the utterly ridiculous and immoral boundaries carved out by Europeans, in Berlin, more than a century ago. Boundaries that had little or no justification either in the humaneness of their approach, or in the political realities of the day, by which I mean the ethnic realities! *We* suffered the consequences of the OAU's myopic vision of Africa and its future."

"You are referring to our Biafra, I take it," said cousin Aloysius. "The OAU wouldn't listen to our point of view, for fear, I imagine, that we would have made the most convincing case possible for the redrawing of the African boundaries."

"Right! And I'm glad you agree with my point of view, *Onwa-n'etili-ora*. The OAU turned a completely blind eye to the age-old principle that every people have the inalienable right to self-determination. But I don't want to get started on politics now."

"I know what you mean," said cousin Aloysius. "Whenever and wherever our people meet, sooner than later, politics takes over. So let's please forget politics today. We are here to welcome my cousin CY and his beautiful wife and daughter to their home in New Jersey. As a matter of fact, I would –"

"Please *Onwa-n'etili-ora*," said Edith, "let it not be as if I am cutting you off in the middle of what you're saying. But I've been looking for a store where I can buy some African things."

"Like scary African juju masks?" asked Mr. Onyeama, amid general laughter.

"You can laugh all you like," said Edith. "But I'm serious. Charity, you said there's such a store in Jersey City. I know Jersey City quite well – or rather, I should say I know several of our people who live there. None has ever mentioned such a store, not to talk of taking me there."

"*Akwa-okwulu*," said cousin Aloysius, "are you saying because you've never actually seen the place with your own eyes, it doesn't exist?"

"Doctor!" cried Edith, laughing. "Won't you leave me alone? You've come with your taunts."

"I've not been there myself many times," Charity said. "Just once or twice. But I am sure of what I'm saying. The store is somewhere close to the junction of Mathieson and another street whose name I never get right. Sounds like community!"

"Must be Communipaw," said Okey Ani. "You've never said anything about this store to me. I wonder why."

"Because, Mr. Ani," retorted his wife, "you've never been interested in things like that. So, what would have been the point telling you? You hate shopping anyway."

"With you especially," Okey whispered in my ears.

"I heard you! But it doesn't matter. Edith, all I can tell you is, there's a store like that in that area. At least there used to be. I even remember the name of the woman who used to run it."

"Okay, madam, tell us the name," Okey challenged her.

"Udozo! Joy or Joyce Udozo – something like that. So, there! What do you have to say, my dear husband?" As she spoke, she rocked her body triumphantly.

I think my heart instantly missed a beat. My body jerked bolt upright, as if stung by an ant in my seat. I looked sharply at Rosemary and Adaku. They had detached themselves from their little groups and were, together, busily arranging the aluminum trays of food on the dining table. There was truly a mouth-watering variety of dishes: *jollof* rice, fried Chinese style; chicken legs and thighs, oven-roasted to perfection; a bean cake known as *moi-moi*, a Nigerian delicacy; soft, fried, ripe plantains; and a rich, tasteful mélange of different vegetables garnished with lemon slices and other condiments. But my thoughts, at that moment, were not about food, however appetizing.

At the same instant, Rosemary and Adaku turned and looked at me. And I surmised, from the expression in both their eyes, that they might have been thinking what I was thinking: that what Charity had just said could be the opening for which we had been searching. I recalled that, not quite two months earlier, Adaku and Theo had told me about a friend of the Udozos who had hinted at Bernard's presence in the country. At the time, they could neither tell me who the friend was, nor when exactly he had said what he said about Bernard. None seemed to know where the Udozos lived.

I recalled what Chikezie Onyeama had said to me at the end of my job interview. And Okey Ani too! They had urged me, after I had told them my story, to do something to clear my name. Now, I looked at Mr. Onyeama, and found him seemingly engrossed in thought, as he stroked his mustache contemplatively. He did not look in my direction. Neither did Okey Ani, though he sat right next to me, strangely silent. He, who never seemed to lack for something to say, appeared lost in thought. I think it was the oddity of his silence that finally compelled me to address him.

"*Ochiora*," I said, "what are you thinking?"

"Nothing," he lied. "And hey! Cyril, go easy with that *Ochiora* thing."

I knew he lied because my sixth sense told me so. I had shared his office with him for just about one month. Time enough to be able, sometimes, to read his body language. He always looked me straight in the eye when we talked. And when he did not do so, as now, I knew there had to be a reason. I was looking steadily at him, but he would not turn to look at me.

"Come-on, man!" I urged him.

Reluctantly, and ever so slowly, he turned his head in my direction. And when he spoke, I knew he was speaking from the bottom of his heart, because he caught and held my eye, steadily, unwaveringly.

"You know what, Cyril?" he said, not rushing his words. "This is very much *your* affair. And I really don't want to meddle in another man's business."

"But –" I prompted him, when he paused.

"But," he went on, "if I were in your shoes, so help me God, I would hunt the son of a bitch down, and see what I can do with him. For starters, that is. Beyond him, there's your other friend – sorry – I mean, Bernard."

"I guess you're thinking about the letter?"

"You guessed right, Cyril. You need to confront him about his denial of its existence."

"After these many years?" I asked. I think I knew what his answer would be. I just needed, I suppose, to hear him one more time.

"Even after – what – twelve years? Yes! The passage of time should mean nothing when you're pursuing your good name, in this kind of situation. For God's sake, Cyril, don't impose some kind of statute of limitations on yourself. Let the lawyers tell you if that statute applies in your case. It's really up to you. If the story you told us is what actually happened, you owe it to yourself, and to your family, to do what needs to be done."

He got up from his chair, and languidly stretched himself. "Hey fellows! I don't know about you all. But me, I'm hungry."

In a flash, Edith was by his side, and whispered to him, but loud enough for me to catch her drift: "She has not announced that we can start."

"That's not necessary," I said. "But if you insist, here's Rosemary. What do you say, Rosemary? Can we go and help ourselves?"

"Yes, of course. I'm only sorry the dining table is not nearly large enough to accommodate us all sitting down. So please help yourselves, and take your food back to your seats. O.K.?"

"Not so fast, gentlemen!" announced Mrs. Obiageli Onyeama, as Okey Ani, quickly followed by my sister's husband, Theo, moved towards the dining table. "It should be ladies first."

Those were the first words I heard her speak, except for our exchange of greetings when she and her husband first arrived. She had been very quiet, sitting close to Mr. Onyeama and, as far as I could observe, saying little to anyone, even those who were closest to her. She was obviously the quiet type, perhaps uncomfortable in company. I had expected the wife of our senior partner to throw her weight around a little bit. It was not as if she did not have a presence. Like her husband, she had a good height, six feet or just under, full bosomed, and probably in her mid to upper thirties. Pretty too, I thought, though I was not at all sure about that. And the reason I was unsure was simply that she wore her make-up just a tiny bit too gaudily, certainly too gaudily for cousin Aloysius's wife, Obiamaka. I saw the way the latter was looking at her, and it was not with admiration.

I knew aunt Obiamaka well. She simply loathed any and all types of garish make-up. In the five or so years I lived with her and cousin Aloysius, during my undergraduate years at Rutgers University, I seldom saw her use any of those cosmetics that women love to apply to their faces to smoothen out wrinkles and other lines of aging. She used regular skin lotions and lip balms (basically the types men also use) only because winter harshly dries the black skin. But she did not paint her lips red, or purple, or whatever other lip color women are slaves to.

"Is there anything my ears won't hear?" asked Okey Ani, laughing. "Ladies first? This may be America-"

"Yes, it is," said Edith seriously. "Let me tell you-"

"But we're in an African home, among ourselves," Okey interrupted.

"Somebody please hold me back," Edith exclaimed, holding her right arm up threateningly, and looking around her expectantly, her eyes flashing false fire, "before I lose my temper and teach this man –"

Charity rushed forward, and obligingly held Edith back. "*Akwa-okwulu*," she said, smiling, "please don't mind him. Don't you know his type? You can take them out of the bush, but–"

"I know," said Edith. "But you can't take the bush out of them. *Ochiora*, you're lucky, because I don't know what I'd have done if your wife hadn't stopped me."

Amid general and hilarious laughter, in which Okey shared, Edith reordered the procedure. "It's going to be like this: children first, then women–"

"And if nothing is left?" Okey asked.

"Too bad," said Edith. "You can stop at the nearest Burger King and buy hamburgers. Now seriously, where are the kids? Chizube!" She turned to me. "That's her name, right?"

But I did not need to answer because, right on cue, Chizube led her band of cousins out from the family room.

"All right, kids," said Edith. "Please wait just a moment, and your mums will help you."

I would have said 'mums or dads', if only so our women do not feel that they always have to carry the burden, alone, of looking after the little ones. But it was Edith, and not one of us men, who had called the mothers to duty. So I relaxed in my chair. Besides, Chizube, at twelve going for thirteen, really did not need her mum or dad looking over her shoulders as she helped herself to some of the food. But I need not have worried. Rosemary and Adaku immediately took charge, and aunt Obiamaka did not have to bestir herself on account of her own two children. "One of the privileges of age," I heard aunt Obiamaka mutter to herself, as she smiled her thanks to Rosemary and Adaku.

Chikezie Onyeama came and drew me aside, as we ate, and said he wanted to talk to me.

"This," he said in a low tone, "is your chance, if you really want to do something about your case. I saw you and *Ochiora* talking after Charity said what she said. And, from the way you two carried on, I suspect you were talking about the same thing. Right?"

"Yes."

"And what did he think?"

"He said pretty much what you just said."

Chapter IX

A WEEK AFTER the house-warming party, on a Saturday of capricious weather, I took my family with me to try to locate the OUA store. Rosemary and I had talked endlessly about the matter. And we were of one mind about our quest. We would pursue the Udozos to the farthest corners, if need be, of the United States. And, when we caught up with them, we would do whatever we needed to do, to get the truth out of Obi Udozo in the little matter of *the letter*. A letter my erstwhile friend Bernard had written to him in 1980, weeks before I was found guilty of being hand in glove with Bernard in his drug-trafficking business. The court put me away for eight nightmare years; years I could never hope to recover, or perhaps even to live down. Solving the riddle of that all-important letter had become my obsession. Failure to solve it would be the ultimate calamity of my life.

We found the store, the OVERSEAS UNITED AFRICA STORE. And we found it, as Charity Ani had indicated, close to the junction of Mathieson and Communipaw Avenues, in the heart of Jersey City. A day that had started out bright and sunny became, by mid-afternoon, a day of freezing temperatures and sleet. I did not mind the sleet once I was inside my car and comfortably warm. The windscreen wiper did its work efficiently, pushing aside the icy particles, so that I could see the road in front of me clearly. But once outside of the car, the particles seemed to come fast and furiously, and I could barely see through my spectacles.

What we saw, when we located the store, turned out to be just as gloomy as the weather. The entire building, a one-story structure that had housed three businesses, was boarded up. The name of the store we had come to see was still there, high up at the edge of the roof. But its lettering was beginning to peel off, suggesting that the store had been abandoned quite a while earlier. Perhaps as many as three or more months earlier, other business owners in the neighborhood told us.

I knew I could not let a little setback discourage me. Had not Charity herself hinted at the possibility that the store had closed down? But there was little more we could do there on that wintry day. No one, to whom we talked, had any idea where the store had relocated to, or indeed if it was still in business.

We did not close the chapter on Jersey City. We could not sensibly do so before we had talked to some members of the Nigerian community who lived in that city, particularly those resident nearest to the junction of Communipaw and Mathieson Avenues. And because the women of the community were more likely than the men to have and to pass on the information we sought, Rosemary readily took on that task.

We were now card-carrying members of the Enyimba Union, and had access to its printed directory. Indeed almost the first thing I did, after I began work in the offices of ONYEAMA & ANI, and knew we were going to live in New Jersey, was to take out a family membership in the Union. Networking is one of the benefits of belonging to an association like the Enyimba Union: that quiet, unobtrusive sharing of information and such-like that goes on all the time, and which can be extremely helpful, especially to newcomers. Or, as in my case, a returning prodigal son! I had been a member of the Union in the two years or thereabouts before my world collapsed around me. That was twelve years earlier.

Assisted by Charity Ani, Rosemary talked to several women, and not only those resident in Jersey City. There were women in the Union, Charity told us, who were known to be obsessive-compulsive shoppers, women for whom shopping was almost therapeutic.

"But you're not one of them, of course," I said, tongue-in-cheek.

She laughed and said: "Me? Of course not! If I were, I think I would have known where the store moved. They had some wonderful things in that store. There weren't only African carvings. They also had tailored, embroidered men's jumpers, and an assortment of women's clothes, with matching pendants, bangles, trinkets and other ornaments. I was there, I think, just twice before I first heard that they might have moved."

"Men's jumpers?" I asked absently, my mind flying back a decade or more, to the day in 1978 when I first ran into my friend, Bernard, in the United States. I remembered the scene vividly: him sitting opposite me, an impish smile lighting up his devilishly handsome face, his eyes riveted on me. We were in cousin Aloysius's house, in Bound Brook, NJ, still my home even after my graduation from Rutgers. At the time, I worked as a security officer at a cookie factory in a nearby town, earning five dollars an hour, while waiting for a better job.

Bernard was not only drop-dead handsome, he had probably the most persuasive tongue of anyone I knew. And on that day, he held me in thrall with his words, though I strongly suspected he was spinning me a web of lies. That was the day he told me the main merchandise in his trans-Atlantic trade was men's clothing. I knew he did not mean European-American type men's clothing: shirts, trousers, suits, ties and suchlike. There would have been little sense in such a trade; like carrying coal to Newcastle.

So now, listening to Charity Ani as she described the things one could buy at the OUA store, I began to wonder if perhaps there might be a kernel of truth hidden in Bernard's story. That perhaps he did indeed bring over, from Nigeria, embroidered Igbo jumpers. Possibly as a cover for his other and shadier commodities! I wondered if there might be any possible connection between Bernard's men's clothing and the embroidered men's jumpers the Udozos sold in their store. I wondered about what the nature of that putative link might be, and if the link was still active in one form or another. But though I wondered about a host of other troubling possibilities, I kept my counsel, and did not breathe a word about it, even to Rosemary.

Something else struck me as just a little odd. Charity never once asked me, nor Rosemary either, why we were so keen to find the Udozos. Perhaps she did not want to let on that her husband, Okey, might have told her something about the matter. If she did not ask us, it could be that Okey had so cautioned her. For our part, Rosemary agreed with me that if she did not ask, we would not volunteer the information. We were well aware, however, that the whole story would come out in the fullness of time.

*   *   *

We were patient in our search. We needed to be. So too was my sister Adaku. Like us, she was searching and waiting and longing for something very dear to her heart. A SON! She liked to say, and I think somewhat blasphemously, that she needed to be patient with God in that regard. Theo, for his part, stoutly declared that he did not really care if their next child was not a son.

"Honest to God," he said on more than one occasion, "I don't. If God, in His infinite wisdom, chooses to bless me with a fourth daughter, I will be quite happy."

I had the strongest doubt that he was telling the truth, the whole truth, and nothing but. Adaku, too! "I suspect he thinks if he says it often enough, he'll actually begin to believe it," she told me. "Anyway, I have faith in God that this thing will come to pass."

It did. On the eve of the ides of March 1993, Adaku was delivered of a seven and one half pound rosy-cheeked boy. They named him *Ifeanyichukwu Somawina*. Ifeanyichukwu is a very popular name, and means that nothing is impossible for God.

"These are heavy names," I said to Adaku and Theo, as we sat with them in their Laurel home on the Saturday following the birth of their son. "Real tongue-twisters."

"For whom?" my sister asked.

"Americans, of course," I answered. "We live here, don't we?"

"That's their problem, not ours."

"Theo, my brother, I know what you mean. But I have another problem with the names, particularly with Somawina. I can understand why you chose the name Ifeanyichukwu. You waited an awfully long time for him, and you must have been near despair. But the other name baffles me. We've only ever known one child named Somawina."

"And that was a girl," chipped in Rosemary

"Boy or girl," said Theo, "what does it matter? It's not a common name, as you say. So, my son might well be the first boy so named. We really don't care. It's the meaning – or shall I say, the reason for the name – that matters to us."

"That's my point," I argued stubbornly. "The full form of the name, as far as we know, is *Somawinajemba*. The mother, who married a man from outside of her village, and was therefore a stranger in her new home, needed a companion, and saw her daughter as that companion. But, in your case –"

"In our case," said Adaku, "the meaning is different. And the name is simply Somawina, period. You know how our people can pluck a name out of a saying, which is what I believe the parents of the girl did. If there are any hard and fast rules for Igbo names, we don't know what they are. But we know we are not doing what has never been done before."

Adaku paused, slowly got up from her chair, and came and sat next to Rosemary on the long settee. She then reached for, and held Rosemary's hand in hers.

"Rosemary," she said earnestly, "it is our wish that our son does not come alone, and that your child, when you are due, will also be a son. I know that's what you want more than anything else. My hope is that as they grow up, they will be like brothers. That's our prayer."

To my utter surprise, Rosemary got very emotional, and turned and encircled Adaku in her arms, and began to sob quietly. Adaku in her turn, perhaps strongly affected by Rosemary's emotion, began to sob too. Theo and I exchanged glances, but neither of us said a word, letting the two sisters-in-law, and old friends, cry on each other's shoulders.

At least Adaku was right on one point. I was not sure about Rosemary, but I was past trying to pretend that it did not matter to me if our next child, quite possibly our last, would be a boy or a girl. I wanted a son. I wanted one so badly that whenever I prayed, I seemed to do so with suppressed desperation, almost screaming my words at God. Rosemary was due in June or thereabouts, a matter of just about three months. But the wait seemed endless.

We were back in Laurel, MD, six weeks later, for the christening of Adaku's son, on the last Sunday of April 1993. Rosemary and I, as we had expected, were Godparents to Somawina. And that was another thing. Ifeanyichukwu is my nephew's first given name. For most others, that is the only name they know, or wish to know. But his middle name caught, and held, *my* fancy. In consequence, from the date of his baptism to this day, he is and remains Somawina to me. This, if I must tell the truth, might also have been because I yearned for a son myself. And the words of my sister, as she explained the reasons for her son's middle name, were carved, as if in stone, in my mind forever. Or at least until the day Rosemary was delivered of her child. The officiating priest for Somawina's christening, in an aside to me after the baptismal service, said he thought I had laid undue emphasis on that middle name when he formally invited us to 'name this child'. If I did, it was not with conscious and deliberate intent.

The family planned an after-service reception. And it was supposed to be a somewhat limited affair, for a handful of relatives and friends. But Theo and Adaku had evidently become rather too well known in the Nigerian – especially the Igbo – community, in the state of Maryland, for that. Their attempt to draw up a short list of guests quickly became an exercise in futility. They did not know whom to leave out; or what to say to those friends – even mere acquaintances – left out of the list.

I was with Adaku one day, about a week before the christening, when a visitor called on her. He looked fortyish, was an inch or so under six feet, and might have weighed about a hundred and fifty pounds. He was quite friendly, but it was easy to see that he was not at all happy with my sister and her husband.

"Where's your *Oga*?" he asked Adaku.

The word is a slang, and means *master*; in this case, master of the house. It is not a term that your typical Nigerian wife cares for, except when its use is clearly understood to be jocular in intent.

"If you're asking about Theo," Adaku replied with a straight face, "he's not back from work. But you are welcome. Please have a seat. By the way, this is my brother Cyril, visiting from New Jersey. C.Y., meet Uzochukwu Ofili, *Eze-amanogechi*."

"Please don't mind her," said Mr. Ofili, shaking hands with me, "though she's your sister. She keeps calling me that name just to provoke me, in the hope of pushing me to take a praise-name. But I'm not ready for that. And I really don't think I'll ever take one. Praise-names are just too pretentious for me."

"I know what you mean," I said in sympathy.

"No!" he fired back. "I don't think you do. But it doesn't matter. I've come on a serious business."

"And what would that be?" asked Adaku.

"Please let me sit down first," he said, suiting action to word, as he sat in one corner of the settee. "You want to know why I've come to bother you? It is simply to ask your husband Theo – excuse me, I should say, to ask *Nwata-kwochal'aka* – and you, why I've not received an invitation to the christening. Is-it because I'm not one of those important persons with some God-forsaken titles? Or perhaps you think I've not washed my hands clean enough to dine with the wealthy?"

That was a not-so-subtle reference to Theo's praise-name, and for just a fraction of a second, Adaku looked as if she would react sharply to Mr. Ofili's protest. But the moment passed, and she quickly brought her emotions under control, and even managed a smile.

"You've come with your palaver," she said, "just to tempt me, because I don't know what I'll say now and, like the frog, water will enter my mouth. I think the best thing is for you to come again when Theo's back. Or, better still, call him on the phone, and ask him your question. He should be back – let me see – in perhaps two or three hours. Today is Saturday. He should be back by five o'clock."

"There's no hurry!" declared Mr. Ofili, stealing a glance at his watch. I looked at mine too; the time was about five minutes past two. "I'll wait."

I watched the man as he coolly reached for a pouffe, dragged it closer until he could place his tired feet on it, and generally made himself comfortable. I glanced quickly at Adaku to see how she was reacting to Mr. Ofili's effrontery, and was surprised to see her wearing a quite affable smile.

It had been on the tip of my tongue to reprove the visitor for his apparent lack of grace. But Adaku's smile instantly killed the thought, as I recognized that there was a familiarity between them that I could not challenge.

So instead I asked: "Is it that important to you?"

"You mean to receive an invitation?"

"Yes."

"You don't understand," Mr. Ofili said. "You see – what's that your name?"

"Cyril," I said. "Cyril Jideofo."

"Thank you, Mr. Jideofo. I was going to say that in this our community, and I know it's the same in your New Jersey – I lived there – there are some people who, if they throw a party, and you're not invited, you feel *somehow*, as we say. I was quite patient, and waited and waited, but nothing came. No card. No phone call. I then decided I wasn't going to swallow my phlegm because of my timidity. So I've come to ask Adaku and her husband: is it that Mgbeke does not know how to shave the head, or that the razor is not sharp enough?"

Adaku was no longer just smiling; she was laughing. It was plain to see that she felt rather flattered by the visitor's remarks. And I could not blame her. I know I would have felt the same way if anyone told me my parties were much sought-after affairs.

My sister was still laughing as she gestured to Mr. Ofili: "*Eze-amanogechi*," she said, "please wait a moment. I'm coming."

She left us in her living room and disappeared for a few minutes. I seized the opportunity to get to know Mr. Ofili a little better. He told me he had lived in Laurel for about three years.

"I lived in New Jersey before then," he said. "You are from New Jersey, so you must know East Orange. Too crowded for my liking. But that was the place that made me what I am today – a systems analyst. I took a course in computer science at the NJIT in Newark –"

"That's the New Jersey Institute of Technology?"

"Yes. Wonderful place, and not too far from where I lived. I also did my Masters there. But I'm trying to spread my wings, and I found a good job here in Maryland with an up-and-coming industrial plant, specializing in manufacturing aircraft parts."

"Wow!" I said, genuinely impressed. But, to tell the truth, I am easily impressed by anybody who has mastered the computer, so unknowledgeable am I in its intricacies.

Adaku reappeared and, a happy smile still lighting up her face, stretched out her right hand to Mr. Ofili. "There! An invitation for you and your wife."

"Me and my wife?" Mr. Ofili asked, putting on his most ingratiating smile. "What about my kids?"

"No children!" said Adaku emphatically. "It says so on the card."

"No children at all?"

Adaku and I exchanged rapid glances. Then I said: "*Our* children will be there of course; that is, hers and mine. But that is different. And I'm sure you understand."

"Please n-o-w, Adaku," Mr. Ofili pleaded in that unctuous tone Nigerians often employ when begging for an unreasonable favor.

Adaku, hesitant, again looked at me. But I could not help her with the decision she and Theo, alone, could make. Then she transferred her gaze to Mr. Ofili, and looked long and hard at him, shaking her head slowly, a few times. At length she said: "Okay, Uzo. The answer is: Yes! Bring your kids."

Mr. Ofili hugged the card to his chest. "'Ask, and it shall be given unto you,'" he quoted. "That's what the Holy Book says. I can't tell you how much I appreciate this gesture. By the way, talking about praise-names, how come the wife of *Nwatakwochal'aka* has not taken a title for herself? A woman like you, with a doctor for husband, and three – sorry, four – children –"

Adaku laughed. "When you take one, Ignatius, I'll take one. And then I'll stop taunting you with that other name. That's a deal?"

"You can't seem to be able to make up your mind what to call me," said Mr. Ofili, smiling resignedly. "But I've told you many times I prefer Uzo to Ignatius. Anyway, you're on! One of these days, I'll surprise you and take a praise-name. Thanks a lot anyway. Please give your husband my regards. Till next time, peace!"

And with that, a hug for Adaku, and a handshake with me, he left. Almost immediately, there was knock on the door. I went to the door, opened it, and Mr. Ofili stood there, staring intently at me.

"Excuse me," he said after a brief moment, and walked past me into the living room. I shut the door, turned, and there he was, still staring at me.

"Excuse me," he said again. "Did you say your name is – ?"

"Cyril," I said.

"Cyril Jideofo?"

"That's me. Why? Have we met before?"

"I don't think so," he said, "or I would have remembered you. I don't forget faces. No, we've not met. And yet there's a familiar ring to your name. Wait just a second! That's it! You're a friend to –" He stopped, and his face that had looked excited one moment, suddenly clouded over and seemed distressed, even haunted.

"Oh no! My mistake!" he said awkwardly, in a vain and bumbling attempt to eat the words he had just spoken. "I think I'm confused and don't know what I'm saying."

"That's all right," said Adaku. "My guess is you've probably heard of Dr. Aloysius Jideofo, or maybe you know him. He's our cousin."

"You know what?" said Mr. Ofili. "You are exactly right. Who, in the New Jersey Nigerian community, doesn't know the revered doctor? We used to call him *Onwa*."

He knew Dr. Jideofo all right. But his confusion obviously had nothing to do with the family name I shared with cousin Aloysius. He had been on the brink of letting on that he knew more than just my name. I believe the realization hit him, a split moment before he uttered the words, that what he remembered about the name Cyril Jideofo was not something he wanted to talk about lightly or off-handedly.

He retreated once more, with as much grace as he could muster, again thanking Adaku profusely for the invitation card, and assuring us he and his family would be there for the christening of Somawina.

"He's a cute baby," he said at the door. "Perhaps, when my wife sees him, she might be convinced to try one more time."

The door closed for the second and final time on our visitor. Adaku looked at me and smiled sadly, shaking her head gently. She did not say a word; she did not need to. But I could tell right away that she sensed what I sensed; actually what I *knew*.

"What was that stuff," I asked after a pause, "about convincing his wife to – how did he say it – try once more?"

"Don't mind the fellow," said Adaku. "He wants a fourth child, but Dinah – his wife – doesn't."

"He has three daughters?"

"You mean, like me, before I had Ifeanyi? Not at all! He has two boys and one girl."

"Two boys!" I said. "I don't understand. He has two boys, and he's not satisfied?"

"He pretends it's not like that," said Adaku. Then, for reasons I could not fathom, she looked at me reproachfully, reprimanding me with her eyes, and said: "All you Igbo men are the same. Boys, boys, boys! But I understand what you mean. However, Mr. Ofili likes to say that he wants to 'balance the equation.'"

"Meaning he would like a second daughter, no doubt."

"No doubt," said Adaku, "if you can believe a word he says. But I'm sure he'll not weep if the fourth turns out to be another boy."

*   *   *

Mr. Ofili was true to his word. He came to the christening with his wife Dinah and their three children. Dinah was as light-skinned as he was dark, as robust as he was slender. They were a study in contrasts, which perhaps served their marriage well. She spoke little, strange for a woman. He prattled on, easily finding a word for every situation. Except when I remarked that their three children looked like triplets! Then he became taciturn, and Dinah waxed eloquent.

"There can't be as many as two years between the first and the second child?" I asked.

Dinah looked for a moment or two at her husband, and then tossed her head disdainfully. "He has nothing to say when people ask him about it. As for me, sometimes I feel as if I had all three in the space of one year, never mind about two years between the first two."

"I see," I said. "You probably wanted to have your children quickly, so you could get on with the rest of your lives, and enjoy yourselves."

"Not at all," Dinah said with conviction. "This is what happens when your husband is a workaholic, and doesn't have other distractions. I wish he would sometimes go out and play football with his friends, or something. All he ever seems to think about when he's home –"

Uzochukwu Ofili, in a movement so fast I did not see it coming, clamped a hand to her mouth. "Enough, Dinah!" he commanded her. But he was smiling. "I believe our friend gets your drift."

*　*　*

Just as I had feared, the reception turned out to be a crowded function. It seemed that just about everybody who was anybody in the Igbo community, in the state of Maryland, was there. I do not know why or how it has come about. But the Igbo, in our diaspora, often exaggerate the scale of our merry-making. In the old country, family and friends gather to celebrate a child's baptism. Good food and wine are served. But there is usually no music. Nor dancing! That, at any rate, was how it was.

My sister and her husband pulled out all the stops, to make the reception grand. They reserved a hall at the Harrison Manor, an imposing structure of cement and red bricks, with a white porcelain frontage, and very tastefully appointed reception halls that catered only banquets and weddings, and suchlike. They engaged the services of the best-known Nigerian DJ in the entire state, and far beyond. He was popularly known as MM LazJazz. Few knew his given and family names, though some people said he was baptized Lazarus. Those persons with a fondness for long names called him Master-Mixer Laz-the-Jazz. Which was something of a misnomer! Perhaps, in his early period as a DJ, he might have mixed jazz music for our African-American soul brothers. But now, his clientele was overwhelmingly Nigerian. And my people really have no ear for jazz, preferring the Highlife, which, as a music form, is next-of-kin to the Calypso.

It was a sit-down, four-course dinner, a sumptuous banquet for a capacity crowd of some two hundred guests. Capacity, that is, for the banquet hall. I had little doubt that if Theo and Adaku had found a hall with a capacity for three hundred guests, they would have pulled a crowd of three hundred. Space limitation, Theo had earlier explained to me, was why they had emphasized, on the invitation cards, that children under the age of sixteen were excluded. They mostly were, though typically three or four couples, in addition to the Ofilis, brought their children along. Some probably lacked the necessities to engage child-minders. More likely, however, they just could not believe that the restriction was seriously meant.

"Trust our people!" said Adaku ruefully. "I've given up on ever expecting that when you say 'no children', the Nigerian parent will respect your wishes."

"Never mind about that," I said. "This is great! Absolutely fabulous! Theo, my brother, how come you went to such expense for this christening? Best DJ, free drinks no matter what, great food. You even let the guests choose what they want, without restrictions. You said you would, but I didn't believe you would go through with it."

"Don't look at me," he said, gesturing with his hands. "If you want to know, the woman you gave me in marriage made me do it."

"That's the old Adam excuse," I said. "But my sister is no Eve. Seriously though, you've both surpassed yourselves. People will talk about this banquet for some time, I guarantee you. Best party I've attended in a long while."

Cousin Aloysius and his wife Obiamaka chaired the occasion. A young doctor colleague of Theo's was pressed into service as the master of ceremonies, my sister having failed to persuade me to take on that role. There was no high table, as such. But Aloysius and Obiamaka's table, which they shared with the closest family members, was the number one table, and was so designated. Chizube was not with us at the table, being just under thirteen years at the time. But arrangements had been made, with the hotel, for a room where the young ones were taken care of. We persuaded those families who, in flagrant disregard of the restriction on children, brought their kids along, to release them to the care of the hotel, to share the children's room with Chizube and her cousins. A magician had been hired to entertain them.

The Deejay had probably the best selection of highlife and *soukous* music I think I ever heard, and we danced until our feet ached. Rosemary and I were in the middle of a dance when suddenly she made an eye signal to me, and surreptitiously pointed a finger.

"Don't look now," she said, gently swaying her body to the music though she was eight or so months pregnant. "There's a fellow there who's been staring at us for some time now. I said don't look!"

But I had immediately jerked my head in the direction in which her finger pointed, searching the faces for the prying eyes. Someone waved to me, and when our eyes met, he smiled. I recognized the man I had met at Adaku's a week earlier, and waved back to him.

"That's Mr. Ofili," I told Rosemary.

"You know him?"

"Yes. Met him at Adaku's last Saturday."

"I didn't like the way he was looking at us," said Rosemary. "And I think – in fact I'm pretty sure – he was one of those who brought their children along, inspite of –"

"Adaku gave him a special dispensation. The fellow was practically groveling, and Adaku finally had to let him bring his kids."

Baby Somawina, whose christening we were celebrating, made two sole appearances during the festivities. The first was at the very beginning, when the officiating priest said the opening prayer. This was immediately followed by the kolanut oblation, which was performed by cousin Aloysius, the oldest male person from the Agu and the Jideofo families present at the party. He asked God's blessings on, and the protection of our ancestors for, the little boy.

The second occasion was the cutting of the baptismal cake, actually performed by Somawina's three sisters, and with Chizube standing hard by, carrying the baby of the day in her rock-steady twelve-year old arms. I was proud of her.

After several minutes of non-stop dancing, I decided to take a break in the corridors of the hotel, where I found an unoccupied easy chair. I gratefully lowered my tired body into its welcoming cushions, and stretched my legs. I sat, immobile and totally relaxed, for about two minutes, and then became aware that someone was standing by my chair. I looked up at the tall slender figure of Mr. Ofili, and smiled. But he did not return my smile. Instead he leaned over and said: "Can we talk?"

"Here?" I asked.

"Yes here, of course," he said. Then he added sarcastically: "Unless you prefer that we go back to the banquet hall."

"Too noisy," I conceded. "All right, Mr. Ofili, let's. I seem to recall we had an unfinished business the other day at my sister's."

"Oh, so you noticed? Anyway, it doesn't matter. What matters is I think I might be able to help you."

I sat up, instantly interested. A week earlier, at our first meeting at Adaku's, he had been on the point of confessing that he not only knew my name, but that he could name one of my friends. He had not said so expressly. Indeed he had tried to cover his tracks by pretending he did not know what he was talking about. But I was not born yesterday, and was not taken in by his sham confusion. However, I decided to play it cool, and not show him how curious I was about his uncompleted confession. And, perhaps perversely, I was not at all sure I really wanted to know what someone like him had heard about me. What were the chances, I asked myself miserably, that what he knew about me would be positive? I had, nevertheless, thought about him day and night since that day.

Since there was no available chair close to where I was sitting, we looked around, and found a bench in the entrance hall of the manor.

"Will this do?" I asked.

"Not terribly comfortable," he said, "which is probably just as well. I'll try and make it brief."

"So," I said, as we both sat down, "what do you have in mind?"

He did not prevaricate. "It's about Obi Udozo," he said, turning to me with an odd smile I could not fathom.

"What about Obi Udozo? And who told you – ?"

"There's someone on my table," he said, pointing in the general direction of the banquet hall. "He comes from New Jersey, like you. Enoch Morah –"

"Of course I know Enoch. We call him *Mba-anabalu-agu*. Tough fellow, as that name suggests. But he's a good man. He's friends with a lady that works in my office."

Mr. Ofili leaned towards me, and cupped his mouth.

"If you ask me," he whispered, "they're much more than just friends. Or let me put it this way: their handshake has gone way beyond the elbow. But that's another story."

I knew that everyone in the office had been invited. But both partners had made their excuses to Adaku and Theo. Okechukwu Ani had, months before he received the invitation card to the christening, committed himself to a wedding, where he and his wife Charity were due to chair the reception. Chikezie Onyeama, the senior partner, was away with his family, on a trip to Nigeria. Edith, however, was present and, as always, bustled around, helping where she could, and even where she was not needed. I had briefly cast about, looking for Enoch, because I knew that wherever the tortoise went, it took along its domed shell. But in a sea of some two hundred faces, sitting at twenty or more tables, it was difficult to spot him. Edith did not help matters by being constantly on the move from one end of the hall to the other.

"So, what did Enoch tell you?"

"That you are eager to get in touch with Obi," said Mr. Ofili. "To tell you the truth, I was the one that started talking about you, you know, how I had met you at Adaku's on the day I went there to plead for my own invitation and all that."

"At least you're honest about that," I said.

"What's the use denying the truth? I didn't want to be left out. But let that be. What I really want to tell you is that Obi Udozo has been in Nigeria for the last I-don't-know-how-long. Business, I'm told."

"When's he expected back?"

"Oh that, I don't know. Joy –"

"Ah, yes, Joy," I said. "How's she? Did she travel with him?"

"Nope! Someone has to take care of the children. It's not yet summer vacation and all that. And there's their store too. That's the business that always keeps Obi in Nigeria for so long. He travels home like twice a year, sometimes three times, buying merchandise for their store in Trenton."

"Trenton! Is that where their store is now? Is it still called the OUA store?"

"Yes," said Mr. Ofili. "The Overseas United African Shop, or something like that."

"That's simply wonderful," I said, struggling to resist the temptation to hug him. "I imagine you know their address, or at least their telephone number, no?"

"How long have you known the Udozos?"

"This is 1993," I said. "I first met them about thirteen years ago. But I was asking if you know –"

"I know what you asked," said Mr. Ofili, "and I'm thinking how to answer the question. You were friends of theirs, you said?"

"No, we weren't really friends. But go ahead about your song."

"About my song? I don't understand."

"It's just a joke," I said. "It's the words of an old song. I just love that line, that's all."

"That's all right," he said. "You were saying you knew them thirteen years ago. That's interesting. I believe, in conversation, Obi has once or twice mentioned your name."

"That must be why, the other day at my sister's, you started to say that my name rang a bell?"

"Yes, but I couldn't quite place it at the time," he lied smoothly. "But when we got talking at our table, and Enoch said he knows you, and that you are trying to locate the Udozos, it all came flooding back to my memory. Yes, I can tell you Obi is at present in Nigeria. Among other things, he also needs to supervise the building of their house in their Ishinkpume village. Big mansion too, from all accounts."

"Ishinkpume?" I asked. "I don't think I've ever heard of it."

"It's a small village not far from Owerri. Odd thing is, there's hardly a motorable road to the place."

"And yet he feels the need to build what you call a mansion there. When's he hoping to go and live there? Do they have plans to return to Nigeria any time soon?"

Mr. Ofili turned and stared at me as if I had completely lost my marbles. "You think that's the only reason our people spend their hard-earned money putting up big houses in their villages? I'm also building something in my village. Nothing fancy of course, mainly because that's all I can afford."

"Meaning-?"

"Meaning that if I could have afforded a big house, I would have built one. It's because of the Biafran civil war."

"The Biafran war?"

"You must be the only Igbo man," he said, looking at me with pity – or scorn, I was not sure which – in his eyes, "who doesn't seem to understand that the reason we build our mansions in our Igbo villages is because of our experience at the time of the civil war."

"I don't understand-"

"I can see you don't. Let me explain. You remember the pogroms?"

"Who doesn't?" I said. "When our people were running for dear life from the North-"

"Not only from the North," he said, shaking his head sadly. "From Lagos and other Yoruba towns too!"

"I know. I had a relative whose wife and kids fled from Lagos, leaving him behind."

"Oh, my God! What happened to him?"

"By the time he was ready to leave, it was too late. And soon after, the war started. He's all right now. But it was not easy for him. He was arrested and jailed for several weeks."

"Just because he's Igbo, no?"

"Of course," I said.

Mr. Ofili stared at me briefly, in silence. I could see the pain of the memory of the long nightmare in his eyes. It was as if he was living the trauma all over again.

"I was still a young man then. But the main thing I wanted to say is that at the time, very few of our people had houses in their villages in which to take refuge. But you should know this."

"I do," I said. "Like you, I was in secondary school –"

"I was just getting to my last year. But I could see clearly what was happening. After that experience, our people swore that never again would we be caught unprepared. That's why –"

"I see," I said reflectively. "But looking at it all from this our Diaspora, which is looking more and more permanent as the years roll by, a big house in the village seems -- you know – somehow like a white elephant."

"The truth," said Mr. Ofili, "is that the Igbo person's mind is never very far from his original homeland – no matter where he lives. Is there any of us who, when the time comes, doesn't want to be carried home to be buried there?"

I laughed, though death was no laughing matter. "Isn't that what we are really doing? We say we're building houses to live in when we return to Nigeria. But we are in reality only building our burial grounds."

"Oh, so you're building something yourself?"

"Who, me? *Who give awo coat?*" I asked, laughing.

But Mr. Ofili was not amused. "Don't sell yourself short," he said seriously. "It doesn't take much to start putting up something at home, even if your ultimate aim is a big house. If you have a steady income here in the U.S., it helps, and you can send money home from time to time. That's if you can find somebody reliable, who will use what you send to actually build your house."

"Where will you find such a person?"

"Right!" said Mr. Ofili. "That's why your friend – I mean Obi – spends so much time there when he goes home. And there's another thing. The fellow is not well."

"Not well?" I asked. "What's the matter with him?"

"If you ask me a question I can answer, I'll answer it."

"Come on! *You* started this. I didn't ask. *You* told me he is not well."

"Well, truth is, I don't really know," said Mr. Ofili, looking very much as if he knew more than he was willing to tell. "He doesn't like to talk about it. The point is, don't you see, he insists on supervising the construction of his house himself, even if it kills him."

"Did he say that?"

"Say what?"

"Even if it kills him," I said.

"No. Of course he didn't. I'm the one saying so. Instead of taking care of his health in this best of all possible worlds, he wants to supervise his building, and to purchase the building materials himself. He says he's been swindled so often by persons he trusted he's thoroughly fed up. There!"

He looked me steadily in the eye, spreading his arms wide in a gesture that said, "That's it!"

But that was not *it* for me. "You've been a great help to me," I said. "But you know what? You've still not told me how or where I can get in touch with the Udozos. But that's all right. Thank you very much. I'll take it from here."

Chapter X

I T WAS REALLY quite simple. All I did was ask Enoch and Edith to find a way to get Obi Udozo's address and telephone number from their friend Ignatius Ofili. Somehow I knew he would not need his arm twisted to tell them what I wanted to know. I think I knew because I had this strong feeling, when he and I talked in the entrance hall of the Harrison Manor, that Mr. Ofili would have been more forthcoming, but was held back by an outmoded sense of loyalty to a friend. Edith confirmed that assessment.

"He's funny," she told me days later, as we talked in her office.

"You mean – ?"

"Uzo Ofili, of course, who else? He said he didn't want to bear the responsibility for directly giving you the address or phone number you were looking for. You know how it is with our people."

"I don't! But did you ask him why?"

She looked at me sharply. "You don't have to snap at me," she said. "And don't be so impatient, or you can forget it."

"*Akwa-okwulu*, you've come with your taunts," I said, smiling ingratiatingly. "What did I do now?"

"Nothing, except talk out of turn," she said, fixing me with her deep brown eyes that smiled, in spite of her efforts to look stern.

"Okay, I'm sorry."

"Good. As I was about to tell you, Uzo knows more about you than he wanted you to know. You know we have talked several times about what happened to you. From what he told us, I think he clearly knows something – at least from his friend Obi."

"They're friends? He didn't tell me – ."

"You're lucky he even told you the little he told you," Edith said sternly. "You must have been at your most charming the day he met you at your sister's. He said he felt drawn to you – or at least he felt something for you almost from the moment you two met."

"You make it sound like love at first sight," I said. "I'm sure I don't know why. And I hope you don't think of me – ."

"Why am I even talking to you?" she wanted to know. "Whether it is love, or just that he likes you, don't you know these things happen by themselves? You like to tell how you first met Rosemary – ."

"Come on!" I said. "You're now – how do Americans say it – you're comparing apples and oranges."

"I'm not, but I can't get into these arguments with you. Main thing is, I've got what you want – here, somewhere."

She rummaged through two or three drawers of her desk before she found the precious piece of paper. She took it out, proudly waved it in front of my eyes, and then handed it over to me.

"That's it," she said. "Address and telephone number."

Okechukwu Ani just then stepped into Edith's office. He took one look at us, and burst out laughing.

"Still exchanging phone numbers!" he exclaimed, with a mischievous glint in his eye. "I thought you already did that ages ago."

I could not tell the junior partner of the firm, and my second boss, to go stuff it. But Edith had no such inhibition.

"*Ochiora!*" she said, using Okey's praise name, usually a bad omen when she was in a caustic mood. "I don't want anyone to say that I said something I shouldn't have. But you know I'm quite capable of giving back – ."

I had heard enough. I was well aware that this was a scene oft repeated in their daily interactions. So I suppose I knew that whatever else Edith was going to say, was not likely to be seriously meant. But sometimes the tartness of her tongue made me just a little uncomfortable.

"Enough, Edith," I cried out, laughing. "You know how he jokes. *Ochiora*," I said, turning to him, and waving the piece of paper to and fro, "this is what I have been waiting for, for several weeks now, as you know."

"Obi Udozo?" he asked, simply.

"Obi Udozo," I confirmed, nodding my head vigorously.

"His address?"

"And phone number," I added.

"What did you think it was?" asked Edith, some fire still in her eyes.

But the fire very quickly went out, replaced by the widest smile I had seen on her face, when Okey went up to her and mightily hugged her.

"Good job, old girl!" he said. "Somehow I knew you'd come through on this thing."

"Who're you calling old girl?" Her tone was acerbic, even as she snuggled closer to him.

*   *   *

That same night, I prevailed on Rosemary to call Joy Udozo on the telephone. We were at table, having dinner. And I did something I normally frown upon; I let Chizube – in fact I did more than just let her – I almost encouraged her to hurry through her meal, and retire to the family room to watch her favorite TV show, *Seinfeld*. *Seinfeld* was a sitcom about nothing, as some have said. But it fascinated her. It was after she left that I broached the subject of the Udozos.

"Tomorrow is Saturday," I said. "I think we should pay Joy a visit. Can you call her?"

"Me?" asked Rosemary. "Why don't you call her yourself?"

"Because, my dear, she might recognize my voice."

"After all these years?" she asked. "It's been a dozen or more years since you last spoke to her or her husband. Unless – ."

"Unless nothing, Rosemary. Just call her."

"But what will I say to her, C.Y.?"

"Oh, I don't know," I said uncertainly. "Anything you like, so long as you don't identify yourself as my wife. You could ask her – let me see – yes! You could ask her about her store. Tell her you want to buy an African dress. Isn't that what you women mostly do when you go to stores – buy dresses, or something? Or tell her whatever comes into your head."

"And?"

"And you want to know the store hours, naturally."

"C.Y., are you saying you want to go and see her at the store? Is that the best way to go about this?"

"What would you suggest?" I asked her patiently. "We have the phone number and address of the store – ."

"Oh!" said Rosemary. "I thought it was her home address."

"No, Rosemary, it isn't. Mr. Ofili may be anything, but he's certainly not a fool. He went as far as he dared to put us in touch with Joy and Obi. I can't ask for more."

"Okay, sweetie-pie!" she said.

I recognized the inflection in her voice, and knew that the term of endearment she used had little or nothing to do with my sweetness. 'Sweetie-pie', the way she said it, simply meant that I had won *this* argument, and that – for the moment at any rate – she would go along with whatever I wanted done.

"Thank you, dear," I said, all smiles.

"So, I call her," she said. "And she tells me her store hours. What then?"

"Oh, I don't know. Mr. Ofili, according to Edith, said that Joy lives not far from the store. We've got to somehow make her tell us where she lives. It's really a shame they aren't members of our big Igbo association, the Enyimba Union. If they were, their address would very likely have been listed in the Union's directory. And it seems they are not even members of Obi's town union, the Ishinkpume Development Union I think they call it. Most of us Igbos are members of our town and village unions, at least. I wonder what's the matter with the Udozos. Their home telephone number is unlisted. And Mr. Ofili said they use a post office box for their mails. If you ask me, I'd say they are a very secretive lot. Can't say I totally blame them, but it is a nuisance when you want to get in touch."

The telephone conversation between Rosemary and Joy lasted barely two minutes. But we got the information we needed: the OUA store closed on Saturdays at five o'clock, and was located at no. 153 Old Newton Avenue, in downtown Trenton, about a half-mile north of the railroad station. I briefly considered going to Trenton by train, until Rosemary pointed out that, in her condition, she could not walk that half-mile. That would have been most insensitive of me, had I made her walk that distance. Besides, for the three of us, it would have cost more dollars than I cared to spend to go by train, and then take a taxi to the store. After all, we had two cars in the family!

*   *   *

I had not set eyes on her for a dozen years and more. But Joy had not changed much in all that time. Perhaps except for a bulging mid-section! That bulge reminded me of the last time I saw her. That was when I was on bail, and only days before my sentence to an eight-year prison term, way back in 1980. The bulge she had then was not quite as protuberant as now, seeing she was then at an early stage of her second pregnancy.

As the memory of that most troubled juncture of my life came flooding back, it seemed to me that Joy's pregnancy was not the only parallel between then and now. Then, I had gone to see the Udozos in the desperate hope that Obi would somehow unearth Bernard's letter, a letter Obi himself had, days earlier, given to me to read, but which – on the most calamitous day of my life some seventy-two hours later – Bernard had mumblingly declared to judge and jury that he never wrote. Now, I was still in quest of the same letter, still desperate to lay my hands on it, but fearful that my quest would end as futilely now as it did then.

The other parallel was no parallel really. Uchenna, Joy's first daughter who, when I last saw her on that ill-fated visit, was bellowing angrily from her playpen, was now a radiantly attractive fourteen-year old, her hair woven in tresses reaching down to below her shoulder line in back. Her resemblance to her father was almost uncanny, notwithstanding that she was significantly lighter of skin than he. She clearly got that complexion from her mother.

I had no illusions whatsoever about how Joy would receive me. I expected her to be cold and, on the matter of the letter, as elusive as she could be. I was assuming that she knew the score; knew that her husband had done me grievous wrong, and had in fact helped our mutual friend, Bernard, to pretty much destroy my life, leaving me to pick up the pieces as best I could. But I knew I had to see her. I needed to see her as I thought I had never before needed to see anybody or anything!

Initially, Joy was all smiles as Rosemary, with Chizube tagging along, approached her where she sat on a high-backed chair behind the store's counter. She smiled, probably because she saw Rosemary as a new customer entering her store, which was good for her business. I did not immediately show myself, because Rosemary and I had agreed on that tactic. Instead, I hung back, moving stealthily, browsing the wares displayed on the shelves, seemingly studying their prices. But I made sure I stayed as close to Joy's counter as I dared, to eavesdrop on her conversation with Rosemary.

"You're Joy Udozo?" asked Rosemary.

"Yes," said Joy. "Welcome to my store. Can I interest you in anything? Is that your – ?"

"My daughter, Chizube."

"Daughter!" said Joy. "You look more like big sister and small sister. You don't look – well, let me put it this way – I could have sworn this is your first pregnancy."

"How old were you going to say I am, eighteen?" Rosemary asked, laughing happily, lapping up the compliment.

"Well, not quite," said Joy, laughing like one who knew that her attempt at flattery had not entirely succeeded.

"At least you did not try to suggest that Chizube is my immediate younger sister."

"I have a daughter," said Joy, looking right and left. "That is, if I can find her. Where's that girl? Uchenna! Where's she gone now?"

Rosemary pointed. "Is that Uchenna, there, in the toys section?"

Joy looked, and then threw her arms upwards in a gesture of resignation. "She knows I don't move too well these days. She's supposed to be here helping me with this and that. She's fourteen, you know."

"I understand what you're saying," said Rosemary. "In fact I'm surprised you're putting yourself through all this. You are here every day, no?"

"Not really," said Joy. "I come as often as my spirit moves me, which is pretty often. Actually we have help from one of my husband's cousins. He comes practically every day, but you know how it is, don't you? I like to keep an eye on things, if you see what I mean."

"Well, at least, I hope you don't live too far from here."

"No, thank God! It's about ten minutes drive away. We made sure about all that by first finding the store to rent, and then we looked for a house as close to it as possible."

"You said your husband's cousin comes to help out. But where is he?"

"He should be back any minute. He needs his break, for lunch or whatever. As we say, the flutist must stop now and again to wipe his nose. Ifeanyi is a good person. It's just that sometimes he takes too long wiping his nose."

"Your daughter, Uchenna, she looks tall for fourteen – just like Chizube, who's actually thirteen years old."

"Which was why I thought she was your younger sister," said Joy, laughing.

"Do you drive yourself?" asked Rosemary.

"In my present condition? That would be madness. No, I don't drive myself. Before my dear husband took off for Nigeria, we made arrangements with a taxi driver, an Igbo man, to pick me up in the morning, and take me home at night."

"Mummy, can I go and look at the toys?" Chizube suddenly asked and, quickly disengaging from her mother's hold, ran to join Uchenna, even before Rosemary could give her consent.

"That's him," Joy said suddenly, pointing to a young man who just then walked into the store. "Ifeanyi Okolo, my husband's cousin."

Ifeanyi, an inch or so under six feet, his arms bulging with muscles, seemed unhurried as he walked over to where Joy sat. Resting both arms on the counter, he made his excuses to Joy. "Sorry I took longer than I should have," he said in a tone that failed to match his words. And then he walked around to the other side of the counter, where he had his own high chair.

"That's all right," said Joy, exchanging knowing glances with Rosemary.

I saw all this without being seen; at least without Joy taking any special notice of me. I was quite content to let the two women chat on and on, to enable me get a feel of the situation before showing myself. Joy had, in the meantime, confirmed what Mr. Ofili told me at the christening of my sister's son, Somawina, that her husband, Obi, was away to Nigeria.

The store was truly an African store. The shelves were stocked full of merchandise from the old continent. There were men's embroidered jumpers and *danshikis*. There were colorful women's dresses of various cuts and styles: the *kaftan* (a straight gown reaching down to the ankles, and worn with a head-tie, both made from the same fabric); the *boubou* (which is like the kaftan, but is loose-fitting); and the *up-and-down*, (a blouse and a long skirt, also both made from the same fabric, but in many different styles, and worn with a head-tie, and with or without *akwa-ntukwasi*, a middle piece that is tied around the waist or thrown over the shoulder). There were artifacts and sculptures of all descriptions, and food items that one did not expect to see in a New Jersey grocery, like stockfish, yams, and *garri* (a farina prepared from the cassava or manioc). There were packets of Maggi cubes (famously delectable in soups and stews), kolanuts and – a major surprise – bottled palm wine.

"You have a great store here," said Rosemary, her eyes taking in the entire store.

"We try, and we pray to God," said Joy modestly.

"I must come here more often," said Rosemary. "There are just so many things you have in this store that remind me of home. Oh, by the way, you said Obi traveled to Nigeria?"

"You know him?" asked Joy innocently.

"I don't think I've actually met him. But I believe my husband has."

"Oh, your husband is here? Where's he?"

"Hello, Joy," I said, stepping forward from behind a shelf where I had been browsing – or pretending to browse – through greeting cards with African designs and pictures.

For one dramatic moment, as time seemed to stand still, Joy gazed at me. Then her gaze changed into a puzzled stare. And, finally, when recognition dawned, horror – total and absolute – seemed to overwhelm her.

"C-y-r-i-l?" she mouthed hoarsely, her lips twitching.

"That's me," I answered, cool as a cucumber, though anxiety gnawed at my entrails. This was the moment of truth, a moment I had dreamed about seemingly forever, certainly since the day of my release from prison, six long years earlier. I held my breath as we stared at each other. At last, Joy sat back in her high chair, and let out a long rasping sigh.

"When – ?" she began to ask, and then stopped as a woman approached her counter.

"I want to buy these," the customer said, holding up two six-yard pieces of a Nigerian tie-dye fabric, both of identical designs, blue and white in color. "You fit reduce the price small if I buy two?"

I saw Rosemary flash the customer a smile of empathy, being, herself, a most assiduous seeker of bargain prices. Joy looked extremely reluctant, confirming the rumors I had heard that it was hard to get a bargain from her. Perhaps my unexpected reappearance disoriented her, and knocked her thinking cap askew. But the customer eventually got what she wanted.

I did not wait for Joy to repeat her question because I had an idea what she wanted to know.

"1987," I said. "Six years ago."

"God have mercy on me!" Joy exclaimed. "Six years! And, if I may ask, since then – ?"

As if she really wanted to know! But since she asked, I felt obliged to answer. "Since then, if you want the truth, I've been trying to piece my life back together."

She looked quite calmly at me as she digested my answer. When she next spoke, it was evident that she had somewhat recovered from her earlier shock, and her voice had become steadier.

"And how are things with you?" she asked.

"I thank God for His mercies," I answered. "All things considered, I'm not doing too badly except that, like the tortoise, the shortness of my arm has prevented me from catching everything I've been pursuing."

There was a long awkward pause. I think she felt ensnared, in spite of her show of bravado. Her eyes became shifty, as her unsteady gaze went from Rosemary to me. I did the best I could to reassure her, with a soft smile, and eyes that I hoped conveyed little or no hostility, if not warmth. I remembered the last time – or two – I saw her. I was on bail then, during the dark days of my trial, back in 1980. I do not know why I remembered such a trifling detail as the fact that Joy was so taken aback by my visit then, that she forgot to offer me even a can of soda, by way of hospitality. At the time, I think I understood how she felt, and I really could not blame her for the oversight. Neither she nor her husband Obi had expected my visit, or was aware of my situation. It was then that I recounted to them how I had been arrested and jailed – on account of our mutual friend Bernard's eight thousand dollars which Obi himself had handed over to me, and which started a chain of cataclysmic events that caused my sun to set while it was yet high noon. My bombshell shocked them almost beyond description. Joy, I remembered clearly, stared at me as if I was the devil himself come to torment her family.

Now, some dozen years later, as she stared at Rosemary and me, I hoped she would not show us outright hostility, though I could see she was struggling with her emotions. Then finally, she shook her head several times, sadly, thoughtfully.

"I'm sorry about what happened, Cyril," she said. Then she added, turning to Rosemary: "I don't believe we've ever met."

Rosemary shook her head. "I'm sure we haven't," she said, smiling warmly. "My name is Rosemary."

"And your daughter?" Joy asked, pointing in the direction of the toys section.

"Chizube," said Rosemary. "I see we are both in the same – er – state of health, you and me. When are you due?"

"My doctor says in another two weeks, three max."

The two women had found a common ground in their shared condition, and they talked and talked, while I stood silently by, hoping they had not forgotten me. By the end of their conversation, I had learnt that Joy's current pregnancy was her fourth; that her second child and first son *Uzoma* (literally, a good road to take, or a good beginning), born a few months into my incarceration, had been a victim of sudden infant death syndrome; that a second son, three years younger than Uzoma, was named *Ndukaku* (life is more precious than wealth); and that ten-year old Ndukaku was at home with Joy's mother, Mrs. Ijeoma Obiora (praise-named *Amalachukwu*, meaning God's grace). Amalachukwu had come to the United States about a week before Ndukaku was born, to help take care of mother and baby. She had come into the country on a visitor's visa, but was now a legal resident. It had taken some doing, but the Udozos did it. It certainly helped that they themselves had, a few years earlier, become citizens by naturalization.

I coughed loudly, just in case they had forgotten I was there. Whereupon Joy turned and said, again: "Cyril, I'm really sorry about what happened."

"Thank you," I said. "So Obi's away?"

"Yes, he went home."

"When is he expected back? I need to talk with him."

There might have been a tinge of desperation in my voice that did not sit well with Joy. I saw her expression change from openness, through guardedness, to suspicion. She certainly took her time responding to my urgent question.

"I don't think he'll be back for a long while," Joy said, refusing to look me in the eye. "Probably a year, if not more."

That answer knocked the wind out of me. But I could not bring myself to believe that a man would leave his wife, whose pregnancy was near term, for that length of time – in the name of business – even though this was her fourth pregnancy. And notwithstanding that his mother-in-law was there in his house, as our tradition required, to look after her daughter and grandson! What kind of a father would name his second son Ndukaku, following the tragic death of his first son, and then abandon wife and children in the pursuit of filthy lucre?

There seemed little point hanging around any longer in the store. We had not fully accomplished our mission, but at least we had established contact – physical contact – with the Udozos. And Joy had been only guarded – perhaps even cold – in her welcome, when she recognized me. But she had definitely not been as hostile as I had feared she might be. Indeed, for a brief moment, I actually wondered if she was aware of the burning issue between her husband and me. But I quickly dismissed the thought. No way, I said to myself, would her husband not have shared his burden with her; the burden of a letter as significant as the one that sent the friend of a friend down to bottomless perdition.

Rosemary bought some yams and plantains, and I, a few black-oriented cards I did not immediately need. Chizube wheedled her mother into buying a fancifully dressed figurine for her; we only insisted that it be a *black* figurine.

"Ifeanyi," Joy called out to the young man, "please help them carry their stuff to their car."

Somewhat reluctantly, or so it seemed to me, Ifeanyi came and grabbed two of our shopping bags, heavy with the yams and plantains, as easily as if they were bags of feathers, and walked ahead of us towards the door. He seemed in more of a hurry than we were. But that was okay with me. I was glad of the help.

We were halfway to the door of the store when a suppressed scream rent the air. I knew it was Joy even before I wheeled round. She was still sitting on her high-backed chair, her body thrown back. Her hands clutched her belly, as she whimpered in obvious agony. I rushed to her, fearing the worst. Ifeanyi, for his part, dropped the two bags he was carrying, and was at Joy's side before I reached her.

"Are you all right?" I heard him ask her solicitously.

"I'm having contractions!" she said, her face reflecting she pains she felt. "Oh my God! My back hurts. I knew this would happen."

"Is it labor?" I asked.

"That's how it starts anyway," said Rosemary, joining me at the counter.

"Okay, so what are we going to do now?" I asked in some alarm.

"I knew this would happen," Joy said again. "But it's still early."

"Do you want us to call anybody?" Rosemary calmly asked. Somebody needed to be calm. "Your mum, or a friend?"

I quickly regained my composure. "Will you close the store, or will Ifeanyi keep it open till your regular closing time?" I asked. "We can drive you home if – ."

"Home?" Joy asked, as another contraction seemed to rack her frame. "What home? I should be going to the hospital, if this continues."

"What about calling your doctor?" Rosemary suggested. "And then, if the contractions continue, we can take you to the hospital. Or we can call 911, whatever you wish. Perhaps your daughter can call your mum so she knows what's going on. As to the store – ."

"I can manage by myself, as you know," Ifeanyi said, looking intently at Joy. "But it's your decision."

"We'll close the store for today," said Joy, without hesitation.

We did what needed to be done. Joy herself made the announcement. "Sorry friends! The store will be closing in another ten minutes!"

Uchenna called home, and told her grandmother about the situation. Joy gave Rosemary her doctor's name and number. It turned out that the doctor was a Nigerian, one Taiwo Oladapo, a Yoruba woman and, in the Nigerian community, a well-known and very reputable obstetrician. Naturally, Dr. Oladapo wanted to know the frequency of the contractions. They talked briefly, and then, apparently satisfied with Joy's answers, the doctor directed us to St. Joseph's Hospital in downtown Trenton.

"This is my first pregnancy with Dr. Oladapo. She says she'll meet me at the hospital within the hour," said Joy. "With my earlier pregnancies, everything went fairly smoothly from contractions to delivery. But my last time was ten years ago. I just hope I've not forgotten what I learned in the Lamaze classes."

"Who attended the classes with you?" Rosemary asked.

"Uchenna," answered Joy. "My husband wasn't much around to be of any use to me for the classes. Uchenna!"

"I'm ready!" announced the bright young lady, preening herself. "I remember everything we were taught."

And indeed she remembered. Displaying maturity somewhat beyond her years, she coached her mother through the gentle breathing exercises necessary at this stage to prepare her, psychologically and physically, for labor. Lamaze exercises are supposed to help the expectant mother go through labor, and its associated pains, without the use of drugs.

We did not call 911. "If Obi had been here now," Joy said, "I know he would have just driven me straight to St. Joseph's, and not bothered with ambulances. He knows I don't like their sirens – just makes me more nervous than is good for me. The hospital is only a matter of two miles from here."

She had her bag of necessaries, ready and packed, in a locker in the store. "I have one bag at home too," she told us. "Just in case. You never know when and where it will start."

As she talked, and with some help from her daughter, she was putting things away here and there, where they belonged. The proceeds from the day's sales she emptied into a handbag with zippered pockets.

"You aren't taking that to the hospital, are you?" Rosemary asked, indicating the handbag.

"My mother will take care of it," Joy said. "I can't just leave the money here."

"About going to the hospital," I said, "do you want to call your taxi? Or – ."

"I thought you said you'd drive me there?"

"Sure! No problem at all. I just didn't want to be – you know – to put you in an awkward situation."

"It will take too long for the taxi to get here," Rosemary chipped in. "There's no time to waste."

The store had emptied quickly, after Joy's announcement. Naturally, several customers, on their way out, came to the counter to ask why. There were oohs and aahs, and expressions of good wishes. One fellow said he hoped it would be a boy. A woman said she was not the least bit surprised at the turn of events. "Your husband shouldn't have let you continue to work until now," she said. "Men never understand!"

I drove her to St. Joseph's Hospital. I drove, fearing that her water might break at any moment, and thankful that Rosemary was present, should anything begin to happen. Happily, nothing happened, and we reached the hospital in quick time. Then, accompanied by Ifeanyi, I drove to her home with instructions to bring her mother and son Ndukaku to the hospital.

*   *   *

St. Joseph's Hospital made a very favorable impression on me, with its clean and shining corridors, and its rooms looking as if they had only just received a coat of paint. Everything looked to be in good order; even the hustle and bustle of the doctors and nurses, as they tended their patients, seemed unhurried, and confident. I felt completely at ease, as I generally tend to do whenever I find myself in a typical American hospital. It never seems to me as if anything could ever go wrong there.

Joy's labor pains persisted for about three hours, during which time she was separated from us. I had no idea where they had taken her; I only knew she was in good hands. We waited in the visitors' lounge, all seven of us, as if we were one big happy family. But we were not part of the family, Rosemary, Chizube and I. If we had not been caught in the wrong place and time, we really had no business there, in the hospital, with Joy. But we could not abandon her, though she now had her entire family, minus husband Obi, in the lounge.

A stern-looking, no-nonsense, black nurse, perhaps suspecting that I was trying to chicken out of my marital obligations, was rather insistent that I be by Joy's side at her hour of travail, until I introduced her to Rosemary. Whereupon the expression in her eyes momentarily changed from mild irritation to wonderment, her gaze flitting from Rosemary's protuberance, to the three children with us, to Joy's mother, to me. Giving up on us, she asked that Joy's mother accompany her to the delivery room.

"The patient asked for her mum," she explained to *Amalachukwu*, "which I imagine is you. I thought she also said something about her husband, but I suppose I might have misunderstood her."

"What about her children?" Rosemary asked. "They're big kids now."

The nurse made a dismissive gesture with her hands. "Doesn't matter how big they are," she said. "Their mother didn't ask for them." Then, looking pointedly at Rosemary's belly, she added: "You look close to term yourself. When it happens, would you like your children – ?"

"Daughter," said Rosemary. "We have only one."

"That's good. Would you like her in your delivery room?"

Rosemary looked questioningly at me, as if I could supply the answer she needed, an answer only she could give. We had never discussed that subject, perhaps because when she had Chizube, I was serving my term. I had, still have, a decided disinclination to being in the delivery room at the point of delivery, though it seems the modern and class thing to do.

"I didn't think so," said the nurse, with a satisfied smile. Indeed, as she walked out of the lounge, with Joy's mother in tow, she was chuckling to herself. I guessed that she herself, though a professional, was not as enthusiastic on the issue as one would have thought.

So Rosemary and I found ourselves baby-sitting two kids that were not our own, and in a situation from which we could not extricate ourselves, though it was not of our choosing. I thought about calling Mr. Ignatius Ofili, as a friend of the Udozo family, but I recalled that he lived close to Laurel, in the state of Maryland.

After what seemed ages, Dr. Oladapo, Joy's obstetrician, came into the lounge. She was bespectacled, fiftyish, very dark in complexion, and quite attractive. The touch of gray in her hair gave her a distinguished aura.

"Good news," she announced, soft-voiced, and smiling from ear to ear. "It's a girl! Seven and a half pounds! Congratulations!"

"Can I go and see her?" asked Uchenna, bounding up and down excitedly. "Please can I?"

"'Course you can," said the doctor. "And you can take your brother and sister with you." She seemed to see Ifeanyi for the first time. "And you too, if you want to come," she said to him.

"I think I'd rather wait here, with them," Ifeanyi replied, indicating Rosemary and me.

Uchenna took Ndukaku with her, but Rosemary would not let Chizube go with them. "We're not family," she told Dr. Oladapo. And she got no argument on that score from our daughter.

I think I was in a brown study, thinking about Rosemary and the coming birth of our second child and, no doubt by force of repulsive habit, chewing my fingernails, when the black nurse burst into the lounge, and drew me slightly aside.

"Mrs. Udozo – is she your sister or something?"

"No," I answered, my senses immediately on the alert.

"I'm afraid," said the nurse, "there's a problem. But – ."

"What problem?" I heard Rosemary ask, from where she sat, within earshot of us.

"It's her breathing. She seems to have stopped – ."

"Oh my God!" shouted Rosemary.

"No!" I said, in a hoarse whisper.

"What happened?" asked Ifeanyi. "What do you mean she stopped breathing? Is she – ?"

"No, she's not," the nurse replied, I thought, a little too assertively. "We're doing everything we can for her. She's on a respirator. Let's stay positive, and hope for the best."

Which was easy for her to say! And what did she mean they were doing everything they could for her? In my untutored mind, her attempt at playing the crisis down fell woefully short of the kind of firm reassurance a family needs; an assurance that the patient, having stopped breathing, could actually come back from the dead.

The stern nurse essayed a smile which, from where I sat, looked more like a grimace. Then she turned and walked towards the door. At the door, she turned, and wagged a finger at us.

"Remember what I just said." She flashed another smile. "Stay positive."

*　　*　　*

In a matter of just over an hour, Joy breathed again though, to this day, I have not understood how the doctors did it. Dr. Oladapo encouraged us to go up to Joy's room, on the third floor of the Women's Wing; Ifeanyi went with us. Joy's recovery was now more or less complete. We found her propped up on her pillows, breathing rhythmically, and smiling, as if all was well with the world. Briefly, I wondered, but did not know how to ask, if she was aware of what she had just gone through. I thought she should have been lying down flat on her back, so as not to unduly jeopardize her recovery, and said so. But what did I know about such matters? And I must have spoken a little more loudly than I had intended, and in English, because Joy's roommate burst out laughing.

The roommate was a Caucasian woman, of an indeterminate age, though she seemed a trifle old for child bearing, and certainly much too slender to find room in her torso for twins. Two days earlier, we soon learnt, she had given birth to two identical girls, each weighing just about five pounds. She was cuddling the twins, one in the crook of each arm, as she spoke.

"You're funny," she told me, and laughed again.

I was unaware that I had said anything funny, even if my concern for Joy's recovery might have seemed a trifle exaggerated. But, to take her mind off me, I complemented her on her twins.

"They look cute," I said.

"It is the Lord's doing," she said.

"Amen!" Rosemary and I said in unison.

"By His crucifixion," the woman continued, as if we had not spoken, "He overcame death. By His resurrection, He breathed new life into us."

"Praise the Lord!" Rosemary said, crossing herself.

I believe my confusion registered in the way I was staring at the woman, because she laughed again.

"Not me, silly," she said, and then pointed at Joy. "It is about Joy I'm talking, not about my twins. The Lord has performed His miracle for her."

I thought to myself: Great! She already knows Joy's name.

"I'm Juliet," she introduced herself, as if she had read my mind.

"If you let her," Joy's mother said to us, speaking in Igbo, "she'll not stop talking. I know you must be eager to be on your way. I'm sure when you left home earlier today, you didn't know you would still be in our area at this time. I don't even know how to begin to thank you for everything."

"Oh, it's nothing," I said. "We did what we had to do, nothing more, and nothing less. And if we've been of help – ."

"If you've been of help!" cried *Amalachukwu*. "How much more can you do than what you've done?"

"Please don't say it is nothing," Joy herself said, speaking weakly. "I don't think it was mere chance that brought you to my store today. God sent you. I thank you and I thank Him."

I looked from Joy to her roommate Juliet. "You know," I said to Joy, in Igbo, "you and her are two of a kind. You make great roommates, the way you both talk. You speak the same language. Anyway, we have to be on our way."

"But not before we say a little prayer," said Rosemary.

I looked blankly at her, then at my watch. It was a quarter of nine o'clock, and pitch dark outside. But I know better than to argue with my Rosemary when she brings up the subject of prayer. It is a battle I lost several years earlier, within a year or two of my release from prison, when I learnt not to fight with her and her God. My God too! Except that I am not as meticulous in these Christian practices as she is, or indeed as I ought to be!

But Rosemary was not done with me. "C.Y.," she said, "can you lead us in prayer?"

"Me?"

"Yes, you C.Y."

For a very brief moment, it flashed through my mind that Rosemary was not serious. Then, in some despair, I looked up to the ceiling, but found no reprieve there. So I smiled my familiar smile of defeat, lowered my eyes befittingly and, holding my palms together in supplication, began to pray.

I mostly seem to stutter when I pray. But on this occasion, the words flowed smoothly from my heart and my mouth. I prayed for Joy and her new baby who, as yet, had no name. I remembered her loquacious roommate, Juliet, who could not of course understand a word of my prayer, said in Igbo. I asked God's blessings on Joy's mother, and on Joy's children. And, yes, on her husband Obi too! I had to remember him as well, because I had always been taught that when you pray, you should forget all grudges, however serious they might be. Nor did I forget Ifeanyi, for whom I asked that God give him the heart and mind to understand that Joy's family would increasingly depend on him till the return of Obi, and not only in the store, but at home. In particular, I prayed for Rosemary's coming travail, when she, in her turn, would come to term.

On our way back to our home in West Brook, NJ, Rosemary complimented me on the breath and depth of my prayer. Then she asked: "Why did you forget your sister Adaku and her family, especially her baby Somawina, for whom we are God-parents?"

Women! But I had my own, very worrisome, question for her.

"Do you think," I said, "that we – me, especially – might have been the cause of what happened today? You know, the shock and all that."

She turned to me, and there was uncertainty in her eyes. "Who knows?" she asked. "But it doesn't really matter. It was God's will that what happened, happened. It isn't as if we even knew Joy was pregnant, not to talk of being almost due."

"Another thing is, we now know where they live," I said. "Let's leave it at that. And as we say, next time we go hunting, we will hunt in the backyard of the quarry."

Chapter XI

THE LETTER FROM Obi Udozo was postmarked 'London, May 27, 1993'. By far the quickest way to transmit a letter from Nigeria to the United States, for close on two decades now, is to give it to someone traveling abroad, usually the United Kingdom or the United States of America, from where it is then mailed. The reason for this is that the regular Nigerian airmail service has been, of its kind, probably the slowest and least reliable known to man.

Chizube met me at the entrance door, before I had properly deposited my bunch of keys into a cup placed, for that purpose, on a low table near the door. As she embraced me, with her usual enthusiasm, and that childlike tenderness that was as warm as it was unaffected, whatever troubles trailed me from the office dissipated into thin air. She had latterly begun to worry about me, and my occasional lapse into a dark mood, brought on – as she sometimes put it – by "what happened to you". For one so young, she evidently understood my circumstances more than Rosemary and I would have wished.

At the end of our embrace, she held out the envelope to me. "I know you like it when all the letters are not for mummy only," she said, smiling.

She was right. Most letters we received, easily nine out of ten, were for Rosemary. I had, I suppose, been making a little bit of a fuss about this, as if I was upset that hardly anybody wrote to me. But what neither Rosemary nor our daughter realized was that it did not bother me in the least. Quite the contrary, if I must tell the truth. Keeping up with correspondence, especially from relatives – and those were almost the only letters I received – was not something I particularly enjoyed doing. Of course unless the letters were from my siblings, Emma and Janet!

The letter came from Obi Udozo. My hands trembled somewhat as I slit it open. I did not know why my hands shook, and I was angry with myself. I was angry because, as I kept saying to myself, Obi Udozo is the one whose hands should tremble, whose heart should palpitate, if he received a letter from me. *He* did me wrong. *I* was the victim.

Perhaps, I reflected, the trembling was caused by my frustration at my inability to get anything going in the matter of my quest for Bernard's all-important letter, and the knowledge that Obi was at the heart and center of it all. I did not expect that Obi's letter would throw any light on, or advance, my quest. And it did not. It was, as I had expected, merely a thank-you note.

"Thank you", Obi wrote, *"for everything. Joy called me yesterday and told me what you and your wife, she said her name is Rosemary, did to help her through her ordeal."*

Did they have telephones in Ishinkpume? Ishinkpume was a mere village, near Owerri, the only town of any size or importance within a radius of several miles. Owerri, if you ask me, was no great shakes itself – at least when I left Nigeria for the United States – in such matters as having the range of amenities that mark a modern city. I had been there several times in the early seventies, when it was burgeoning in population, as well as in the unsightly disorder that so often marks our growing cities and towns.

"Joy told me how you two came to our store in Trenton," wrote Obi. *"She said she was surprised to see you after so many years, and that you said you would like for me and you to talk about things.*

"I want you to know that I fully understand, and promise you that on my return to the States, we will talk. Let me say straight off that I am really sorry about the way things went. But this is not a subject I should discuss in this letter."

It was not a long letter, though he did mention some details of the events of that day, as recounted to him by Joy. There was no direct – or even indirect – mention of Bernard's letter. No surprise there!

I suppose, all things considered, that he had to write the letter. It would have been passing strange had he not found a way to show some appreciation to Rosemary and me for what we did. Perhaps I respond too easily to such gestures, but I confess that I was deeply touched by the letter. I think I was particularly touched by the fact that he wrote the letter not quite two weeks after the birth of his daughter on May 14, 1993. He could have taken his time writing the letter, and found a hundred different reasons to justify his tardiness. And the fact that he readily referred to my wish to talk with him about the past seemed a positive sign. He gave no indication when he would return to the United States, but I hoped it would be soon – if only because of the birth of his child.

"Let's keep our fingers crossed for luck," Rosemary said. "I can see that this thing is beginning to eat at you. If you don't watch out, it will eat you up, and you'll be sick."

*   *   *

Three happy events have really given some meaning, and uplift, to my life. First, Rosemary married me. Against all odds, she had remained steadfast in her love for me during the dark days. Her parents, particularly her father, had not wanted me for a son-in-law. But Rosemary rode out that storm. And then we wedded in secret.

I say that my marriage to Rosemary was the first of the three happy events. What I mean is that it should have been. I am a struggling, but believing, Christian man, and have always been taught that marriage should come before procreation. But the birth of our daughter came first. I was not free to be present at Chizube's birth even had I wanted to be there. But when the news reached me in prison, it was the freshest breath of life and hope that ever came to me in that dark and sometimes very dank hellhole. If it did nothing else for me, it lifted my spirits wonderfully, and gave me renewed vigor and a fresh determination to serve out my sentence, without that sense of utter hopelessness that is sometimes the lot of persons in my situation. I could, and indeed began to look forward to the day my captivity would end though, at that moment, my eight-year sentence had only just begun. In other words, the birth of my daughter Chizube gave me an additional reason to live – additional, that is, to my love for Rosemary.

Our son Ndubisi was born on June 10, 1993, about a week later than his due date. And I was there – literally! I had not wanted to be there. But, in the face of Rosemary's insistence that I be a modern man, I capitulated. So I sat, immobile, by her bedside when the miracle of the birth happened. I put on a show of stoicism that I did not at all feel, and contented myself with merely holding her hand. That is, when she let me! I made sure not to talk too much, or out of turn, for fear of saying the wrong thing. I had been told that a woman, at the most critical moment of labor, was apt to turn on her husband, and heap verbal abuses on him for her agonies and pains. And when the, as yet unwashed, baby was first put into my arms, I did not pass out, as I had feared I would, though Rosemary, to this day, swears that I looked petrified. Of what, for crying out loud! She should have had other things to worry about than watching to see how I would carry the cute but squealing, eight-pound, slimy baby-boy.

We knew, when Ndubisi was born that, baring a delicious accident, he would most likely be our last child. Rosemary and I had talked endlessly about it, and we had, happily, a total concordance of minds on the issue.

What weighed most heavily on our minds was the notion – right or wrong – that Rosemary was getting to an age, if she was not there already, where it would be like tempting fate to go on procreating.

The other consideration had to do with my uncertain status in the country. I might not still be in prison, but my situation vis-à-vis the INS was not where I would have wished it was.

"In other words," I said, "anything can happen to me, anytime."

"Meaning what?" Rosemary asked.

I laughed, though without mirth. "You know what our people say, that the mother-hen, with a brood of chickens, does not know how best to run for shelter when it rains."

"I don't know about that," said Rosemary. "I think what matters most, next to the question of my age, is whether we can even afford to have more than two or three children – ."

"Did you say, or three?"

"I'm serious C.Y. And wipe that silly smile from your face."

I was not aware that I was smiling, but the scowl on my wife's face told me it would be futile to argue the point.

"I'm sorry," I said. "You were saying?"

"You know how it is in this country, when a family has many children. At home, where it is not too difficult to find nursemaids, it would have been a different story. At least it didn't use to be difficult, or even too expensive, to engage a domestic help."

"You're right," I said, "as always."

She looked sharply at me, and for a moment I thought she would come back at me with a rebuke. But she evidently thought better of it, shook her head regally, and smiled. We knew one thing though: we just could not stop at Chizube. She had been born – even conceived – when my world was upside down. Which was the reason Rosemary argued that we needed a child conceived and born in more regular circumstances. She did not get an argument from me on that.

Chizube had kept at us with an unceasing plea that she wanted a sister. And when Rosemary commented that it might please God to give us a son, Chizube had shrugged her slim shoulders. "It's all the same," she said, very sensibly but not very truthfully, as both her mother and I knew.

Ndubisi brought us contentment, and a deep appreciation of God's grace. We had agreed on the names: Ndubisi Ogonna, if a boy; Chioma Nkechinyelu, if a girl. The name Ndubisi is an acknowledgment of the paramountcy of life over every other consideration. Ogonna is a source of joy to the father or, to put it a little more grandly, to God, who is the Supreme Father. My people choose names – that is, Igbo names – with care and attention to their meanings. Sometimes with too much care!

We celebrated with family and friends on the occasion of Ndubisi's christening. Rosemary's uncle Frank Akamelu and his wife Nwamaka were there. So were Aloysius and Obiamaka Jideofo. Uncle Frank, regally resplendent in a long, embroidered Igbo jumper, chaired the reception, and did the kolanut ceremony. When it came time to pour the libation to our ancestors, he invited the oldest member of my family, cousin Aloysius, to do the honors. With tradition duly observed, the chairman next called on the baptismal priest to say the opening prayers.

The reception was relatively low-key, certainly nothing to compare with the lavish banquet that feted the christening of my sister Adaku's son, Somawina. But I scored one over Adaku. Our brother Emma – I should rather say, with due respect,

Mr. Emmanuel Jideofo, MRCS, Surgeon at Guy's Hospital, London – came over from England to be with us for the occasion.

This was the first time, in close to two decades, that we had set eyes on each other. He had made it a point to come to *my* son's christening because, he said, the weight of all those barren years had latterly begun to weigh very heavily on his mind and conscience. He came all by himself, though he had hinted he might come with his wife Irene.

"I know you cannot travel out of this country for the moment," he told me. "And I've been feeling guilty about things for some time now. Maybe it's terribly selfish of me to have come alone. I'm not sure Irene will ever forgive me for not bringing her to this wonderful country. Everybody wants to come to America. But it's been one heck of a long time I've not seen you. And it is very important to me to come to this event without distractions from wife or children."

Emma stopped, and moved closer to me on the settee we were sharing. Even sitting down, he towered over me. His eyes, as he stared into mine, shone with such tenderness, I was almost moved to tears. And when he reached for me, pulling me into a bear hug – for perhaps the third or fourth time – the lump in my throat literally threatened to choke me. And like a child, though I was all of five years his elder, I unashamedly let my head come to rest on his chest.

He had lost some weight, indeed quite some weight, and looked almost svelte. At thirty-eight or so, he had not altogether lost that youthfulness of face that had been his hallmark from as far back as I could remember. And he still talked with the same vigor, and a touch of that boastfulness which used to sometimes make me mad with him.

At the beginning of the party, Emma insisted that I introduce him as *Mr.* Jideofo, Surgeon, after the manner and style of the British. And I did, to please him, and because I was aware that British surgeons set a high store by that designation. That insistence, on Emma's part, to be addressed as Mister, was perhaps the thing that most stands out in my memory of the events of that day. I do not recall how well he performed his duties as Godfather to Ndubisi, during the service of baptism. He had to be my son's Godfather or, as he so flatly put it, what would have been the point of his long flight, across the wide Atlantic, to be with us? I knew he said that to get a laugh out of the guests at the reception, and I paid it no mind.

He got another laugh when he told a little fib about how, on the day I received our cousin Aloysius's letter in 1973, inviting me to come over to the United States for my college education, I was so excited I began to quake all over. "And if I had not physically held him up," he shamelessly lied, "I honestly believed he would most likely have fallen on the cemented floor, and probably broken a bone or something." Well, perhaps it was not a *complete* fib, as I did indeed seem to have blanked out for a split second. But though I came to very quickly, Emma never thereafter missed an opportunity to exaggerate his role on that occasion.

He could not get enough of me, nor I him. Ours was a reunion to beat all reunions. I reveled in his presence and his physical closeness to me. I had been starved of his face, and yes, his idiosyncrasies, for most of my adult life. Having him this close to me, after the long years of our separation, inevitably made me long also for the face of my sister Janet, fifteen years old at the time I last saw her. That was at the Enugu airport, from where I caught my flight to Lagos, on the first leg of my journey to the United States, in 1974.

I do not think I will ever forget the way Janet silently held on to my hand, and refused to let go, as I walked towards the boarding gate. But she had to let me go when we reached the gate. And then she continued to wave to me until I passed beyond her view, and into the plane. The picture of the pain etched on her innocent adolescent face, and of her eyes from which all sparkle had gone, remain vivid in my memory as if carved ineffaceably in stone. I will probably never stop worrying about her until her luck changes, and she and her husband and children obtain visas to at least visit the United States.

Emma and I talked until there was almost no more talking to be done. We paid scant attention to the clock, or to Rosemary's mostly good-humored complaints that I was abandoning our conjugal bed. My bosses in the office – Messrs Onyeama and Ani – let me have two days of my annual vacation on the Monday and Tuesday following the christening. They understood – I made them understand – the importance to me of my brother's visit.

Adaku stayed back one extra day after the christening, and did not travel back to Laurel, Maryland, with her family. She kept baby Somawina with her, notwithstanding her husband Theo's protestations that he was quite capable of taking care of his son "for one bleeping day!" as he so colorfully and indelicately put it. Adaku merely laughed at him, as did Rosemary, though Theo had not meant what he said as a joke.

Rosemary, bless her heart, mostly let my siblings and me be. On the Sunday night, after the reception, we stayed up talking well beyond midnight. Then Adaku withdrew, leaving Emma and me to catch up on the long period of our separation. Adaku did not need all that catching up with Emma. Over the years, they had seen each other quite regularly. On her annual Christmas trips to Nigeria, Adaku usually arranged her flights through London, so as to visit with Emma and his family. Or they had met at home, if Emma also traveled to Nigeria for Christmas.

"The main reason I stayed this extra day," she explained, as if she needed to explain the obvious, "is to be with both of you. This is the first time for God knows how many years we've been together like this. It's just like old times. How I wish Janet was here."

Adaku returned to Laurel, MD, the next day, Monday. That same evening, I took Emma to my favorite all-you-can-eat Chinese restaurant, The Ming. Not quite a mile from our apartment, The Ming was located in the Brook Plaza, our local shopping center. Rosemary and I, whenever we wanted to eat without counting the calories, would take what I liked to call our "preprandial walk" along the tree-lined Kennedy Avenue that runs straight from our Mount of Olives Gardens estate to the Plaza. Chizube, whenever we did this, would trot reluctantly alongside of us, grumbling the while. Sometimes, if we drove to The Ming, and then ate more than was good for us, I would elect to walk the mile back to our estate – my postprandial walk – to help the digestive process.

Emma had evidently not been in any all-you-can-eat restaurant before coming to America. He kept asking how the restaurant could make any profit if the customers ate as much as they wanted, and for a cost significantly lower than one would pay for a sit-down dinner in an average London restaurant.

"This is America," I said. "There's enough food in this country to feed the entire world. But surely, even in your poor England, there must be places where you can – ?"

"Eat like this?" Emma asked. "I'm sure there must be, but I just haven't been in one, that's all. The U.S. is obviously blessed beyond measure. Things are so much cheaper than in England, and I imagine life is good here."

"Very good," I said, nodding vigorously.

"So good, I take it, you want to stay on in spite of everything?"

"Yes, my brother," I said, with a sad shake of my head. "What else can I do? Return to – ?"

"Don't even mention it!" said Emma forcefully, the piece of scallop at the end of his fork suspended in mid-air. "I would not wish that on my worst enemy. I was only thinking, with all the things that have happened to you here, a change of scenery might not be a bad idea. England, for example."

I looked across at Emma, and saw that he was deadly serious. A Chinese Emperor, fiercely mustached, peered down at us from his framed immobility on a wall of the restaurant, with an expression that seemed to be asking me: "why not?"

I looked away from the Emperor's piercing eyes and into the tender eyes of my brother. We stared at each other for a moment or two. Then I looked away because, strangely, I could not bear the softness of his stare.

"What about my family?"

"Of course, you must come with them," he said without the slightest hesitation. "I have to confess I already made some enquiries and, though it might not be easy, I think it is possible to arrange something."

"I don't think so," I said. "If I leave this country now, I might simply end up in Nigeria. I don't even want to expose myself applying for a British visa. I'm lucky to be still where I am and, in any case, I have unfinished business here."

"What unfinished business?"

"Emma, it's a long story, and I've told you only the half of it. But let me put it this way: I'm waiting for a friend – well, actually, I shouldn't call him a friend, just an old acquaintance – I'm waiting for him to return from Nigeria. He and I have some serious talking to do. Yes, I would say very serious talking, and very important for me in my quest to clear my name."

"You're still hoping to do that – I mean, clear your name?" asked Emma, very softly. His voice was barely above a whisper, I suppose, so as not to be heard by the diners at the tables closest to ours. "How do you hope to do so?"

"Oh I don't know. But I'll go on trying until thy kingdom come, and then most likely, I'll present my case to the Almighty. I've told you I don't know where Bernard is."

"Yes," said Emma. "And I told you he's at home. At least that's what I've heard."

"But you haven't actually ever seen him on your trips home?"

"I haven't, I'll admit," said Emma. "He's a slippery fellow, that one."

"He is," I said. "Bernard obviously doesn't want to be seen, especially by anyone close to me. But he has this friend, Obi Udozo, who can help me – if he wants to – when he returns to this country. I don't know what's keeping him at home. His wife had a baby recently, and he should have been back by now. I call his wife occasionally to ask how things are with her and her baby, and of course I ask about Obi. That's how I know he's not back. Unless of course his wife is lying to me!"

"Is this the same Obi who received the letter from Bernard that got you into all this mess?"

"The same," I replied. "As far as I'm concerned, other than family, Obi is the most important human being in my life right now. Whatever it takes – ."

I stopped because of the expression on Emma's face. Brows furrowed in concentration, he seemed to be struggling to remember something.

"What's the matter?" I asked.

He stared at me for a long moment, but I doubt he saw me. The stare seemed to go through me, as if I was temporarily immaterial.

"You said Obi Udozo?" he finally asked.

"I did," I said, "about a million times already. Why?"

"Because –," he said, and then stopped for a moment. "Because I think I've met him."

"You met him in Nigeria on one of your visits?"

"No, Cyril. I did not meet him at home. Right now, as we talk, he must be in London, unless he returned to America within the last week or so, while I've been here."

It was my turn to stare at my brother. "But that's quite impossible," I said. "What would he be doing there, with a wife and a new baby waiting for him here?"

Emma shook his head slowly. "You don't understand. Unless I'm totally off course, he's in London. You see – there's a doctor, well known in the Igbo community in London, one Dr. Josiah Udozo, who's something of a friend. We meet occasionally because he sometimes comes to my place, and I go to his. On a recent visit – I went to see him to discuss about our association of Nigerian doctors – he took me to see his brother who, he said, lives in America, and stopped over in London for a few days. At least that was his intention – ."

"He took you to meet his brother? Wasn't his brother staying with him? Anyway, what's keeping him there till now?"

"Quite simply because he can't travel as yet," said Emma. "He stopped over to visit his brother, but right now, he's lying in a hospital bed, in Brixton General Hospital, where his brother works."

You could have knocked me down with the old feather, if I was not already seated. "In a hospital bed, in London? What happened?."

"He's seriously, even critically ill," said Emma. "He had something of a crisis, apparently quite unexpectedly, within a day or two of his arrival in London. And his doctor brother knew how to use the National Health Service. Costs him nothing. Anyway your Obi has to stay in the hospital until he gets well enough to continue his journey to the United States."

"I'm sorry to hear that," I said. "I really am. Did you get to talk to him, because if you did, and with your name, he surely would have asked – ."

"We did not talk," said Emma. "*He* could not talk. You see – he was in a coma."

"What seems to be the matter with him?" I asked. "I had indeed heard that he was quite sick, but not *this* sick."

"He's not just sick. He's gravely ill. Josiah told me his brother probably doesn't know how very sick he is. It is, I'm afraid, terminal. Best prognosis is a year to a year and a half. He has leukemia, but too far gone to be reversible. Diagnosed rather late, it seems. Josiah doesn't have the heart to tell his brother all this, and who can blame him? But then, Obi is returning to the best of all medical worlds, if I may put it that way: the United States of America. And miracles still happen, or I'm not a good Christian."

I immediately went on my guard, as a good Christian ought to, against putting my selfish interests first. Yes, I had an acute need for Obi's early return to the United States. But Obi himself needed even more acutely to be saved from his devastating illness. And there was Joy, his wife. She needed her husband, and father of her children, to return to the family in sound health and mind. *Those* were the paramount needs. And if indeed Obi's disease was terminal, my first duty was surely to pray that he and his wife should find that inner peace without which, I imagined, they would be unable to reconcile themselves to the ultimate calamity.

But I am human, and fallible. And so, even as those pious thoughts went through my tortured mind, I could not easily overcome my self-centeredness. I wanted Obi healthy as I had seldom wanted anybody, other than myself, healthy. The fear that I might lose him, before I got properly started on my quest to have my conviction judicially quashed (I think I knew that in the eyes of God, I was guiltless), seared through my brains, leaving me temporarily stunned.

"Cy – ri – l!" My brother was waving his hand from side to side right in front of my eyes. "Where are you? Come on, brother! This is not the end of the world."

"That's easy for you to say," I countered wretchedly. "For me, this is the virtual end. Can you not see how it will look if, when he returns to America, I start pestering him to get me what I want?"

"You mean the letter?" Emma asked. "Aren't you assuming that it has not been – how shall I put it – destroyed?"

"Of course I mean the blasted letter! And as for destroying it, that has, needless to say, been my central prayer to God: that in His mercies, He will thwart the works of the devil, and save that letter for me. But now, in the face of Obi's condition, the letter might still exist, but how do I get my hands on it?"

*   *   *

In bed that night, I tossed from side to side, cursing my fate. Sleep would not come, until the wee hours of the morning. Rosemary could not sleep either, because my constant motion would not let her. She was already in bed when Emma and I came back from The Ming, and I did not have the heart to wake her up just to tell her the story about Obi Udozo in a London Hospital. I threw myself into bed and pulled the comforting sheets around my body, hoping to drop off immediately into slumber. But the sheets brought me no comfort. Indeed I was only emotionally drained, not physically tired. All I achieved was wake my wife up from her slumber, without the compensation of any endearments and that sort of stuff from me.

"Tomorrow is Tuesday, C.Y., not Saturday or Sunday."

I turned and saw my wife staring at me, propping her chin in the palm of her hand.

"I've watched you these last five or so minutes," she said sternly. Then in a more compassionate tone: "What's the matter?"

I decided to give it to her straight. "It's our friend Obi – ."

"Which Obi now?" she asked sleepily, rubbing her eyes with her free hand. "There are many Obis in our community here in New Jersey."

"Obi Udozo," I told her. "That's the only Obi we've talked about in a long, long time. You won't believe this – ."

"He's back from home?"

I clamped a firm hand over her mouth. "Any more interruptions," I said, "and this story will wait until morning. What I'm trying to tell you is that the fellow, as we talk, is in a London Hospital, probably still in a coma."

Rosemary abruptly stopped her feeble effort to push my hand off her mouth, and I saw her eyes dilate with wonder. Two sure signs that I had gotten through to her! I slowly withdrew my hand from her mouth. But, for a long moment, she said not a word.

"You heard what I just told you?" I asked, knowing well that she did, but only seeking to draw her out of her shock.

"Obi? In a hospital! In London! Who told you? Joy?"

"Emma – ."

"Does Emma know him?"

I resisted the urge to clamp my hand once again over her mouth, as I went on and answered her question. "They met at Obi's bedside a few days before Emma left London for America. And if you'll keep quiet, and not keep interrupting me, I'll tell you what he told me."

And I did. She listened with rapt attention, and no interruptions, until the end of my story. Then she looked steadily at me for a moment or two, shaking her head sadly.

"You know what this means, C.Y.?"

"It's the end of the road for my quest," I said.

"It may well be, but I don't think so," said my wife, reaching for me, and enfolding me in her arms. When next she spoke, she spoke directly into my ear.

"We'll go into reverse gear," she said softly, "and not pursue the matter of the letter for as long as Obi needs to take care of this illness. But there should be no question of giving up, do you hear me, C.Y.? As long as there is life, we must hope. Let's put it in God's hands in prayer, and I believe that in the end, this terrible wrong will be set right. It may be difficult, but I have faith in my maker. Are you listening to me? We must never lose hope. You have not forgotten what Evangeline said, have you?"

I had not forgotten. How could I ever forget the day I first met Evangeline, the prophetess of the Church of the African Martyrs, in Washington, DC? Or her prophecy about God's judgment, which has rung ceaselessly in my head from that day on? I certainly remembered, and now thought about that prophecy for a second or two.

Then I spoke into my wife's ear. "Keep hope alive, as Reggie Jackson likes to say. Keep hope alive!"

*   *   *

My brother Emma returned to London three days later. Within hours of his arrival there, he called us to report that there had been some improvement in Obi's condition. At least he was out of his coma and, with continued improvement, might be able to complete his journey to America in a matter of days.

*   *   *

Two weeks later, Joy Udozo called to inform us that her husband had finally returned, and had been driven straight from Newark International Airport to the Robert Wood Johnson Hospital, in downtown New Brunswick, NJ.

END OF BOOK I

BOOK TWO

BOLA AKANDE'S STORY

Chapter XII

BY NAME I am Yoruba, but I speak Igbo just about as well as most young men my age do, who grew up in a typical Igbo town in Eastern Nigeria. I was born, and grew up, in the most important Igbo city, Enugu. I went to school, both primary and secondary, there.

I am rather proud of my academic career. I won a scholarship to my secondary school, the College of Immaculate Conception, better known as C.I.C. In my final year there, in 1994, I achieved Distinctions in seven subjects in my West African School Certificate examination.

I was in my first year, 1994/95, in the University of Ibadan, when the unimaginable happened. My mother wrote to inform me that she had won the best of all possible, non-monetary, lotteries: a resident visa to the United States of America! And just like that, I found myself in the U.S. of A, a young man of eighteen, in 1995.

To this day, I have not figured out how my mother did it. She has steadfastly refused to tell me how she raised the money to enable us actually take advantage of that splendid, magnificent stroke of luck. It is one thing to win this lottery, but quite another to finance the relocation from Nigeria to America.

And that's another thing! I did not know who my father was. I must have asked about him a thousand times, but my mother always put me off with vague answers that I never understood, and with promises that in the fullness of time, all things would be revealed. In the end, exhausted beyond human endurance, I gave up. At least I gave up pestering her with my importunities though, in my heart, I never gave up the desire to know. As my baptismal certificate shows, I was given my mother's family name, and it has remained so since. I bear that surname – Akande – with pride, because I learnt not to be ashamed of the woman who bore me.

The need to know came back with a surge the day I met this gorgeous girl. She wore a simple *accra*-type outfit: a two-piece dress of blouse and long skirt of the same flowered cotton material, cut to fit the body closely but not so as to hinder easy movement. She looked extremely fetching in it, and it was all I could do to restrain myself from perhaps making a fool of myself by rushing to engage her in some silly conversation. That's not my style. She was not the first girl to make a favorable impression on me, and I did not think she would be the last. But this was different. Something – and I did not know what it was – told me this was not your usual flighty, skittish girl one so often ran into on college campuses.

Actually this was no college campus; and the party was a packed, late-winter affair in the middle of March 1999. We were at a get-together of Nigerian students, in the church-hall of St. Mary Magdalene (an Episcopal Church), in New Brunswick, NJ. They have a Nigerian Students Union of sorts in New Jersey though, from my observation on the day of the party, the students were probably eighty percent Igbo. But that was all right with me. If it were not for my name, I could pass for an Igbo. I like parties. Good highlife music, good company, sometimes good food; what more could one ask for? All those ingredients were there, the music especially.

The deejay was – so I was told – the father of one of the students. For an Igbo, it came as a bit of a surprise to me that he favored Anikulakpo Kuti's slow, almost solemn-sounding rhythm. Anikulakpo was of Yoruba ethnicity. But he also had a good selection of *soukous* numbers, as well as songs by the late, lamented Cardinal Rex Lawson. Rex Lawson was of course not a Cardinal, but his sweet tunes affected the soul in a manner few others did.

I nudged my friend, and pointed. "Who's that girl?"

Kojo Ankrah gave me a brief, uninterested glance and turned away. "Which girl?" he asked offhandedly.

"If you look where I'm pointing –"

"O.K., I'm looking. But there are many girls –"

"The one in the brown *accra* dress, with her arm up."

"Oh, the quarter-miler?"

"The what?" I asked.

"C'mon!" said Kojo. "Don't tell me you don't know her."

"If I did, would I be asking you? A quarter-miler?"

"Oh, so you heard me," said Kojo. "Everybody knows her."

"I don't!" I said with some feeling. "But wait! I think I've seen that face somewhere."

"On T.V.," said Kojo. "She came second in the four hundred meters at the intercollegiate meet last Saturday. It was on T.V. That's just a week ago today."

"That's it! It was an indoor meet. But she looks different somehow."

Kojo looked at me with pity in his eyes. "Of course she looks different. You would too if you had only your running trunks and a singlet –"

"I get it, thank you."

"So-o?" Kojo asked after a pause, his eyebrows raised, his eyes boring into my face.

"So, what?"

"So plenty," said Kojo patiently. "Why did you ask?"

"Can't I ask a simple, innocent question – ?"

"Your question may've been simple, but there was nothing innocent about it. Look, Bola. I've known you rather well these past ten years or so. So don't try to play any games with me." Then slowly, deliberately, he asked: "Are – you – interested?"

"In what?"

"So she's now a *what*!" Kojo observed, talking more to himself than to me.

"What's the matter with you, my friend?" I asked. "You know, you're beginning to get on my –"

I stopped because I found I was talking to myself, and I don't like that. Kojo had plugged his ears with his fingers, which is something he tends to do to tell you he's heard enough of your stuff and nonsense.

"Can't you answer a simple question?" he asked, ears still plugged. He removed his fingers from his ears, but held them threateningly close, just in case I went off on the wrong track again. "Just tell me if you're interested."

"And if I am?"

There are moments when words are strictly unnecessary between friends who know each other, and I knew Kojo pretty well. I could see the temperature rise in his eyes, and immediately recognized the signs. The fire went out of me.

"If you really want to know," I said, deflated, "I think I am."

"Now you're talking!" said my friend, finally letting his arms drop to his sides.

"D'you know her?"

"Nope! Do I have to?"

"You don't?" I asked disbelievingly. "So what's all this – ?"

"Neither do you," said Kojo, brushing aside my protests. "You're here. She's there. What more do you need?"

"You mean I should – ."

"Yep! Close the distance between you and her, and you'd be surprised at what might happen."

"You really expect me to walk straight up to her, and – and – do what exactly?"

"Talk to her! Very simple. What's the worst thing that can happen? She might not be interested. So what?"

"I can't! You must be out of your mind."

Kojo got up from his chair, stretched himself, to relax his body I supposed, and looked me directly in the eye. "Watch me!" he commanded.

I knew what the fellow had in mind and, for just a moment, I thought about pulling him down back into his chair. But the moment passed, and I sat back and watched him stride purposefully away from our table, and make a beeline for the quarter-miler.

All my senses were aroused, as I waited to see what would happen. As I watched, it occurred to me fleetingly that I might regret my own inaction.

Kojo had dash – had it in abundance. Good looks too, in a square-jawed kind of way. He was as black as midnight which, in a manner I cannot explain, added dazzle to his smile. Just under six feet tall, lean but strong, he was a soccer player of considerable skill, and had represented Ghana in a junior world cup soccer tournament two or three years before coming to America. An American soccer enthusiast in Ghana suggested that Kojo apply to any number of U.S. universities that offered soccer scholarships. But Kojo ended up in Columbia University, where I have yet to hear that anyone won an athletic scholarship!

I watched, entranced, as he walked up to the girl, said something to her, flashed his million-dollar smile, and held out his hand. I think he rather surprised the girl, who had seemed engrossed in conversation with a coterie of friends and obvious admirers. She hesitated briefly, but eventually took the hand Kojo offered her, and smiled – I thought – shyly.

I suddenly became aware that Kojo had turned and was pointing in my direction. If I could have saved the situation by so doing, I might have dived under a table. But my trancelike state had slowed my reflexes, and the girl had quickly turned, following the direction of Kojo's finger. She stared hard in my general direction, and continued to do so until I was more or less compelled to raise a slow arm in acknowledgment of my connection to Kojo.

To this day I cannot recall if she actually smiled at me. Perhaps she only smiled faintly. I know I saw a corner of her mouth lift slightly in a manner that lit up her face wonderfully. So she must have smiled. Anyway, I hate it when I get into a bother over so simple a matter as whether or not a beautiful girl smiled at me.

Someone whispered in my ear, and I turned. Cletus was frowning, and gesticulating forcefully, though he seemed to be doing so in a way not to attract attention.

"What's wrong with you?" he asked. "You don't have eyes again?"

"What–?"

"Can't you see what Kojo's telling you?"

Kojo was still talking to the girl but, from time to time, he would turn in my direction, and smile.

"I'm sorry," I said to Cletus. "I must be slow today."

"You are, Bola," said Cletus, none too gently. "You'd better get your ass over there pronto, or you might regret it."

Cletus Ozobi is a friend of relatively few words, unless you provoked him. A Rutgers University sophomore, he was the reason Kojo and I were at the party. We were some kind of a triumvirate from our high school days in the College of Immaculate Conception, in Enugu, Eastern Nigeria. Yes, Kojo was there with us, one of the star soccer players in the school team, and who should, by rights of long domicile in the country, perhaps have played for Nigeria. But Ghana found a way to entice him into their junior soccer squad. He never told us what inducements might have been offered to him. I doubt any was, and prefer to think that he merely decided that the honor of playing for his country of origin was one he could not pass up.

We were very close friends, Cletus, Kojo and I. We were so close that an offence against one was an offence to all three of us, and so tight that nothing seemed capable of coming between us. Not even girls!

Now I looked across at the quarter miler, and for some odd reason that I could not understand, and which made me extremely cross with myself, I could not work up the courage to do what my two friends were urging me to do.

"I don't believe this, Bola," said Cletus, shaking his head. "I've never seen you like this before, man. You want me to regret I invited you to this party?"

"What did I do now?"

"It's what you're not doing, man."

"What I'm not-?"

"Oh, shut up, man! Look at the girl! Look at her, Bola! She's perfect."

"For whom?"

"For you now-w-w," Cletus said. "Who else?"

"How would you know?"

"Bola, please look at me," said Cletus. "If I know nobody else in this world, I know you. And I know Kojo. You remember what they used to call us in CIC?"

"A band of brothers," I said.

"Good. What did we not do together, we three? We were inseperable, man. I knew what you liked, you knew what I liked. That's how it was with us, no?"

"Right!" said Kojo at my elbow, startling me somewhat. "Bola, if you dare tell me Chizube Jideofo is not – how to say –"

"Perfect for me? That's how Cletus put it."

"Right! You know who she reminds me of?"

"Who?" I heard myself ask.

"As if you don't remember," said Cletus challengingly.

"You mean – ?"

"Yes, Bola," said Cletus. "We mean Sarah, the one with the longest leg you ever saw."

"But that's way back –"

"Way back?" asked Kojo. "That was only three or four years ago. What was the name of that their girls' school, just outside Enugu?"

"Holy Rosary College," I said, "in Okunano."

"You remember very well," said Cletus. "You couldn't stop talking about her legs. Listen, my friends, let's cut out the shit. D'you know why I made sure to invite you two to this New Jersey party, even though you New York fellows think New Jersey is some kind of bush country?"

"No!" I said, looking at Kojo, seeking confirmation that he too did not know. But the blighter only smiled at me.

"I've known Chizube for some months now," said Cletus. "We do the same classes in Chemistry and Physics, though I believe she hopes to major in Chemistry. It's one of those strange things that happen, but the first moment I saw her, my mind went to you Bola. I called Kojo –"

"So you were in on this too?" I asked, turning to Kojo. "You knew about this?"

Kojo spread his arms wide in a – for me – futile gesture of innocence. He couldn't even look me straight in the eye.

"So what was all that stuff and nonsense when I first tried to draw your attention to the girl, and you pretended – ."

"What was I supposed to do?" asked Kojo. "I told Cletus that if the girl turned out to be exactly as he described her, you would fall for her at first sight. And you did."

"Who said anything about falling – ?"

"Man," said Cletus, "you are talking to us, Kojo and me. Not to some strangers. I bet him –"

"You were betting on me behind my back?"

Another thought struck me, and I took Kojo by his shoulders, and made him turn so we faced each other.

"Let me guess, Kojo. You never saw the girl on TV, did you? You said she came second in the quarter-mile –"

"Four hundred meter race," said Kojo.

"Same thing! Did you?"

"Did I what?"

I knew he was deliberately playing dumb to needle me, so I played along. "See her on TV doing track? The truth!"

"You want the truth? Hell, no! It was Cletus –"

"You don't have to explain further. You both just played me for the sucker that I was."

Then I burst out laughing. I was still laughing when someone tapped me on the shoulder. I turned, and did a double take. The quarter-miler was standing just behind me, a gentle, rather shy smile playing on her lips.

"Would you like to dance?" she asked, her voice the sweetest musical sound I ever heard. It took me a split second to collect myself.

"The pleasure is mine," I said, and instantly hated myself for not coming up with a better answer than that hackneyed old phrase. "Excuse us," I said, turning back to my two friends. But they were already beating a hasty retreat, pausing only briefly to high-five each other exuberantly, as they melted into the crowd.

"Let's dance," I said to the quarter-miler, leading her by the hand as we jostled our way through the crowd, on to the packed dance floor. And did we dance!

It mattered little to me what music was playing. We just danced! Again and again! I did not ask her if she came to the party alone. I did not *want* to ask her that question. I suppose I was just plain scared of her answer. I did not even ask her her name, until we had danced for perhaps ten or fifteen minutes. In any case, I already knew it – Chizube. It was just that I was concerned about the etiquette of the situation.

We had not been formally introduced to each other, and I worried whether or not I was supposed to ask the question.

"My name –" I began.

"I know it," said the girl, swaying her supple body to the pulsating rhythm of SUZANNAH, a *soukous* song. "Your friend – what's his name – ?"

"Cletus?"

"No, the Ghanaian boy. Yes – Kojo. I forget his family name."

"Ankrah," I said. "As in Roy Ankrah, the famous Gold Coast boxer of the fifties."

"Who?" She asked. "Anyway, *he* told me. Actually I knew you were coming to this party."

"You knew? How – oh, no need to ask. Cletus!"

"Cletus," she confirmed. "He told me he was bringing an old friend –"

"I don't know about old," I said, smiling.

"You know what I mean. An old friend he'd like me to meet."

"What else did he tell you about me?" I heard myself ask, not quite knowing why.

"Oh, that you were in C.I.C together, and that you're Yoruba, though you speak my language much, much better than me."

We both laughed. Conversation, on account of the excessive loudness of the music, was not at all easy. But I was like a spirit floating on clouds, and not subject to the normal human limitations of the senses. I did not need to look at her to *hear* her smile.

"I think you know my name already, no?" Chizube asked. Or said.

"Chizube," I said proudly. "Chizube something-ofo."

"Jideofo," she said. "So you were in C.I.C. in Enugu. My grandmother lives there."

"Oh, you know Enugu? That's where I grew up. But I don't think I ever ran into your folks there."

"It's a big city. I've only visited three or so times, and can't claim to know it. So you speak Ibo. How wonderful!"

"You mean, Igbo, not Ibo," I said, dancing slightly away from her, but looking at her steadily, to satisfy myself she did not take offence at my daring to correct her. Oliver de Coque's music, but especially his jumping rhythm, sometimes intoxicates, and sometimes disorients the senses. But as I once again held hands with Chizube, I knew exactly where I was, and with whom. And I knew that I had to be careful how I spoke to her at this, our very first meeting. Mostly I held her close to my body, though body contact is not of the essence when the music is our type of music. But it had the advantage that I could talk directly into her ear, and she would hear me, regardless of the ear-shattering volume of the music.

"I'm sorry," she said. "Igbo! You're right. My dad's always telling me –"

"Your dad's here, in America? And your mum?"

"Right here, in New Jersey. In a town called West Brook."

"West Brook? Never heard of it. But then, for a small state, New Jersey has a thousand and one towns and cities."

"And your parents?"

I immediately wished she had not asked that question. It is the type of question, in my particular situation, that never comes alone. If I answered truthfully, she would inevitably ask a follow-up question. But who wants to confess to a girl he has just met, a girl whose immediate impact titillates his senses in many different directions – dreamed and undreamed of – that he does not know where his father lives? Worse, that he does not know his father!

In the fraction of a second that it took for these thoughts to rush through my mind, I knew also that I had no option but to bare my soul to her, then or later. I held her tightly, as I whispered my answer.

"My mum lives in Queens."

She immediately turned her head to look sideways at me. At least I felt her head turn, and some kind of extrasensory perception told me she looked briefly at me. I think I felt her body tense ever so slightly, and then very quickly relax. And I knew then that she would not ask the question my extra-sensitized nerves had feared she would ask. I, too, relaxed and even executed a pirouette or two with her. Then somehow, suddenly, I found the courage to ask the question that I knew, from the very moment we began to dance, that I would – that I *had* to – ask her. Or all else would have been vanity!

"When can I see you again?"

She did not immediately answer my question. Instead, she leaned a little back and away from me, and looked me in the eye for a moment or two. Then she fired her own question.

"Why do boys always ask that question?"

"They do?" I said. "I mean, do we?"

"Why?" she asked again, still looking steadily at me, and somewhat slowing down the frenzy of our gyrations.

"Why? I s'pose we can't help –"

"I mean, why d'you want to see me again?"

I had not read any manuals on chasing girls and, though I had dated a girl or two in my time, none had ever asked me such a question. It seemed a silly question too, because I thought the answer was pretty obvious. My instincts, however, told me to avoid the obvious this time. "Think of something unusual!" my mind commanded. I did, quickly too.

I cleared my throat. "Because, Chizube," I said, "don't you see, we were destined to meet, you and me."

She looked at me skeptically for a moment or two, and smiled. "You don't really believe –"

"I do," I said seriously. "Look at us. We're dancing like we came here together. An hour ago, I did not know you existed, and you didn't know –"

"That's not quite true," she said sweetly. "Cletus told me you were coming –"

"He told you about a friend he wanted you to meet. Don't you see? That's exactly what I mean. Cletus and Kojo kind of prepared the stage for us – two people who had never met, or known of each other. But somehow they knew we would be – how do I say it? They just knew."

On the jam-packed dance floor, Chizube and I danced as if we were all by ourselves. We talked as we danced, effortlessly. The music, the frenzied crowd, the noise and bustle of uproarious merriment, all formed the perfect backdrop to this, my first meeting with Chizube Jideofo. There is a form of intoxication that good highlife music induces, and that tends to free one from all kinds of inhibitions, and liberates the shy and bashful soul.

I rode on the wings of that intoxication to a state of euphoria such as I had never before experienced. Nothing else seemed to matter. Indeed nothing else mattered but the beautiful and stately girl who wove her sinuous charms opposite me, when I let her dance freely. Or who let me hold her close – but not too, too close – when I wanted to dance cheek to cheek! She was regally tall. When I held her close, my eyes looked straight at the top of her forehead, by which I judged she must have been just about six feet tall.

"So?" I asked.

She looked innocently at me, her expression puzzled.

"I mean about the question I asked you."

"Oh," she said, "about when we'll see again?"

"I don't want to press you, if you'd –"

"It's okay, really. I have no problem with that."

"Meaning – ?"

"Call me," she sang, "and we'll talk."

I did the best I could to contain my joy, and asked, very businesslike, for her number. I took my pen out of the pocket of my jacket, and fished around in my trouser pockets for a piece of paper. But she cut me short.

"Cletus knows my number. He'll give it to you."

As if on cue, Cletus and Kojo reemerged from the shadows. They were still smiling, but if they expected me to ask them what made them so happy, I must have disappointed them.

"Excuse me," said Cletus, fixing me with his smiling eyes. "It's my turn to dance with her."

He made to interpose himself between me and her but, playfully, I would not let him.

"No one said this is an excuse-me-dance," I said.

"It is now," said Kojo, though no one asked him. "You must let Cletus dance with her."

"Why?"

"Because she's his date for this party. That's why."

"Oh – oh!" was all I could say. As I graciously stepped aside, Chizube smiled at me, and her smile was full of the promise of joys yet to come.

Kojo then linked arms with me, and forced me to give the dancers some space.

"I won't ask you how it went," he said, "because we practically saw everything that happened. I didn't know you could dance, you know, holding the girl close to you, and all that."

"It was unbelievable," I said. "I never expected anything like this."

"I know," said Kojo softly. "I know. But you have to cool your heels for a while. When Cletus is done, it'll be my turn next."

"Oh, I can wait, my friend," I said, my mind in a heightened state of elation. "Take your time. Something good is happening, and I'm going to make darned sure whatever it is doesn't slip through my fingers."

"H'm!" said Kojo, his eyes, as he stared at me, shining with the light of perfect understanding.

Chapter XIII

I TOOK A peek at the mirror, and liked what I saw. That was something I seldom did, but I needed to be sure that I looked good for my first real outing with Chizube. I do not mean that I put on my Sunday best. It was not a Sunday, and we were not going to church or to a party. But it was our first, and therefore probably our most important, date. It was, in a manner of speaking, my second chance to make a good first impression.

I do not go for fancy clothes. I had been told repeatedly, and by sundry persons, that I looked good in almost any garb. It was all very flattering, and I had gradually come to believe that it was true. My mother strained herself, she liked to tell me, to bring me up as a Yoruba boy. But the odds were heavily against her, and I grew up more or less Igbo. I spoke the Igbo that my playmates and classmates spoke; the Igbo that the servants and our neighbors spoke. That is, when we were not speaking pidgin English! I grew up favoring the Igbo embroidered jumper over the loose and voluminous Yoruba *agbada* and *shokoto*, for festive and sometimes religious occasions. My main concession to my Yorubaness was the *danshiki*, itself also a loose top garment, though not as voluminous as the agbada. But of course I had a wardrobe full of all of the above, with a few European-American style suits thrown in. For color, my preference has always been more somber than bright.

I had called Chizube the day after the students' dance party, and we had talked and talked. I called her again the day after that; and the day following! In truth, I called her every day for one week straight. And then I held off, and waited. Three excruciatingly slow days passed. On the fourth, she called me. It had been a deliberate and calculated tactic on my part. And it had worked, just as I had hoped and prayed it would work. Indeed, I had more than just hoped. I had a strong suspicion, bordering on certainty, that it would.

She went straight to the point. "You didn't call since the other day," she said.

"I did. At least I tried a few times, but –"

"You did?"

"Your line was always busy," I lied.

She was silent for a moment or two. "You couldn't have been dialing this number. I don't make hardly any calls –"

"You don't? You expect me to believe that?"

A brief pause, and then she came back. "Why not?"

"A girl with your looks –"

"Looks have nothing to do with anything," she said. "It depends on – well – you know –"

"I don't."

"Like I was saying, I hardly make calls except to my parents. So my line is not that busy –"

"Perhaps I dialed the wrong number. Anyway, I'm glad you called, Chizube. I've missed you."

"Say what?"

"I said I've –"

"I heard what you said," Chizube cut in, in a voice at once incredulous, and amused. "We only just met the other day, Bola."

She spoke my name like a caress and, briefly, I thought to tell her so. But I was not sure how she would react to that kind of flirtatious remark. So I desisted, and instead said: "A few days is long enough for me to know – well –"

"What?" she asked, noticing my pause.

"Well," I said, rather lamely, "to know that I really want to know you better."

This conversation was not quite going the way I had planned. Not that anyone can plan a conversation, if you see what I mean. I was desperately casting around in my mind for a way out, when she unexpectedly came to my rescue.

"Meaning," she said, "you want us to go out, or something?"

"Something," I said. "Let's just meet, in your place, or mine."

She was silent for a pregnant minute or so, no doubt pondering the alternatives I had held out to her. "I don't know about your place –"

"Then I'll come to see you in your college," I quickly suggested. "It's much easier for me to come to New Brunswick than for you to come to New York."

"Especially to Harlem," she said. "It's easy to get lost in upper Manhattan and Harlem."

"As if I'd ever let that happen to you!" I assured her. "When you come here –"

"When?" There was a faint sound of laughter at the other end of the line.

"I mean, *if*. If you ever come here, I'll make sure to meet you at your point of entry into the city, say at the Port Authority Bus Terminal –"

"Or Penn Station," she said. "I prefer trains to buses any day."

"Or Penn Station," I repeated after her. "So, when is it convenient for you – ?"

"To come to New York?"

"Oh, no! I didn't mean –"

"Just kidding, Bola." She paused for a moment. "When? Well, it would have to be a Friday."

"Late afternoon or –"

"Of course," she said. "Say, around five."

"Perfect. Today is what – Tuesday. So I'll see you in three days time. How about you give me your address? I know it's Rutgers College."

"Yes, in downtown New Brunswick, very close to the railroad station. How're you coming?"

"By car," I said. "So I'll need street and number, or the name of your hall, whatever."

"You know New Brunswick well?"

"Oh, no. But I'll manage. I know the station, and the University bookstore opposite it."

"And no doubt the McDonald, also opposite the station?"

"Of course," I said. "But I'm not much into junk food, that sort of thing."

"Don't worry about that," Chizube said, laughing. "I don't plan for us to go there, unless it's just for coffee or hot chocolate."

*   *   *

Kojo Ankrah lent me his car – an old Volvo that had already clocked a hundred and fifty thousand miles before its odometer lost its vitality, but which he kept in fair condition by virtue of his uncanny knowledge of car engines. His father owned a car-maintenance garage in the Ogbete quarter of Enugu, Nigeria. Amazingly, for such a fun-loving boy, Kojo loved to get his hands greasy working and lubricating car engines. He was, not surprisingly, the only one of our small circle of friends – mostly Africans – who owned a car. My mother would not give me the money to buy one. Neither did his old man give Kojo a cent. But he somehow scraped together enough cash to buy the Volvo, *as is*, at a government auction of seized and unclaimed cars, for just over two hundred dollars. He always boasted that he could restore life to a dying vehicle, so long as a few essential parts were in fair working order.

Until now, I had never driven his Volvo, alone. Whenever I needed it, especially for distances over ten miles or so, I persuaded him to come along with me. I suppose I was often concerned that something or the other would malfunction in the old jalopy. He would let me drive because he knew I was the better driver of us two. When I asked him for his Volvo, for my first visit to Chizube, he offered to go with me. But I would have none of that.

"Not this time, man," I said.

"Just because you're going to see her?"

"Just because I'm going to see her," I echoed, looking him straight in the eye. "I'll take my chances on the grease-box." That was our affectionate name for the Volvo.

"Good luck," he said, and handed me the car keys.

"I hope I don't need it."

Thankfully, I did not. Which is not to say that I did not worry, especially whenever there was a noticeable change in the humming of the engine! I drove to New Brunswick at a fair clip, spurred on by thoughts of Chizube, and maybe just a little bit nervous about how my first date with her would go. I think I knew it was going to be the first of many dates, because the thing – whatever that was – that had developed between us on that unforgettable night of dancing, was unalloyed and beautiful chemistry. My senses, even as I drove, tingled all over with excitement, as the memory of the crush of her body against mine came flooding back.

There might have been a thousand Rutgers College students milling about on the college grounds as I turned the grease-box off College Road, and headed for Chizube's hall. Washington Hall is a five-storied structure of brick walls and slate roofs, and white window frames that contrasted nicely with the burnt red color of the walls. It was the beginning of the weekend, in the fourth week of March. The golden rays of the setting sun lit up the western sky, even as the spectral colors of the rainbow arced across the eastern sky. The students lolled around unhurriedly, in groups and pairs, representing a fair sprinkling of the totality of the human condition: black eyes and blue eyes, straight hairs and curly hairs, wide eyes and slit eyes, white skins and black skins – and all the shades in between.

But I had eyes only for her. She stood by the main entrance of the hall, as she had promised she would, dressed very simply in a modest long-sleeved white blouse, and dark-blue pants. Her lips parted in a radiant smile as I drove up to her and stopped.

"Hi!" she said cheerily, melodiously. Amazing how the simple American 'hi', when *she* spoke it, could convey so much more than your honest English 'hello'!

"Hi!" I responded, following her example, though my preference is for the British version of the greeting.

I leaned out of the car windows. "Where can I park this thing?"

"Certainly not here," she said, walking round to the other side of the car. She opened the door, and took the passenger seat. "I'll show you. Go to the next traffic lights, make a left, then another left. The lot is behind the Students' Center. Let's go."

The parking lot was half empty, on account perhaps of many students having gone away for the weekend. As we walked back to her hall, I felt an urge to take her hand. But I resisted the temptation. Chizube might be American – born and bred – but I knew her parents were Igbo. And I know the Igbo parent, and how his or her mind works. It was therefore a safe assumption that Chizube must have been brought up to eschew easy familiarities with men, especially this early in a relationship.

I watched her with the corner of my eye, as she led the way, and could not help but notice how she looked the other way whenever we came across a couple lovingly holding hands or, worse still, smooching or drooling over each other. Once or twice she looked at me and pursed her lips, and I thought I knew exactly what wordless feelings of disdain she sought to convey. I also knew that I could take nothing for granted with her. "Boy!" I said to myself. "I'll have to play this relationship by ear."

She shared a studio apartment with two other girls. One of the two, an African, was standing before a stove in a small kitchen to the far left as one entered the living room. On the stove was a steaming, odorous pot. The other, of East Asian stock, lay totally relaxed on a long sofa which was set by a wide, three-paneled window opposite the kitchen. She had ear-phones on, and one leg twitched rhythmically to the tune that doubtless filled her ears and head.

"Hi!" said the African girl, waving her cooking ladle in the air, as she turned at the sound of our entry.

"Hi!" said her companion, half-raising her body from its recumbent position. She smiled fleetingly, and then threw her body back on the sofa.

"Don't mind them," said Chizube. "They're playing cool –"

"I'm cool," said the African.

"I'm cool too," said her Asian echo. The leg twitched one more time and then she sat fully up, and took the ear-phones from off her ears. She stood up and came towards me, her right hand held out in front of her.

"You must be Jacob," she said with a smile. "I'm Sue, Sue Chan."

I took her slim, delicate-looking hand in mine, and very gently squeezed it. "Yah, I'm Jacob," I said. "I'm pleased to meet you."

"And I'm Nenaia," said a voice slightly behind me.

I turned, and almost bumped into her. The hand she too held out to me had artificial nails at least an inch long, possibly two. Her face, not smiling, was calmly reposed. Her eyes shone with a luster that gave her face a brilliant sheen, and that exuded confidence and high intelligence.

I shook hands with her, deftly avoiding the nails. "Nenaia? What nationality are you?"

"Don't mind her," said Chizube. "Her name is Nnennaya Oboli."

"But that's Igbo," I said.

"Of course," said Chizube. "She's as Igbo as you're Yoruba. But Americans have difficulty pronouncing her name –"

"Except you, I suppose?" I asked jokingly.

"I'm not American," declared Chizube instantly, and then thought better of her answer. "Well, o.k., I'm American, since I was born here."

"So was I," chimed in Nnennaya. "But I'm tired of trying to make people pronounce my name –"

"You mean you succumbed to it, and adopted the way they say it."

Chizube's voice was entirely teasing, and I was glad to note that Nnennaya took the teasing in stride, and laughed with her tormentor.

"They're both as excited as hell," said Chizube after a slight pause. "They've been waiting for your visit since – I don't know how many days ago."

"She told us you're good-looking –" said Sue, as her gaze swept my frame, from head to foot.

"Sue!" Chizube shouted in protest.

"You are too," said Sue, paying Chizube no mind.

"C'mon, you're making me blush," I said, very embarrassed but, as ever, lapping up the compliment.

"Africans don't blush," said Nnennaya, laughing.

"That's only because you can't see the redness," I said.

"You're funny too," said Sue, joining the laughter at the tired old joke. "Welcome to the most untidy, messed-up apartment in the entire hall."

"She always says so," Chizube whispered rather loudly in my ear. "But she knows that's not true. Okay, look around you and tell me if –"

"That's because we made some effort to clean up this living room," Sue interrupted. "If I take you to our bedroom –"

"You wouldn't dare!" shouted Chizube.

"I rest my case," said Sue with a triumphant smile.

Chizube turned to me. "If our bedroom is untidy, it's because of her. You should see her walking into the bedroom."

"It's quite a sight," said Nnennaya, giggling. "As she takes off her clothes, her shoes go in one direction, her blouse in another, her –"

"As if I'm the only culprit!" Sue protested.

"Perhaps not," said Nnennaya. "But you're the worst. Which makes it odd you're the one that's brought up the subject!"

"As always," said Chizube.

This quick-fire thrust and counter-thrust was accompanied by some hilarity. At first puzzled, I finally understood that it was just good-natured ribbing. They were so caught up in their banter that they completely overlooked the fact that I was still on my feet. So I had to ask the question, laughing.

"Can I sit down somewhere?"

"Sorry, Bola, my fault," said Chizube. She pointed to a two-seater placed at right angles to the sofa, and then hastened ahead of me to remove four or five thickly bound books heaped on it.

"See what I mean?" asked Sue, with an impish wink.

"Thank you, Chizube," I said, sitting down.

"She called you Bola," remarked Nnennaya.

"My middle name. Jacob's my first name."

"So how d'you want to be called?"

"As you like."

"I'll call you Bola, like her. That's if it's okay –"

"Me too," said Sue.

" . . . with her." Nnennaya was looking keenly at Chizube.

"With me?" Chizube asked, somewhat embarrassed. "I've no claims –"

"I'm sure she wouldn't mind," I assured Nnennaya, stealing a quick glance at Chizube. She looked away stiffly.

I looked around the living room. In addition to the long sofa and the love seat, there was a single easy, reclining chair, all three with the same dirty-brown upholstery. A low, round, center table, on which Chizube had dumped the offending volumes from the love seat, an old seventeen-inch TV set placed on its own hexagonal support opposite the sofa and the love seat, and a six-foot-high wooden bookshelf, completed the room's furnishings. The bookshelf stood by the wall closest to the bed room.

Nnennaya, ladle still clutched in her hand, quickly came and sat by me, and then made a playful face at Chizube, who smilingly pretended that her tormentor did not exist. But before Nnennaya could get too comfortable with me, a fizzing sound from the kitchen quickly brought her to her feet. For a girl built rather heavily – though not unattractively so – she was quite brisk as she made a dash for her bubbling pot. She had very quickly made a favorable impression on me, with her twinkling, kindly eyes, her round attractive face, and her general congeniality. She was Nigerian, but her sound was totally American. In this regard, she was exactly like Chizube who, the first time I met her, had an accent as un-Nigerian as that of an un-traveled native-born American. I am not quite sure exactly what I had expected, but I must confess I loved the way she talked. I suppose I notice these things because as a Nigerian, born and bred in the old country, I carry my heavy accent with me like an African burden, whenever I try to communicate with Americans.

"Hope you'll like my concoctions, Bola," Nnennaya shouted from the kitchen.

I was caught, as it were, off guard, and uncertain how I should respond. I quickly looked at Chizube. She had chosen, for her own reasons, to sit away from me, on the single chair. She nodded, smiling.

"Nnenna," she said, shrugging, and then turned to me. "That's what I call her, Nnenna. She loves to cook. Comes up with all types of dishes too, but they're all great."

"I'd say, *mostly*," said Sue. "Sometimes she cooks things that have no name."

"In Korean, perhaps," Nnennaya shot back. "In my language they have."

"Oh! D'you speak Igbo?" I asked her.

"She doesn't," said Sue.

"How'd you know?" asked Chizube, laughing.

"Because I listen to you when you talk about Nigeria and suchlike! Bola, let me tell you, Nenaia doesn't speak a word of your language."

"But I understand it enough to get by. And I know the names of several of the things my mum cooks. There!"

"Chizube is the better of the two," Sue told me. "At least that's what they tell me."

I looked questioningly at Chizube. She shrugged vaguely, and said, "I don't speak it as well as I should."

"Meaning –"

"I speak some. And, for that, I thank my mum and dad, and especially my aunt Nwamaka – I should really call her my grand auntie. She made it her business to force me to speak Ibo, I mean Igbo.'

"And you, Bola?" asked Sue. "Do you?"

"Yes."

"Ibo or Yoruba?" asked Nnennaya. She pointed to Chizube. "She said –"

"I speak both, Igbo in fact better than Yoruba. I grew up in Enugu. You know Enugu, I hope."

"You trying to find out how much I know about my country? Of course I know about Enugu. Never been there, though."

Chizube waved an arm to attract our attention. "Enough of all this stuff about Ibo or Igbo –" she said.

"Not before I ask Sue if she speaks her – what – Korean language," I said.

"Of course," said Sue with pride. "I was bilingual from the get-go."

"And that precisely is the difference between your people and us Igbo people,' said Chizube. "Sue, you know we've talked endlessly about it. I suppose that's why people say Igbo, as a language, is in danger of extinction. Anyway, Bola, what I wanted to tell you is that we are dining here. Nnennaya absolutely insisted on it."

"You must," added Nnennaya.

"Thing is, we take turns to cook," said Chizube. "But when I offered –"

"She wanted to take *my* turn. That's what she's trying to tell you. But nobody takes my turn. Not especially when I have something special –"

"What's it this time?" asked Sue.

"Something my mum taught me. It's a special kind of vegetable *melange*, something like your Chinese *moo-shu*, only richer. There's steamed white rice to go with it, as well as your favorite *jollof* rice."

"You should taste her *jollof* rice," enthused Sue. "Absolutely heavenly! Nenaia, I hope you used bacon bits and anchovies –"

"And corned beef, yes," said Nnennaya.

"When *she* cooks," said Sue, "it's better than anything you'll find in a restaurant. Real home cooking."

"She's good," said Chizube. "And she's a straight A student too. It's downright unfair!"

"Well, well," I said. "It looks as if we're set for the evening."

The kitchen was large enough to accommodate a medium-sized rectangular table, seating six. Nnennaya's vegetable pottage was finger-licking delicious. So delicious indeed, I would have had a third helping if I had not insistently reminded myself that this was my first date with Chizube. A girl who, in the space of barely one week, had irrevocably turned my mind away from the worries of things past and present, to a guardedly blissful contemplation of the future. A future pregnant with all sorts of possibilities, at the center of which she sat in gentle majesty, robed in purple. "Easy, man!" I said to myself, and curbed my appetite.

Contrary to what I had thought, we were not done for the evening. Chizube had a surprise for me.

"I have two tickets for an evening show in the city's Arts Theater," she announced. "I think you'll like the show."

"A theater? What's showing?" I asked excitedly.

"Shakespeare."

"Romeo and Juliet," said Nnennaya. And then she added, with a wink and a smile: "If you ask me –"

"I didn't," Chizube interrupted.

"I know you didn't," said Nnennaya. "But I'd say if you had to do the theaters, that's the one play I'd recommend." She turned to me and winked again. "And don't you worry about Sue and me tagging along. You're going by your lonely ol' selves."

Chapter XIV

I HAD READ *Hamlet*, perhaps the greatest of Shakespeare's tragedies, in high school. I had read *Julius Caesar, Macbeth, Othello*, and *The Merchant of Venice*. But I had never read *Romeo and Juliet*. Like most kids my age, who went to any reputable high school, I vaguely knew the story of the two famously star-crossed lovers of Verona, in Italy. But that was it.

For just a moment or two, I wondered if Chizube's choice of our evening entertainment was perhaps indicative, even if only subconsciously, of her state of mind. Towards me, that is. I fervently hoped it was. Then a second thought hit me. If there was love, or the beginning of it, in the air, wasn't this particular play, about two ill-fated lovers, a strange, if not an ominous choice for our first outing?

Suddenly, intuitively, I felt her eyes on me, and I turned in her direction. She was looking at me with a smile that was at once soft and mysterious, and that seemed to reach the innermost recesses of my mind.

"It's the only play in the city at this time, as far as I know," she said, as if in answer to my unspoken thoughts.

"Do you often go to the theater?"

"As often," she said, "as there's anything worth watching. This one is a kind of modernized version of the play, according to Nnenna who's seen it."

"Meaning – ?"

"That the actors," said Nnennaya, "are not dressed in your typical Shakespearean costume, and the dialogue has been slightly changed to make some of the ancient words and expressions more easily understood."

"I've got to see this one,' I said. "Tell you the truth, I can't imagine Shakespeare in modern clothes. Chizube, whatever gave you the idea that I might like –"

"Something you said several days ago. Something about New York being a great city because of her Broadway district, with its uncountable theaters –"

"You're sharp. I love going there, especially in fact the off-Broadway shows. They're cheaper, but some of them are just as good as the ones on Broadway."

"You'll be late," said Sue, peeking at her watch.

"I'm ready." I said.

"So am I," said Chizube. "Let's go! We'll walk. I hope you don't mind walking? It's just about a mile from here."

I think she caught me looking at her long athletic legs, and smiled. "It's nothing to do with that," she said. "It's beautiful outside, and you'd be surprised how quickly we'll get there."

"She'll probably kill you with her pace," said Sue, "if you let her. Anyway, off with you!"

I remember remarking to Chizube, as we walked, that Nnennaya did not look the theater-loving type.

She laughed, and said: "She's an amazing girl. And, as they say, you mustn't judge a book by its cover."

*   *   *

It probably did not matter that I had not read the original play. If the producers changed some of the text, it still came across as vintage Shakespeare. Whatever changes they made, almost certainly made the dialogue (still overwhelmingly in verse) more easily digestible. I knew the story in outline, *Romeo and Juliet* being, without question, the most famous love story that there is. I was familiar with the famous cry by Juliet, 'O Romeo, Romeo! Wherefore art thou Romeo?' Happily, the producers – or editors – did not touch that cry from the heart. Now, I understood, watching actors and actresses who were masters of their craft, that she was not asking the absent Romeo *where* he was, but *why* he was a Montague. I had not known, but knew now, the original source of that other oft-repeated phrase, 'A rose by any other name would smell as sweet'.

I was so completely absorbed in the unfolding plot of the play that I came very close to tears at the end of it all. And it set me thinking about my country Nigeria, and the eternal feud between my Yoruba people and Chizube's Igbo people. Two peoples, each blessed with a large enough population (easily twenty to thirty millions), and abundant natural resources, to be a viable nation by itself, but who were forced, along with two hundred other ethnic groups, into an artificial creation called Nigeria. It bears repetition: two hundred ethnic groups! The Igbo and the Yoruba are always, so to speak, at daggers drawn. Their never-ending struggle for primacy in the country has been largely responsible for the lack of cohesion in the Nigerian body politic. Their mutual distrust is so tangible you could slice it with the proverbial knife. It is rare for the two to intermarry, the prognostication for such unions being, routinely, disastrous failure.

I put myself in Romeo's shoes, and Chizube in Juliet's, and worked those placements over in my mind. But I quickly dismissed the comparison. I was no Yoruba Romeo to her Igbo Juliet. My background combined my mother's Yorubaness with my Igbo upbringing in every other respect that mattered. Therefore I was no Romeo.

I do not know what thoughts went through Chizube's mind as we watched the unfolding tragedy on the stage. She had confessed to not having read the play though, like me, she was familiar with the story. Did she see herself as an Igbo Juliet? I wanted to know, but I was afraid to ask. I was afraid she might think I was presuming a lot about our relationship.

The night was overcast by the time we emerged from the theater. The moon, struggling to penetrate obscuring clouds, shed an uncertain light on everything. Chizube was subdued as we began to walk to her college campus. I must have reached for, and held her hand three or four times – very experimentally – before we had walked a couple hundred steps. Each time, she left her hand limply in mine. Once or twice she turned her head to look at me with eyes which, even in the feeble light of the moon, seemed quizzical. Because of that limp hand and her questioning eyes, I soon thought it best to desist from any further gestures of endearment.

All of a sudden, Chizube stopped, and pointed to the door of a café. "Let's go in and have a cup of coffee or something," she said, flashing me a smile.

"But we're very close to your dorm," I said. "Just another half mile or so."

"Too many people in the dorm," she said. "I know my roommates, especially Nnenna. She doesn't go to bed until well after midnight."

"Even on a Friday night?"

"Especially on a Friday night. She likes to catch up on her books before the weekend properly sets in."

"Amazing," I said. "She just doesn't – you know –"

"Look like a bookworm? That's what people say."

I pushed the café door open, and held it for Chizube. She smiled as she walked past me, and said softly: "Quite a gentleman. You're learning fast, I see."

"Learning? From where?"

"America, of course," she said.

"Which America? If this country has taught me anything –"

A waiter emerged from behind the counter. "Smoking, or non-smoking?"

"Non-smoking," I answered slowly, looking at Chizube, who nodded.

"This way please," the waiter said, with a bit of a flourish. He grabbed two menus from off the counter top, and led us to a table set deep in the non-smoking section, close to a window giving onto the road. I made sure I held a chair for Chizube before taking mine. We did not need the menu, except to check out the prices.

"You were saying – about what America has taught you?"

"Nothing! I mean America has taught me nothing about politeness, courtesies, things like that. Quite the contrary! I've learnt here *not* to hold doors for women, because you never know who might take offence –"

Chizube burst out laughing. "So why did you – ?"

"Because you're not an American girl."

"Wrong!" she said. "Born and bred. That's what I am."

"By a Nigerian couple, no? That makes all the difference in the world."

The same waiter approached, pad and pencil at the ready for our orders.

"Coffee for me," said Chizube. "Hot please. Real hot."

"Same for me, but make mine decaf."

The waiter scribbled down our orders fast, and looked up, expectantly.

"That's it?" he asked, when we remained silent.

"That's it," I confirmed, giving the man a wide smile.

"Right on!" he said – or words to that effect. Some Americans speak with the speed of lightning.

There was an awkward silence for a long moment. Then Chizube startled me with a question I had not expected. Not in so public a place, at any rate.

"How many girlfriends d'you have?" Her voice was deadpan, her eyes studiedly vacant.

"What d'you mean girlfriends?"

"You don't know what girlfriend means? It's like –"

"I know what it means," I said. "But I don't know where you're coming from."

"You're just trying to buy time. I asked you a very simple –"

"And here's my simple answer: none."

"None, as in – shall we say – currently?" she asked, smiling in obvious disbelief.

"None currently, or for some time now," I essayed, not quite sure what I meant by 'some time now'. "Satisfied?"

"Reasonably, but –"

"No buts, please! Here's a counter question for you. How many – ?"

"None. Not now, not ever!"

"Impossible, Chizube! A girl with your looks. Perhaps you've been living in another world, a world where there are no men."

"Sometimes," said Chizube, "it is best to keep a low profile."

"Then you shouldn't have been doing track on TV. Everyone knows you. What was it, three or so weeks ago, I saw you on TV burning the tracks. You were superb. The way your legs –"

I stopped because of the expression in Chizube's eyes. All of a sudden, she had gone somber. The same eyes that, moments earlier, had sparkled with vitality now were solemn. She was staring at me, but I had this feeling that she did not see me. I sat, immobilized, staring back at her, respectful of her silence, and unwilling to intrude into that other world into which she had retreated temporarily. I watched as she slowly came back to me, out of that sad gloomy world, a soft smile playing on her lips, her eyes focused once again on me.

She spoke slowly: "What – do – you – want – from – me, Bola?"

The question was non-confrontational. The smile was still there, her voice was soft, and her eyes, though still quizzical, looked at me with kindliness. But it was a loaded question, and I suspected that my answer could be important to her. I took a second or two to reflect on that answer, and quickly decided that Chizube deserved nothing less than my total candor.

"I think," I said slowly, "that I have fallen in love."

Her smile widened, but she shook her head, slowly, from side to side. "That's no answer to my question," she said. "What d'you –"

"Want from you? Nothing that I have any rights to. I'm in love. That's all I know."

"Still –"

"Still what?" I asked.

I stared at her for a moment or two. Around us, the café buzzed with the noise of laughter and the rattle of cups on saucers. Our waiter came and placed our check on *my* side of the table, with a smile that said he knew who would pick up the tab for the two coffees. A TV set, placed high on a shelf above the café's counter, showcased The Boss, New Jersey's Bruce Springsteen, doing his signature song, *Born in the USA*. I was no great fan of The Boss. But had it been the incomparable Michael Jackson himself on that screen, at that particular moment, his impossible bodily contortions and his amazing shuffles would have meant nothing to me.

I had eyes only for Chizube. What did I want from her? My problem was that I did not know what she wanted to hear from me. That she should love me back? I suddenly realized I had not told her I was *in love with her*, only that I was in love. But surely she knew. I shrugged.

"Chizube, I love you. There! I've said it. And if you still insist on my answer to your question, I suppose what I want from you is – well – your – how do I say this – your friendship. That's it! Your friendship! I have no right to expect anything more, now or ever, than your friendship. But I can still hope –"

"I must be raving mad, because I think I love you too."

"What – what did you say?"

"I love you, Bola," she said again, more clearly, perhaps thinking I had not heard her.

I looked around us, suddenly conscious of the milling crowds of diners in the café, worried that our conversation could be overheard at the nearest tables. But everyone seemed to be minding his or her own business.

I reached across the table and took her hand in mine. Time was of no essence. Only our mutual declaration mattered. I could have held her hand for eternity, if she had let me. But, after a long moment, she slowly withdrew her hand from mine, her eyes the while steadfastly looking into mine.

"But we know so little about each other," she said softly, almost sadly. "I only know you're Yoruba and I'm Ibo –"

"Igbo," I corrected her. "You keep forgetting."

"I know," she said. "I know. Funny a Yoruba man should be teaching me how to pronounce the name of my own people. But you're right. Igbo."

"I didn't think our being Yoruba and Igbo would matter to you."

"Why?"

"Because you're not, so to say, homegrown," I said. "You may be Igbo, but you're American, born and bred, as you told me not quite ten minutes ago. All that Nigerian way of thinking must be foreign to you, surely."

"Perhaps, yes," she said. "But my parents are what you'd call dyed-in-the-wool Ibo – I mean, Igbo. Especially my mum! My dad isn't so bad."

She cupped her chin in the palms of her hands and silently gazed at me with such intensity, and for so long, that I got a little flustered. Then she lowered her gaze. Her lips moved, but no words came. I am not a lip-reader, but I thought I recognized my name when her lips formed the word.

"Why are you calling my name?" I asked her.

She looked up, surprised. "I didn't –"

"Don't give me that," I said. "You clearly said Bola two or three times."

For a moment or two, I thought she was going to persist in her denial. Then she threw her head down in surrender.

"You're sharp," she said. "I hope you're not a mind-reader too, because that'd be too much –"

"So tell me why you were calling my name."

"You weren't supposed to know I called your name. In fact you're not supposed to be here at all."

"And what's that supposed to mean?"

"Don't you see?" she said. "I wanted to pretend you're not here. God! This is embarrassing –"

"Come on, Chizube. There should be no embarrassment between us, not now, not ever again. We just –"

"You really want to know? O.K. I'll tell you. What I was saying – asking, really – was: Oh, Bola! Bola! Wherefore – ?"

"Art thou Bola?" I completed her question, and then burst out laughing.

She raised her eyes to mine. "It's not funny," she said.

But she too was laughing. Not perhaps laughing out loud. But I could see laughter in her eyes, which sparkled with the utter deliciousness of the moment. Within seconds, the smile spread all over her face.

"You're no Juliet," I said finally. "And I'm no Romeo. Those two were lovers of a different time and place. Juliet was not yet even fourteen. How could a girl so young work up such intense passion for any man? That's why it all turned out so tragically. You and me, we're different. Our families are not feuding, never mind about the stupid thing between the Yoruba and the Igbo. It doesn't touch us."

"That's quite a speech," Chizube said.

"You inspired me," I told her.

"And you seem so sure –"

"That's because what we have between us is pure and golden. I know I've never experienced anything like this before. I mean it. Whatever I might have felt for any girl in the past –"

"What past – ?"

"That was a long, long time ago. At least four years or so." It was actually more like one year ago, if truth be told. But I wasn't about to spoil a good thing by telling inconvenient truths. I could always try to explain later, if the absolute need arose.

"O.K. I'm sorry. I have no right –"

"Oh yes, you have. But what's past is past, and gone. Question is, where do we go from here?"

"Back to my dorm," she said, "or rather, to your car."

That was not exactly what I had in mind. But I let that go. There is a time to be persistent, and a time to play it by ear.

She took a peek at her watch. "What time is it?"

"Why do you even bother to look at your watch? Ladies watches are just an ornament, not to tell time by. Anyway it's close to midnight, and I have a few miles to drive, back to Harlem."

"So let's go," she said.

I beckoned to the waiter, and gave him my visa credit card, with the bill. I calculated fifteen percent of four dollars, and brought out sixty cents from my pocket. On an impulse, however, I changed my mind, took a dollar bill out of my wallet, and placed it on the table.

"Generous!" said Chizube.

"I only wanted to impress you." We laughed.

"I'm impressed. But you know something? I'm the one should've paid for the coffees."

"Well spoken," I said, "like a true young lady of America. But no girl pays for me. You'd better get used to that."

"Careful now," she drawled. "I might take advantage of that."

"I don't think you would. You don't look the type."

The waiter returned with my credit card and the payment slip for my signature. I drew his attention to the dollar bill on the table, and he beamed his appreciation.

"Come again," he called after us, as we left.

Chizube insisted that we went straight to my car. "I'll be all right walking by myself to my dorm," she assured me.

I was in the car, and inserting the key in the ignition when Chizube leaned forward through the window, and said: "I'm surprised your parents let you have a credit card."

"My mother actually," I said.

"Oh!"

There was a pregnant pause. Time enough for me to weigh the significance of that 'oh'. On the day we first met, she had asked me about my parents and, very carefully, I had replied that my mum lived in Queens. She had not gone on then to ask me specifically about my dad, but I knew then that that was a score I had to settle, sooner or later. Perhaps Chizube had forgotten my answer to her question. The 'oh!' was said in a manner that suggested a faint stirring of her memory. But whatever it signified, Chizube was clearly a girl who was not inclined to press an issue, preferring to let me tell her *what* I wanted to tell her, *when* I wanted to do so.

"You don't have one?"

"A credit card?" she asked, making a face. "You must be joking. I'm still daddy's little girl. That's what he calls me sometimes. He tells me I'm still too young for the wiles of the world. Doesn't bother me actually. In time I know I'll get one."

"You *are* patient," I said, with appropriate emphasis.

Chapter XV

I BELIEVE I startled her with my question. I startled myself too, come to think of it. I had not meant to. Indeed I had not intended, in a conscious, deliberate way, to ask the question. It just popped out of me, like that. I know now that if I had thought about it, if I had paused long enough to reflect on the matter, I might have developed cold feet. But I suppose it was a question I needed to ask, else it would not have come out the way it did.

It was not really a question, except that it required some sort of a response. "I'd like," I said to Chizube, "to meet your guys one of these days."

She looked at me for a moment or two. "You must be out of your cotton-picking mind," she said, reminding me how very American she could sometimes be. She paused, and then added: "Why?"

"Why not?"

"I mean it, Bola. Why? This is the first I've heard you say anything like that. And please don't give me your 'why not' again."

"Why?" I said mechanically, more to myself than to her, reflecting that some questions, particularly impulsive questions, are often difficult to explain. I might have tried to prevaricate, if I could have. But I was not smart enough to quickly think of a clever, evasive answer. In the end, I was compelled to tell her my truth, plain and simple.

"Because," I said, "it's just about the right time to do so –"

"That's not saying much," Chizube countered.

"Let me finish what I wanted to say. Chizube, we've known each other now for just about a year. There's very little, I think, that we've not told each other about ourselves. We've talked endlessly about your parents, and mine. I know the pains your dad, in particular, has gone through. You know I'm searching for *my* dad. Let's complete the cycle. I should meet your folks, and you, my mum. What d'you say?"

We were at the Franklin Diner, a restaurant of bright lights, and moderately priced meals. The Diner is centrally located in the Easton Plaza, at the junction of Easton Boulevard and Van Wyck Street, not far from Rutgers College. I am particularly partial to breakfasts at any time of the day or night, and the typical American Diner, so called, gives one that flexibility. Though it was evening, I ordered a combo of scrambled eggs, three fluffy pancakes and two sausage links. Chizube, whose athletic program required that she watched what she ate, was content with a plate of un-garnished Caesar salad.

The Franklin was Chizube's favorite place to dine out. Indeed in the months she and I had been going steady, I lost count of the number of times we went there. We did not always dine out. When we did, it was, more often than not, at my insistence. She enjoyed preparing something special for us to eat, when I visited her, which was something I did more frequently than perhaps I should have. Once or twice she felt impelled to ask me how my studies were going, which made me think that perhaps I was taking up more of *her* time than was good for *her* studies. But because both our grade point averages hovered just under four apiece, there seemed – indeed there was – little to worry about. Chizube apart, the occasional game of tennis and a fairly regular visit to the swimming pool were my only distractions. I was also something of a party aficionado. It did not take long for me to see that Chizube also enjoyed going to parties.

We had done eating, and were waiting for the waiter to bring me a doggie bag for my left-over scrambled eggs and one sausage. Chizube, almost as a matter of principle, never took away a doggie bag. She always ate what she wanted to eat, and that was it for her. Happily she never raised any objections if I wanted to scoop her leftovers into my doggie bag. "For my dog," I would tell her. "Yah," she would respond mechanically, meaning it was a tired old joke.

I watched as she struggled with my proposition. I had no wish to put any pressure on her. I thought I knew what she was concerned about, what might have been preying on her mind. Then she surprised me, because when she looked up at me, and nodded her head slowly a few times, somehow I knew I was no longer out of my cotton-picking mind.

"You know," she cooed, "it's not such a bad idea. They might as well get used to the fact that we're – you know –"

"Dating," I suggested.

"Don't care too much for that word. Let's just say you and me, we're – well – friends. Yes, friends."

"Only *friends*?" I asked, looking steadily at her with as much tenderness and yearning as I could inject into my eyes, my head tilted expressively to one side.

"Oh, stop it, Bola!"

"What did I do now?"

"You know very well –"

"I don't," I said, though I did know.

"You do. Stop looking at me like that –"

"Why? Does it affect you?"

"And if it does?" she asked with a smile.

"Then don't expect me to stop it. But okay, let's get serious. You were saying –"

"I think I know how my parents will react, especially my mum," she said reflectively.

"I think I do too."

"I can just see her," mused Chizube, "looking at me, her eyes asking all sorts of questions –"

"About me and you, no?"

"Of course, about you and me. They're of the old school, you know, who want explanations for every move their children make, especially –"

She left the thought suspended in mid-sentence. But she did not need to complete it. I am myself somewhat of the old school too. I might not be as deeply traditional as my parents' generation is. But I was not born, and certainly did not grow up, in America either. I knew that if I was a parent, and my child brought a friend of the opposite sex to introduce to me, I would have a question or two to ask. Come to think of it, even an American parent might have questions too.

"So?" I asked.

"Why not?" she asked, in turn. "Let's go for it."

*   *   *

I ran the idea by my band of brothers because I was suddenly assailed by doubts and misgivings about the wisdom of the step I was about to take. Kojo and Cletus more or less knew what there was to know about my 'progress' with Chizube. The two had conspired to set me up with her, and had demanded, as their pound of flesh so to say, that I kept them apprised of developments. Which was something I did with the utmost reluctance. I could easily dodge Cletus who, being a Rutgers student, lived several miles away from me, and did not share in my daily life. He was forced to glean what he could from Kojo, who was like my shadow. Kojo and I shared an off-campus apartment, about which he continually irritated me. "With a mother in near-by Queens," he would say, "you should live with her, and commute to Columbia University. Could have saved her lots of money." As if it was any of his business! Perhaps he was really only interested in my mum's cooking, which he would have had frequent opportunities to sample if I lived with her.

Kojo pestered me on an almost daily basis about the 'Quarter-miler'. He seemed to have some difficulty calling her Chizube. I tried to insist, but it was useless. For old times' sake, however, I gave in to his pressure, and related as much of my story with Chizube as I could not withhold from him. Whatever I told him, he dutifully passed on to Cletus. Poor Kojo! He had no real choice in the matter. Cletus, he told me, had threatened never again to invite him to a Rutgers or other Jersey student party if he was kept in the dark about what was going on. Cletus might have extended the threat to me, but he knew it would have been pointless. I had Chizube!

I made sure Cletus was visiting when I told them about my move. The words were scarcely out of my mouth than they reacted in their different ways. Kojo pumped a fist, and let out a loud and triumphant "Yes!" Cletus, stunned, ripped into me.

"What would you go and do that for?" he asked, frowning.

"What's your point?" Kojo asked him.

"As if you don't know!"

"I don't know nothing," Kojo shot back, "about what goes on in that misshapen head of yours."

I flinched. It was a definite no-no to refer in any negative manner to the shape of Cletus's head. It used to be, for him, like a red rag to a bull. But I quickly relaxed. Cletus was no longer the Cletus of our high school years. *That* Cletus would have reacted to the cruel taunt with clenched fists. The boys taunted him about the elongated shape of his head. They sang him a juvenile Igbo song that mocked the five protuberant points of his head. But maturity had done wonders for his temper, which was now so much under control that he actually laughed at Kojo, and threw one back at him.

"At least I have only one jaw," he said to his tormentor. "Yours is double pointed. What I'm saying is that unless Bola intends to show his hand this early in the game –"

"Hold it there!" commanded Kojo. "You've got me confused, the way you moved smoothly from the shape of your – I mean, from your head to Bola's hand –"

"And what d'you mean 'this early'?" I threw in.

Cletus took a moment or two to look from Kojo to me, and back again to Kojo. Then he slowly got up from the two-seater he was sharing with Kojo, and walked over to a picture of Kojo's father which hung on a wall of the apartment. He stood gazing at it for a while. Then he turned back to us.

"Let me tell you something," he said, pointing to Kojo. "The day you take a girl to introduce to your old man, he'd want to know if it's a serious relationship. It's even worse if it's a daughter that brings her boyfriend –"

"Have you finished talking?" Kojo asked Cletus, but did not wait for his answer. "I have no sister, as you well know. But if I had –"

"Oh please stop all this babbling," I said. "There's something serious going on here. What's your problem, Cletus, with me going to meet Chizube's folks?"

"Simply this, if you really want me to spell it out: they'll think you two are trying to say something to them. Like, that this is serious –"

"Isn't it?" asked Kojo.

"Well –" I began, then stopped.

"Well, what?" Kojo urged me. "Is it or isn't it?"

"If you press me, I'd say it is. Most definitely! She's *it* for me."

Cletus snorted. "She may well be," he said. "But if you ask me, it's a little too early for you to show your hand to her parents. You know, there are still many Igbo parents who do not like the idea of their daughters having boyfriends. How long have you known Chizube?"

"Funny you should ask that question, when you and Kojo planned the whole affair."

"You think I keep a count of the months that have passed?" Cletus asked.

"Okay, ten months, but who's counting?"

"And it's a very common thing in America," Kojo said, "for parents to meet their children's friends."

"This is not America!" said Cletus. "I mean, we're not talking about Americans. Chizube's parents are Nigerians; they're Ibo –" He raised an imperious arm to stop me from interrupting him. "Okay, Igbo people. Doesn't matter how long they've been in the U.S." He paused, and then added: "That's it. I'm done. That's my opinion."

For what seemed like a full minute, no one spoke. I could not recall when last we had such a prolonged period of silence between us band of brothers. Kojo gazed at me, in expectation of some reaction from me. Cletus resumed his seat, and rested his head in his hands, the fingers of which were intertwined at the nape of his neck.

"So – ?" asked Kojo.

"*You* tell me," I said. "You haven't really said a word other than the unkind things you said to Cletus."

"You want it in words? Okay, my brother. I don't know what Cletus is afraid of. I've had a strong feeling about you and the quarter-miler right from the beginning –"

"We know you have," said Cletus. "I do too."

"Nothing that has happened has caused me to change how I see things. We're still young, I know. But if I were to have the good fortune to meet my own quarter-miler today –"

"Chizube!" I said.

". . . My own Chizube today, I'll be ready to meet her folks any day of the week she wants."

Nothing more was said. Nothing more needed to be said. As I had expected, Cletus was distinctly unenthusiastic about what he saw as my rush to jump in where an angel might have been more circumspect. Kojo, ever the adventurer, was more gung-ho. If I must tell the truth, I think I shared Cletus's reservations about my venture. But I was now set on a course that I had no wish to reverse. For me, the die was cast.

*　　*　　*

The Mount of Olives Gardens, where Chizube's parents lived in West Brook, was a beautiful estate. What I liked most about it was the pervading greenery, and the gardens full of flowers. There were trees everywhere, along the streets of the estate, and in clusters here and there. When I parked, and stepped out of my rented Toyota, I could hear the faint murmurs of a stream that flowed along one side of the estate.

Chizube did not bother to knock on the door, or ring the door bell, before letting herself in with her key.

"Don't you think you should have knocked?" I chided her softly, following her closely into the entrance area.

"Knocked?" she asked. "This is where my dad and mum live, the home where I grew up. In any case, they know I'm coming."

"Just you," I asked in some alarm, "or us? I don't like surprises."

Chizube turned to me, and smiled enchantingly. In the brief moment we had to ourselves, I looked around me. I saw the masks almost before I saw anything else. They hung on the walls, in pairs, in some kind of silent assertion of Africa. A large framed photograph of Chizube's parents was placed between two of the more terrifying masks, in a manner to immediately draw the eye when one entered through the front door. I said to myself, as I gazed at that odd arrangement, "perhaps this is their way of ensuring the protection of the ancestors".

The other thing that struck me, almost immediately, was the strong resemblance between Chizube and the beautiful woman – more like a girl really – in that photograph. But I did not have much time to reflect on that striking resemblance, because Chizube's dad just then joined us from an inner room. Chizube ran into his outstretched arms for a hug that warmed the heart, and that inevitably put me in mind of my own father whom I did not know. Then he saw me, and his expression was one of utter surprise.

"Where's mum?"

Her dad slowly disengaged from their embrace. Still with an eye on me, he gestured behind him. "She's coming," he said. "We've been expecting you this last hour or so." His eyes resolutely held mine. "Who's your friend?"

"Let's wait for mum. I'm not going to do this twice over."

Her dad shrugged, perhaps in recognition of the futility of arguing with her. What he did do was take a step in my direction, and hold out his hand. I took it, bowing respectfully to him.

"My name –"

"Hold it there, young man," said Mr. Jideofo, albeit with a smile. "My daughter wants to do this thing properly."

Just then, the door, through which he had earlier emerged, opened once more, and Mrs Jideofo stepped into the entrance area.

"Chi-Chi!" she exclaimed, throwing her arms around her daughter. "You finally made it. You're late." She did not seem as surprised to see me as Chizube's dad had been. I understood better when she added: "Aha! I thought I heard more than two voices."

The only way I know to say it, is that she was a somewhat more matured version of Chizube. They could easily have passed for sisters. They both had the same softly appealing, quietly satisfying, beauty, a type of comeliness that gives one the feeling that all would be well in their joint orbit, so long as one belonged in it. Chizube was much taller than her mum; indeed when she stood by her dad, they looked to be the same height – about six feet.

I saw Chizube's resemblance to her dad when I was not looking for it. It was not the total physical resemblance, which she shared only with her mum. But I saw it when both their faces lit up with joy at their reunion, and the radiance of their shared joy illuminated the subtle facial resemblance between parent and child that one sometimes sees only in flashes.

Chizube came and stood by me, and suddenly, clearly on an impulse, took and held my hand. I had not expected anything like that, not on this, my first meeting with her parents. But I gratefully closed my fist on her fingers, and we stood like that, side by side, facing her parents. I was nervous.

"Dad, mum, this is Jacob Bola Akande." Or words to that effect!

As she said this, she withdrew her hand from mine, and then linked arms with me, which made me even more nervous. There is a difference – perhaps only a subtle difference – of emphasis between the two gestures. When Chizube linked arms with me, face to face with her dad and mum, I could only think that she wanted to make a statement about the nature, the closeness, of our relationship.

I saw a wild flash in Mrs. Jideofo's eyes, a reaction that immediately set me thinking about Romeo and Juliet. It was evident to me that Chizube had never told them about us; evident also that my Yoruba name came as something of a shock to them. I felt Chizube, who had clearly observed her mother's reaction, momentarily stiffen.

"Mum!" Chizube called out to her.

"Take it easy, Chizube!" her dad quickly said to her, in a soft pleading tone. "It's all right."

Those were not the first words her parents had spoken to Chizube in Igbo since we came into the apartment. But those words, spoken in innocence by her dad, came as a bit of a shock to me. Then I understood. If, as was now clear to me, Chizube had never told them about us, there was no way they would know that I understood and spoke Igbo. They would not know that Igbo was the language I spoke growing up in Enugu, in the heart of Igboland, though my Yoruba mother made sure I also spoke *her* language.

For the next several minutes, as Chizube and I answered her parents' questions about me, I felt tormented in spirit. At what point, I kept asking myself, would it be appropriate to tell them that I was, in a manner of speaking, more Igbo than their daughter. My nervousness – indeed my discomfort – increased with every passing minute. To this day, I cannot recall how I lived through those harrowing minutes, as I struggled to come to terms with the situation. I think I remember that I tried to put some space between Chizube and me, and that at one point I went and sat by myself on a dining chair. Why I did that, other than to pretend that Chizube and I were not particularly close, I have no idea.

Then Mrs. Jideofo gave me an opening, and I grasped the opportunity with both hands. I was not sure it was the best moment to do so. But I suppose I reckoned that if I did not, the moment might never come again, and worse things might, in the meantime, be said in Igbo by Chizube's dad and mum, in their innocence.

Mrs. Jideofo asked her daughter a very simple question. A question, I had not the slightest doubt, she would not have asked – at least not that openly – if she knew I would understand her words. Had she known, she would assuredly have taken Chizube aside for that purpose.

"Chizube," she asked in Igbo, "what's the reason for this visit? You didn't tell us about your young friend."

That was my moment of truth. "It's my fault entirely, ma," I said, in English. "I've been wanting to meet you for a very long time, and I talked her into bringing me here today."

To say that Chizube's parents were surprised by my answer would be a gross understatement. They were in shock. I saw both their mouths drop open, and stay open for the longest time. Mrs. Jideofo's eyes, as she stared wildly at me, dilated with horror. I quickly stole a glance at Chizube. She was smiling! I looked again, and this time she, too, turned to look at me. Her smile widened; worse, she winked at me. I scarce believed my eyes. Chizube was enjoying herself; she who should, by rights, have been covering her face in shame.

I decided to go the whole hog. At the next opportunity – when Mrs. Jideofo asked me if I was a Catholic – I answered in Igbo. Indeed Mrs. Jideofo had asked the question, with an infectious smile, in Igbo.

I was not at all sure how the visit was going. This was a visit I had hoped would mark a watershed of sorts in my relationship to Chizube's family. The question I kept asking myself – a question I decided I would ask Chizube the very first moment I had her to myself – was: why did she not tell them about me? If I could have, I would have been very mad at her. But I couldn't. Or rather, I was just a tiny bit angry. But her smile, not to talk of that devilish wink she gave me, somewhat illogically blew my anger away. Perhaps that was my first lesson in the power of love.

The rest of my visit went reasonably well, I thought, thanks in large measure to the uninhibited and overflowing joy with which Chizube was welcomed. And perhaps a tiny bit too to the odd fact that I could converse with my surprised hosts in fluent Igbo, which their daughter could not, or at best could only very sketchily, do. They warmed to me by the end of the visit and, in answer to Chizube's hesitant question, said I was welcome to come again.

There was one last surprise – for me. Chizube and I were half out of the door, when she stopped and turned to her parents.

"Where's he?"

I remember particularly her mother's answer, because it was strikingly expressive, and a quote from the Bible. "Why do you look for the living among the dead?"

Chizube saw the puzzlement on my face, and whispered in my ear: "That's my little brother." Then she added aloud, taking me by the hand: "Come, Bola. Pay no mind to my mum. You never know what she'll come out with. Let's go to the village park. You have to meet the little devil."

Once the door had shut behind us, I pulled Chizube up. But before I could get a word out, she pulled me to her in a manner I could not resist. Then she spoke softly, her eyes looking directly into mine, her expression pleading.

"I'm sorry, Bola, I never told you I have a younger brother, Ndubisi. He's what, only seven or so years. You'll meet him in the next few minutes."

"This is a day of surprises –," I said, but got no further.

"I know," she said quietly, a tentative smile playing on her lips. "I should have told my parents about you and that you speak Ibo – I mean Igbo."

"They were shocked."

"But it doesn't really matter," she said. "A little shock now and then is good for the old folks. If you ask me, it was well worth it, to see how surprised they were. Does them good too, especially my mum! She needs to be more careful how she talks about people when she thinks it's safe to do so."

We found the little devil in the park all right. He was quite tall, for a seven-year old. As soon as he saw his sister, he abandoned his three friends, with whom he had obviously been taking turns at the swings, and ran over to us. He got his hug and a peck on his forehead. Then he turned and gazed at me with wide eyes that were full of questions.

"That's Bola," Chizube told him.

"You must be Ndubisi," I said, extending my hand to him. "I'm glad to know you."

"Are you her boyfriend?" the little devil asked, with the refreshing artlessness and candor of a child's innocence. He gave me his hand.

As we shook hands, I beamed at him. But I did not answer his question. I was caught, as it were, unawares, being totally ignorant of his existence until just moments earlier. Besides, no one had ever asked me such a question before.

Nothing daunted, Ndubisi turned to his sister. "Is he?"

"Why d'you want to know?" Chizube asked him.

"Because!" said the little boy, wide eyes looking from me to his sister.

I too looked at Chizube, and she looked back at me. I shrugged, smiling. She made a face at me, and then nodded to Ndubisi.

"Yes, he is."

Ndubisi gazed at me for a brief moment, and then spoke the words that rang in my head for several weeks and months thereafter. "I like him," he proclaimed, and turned and ran back to his friends.

"Bye, little brother!" Chizube sang loudly, waving to him.

"Bye!" Ndubisi shouted back, already claiming his turn at a free swing.

"Bye!" I echoed, though no one seemed to need my input.

As we stood and watched him clamber on to his swing, and begin to urge it into motion, I smiled at Chizube.

"Can you explain something to me?"

"What?"

"How can Ndubisi resemble you, and yet be a spitting image of your dad?"

"Why not?" asked Chizube, looking at me with mock reproach. "Don't I resemble my dad?"

"Only in flashes," I said. "If you weren't much younger than your mum –"

"That's what many people say. But I've met others who, when I'm introduced to them, say I look like dad."

"Great name, Ndubisi," I said. "Can I shorten it to Bisi?"

"Nope!" she said emphatically, and without hesitation. The tone seemed to leave little room for negotiations.

"Why?" I asked.

"D'you have to ask? I think it's pretty obvious."

"Not as obvious as you'd think," I said. "But if your reason is what I'm thinking, I'm really surprised you're familiar enough –"

"With Yoruba names?" Chizube asked, feigning wounded pride. "In my college, I know two Bisis, both Yoruba, both girls. There!"

"Correction! Boys answer Bisi too."

"That's your typical Nigerian English," said Chizube. "But I know what you mean. My answer is still No!"

"O.K. Whatever you say, my dear."

She looked at me quizzically for a moment or two, on account of that 'my dear', a term of endearment I had not, until then, added to my vocabulary. Then her face broke in a smile, and she took and held my hand, and nestled closer to me, as we walked towards our rented Toyota Camry.

"I like that," she said, looking at me. "I never thought to hear you say anything like – you know –"

"Like 'my dear'?"

"Or 'honey'. It's just not you."

"You mean you accept my love without all that stuff? I could learn to, you know. Isn't it what you young ladies of America seem to thrive on?"

She made me stop, though by this time we had reached the car. She held both my hands as we stood, facing each other, in the parking lot of the Mount of Olives Gardens. People passed by us, though none seemed the least bit interested in us. Happily, too, our car was parked far enough away that we could not be seen by anyone in Chizube's parents' apartment.

"*Nigerian-American*, please," she said earnestly. "Not just American. Bola, you and me, we don't need those words. I'd rather be your Chizube than your 'honey'. Sooner or later, there's no honey left in the jar, and that's when trouble starts, if you see what I mean."

"Wow!" I said, as our eyes held. "You'd like to be my Chizube? Is that some sort of a proposal?"

Chizube let out a growl, and playfully hit me across the chest and shoulder. She disengaged from me, and reached for the car door. "Please unlock the door, and let me get in. Men!"

I did, and then held the door open for her. She hit me one more time, with a softer growl, before letting herself into the front passenger seat.

I turned the key in the ignition, and let it idle for a moment or two. I leaned over to Chizube, and said: "You know I was just kidding."

Her eyes said she did, but her lips said: "Were you now?"

"Seriously," I said, changing the subject, "what d'you think of our visit?"

"No," she said. "*You* tell me. *You* met my folks for the first time today. How d'you feel about it?"

"You mean, other than the two surprises, shocks actually? I cannot tell you a lie. I think it went very well, even with your mum. I honestly think in the end, she was – how shall I say it – okay with me, I mean, with us. No?"

"My dad and mum are two open books," said Chizube. "What you see is what you get."

There was still enough daylight, as we drove away, for me to take in again the beauty of the estate, the undulating landscape, the flowers just beginning to blossom, the well-kept lawns. The trees, majestic in height and in the breadth of their branches, though they were not yet in leaf, dominated everything.

"How will *your* mum receive *me* when we see her this time next week?" Chizube asked. "That is the question now."

I shrugged, and raised my right hand. "My fingers," I showed her, "are crossed."

Chapter XVI

MY MOTHER'S ATTITUDE to the girls I had more or less seriously dated since I came to America, three girls in all, had been cool to lukewarm. She usually found one reason or the other to disparage them. One was 'too short'; the second, 'too skinny'. She watched the third briefly, and then whispered in my ear: "Do you see how her eyes flash? The girl is sharp. She won't miss anything." She once said to me: "Look at yourself. Any girl would be lucky to catch you."

Chizube was different. *I* was the lucky one, not the other way around, no matter my doting mother's exaggerated perspective on the matter. I was, after all, her only child.

"Tell me about your mum," Chizube excitedly asked me, a day before I was due to take her to Queens, NY, to meet my mother.

I thought briefly about that request, and shook my head. "Not a good idea," I said.

"Why? Is there something – ?"

"Like what?" I asked, smiling. "There's nothing to hide, if that's what you're thinking. I just don't want to prejudice you one way or the other."

"But I told you about my parents – ."

"Oh no, you didn't. You merely said your mum would be wondering what we were up to, you and me – something like that. I didn't know anything about either of them before I met them – I mean, anything about how they would react to me as your – you know – boyfriend."

"And – ?"

"And it turned out pretty well," I said. "So, I pray, it will be with my mum. However, there's one thing I can tell you about her. Something you'll be able to confirm the first moment you meet her."

"What's that?"

"She's beautiful."

"I knew that. She –"

"Impossible," I said. "You've never met her."

"Don't need to have met her," said Chizube. "She had you, didn't she? Unless you think you got your looks only from your dad, or something."

"Or both," I said, flattered by her compliments. At the same time, a stab of pain went through my heart. If I ever needed my dad, I mused, tomorrow would be the day. I knew I could not change my situation. But the thought that I would be taking Chizube to meet only my mum – when just days earlier, I had met both her parents – left me feeling incomplete, and inadequate. The more I thought about it, on the eve of one of the most important days of my life, the more worried I became. I knew in my heart that this thing that I had with Chizube was not a fleeting feeling. How, I asked myself, could I expect Chizube to be willing to go along with me, and take our relationship to the next and perhaps most crucial level of all, if I, myself, did not know from whence I came?

Chizube did not press the issue. I knew she would not. That was one of the things I loved about her: she was a very considerate person. She knew my situation; knew I was hurting on account of the gaping hole in my life. It was easy to see that she was acutely curious about the matter. But she managed to keep her curiosity in check.

My mother was curious too. From the moment I told her that I would bring Chizube to meet her, she wanted to know everything there was to know about her. Naturally! But I gently declined to satisfy her curiosity. What's good for the goose, I said to myself, is good also for the gander. If I would not tell Chizube about my mum, it seemed only fair not to tell my mum about Chizube. "Warped logic" Chizube commented, when I told her about it. "If I was your mum, I'd tweak your ear."

Part of my problem was probably that I did not know, even if I wanted to, how to describe Chizube to my mum.

"I'm in love with her," I told my mum. "That's all that matters."

My mother fixed me with her eyes in a manner with which I was all too familiar, growing up. Time was when that fixed stare had the power to make me go weak in the knees, especially when I was not being a good boy, or was hiding something from her. It was always a battle of wills between us. She was moved once or twice to mutter that if my father had been there, *he* would have gotten the truth, one way or another, out of me. I was very young then, in primary school. But I never forgot.

On one such occasion, I so far forgot myself as to ask her: "Why isn't he here, to make me talk?" And for my pains, she laid into me to such effect that I do not remember ever again asking her about my dad in a defiant, rebellious spirit.

Happily, I had learnt, over the years, to take my mum's hard stare in stride and, far from turning rubbery-kneed, I now smiled expansively at her. I had learnt to smile, and smile, at her, and still refuse to give her what she wanted from me. And as I progressively grew beyond her strictly physical control, *she* learnt to accept my smile for what it was: a gentle, loving tactic on my part, in the face of her inquisitiveness, especially as regards my female friends.

When she tired of trying to make me tell her about Chizube, she showed her frustration and impatience in the way she rapidly shut her eyes, as she turned her head away from me in a slow disgusted motion. "Lord, help me!" she said in her sweet, sing-song Yoruba. "I hope she's not like one of them." She pointed a disparaging thumb backwards over her shoulder.

My mother was never a particularly tidy person. It was not unusual, whenever I visited her, to see piles of letters and other papers strewn around the living room: on the low rectangular center table, on the chairs, on the TV set, on any shelves or ledges that offered flat, usable surfaces. She loved to read. But she had this maddening habit of starting two or even three novels at about the same time. And then she would struggle mightily to finish any. The books, dog-eared or otherwise book-marked, would lie in some kind of magnificent disorder by, or on top of, the piles of papers.

Two days before Chizube's visit, I made a special trip to Queens, NY, to clean up the apartment, or at least the living room. My mum was surprised, but delighted, to see me. But scarcely two minutes into my visit, she stopped tinkering around the kitchen and, for a long while, just stood leaning against the kitchen door, watching me.

"Someone has to do this," I said to her, dumping a handful of papers I had carefully sorted out, into a wastebasket. "I intend to hide some of these papers in your bedroom."

"Because of *her*?" she asked, a cynical smile contorting her comely face.

"Because of her," I conceded.

"You never did this before."

"That's because none of the others was –"

"Chizube?"

"I'm glad you remember her name," I said.

"Is that surprising?" my mum asked. "I've heard nothing else from your mouth than Chizube, Chizube, in the last how many months."

"She's special," I said. "That's why."

"And you're bringing her here tomorrow –"

"Not tomorrow," I hastened to correct her, "but the day after. That's Saturday. Today's Thursday, right?"

"Good thing you reminded me," said my mum. "Otherwise I was going to do some special cooking tomorrow for you. Except of course that you've never told me what she likes."

"Nothing to worry about there," I said. "If the food tastes good, she'll like it. That's one of the reasons she's such a great girl."

"Hey, Bola!" she suddenly screamed, abandoning her post by the kitchen door. She took three or four steps towards me, and placed her hand on my left arm, which clutched a sheaf of papers I took off the top of the TV set. "What are you doing?"

I looked at her hand on my arm, and then at her face. "What's the matter?" I asked. "And what d'you mean, what am I doing? I told you –"

"I know what you told me," she said, as she not-so-gently took the sheaf from my hand. "But –"

"What's the matter?" I asked again, as she paused. "Anything special about those papers?"

"Nothing," she said, I thought, a trifle too quickly. "It's just that I might not be able to find anything after you're done and gone."

I looked steadily at her for a long moment. I looked at her because she knew I was not at all careless about what I was doing. She knew that I had a sense of what papers were important to her. She must have observed that I was making a neat pile of such papers, with the express intention of transferring the pile to the privacy and sanctity of her bedroom. I had earlier told her so. What papers I discarded were mostly advertising material, and letters offering 'low interest' credit cards, or guaranteeing instant approval of life insurance policies, 'no health-related questions asked'. I simply had not had a chance to scrutinize the sheaf she so abruptly snatched from me.

It flashed through my mind that some of those papers might be sensitive documents that my mum did not want me to see. My visit had been unscheduled; therefore she was caught off guard. To my eternal shame, my first thought was that, in that sheaf, there might be a letter, or something, from a secret boyfriend. My mum, at forty-five, was beautiful in a not quite yet middle-aged sort of way. I was personally aware of three men, one of them a handful of years younger than her, who – as they say – had the hots for her.

My second thought, which I quickly dismissed, was about my father. Who knew if I had held in my hand, for a too shatteringly brief moment, a paper that might have given me a clue or two as to his whereabouts. Or who he was! Or what he was up to! If I must tell the truth, this was something I often did, whenever I thought an opportunity presented itself. I would, unashamedly, read her letters, if she left any lying around. But I never stumbled on any tell-tale document. My mum must have developed an ironclad system to hide any such letters from my prying eyes. That is, if the man – my father – ever committed himself to paper.

I quickly dismissed the thought because I could not bring myself to seriously believe that my mum would have come this close, now, to lowering her guard. I quickly completed my task in the living room, and did the over-night dishes that had cluttered her kitchen sink.

"Anything else I can do?" I asked.

"You've done more than enough," my mum said with what sounded to me like a trace of sarcasm in her voice. "Thank you."

"You don't have to thank me. I did it for me actually."

"I know. Thank you anyway. You'd better make haste or you'll miss your train."

Whenever she said that, which she almost always did at the end of my visits, I would smile, and shake my head.

"We never grow up, do we?" I said. "O.K. I'm out of here."

I embraced her warmly, and then tapped my knapsack, already slung over my shoulder, in which I carried a big bowl of my mum's incomparable okro-and-dried-fish soup. "And thanks, mum, for my doggie bag."

"Hey, Bola," she said. "Make sure your friend Kojo – ."

"D'you need to remind me? I always share the soup, or whatever, with him."

"Always?"

"Always," I assured her. "If I know my man, he's even now waiting to pounce on me the moment I show my face. God help me the day I return to the college without a doggie bag."

"Will you stop calling my soup that name. Off with you."

"O.K., O.K.," I said, and turned and waved to her. "I'll see you in two days time."

*   *   *

Two excruciatingly slow, nerve-racking, nail-biting days later, I returned to no. 56 Village Road, my mum's apartment block in Parkway Estate, Queens. The six-storied edifice is located a couple hundred yards down the road from its junction with the Union Turnpike. My mum loved its location because the complex stood directly opposite a plaza dominated by her favorite supermarket, *Food Town*, and the all-purpose store, *K-Mart*.

Why I set such a high premium on the coming interaction between my mum and Chizube was something I never attempted to understand. I just knew it was terribly, terribly important to me that the two women who mattered most to me would hit it off at first sight. Or, if that was too much to expect, at least that they would be courteous to each other.

Chizube came with me, sporting a not-too-close-fitting long gown, reaching down to almost her ankles, and made of rich light-blue brocade. She wore it because she knew that, of all her long gowns, it was my favorite. She looked absolutely stunning in it. In my eyes, that is. She not only looked ravishing, she was cool, calm and collected, this girl, though she was meeting my mum for the first time. Perhaps these things are different for girls. *I* was a bundle of nerves the day I met *her* folks.

She smiled expansively at my mum, and did what I can only describe as a little curtsey to her. She then waited to see how my mum would welcome her. She had indeed asked me about that matter on our drive to Queens. "Is she a hugger, or a hand-shaker?" To which I had replied: "We'll soon know, won't we?" The truth was that I did not know, in that regard, how to classify my mum. I was nervous, and understandably so because, to judge by her history with every girl I had dated, no one could accuse my mum of being overly welcoming, no matter if she was hugging or shaking hands.

My mum came forward, with her arms outspread, and a careful smile on her lips. Careful, because it seemed tentative to me, though just warm enough to put Chizube fairly at ease. Not that Chizube needed to be put at ease. Nevertheless, I put a loving, protective arm around her shoulders, and drew her close to me, just in case she needed the comforting reassurance of my closeness, as I did the introductions.

"Mum, this is Chizube – ."

My mum cut me off with a wave of the hand. "As if I don't know already!" she said to me. Then, embracing Chizube, she did what I knew, from the long experience of being her son, she would do. She spoke to Chizube in Igbo.

"Welcome, my child. How are you?"

If Chizube was the least bit surprised by this, she did not show it. Indeed her smile widened, as she looked from my mum to me.

"I'm well," she replied in Igbo, as they disengaged from their embrace.

It was one of the very few times I had seen Chizube literally forced into replying in Igbo to the standard welcoming Igbo greeting. My mum, as I had expected, caught the American inflection in that very short response, and raised an eyebrow. If she had been content with that raised eyebrow, all might have been well between her and me. But she could not help her nature, which was never to miss an opportunity for critical commentary, even when the circumstances cried out for warm cordiality.

"You don't speak your language?" she asked Chizube, still in Igbo, shaking her head disparagingly.

"Not as well as I should," Chizube replied smoothly, looking at me, "or as well as Bola. But I do the best I can."

"But – ."

"Mum, enough!" I cut in. "If you were born and grew up here, you too – ."

My mum was immediately apologetic. "I'm sorry," she said, this time in English, putting a hand on Chizube's shoulder. "I didn't mean – ."

"That's all right," said Chizube. "I must say I'm surprised you speak Igbo so well."

"You shouldn't be," said my mum. "I lived in Enugu for more than twenty years."

"But she doesn't speak it all that well," I said, just to take her down a peg or two.

"That's not true," said Chizube. "She sounds good enough to me. And I can usually tell that sort of thing."

"Thank you my child. Don't mind him."

"C'mon, Chizube! Sit down somewhere, and make yourself comfortable."

"You're beautiful," said Chizube to my mum, "just as he told me."

My mum's face absolutely glowed with pleasure at the compliment. "He did?"

"Now, now, Chizube," I said. "You're making her head swell."

"Hey, Bola! Careful how you talk about your mother! But don't mind him, my dear. He likes to pull my legs."

Did I just hear my mum call Chizube 'my dear'? That was a first. And she had used the term within seconds, literally, of meeting Chizube for the first time. This was heady stuff, and thrilled me to the bones.

I guided Chizube, who had remained standing, to the two-seater and made her sit with me. When I looked up, I saw my mum staring intently at her, brows furrowed in concentration.

"It's funny," she said. "I don't believe we've ever met before. But I swear I've seen your face somewhere – ."

"Mum, you're just imagining things."

"Perhaps," my mum said. "Anyway, it doesn't matter. You're welcome. Where d'you live?"

"Westbrook. That's in New Jersey."

"But mum, I already told you."

"So? Don't you ever forget something you've been told?"

"Obviously not like you."

"Maybe it's a sign of old age," said my mum, smiling. "Did you also tell me her last name, or can I go ahead and ask her?"

I laughed. "You know very well I didn't."

Chizube did not wait for the question. "It's Jideofo."

"Thank you dear," said my mum. "My son makes a fuss about every little – ." She stopped, then asked, "Jideofo?"

"You know the name?" Chizube asked, expectantly.

"Yes – I mean n-no. I d-don't think s-so," my mum stuttered.

"Maybe in Enugu?" asked Chizube, smiling. "My dad grew up there. My granny still lives there."

"And your granddad?" I asked, fearing her answer.

"Died about two years ago,"

"You never told me," I said.

"I believe I did," said Chizube. "The very first day we met at the party. We were talking about our folks in Enugu. I remember telling you then that my granny lives in Enugu. Perhaps you didn't notice I left out my granddad."

"I'm sorry," I said.

"That's all right," said Chizube. "He lived a long life, nearly eighty years when he died."

"Jideofo?" asked my mum. "No. Definitely, no. Can't recall the name. But wait a moment! I think I remember now where I've seen your face – on TV. Yes, on TV. Must have been last summer."

"If you saw her on TV," I said, "you must have been watching a sports program."

"That's it!" said mum. "I told you I'd seen your face somewhere. I don't forget faces – ."

"You watch sports on TV?" Chizube asked excitedly.

"You're surprised? He didn't tell you – ?"

"What?" I asked. "That you were a sprinter in your secondary school years?"

"Not just a sprinter, my dear. I did the Long Jump also. In Lagos and Enugu. I was in the Enugu Campus – you know – University of Nigeria – ."

"You did Law?" Chizube asked.

"Not Law. Accountancy."

"They call it Accounting here in America," I said.

"I know. I didn't actually finish the course because my parents couldn't cope with the fees."

"What a shame," said Chizube.

"That's all right," said mum. "I learnt quite early in life to accept what I can't change. And look what God and America have done for me."

"She always says that," I said to Chizube, whose puzzlement showed in the way she was staring at my mum. "God gave her a son, is what she means – ."

"And America?" Chizube asked, looking from me to my mum.

"America gave her what few countries give to persons like her – ."

"Meaning us old folks," said mum.

"I didn't say that – ."

"But that's what you meant, son. It's all right, dear. It's the truth."

"No, it's not, mum. What I was going to say, if you had let me, is that you were able to work and go to school. It wouldn't have been that easy in England, for example."

"Oh, so you were able to complete your accounting course," Chizube asked. "My father – ."

"I didn't," said mum. "I got some credits for my accountancy studies, but I took a degree in Nursing."

"She's an RN," I added, "and the pay is good. Hey! Enough talking! I'm hungry. How about you, Chizube?"

"Don't rush her," said mum. "Have something to drink, my dear, before you eat. I have – ."

"Don't worry, mum. I know what you have, and what she likes."

"O.K.," said mum smiling. "I know when to take a back seat. Food will be ready in a jiffy."

At the kitchen door, she turned back to us. She spoke to Chizube. "You were going to say – I mean about your dad – ."

"Oh, yes. He's sort of an accountant."

"Sort of – ?"

"He's actually an MBA, but he is in an accounting firm."

"I see," said mum. She hesitated for a second or two and then, shrugging slightly, closed the kitchen door behind her.

"She likes you," I whispered triumphantly to Chizube. "I could have told you – ."

"But didn't." said Chizube softly. "I hope you're right."

I looked sharply at her, struck by the oddly sad tone of her voice. She was pensive, with a faraway look in her eyes. She was looking at me, but her thoughts were clearly elsewhere.

"I hope you're right," she said again.

I got up off the love-seat. "I'll get you your drink, and something to snack on."

"Sorry! What did you say – oh yes, the drinks," said Chizube. "But your mum said food will be ready in a minute or two."

"Don't believe everything you hear. If I know my mum – and I do – it'll be at least a half hour before we eat. Trust me."

Almost an hour later, we fell to. Mum had prepared her signature dish of macaroni and cheese, with mashed sweet potato flavored with cinnamon, and roasted turkey drumsticks seasoned with honey barbecue sauce.

Mum said hardly a word throughout dinner. She sat opposite Chizube and me, and for long moments all she did was shift her stare from the one to the other of us two. She was not too obvious about this; at least she tried to pretend that she was not looking at us, Chizube in particular. And, she only really pecked at her food. Whenever I caught her in the staring act, she would daintily lift some food into her mouth. Poor Chizube! It was easy for me to see that she too felt my mum's eyes on her, because she seemed tense, not at all as relaxed as she had been, and occasionally darted her eyes sideways at me.

Once or twice I thought to tell my mum to get on with her food, or to leave us alone. But I could not find the words appropriate to the thought. All my grown-up life, I had seldom found it really difficult to admonish her, when I thought she needed be rebuked. But it was different this time. Chizube was present. Plus there was a special significance to this particular visit which, kind-of, tied my tongue.

I had to find a way to talk to my mum privately because her strange attitude at the dinner table seemed to cast a long gloomy shadow over Chizube's first visit; a visit that was supposed to point the way to the future. That is, *our* future: Chizube's and mine. Sitting, as we were, facing my mum, I tried in a number of different ways to convey to her that I wanted a word with her urgently. I made a face at her. I even leaned slightly back so Chizube would not see what I was up to, and gestured with my head in the direction of her bedroom. But mum did not catch on; or, if she did, she deliberately played obtuse. So I knew I had to force the issue.

I got up from my chair. "I'll be back in a second or two," I said to Chizube. "I need to get something from my bedroom."

"*Your* bedroom?" Chizube asked.

"Well – yes. It's mine, though mum uses it when the need arises."

"What are you looking for?" asked my mum.

But I was already several steps away from the dining table, and chose not to answer her question. I knew she would come after me. She did. I also suspected she had an idea why I had to employ this tactic. Her first words confirmed my suspicion.

"What's the matter, Bola?" she asked, closing the bedroom door behind her. "What did I do now?"

"Why do you keep staring at her? Is something wrong?"

"You forget I'm meeting her for the first time," mum said.

"But it's not nice to keep staring at her like that."

Mum looked steadily at me for a moment or two, smiled her Mona Lisa smile, and then spoke the words that knocked my world askew.

"I don't like her," she said simply. "She's not right for you."

For a very brief moment, I think my mouth hung open. In shock! But I quickly recovered.

"You're not serious, of course," I said, smiling at her.

"I am," she said simply, her eyes boring into mine.

The smile faded from my lips, because I was well aware of the significance of that ominous stare.

"But mum, you two seemed to get on very well – ."

"Oh, she's all right," said mum. "She seems a nice person, and all that."

"So what happened? I don't understand."

"Nothing happened. Just my instincts; what you'd call a mother's instinct."

"That's not good enough, mum. You've got to give me some other reason. Didn't I hear you call her 'my dear'? Or were my ears playing tricks on me? You never called the other girls – ."

"Those ones don't even compare with this one."

"Then what seems to be the problem, mum? You remember what you said about Audrey: too short. Chizube is tall. Plus she's not as skinny as – ."

"Come here, Bola."

She took me by the hand, and led me to the bed, and made me sit down by her. She held my hand in both of hers, and would not let go. We sat like that, in silence, for a moment or two. My head was spinning from the shock of my mum's unexpected and – as far as I could see – totally irrational reaction to Chizube.

"Mum, please let's be reasonable about this – ."

She put an imperative finger to my lips and would not let me say more, and held it there while she spoke.

"Bola, there are certain things in this world you cannot give perfect answers to. A mother has instincts about a lot of things concerning her children. But though that's all they are, instincts, they're not to be taken lightly."

"And your instincts about me and Chizube tell you that – ?"

I left the question suspended in mid-sentence, but mum was in no hurry to supply an answer. She let go of my hand, and leaned her trunk forward, covering her face in both her hands. For a long and pregnant moment, she stayed like that, bent over, deep in thought. I did not want to rush her because I thought that if I did, I might only push her into making another unwelcome, perhaps even ill-considered, remark.

A full minute must have passed before she slowly raised her head, and turned and looked at me; and gave me the second shock of the afternoon! She was crying. Tears coursed down her beautiful face, in a steady, silent stream. Reflexively, I put my arms around her, and drew her to me, so that she rested her head on my chest.

"What's the matter now, mum?" I asked solicitously. "Come on, mum. You've got to stop this. And Chizube must be wondering what's keeping us so long."

Mum raised her head and, between muffled sobs, said: "You two would have been perfect for each other."

I think that, for the second time in barely five or six minutes, my lower jaw must have dropped open. I looked sharply at her. And though my faculties were in total chaos and disarray from an inability to follow the twists and turns of her logic, I kept my voice low and my tone controlled as I asked the inevitable question.

"I thought you said she's not right for me?"

She took a moment or two to calm down. "You don't understand," she finally said. "You two would have been okay, but I just sense there'll be trouble ahead for you."

"For me, or Chizube and me?"

"Both."

What she was saying made no sense to me. Nothing she could have said, in opposition to Chizube, would have made any sense to me. I had not brought the girl I loved, to meet my mum, so my mum could talk from both corners of her mouth. I had been supremely confident that Chizube's magnetic personality would bowl her over. And it apparently did, if what she said from one side of her mouth could be taken literally. I just had not reckoned with the other corner spewing poison and pollutants into the air.

"Mum, you don't know what you're saying," I said, very gently, after a moment of silence. "You don't know Chizube. So how can you sit there and say what you're saying? What kind of trouble do you foresee for us?"

"That's not fair, Bola – ."

"What's not fair?" I asked, in exasperation, a cutting edge now to my voice. "Am I supposed to plan my life, and who I want to be with, on the basis of *just* your instincts?"

"I'm sorry, Bola. I know I've hurt you – ."

"You have, mum. And what you're saying – *that's* what's not fair!"

"Didn't I say that the girl would have been right for you – ?"

"Except for your maternal instinct about some future trouble? Yes! Thank you, mum. I've heard you loud and clear."

"Think about it, son. Don't rush into anything."

"I won't. We never ever intended to rush into anything. Now, let's rejoin Chizube. And I think it's about time we left, so I can take her back to her dorm, and get back to my own place before it gets too dark. I hate driving in New York late at night."

"And you have to return the car to your friend."

"That's the least of my problems," I said, as I got up off the bed, and walked ahead of my mum out of the bedroom.

Chizube had left the dining table, and returned to the love-seat in the living room. She sat demurely, hands clasped and resting on her lap. She looked up at my entry, and gave me a smile so radiant and innocent it rent my heart.

"You found it?" she asked.

"Found – ?" I began to ask, and quickly remembered. "Oh, no, I'm afraid. But it doesn't matter. Mum will take care of it. Won't you, mum?"

"Of course," said mum, giving me a sorrowful look.

"And when you find it, you'll make sure you call me?"

"Okay."

I gave my mum a long look. And the way she stared back at me convinced me that she understood that look, and the undertone of appeal that went with it: an appeal to her gentler, more generous, spirit; an appeal to her love – her abundant, unconditional love – for me; above all, an appeal to her to revisit that maternal instinct that would cast a dark cloud over my life.

I turned to Chizube. "I think it's time for us to leave, if you're ready."

Chizube went from her sitting, to a standing, position in the blink of an eye, seemingly with a mere flick of her body. I had almost forgotten what a superb athlete she was.

"I'm ready," she said. She turned to my mum. "Thank you very much, mama. I enjoyed my visit. I hope I can come again."

"Of course, dear," said my mum smoothly, with a smile.

I could not bear to look my mum in the eye, as I gently led Chizube out of the apartment.

As I eased Kojo's Volvo out of the gates of Parkway Estate, Chizube turned to me, and once again smiled radiantly. But I was not prepared for her question.

"You didn't really go to your bedroom to look for anything, did you?"

"What are you talking about, girl?"

"You sound like Gary Coleman in – ."

"In *Different Strokes*? I've been watching the re-runs. Great sitcom!"

"One of the best," said Chizube. "But I was serious."

"Of course I went to look for something – ."

"Bola! Bola! You know, I wasn't born yesterday."

"What's that supposed to mean?"

"You were – I sensed it – angry with your mum, weren't you?"

"Why would I – ?" I began to ask, but she cut me short.

"I saw the way you were looking at her while we ate. I don't really know why, but I had this uncomfortable feeling things weren't quite right. A girl's instincts, I suppose."

That hateful word again! What's with all these women and their instincts, I asked myself, wretchedly, feeling as forlorn as an insect caught in a spider's web. I had not the least intention to admit to her that our visit had not quite yielded the result I had hoped for. How could I, in one breath, tell her that my mum thought she was a great girl, and in the next, that mum did not think we were right for each other? How explain the easy facility with which my mum could smile like an angel one moment, and in the next, turn round and damn our joint future with dark forebodings?

Suddenly, I knew what I needed: time; time to work on my mum, in hopes of bending her to my will. I was confident that my mum would eventually come around.

"You know something else?" asked Chizube.

"What did I do now?"

"Nothing," she said sweetly. "But there's a strong resemblance between you and your mum."

"So I've been told."

Chapter XVII

MY MUM SUMMONED me to Queens a week or so later. Her voice brooked no argument on the matter. She wanted, she said, to see me on a matter of some urgency.

"I've been expecting your call for some days now," she grumbled. "Why didn't you?"

"It's close to my final exams, mum. You know that."

Mum snorted over the phone. "I don't know anything," she said bitterly. "You tell me nothing these days. Is it because of her?"

"Chizube?" I asked. "Actually I've been thinking of coming to see you."

"About her?"

"About her, yes. I hope you've had time to think things over, mum. It's very, very important to me."

"We should talk, yes."

"Is that why you want to see me?"

"Perhaps," said my mum, teasingly. "So I'll see you tomorrow?"

"That's Friday. It'll have to be after my classes and things."

"What things?" she asked sharply. "Are you seeing her tomorrow?"

I chose not to answer her question. "I'll be there, mum. About seven p.m., okay? Can I bring my friend Kojo?"

"Are you crazy or – ?"

"I'll see you tomorrow," I said, laughing. "I was just kidding."

But there was no laughter in my heart as I hung up. I rehearsed the likely scenario over and over in my mind, as I drove Kojo's Volvo to Queens. For an April day, it was unusually cool. But it was nothing like the chill in my heart on account of what I could only see as my mum's totally unreasonable attitude to Chizube. It was something I could not understand. I did not want to think that her opposition had anything to do with Chizube's being Igbo. My mum had lived too long in Enugu, in the heart and soul of the Igbo country, and got on too well with most of her neighbors in all those years, for her to be *this* negative on that score.

There had to be something else. Perhaps jealousy? But I could not bring myself to believe she would feel seriously threatened by another woman in my life. She knew – she *had* to know – that the bond that held us together was strong and unconditional, being God-given and in the very nature of things. But then it could be that it was also in the nature of things that a parent might be loath to see a child out-grow the parental nest. Especially a single-parent mother of a son on whom she perhaps doted! Which is not to say that my mum doted on me, as far as I knew. I was certainly no mama's boy!

As I negotiated the turn into Village Road, in my mum's Parkway Estate, Queens, my heart was beating uncontrollably. I suddenly found myself mouthing a short prayer. I am, I suppose, one of those easygoing, laid-back Christians who remember the power of prayer only in moments of crisis. But this too-convenient devoutness did me little good because, when I embraced my mum, and held her tightly, she felt something.

"You're shaking," she said, holding me at arm's length the better to look me over.

"Oh, it's all right," I said, doing my best to look the part.

"It's not all right. You're my son. I know your moods. Even before you were born, when you were still in my womb, I could tell how you felt."

I laughed, in spite of myself. "I'm sure you did. You've never stopped reminding me –"

"Why should I?" she asked earnestly. "You sucked these breasts until they were almost bone-dry."

"*You* let me. In any case, for whom would I have left some of the milk?"

Strangely, this conversation, short as it was, restored my composure. Most of it, at any rate! I really believe it was a trick mum developed – over the years – to calm me down whenever I was agitated or restless.

She hugged me one more time, and then let go. "Let's talk, Bola," she said softly. "Come and sit down, because I want you to listen very carefully to what I'm going to say. And in case you're wondering, I've prepared your favorite *egusi* soup, with dried fish, just as you like. And you can take some to your friend, Kojo."

She sat with me on the two-seater, and switched off the TV. She would never have the TV on, when there was serious business to discuss, or she wanted to say a prayer.

"Have you thought about the matter some more?" I asked, because I saw no point in beating about the bush.

"Yes, son, I have," she said, and paused.

"And – ?"

"I can't give a simple answer to your question. It is somewhat complicated."

I looked sharply at her, wondering – desperately wondering – if 'complicated' somehow held the promise of a chink in her strong opposition to Chizube. If she was, even slightly, confused about her attitude to my hopes regarding Chizube and me, I would have to find a way to widen, to break open, that chink.

"Mum, you've met Chizube. You said yourself she's a great girl, or at least we'd have been good for each other."

"Honest to God," said mum, reverently touching her chest, "I have nothing against her. And before I say anything else, I want to say this. You are a grown man, and soon you'll be a doctor, God willing. She's a grown woman herself, Chizube. I don't remember what profession she's studying for –"

"Medicine too. Or Pharmacy. Not quite sure which, yet."

"That's good. I'm your mum. If I have a feeling about anything concerning you, I must honestly tell you about it. Two of you will decide where you want to go with your lives. You heard what I said when you two were here. I just have a feeling about trouble ahead –"

"But mum –"

"Please don't ask me to explain –"

"I must," I said. "I've no choice. As clearly as you can, you must tell me why you don't approve of Chizube and me. Let's call a spade a spade. Why are you so against my marrying her? That's what this is all about, no? So, is it because she's Igbo?"

"Of course, no," said mum emphatically.

"Good! How about: she doesn't speak any of our Nigerian languages?"

"It's nothing to do with that," mum said. "I understand her situation. She was born, and grew up, here."

"Okay. Is she perhaps too tall, in your eyes, for a girl? At least she's not taller than me, which might have been a problem for some people."

"Bola, please stop it!"

"So, tell me, mum, why are you not happy for me – for us? You've had a week to make enquiries about her. Is there something bad about her you want to tell me? Is there something you know, something I don't know?"

"You don't think it's enough that a mother has her instincts – strong instincts – about these things?"

"Not good enough, sorry, mum. You've got to do better than that. If you can't, I'll be left with only one supposition."

"And what's that?"

"That she's Igbo."

"Bola! You really don't think that I –"

"You leave me no alternative, mum. The Igbo people are in the East of Nigeria, and the Yoruba are in the West. And as they say, East is East and West is West, and never the twain shall meet."

"That's ridiculous."

"What's ridiculous, mum? You're Yoruba, and you're pretending you don't know how it is between the Yoruba and –"

"That's not what I'm saying. I mean, it's nothing to do with all that stuff."

"I'm glad to hear that," I said, genuinely relieved. "I'm really glad. Because, if you oppose us on that ground, I would have to say I consider myself more Igbo than Yoruba, because I grew up among the Igbo. And, in any case, Chizube is probably more American than Nigerian, never mind Igbo. She's the most delightful person I could ever wish to meet. She's gorgeous, and a great athlete. I thought that should have meant a lot to you, of all people, since you were not bad at all on the track –"

"It's her dad, Bola. I know about her dad."

It was perhaps fortunate that I was sitting down, or I do not know what might have happened. I think I went numb, literally. The juices – whatever they are – drained out of me. For perhaps a second or two – long enough for my mum to notice – I froze.

She put her arms around me, and pulled me to her. "I'm sorry, Bola. I didn't mean to shock you."

"What – ?" I stuttered. "What – did you just s-s-say?"

"That I'm sorry –"

"No," I said. "I mean about her dad?"

"I know about him."

"You can't, mum. I've never said anything about him to you."

"I take it you know what I'm talking about? That he was –"

"Don't say it, mum! How in the world did you hear about it?"

"I didn't need you to tell me anything. If you must know, on the day you brought her here, everything came clear the moment she mentioned her family name, Jideofo."

"There are many Jideofos,' I said. "It's not an uncommon Igbo name."

"But she also said that her dad is an accountant."

"So – ?"

"Simple," said mum. "I put two and two together, and I knew. The Jideofo I knew – or at least heard about – did Accountancy – I mean, Accounting – in Rutgers, years and years ago."

"You seem very well informed, mum. So, tell me one thing. In your long years in Enugu, did you know the Jideofos?"

"I told Chizube when she asked that same question –"

"The truth, mum! Please tell me the truth. Did you know the family?"

"You want the truth?" asked my mum. She stood up.

"God's truth," I answered, almost shouting.

She walked away from me, taking three or four steps. Then she stopped, spun round, and looked at me with eyes from which the light had gone completely out.

"I never met the family. But I knew about them."

"So you told us lies the other day –"

"I had to, Bola," said mum, her tone pleading. "I had no choice. There was no way I was going to admit to Chizube that I knew about her family, especially her dad. Not at that first meeting anyway."

I too stood up, and went and stood in front of my mum. On an impulse, I reached for and took her hands in mine. My eyes were steady as they bored into hers. And there might have been a steely edge to my voice.

"So mum, what are you really saying to me?"

"That you have to let her go, my son."

"Because of her dad?" I asked.

"Because of her dad," she echoed. "Yes."

"Would it make any difference to you if I told you that Mr. Jideofo might very well be innocent of any crime?"

"How would you know?" she asked me. "Is that what *she* told you?"

I saw no point in pursuing that line, and changed my tactic. I led her gently back to the sofa on which we had been sitting.

"Are you telling me, mum, that if her dad had been a regular okay dad, you would have had no problem with anything?"

"I think I can say, yes."

"And if I proposed to her, and she accepted, you'd have given your blessing?"

"You're full of questions today, Bola. But, yes, I probably would have."

"So, it would have been okay for her to accept *me*, when I don't even know who my father is. At least *she* has a father. *Where* is my father? *Who* is he? What about what the Bible says: that we should remove the beam in our own eyes, before trying to remove the mote in Chizube's eyes?"

Cool as a cucumber, my mum replied: "That's a question only *she* can answer. I don't fight other people's battles."

"One of these days, mum, you're going to reveal who this man is, or was, who bore me. All you've ever told me is that he abandoned you even before I was born, and you think he might be long dead. You tell me that, among the Yoruba, it is all right for a child to take the mother's family name. But that's not good enough for me."

"Bola, please –"

"No, mum! Let me finish what I'm saying. This is exactly my moment of truth, mum; the crisis point in my life. Mum, I love you, and always will, no matter what. But I have come to my crossroads. I must now really begin to make the decisions that are important in my life."

I stopped because I needed to. Somehow, I had to marshal my thoughts carefully in order to avoid a headlong rush into saying things I might later regret – if I had not already overstepped the mark! I knew what I owed my mum: in a word, my life! And every important step I had ever taken! Including my being a student in one of the most prestigious universities – an Ivy-League college – in America! The gravity of the moment also affected my mum, because she sat quite still, staring at me as if mesmerized. I cleared my throat.

"I'm very thankful to God that you're my mum. Where would I be today if not for you? But in this matter of where I go with my life, and who I have by my side, the decision *has* to be mine. I intend to propose to Chizube the first chance I get to do so, her father's past notwithstanding. My prayer is that, in time, you will be happy for me; for us."

I leaned across and kissed her on the cheek, and she raised tear-stained eyes to mine. Gently, I wiped the tears away with my fingers, before I got up. She did not attempt to stop me. Instead, she folded her arms across her breasts, and continued sobbing.

"Mum, I love you. We'll talk again about all this."

I was half-way to the entrance door when her voice stopped me.

"Bola, you forgot about the food."

My first, rather irreverent, thought was to say, in Igbo, *"Nni gbakw'oku!"* food being, at that moment, the least of my problems. But I remembered what she said, that she had prepared *egusi* soup for me, the way I most liked it, with dried fish. So I held back that first, irreverent, disrespectful wish that fire should engulf and burn the food to cinders, for all I cared.

"I did forget," I said. "And I wouldn't have forgiven myself if I had left without it."

"Neither would your friend, Kojo," my mum found the voice to remind me.

I struck a happy compromise with her, and took all of the soup with me, in a take-away container, when I left.

Chapter XVIII

FOR THE MOST important day of my life – other than the day my mother bore me, and I took my first breath as a viable, vibrant baby – I wore probably my most casual outfit. I did not do this in a pretended show of nonchalance, as if the day was like any other day in my life. To be sure, the weather started out more clement than the weatherman had forecast. But I feared it would sour later in the day, because the New York area meteorologists were, in my admittedly limited experience, correct in their forecasts nine times out of ten. I armed myself with a pullover, just in case.

No, I wore my casuals because that was how Chizube most liked to see me. She never, to my recollection, told me so in so many words. Even when she said, as she did now and again, "You look good", she did so without any direct reference to the clothes I wore. She was not very free with her compliments. But I had observed, over the many months of loving her, how her eyes light up, whenever I showed up for our outings in my simple *danshiki*, or other type of short jumper, worn over a polo shirt and a pair of gabardine or other cotton trousers. Besides, her room-mate and friend, Nnennaya, once told me, in strict confidence, that the two of them had talked about it several times. Nnenna, as I always called her, was a true friend, who took uncomplicated, unalloyed delight in Chizube and me.

I told my band of brothers what I had in mind, and the day I would do it. I had to, because I just could not seem to take any important step without letting them in on it. It was, I suppose, a mutual thing; else we were a hollow band of brothers. Happily, neither Kojo nor Cletus strongly demurred, except that Cletus would have delayed the step another two or three months.

"Till after your finals, man," he said. "For your BS."

"BS?" I asked.

"You know what I mean," he said, laughing.

They both had their say as to my choice of a ring, with Kojo, more a man of the world than Cletus, having the weightier voice. They went with me from store to store, till my limbs ached and my spirit was weary. It took a while to find what I sought because, if truth be told, I was seeking the best bargain that my slimmer-than-slim purse could afford. I was not about to go to my mum, cap in hand, seeking help. She would, probably with good reason, have enjoyed my embarrassment.

"That's another reason to delay this thing till summer," Cletus persisted. "You could earn a few dollars with which to buy something better."

Kojo disagreed. "This is the best time of all," he said, "now in your full glory as a cash-strapped student. The Quarter-miler – okay, Chizube – will find it so much more romantic than if you came to her with a pocketful of jingling coins and jewelry. Trust me."

I trusted him; trusted him also in his advice that I take the plunge with Chizube. I took the ring he finally picked out, a quite simple affair whose value – romantic or otherwise – far outstripped the number of its karat. At least, I hoped Chizube would see it my way: that we did not need the ring's karat measure to appreciate, and rejoice in, the pristine and immaculate purity of our mutual love.

*   *   *

The good weather held; one of the very few times I had known the weathermen to fail to deliver. Nnenna knew my designs on Chizube for that day; Sue, their oriental roommate, did not. At least I had sworn Nnenna to secrecy on the matter, though she was somewhat of a chatterbox, and might have blabbed. They were both watching a tape-recording of an NCAA Track and Field meet, televised a week earlier. In the meet, Chizube had, once again, finished a close runner-up to Julia Henshaw, her old nemesis in the quarter mile.

When Sue let me into their apartment, Chizube was in the bedroom, doing some ironing. I joined her there, at her invitation which she shouted through her partially open door.

"Come right in! It's tidy enough!"

The bedroom was surprisingly large; large enough to accommodate three single beds, with their bedside tables. On each bedside table were a shaded lamp, and an assortment of books. A door in the far right corner as one entered the room opened into the bathroom.

"Why aren't you watching the videotape with Nnenna – ?" I asked as I took her in my arms, and kissed her. But I knew what her answer would be before she spoke it.

"You know I usually don't," she said, sweetly smiling her welcome that needed no words. "I have no desire to see myself on TV."

"It might help you learn what you're doing wrong."

"You're referring to Julia of course."

"Of course," I said.

"Well, I don't think so. But I know this: one of these days, I'll beat her. But it won't be from studying the tape of our races. The coach and I have done that – how many times? Julia just has, for now, more explosive endurance than I have. It's not anything I'm doing wrong."

"For me, as you know, you never do anything wrong."

"I know – ." She smiled from ear to ear.

"Except –"

"Aha!" she said, putting her iron back on its stand. "Like what – ?"

"Well, you know, I've asked you recently – two or three times – to come with me for another visit to my mum, and you turned me down."

Slowly, Chizube picked up her iron. "Bola, you know your mum isn't exactly – how shall I say it – ?"

"Don't say it, please. All the more reason, it seemed to me, another visit or two – you know – might change things."

She stopped ironing altogether. Pursing her lips, she stared at me for a long moment, in silence. Then she shook her head, sadly.

"Bola, it won't do any good. In fact, exactly the reverse might happen. I think it best for me to give your mum her space. Come, let's go join Sue and Nnennaya. I've done enough ironing for the day."

I waited as she put away the pile of ironed blouses, skirts and pants, and kicked the basket of un-ironed things to one corner of the room. Then she led the way back to the sitting room. I hesitated just long enough to dip my hand into a pocket of my *danshiki,* to caress the small, velvet-covered case, containing the ring. Reassured, I held my head high, and walked with resolute steps after Chizube.

Sue and Nnennaya were setting the dining table when we walked into the sitting room. And they were setting it for two, which surprised Chizube.

"What's going on here?" she asked. "You've already eaten, or what?"

"What!" said Sue, in some kind of an answer to the question.

"Is this the first time we've set the table for two?" asked Nnennaya, looking at me with the faintest wink I ever saw.

"I know it isn't," said Chizube.

"And we do it for *him,* not for you," said Sue.

"Of course," said Chizube, all smiles.

"So relax and enjoy it when we do," said Nnennaya, pulling Sue away from the dining area. "Come, Sue. We'll be late."

"Where're you going?" asked Chizube.

"None of your beez," said Nnennaya. "But if you really want to know, we're off to a movie. Don't blame us you're not going with us." She paused for a nanosecond, and then pointed at me. "Blame him. When *he* comes, you need your space."

I had little or no time to react to all of this before the door of the apartment shut behind Sue and Nnennaya. And I found myself wondering about Sue. She had behaved as if she was in on my plans, which made me think that perhaps

I had not *specifically* asked Nnennaya not to share my secret with Sue. Sue was probably as good a friend to Chizube as Nnennaya was. But I just had not learnt to look at both girls with quite the same level of relaxed comfort – for perhaps a rather obvious and not particularly ennobling reason.

Chizube came to me, and took and put my arms around her. I kissed her a second time; this time, a long lingering kiss – which was something I had learnt to do through the many months of loving her; something I had not really done with any of my previous girl-friends.

"I hope you'll like the spinach and *okro* soup I prepared for us," said Chizube into my ear, as we still held on tightly.

My moment was on me before I quite realized it was close. The truth was that I had formulated no particular plan as to the timing, and the place, for what I wanted to do. I had not envisaged the scenario that developed: Nnennaya and Sue taking themselves out of the apartment, without – as had become somewhat customary with us – even sharing a meal. I could, I supposed, have done my thing when I was alone with Chizube in the privacy of the bedroom. But no part of my brain supplied the spark, the impulse I needed to drive me to that act, at that moment.

I did not go down on my knees. I have nothing against the culture – principally, I suppose, Western – that would require that I genuflect to my girl in popping the question. I take, or copy, what I need from cultures alien to my own. But I draw the line at genuflecting; this, notwithstanding that the Yoruba, my mother's people, are customarily given to extravagant gestures of obeisance. The other half of me – my father's – must be Igbo. At any rate, I grew up among them, and was formed by my long closeness with them. Among the Igbo, really the only genuflection that matters, in my particular context, is traditionally done by the girl. When she ceremoniously carries the cup of wine from her father to the man who seeks her hand in marriage, she bends her knee, sips the wine, and then gives the cup to him.

I crossed myself, without visibly doing so, and said a quick, silent prayer. Then I held Chizube at arm's length, and looked deeply into her eyes.

"The soup," I said solemnly, "can wait. But *this*, cannot."

"What – ?"

She did not complete her question. She did not need to. In a flash, I put my hand into the side pocket of my *danshiki,* and produced the small, but precious velvet box, and theatrically waved it in front of her. Her mouth dropped open, her eyes dilated, and her face shone with surpassing radiance.

I let go of her, and took one step back. I opened the box, and calmly took out the ring. And then I popped my question in the time-honored words.

"Chizube, will you marry me?"

I held my breath for what seemed an eternity, but might have been only one or two seconds. Chizube was looking at me with eyes that held mine, at once magisterially and tenderly. And I saw her answer in those orbs a split second before she joyfully walked into my arms, and whispered it into my ear.

"I will," she said, "but what about your mum?"

"I'm afraid I can't marry her."

Chizube hit me across my chest and shoulder. "I'm serious, Bola. She might not approve."

"Does she need to, before I can marry my girl?"

"Did you tell her you were going to do this?" she asked, the smile gone from her face.

The telephone rang, giving me a temporary relief, and some time to think about my answer. Chizube picked up the phone from the low center table, identified herself, and then listened for a moment or two.

"Dad, can you hold on one moment?" Chizube covered the mouthpiece with one hand, and turned to me with pleading eyes. "Bola, can you hold this phone for a second? I have to take this call from the bedroom extension. Don't hang up until I shout to tell you to. Please, it's important."

"Can I at least say hello to your dad?"

"Good heavens, Bola, no! Whatever you do, don't say a word. Please!"

She rushed to the bedroom and, a second later, shouted to me to hang up. I dutifully obeyed, and sat down and waited. My mind was in a state of flux, hopping from one thought to another.

I heard Chizube's shout, and quickly came out of my brown study. But before I could so much as get up from my chair, Chizube burst into the living room.

"That was dad."

"I know –"

"Best piece of news he's had in a long, long time," Chizube went on, her voice breaking, "my poor, dear dad."

"You just said it's good news."

"You don't understand," she said, breaking down completely, as tears welled up in her eyes.

I led her gently to the love seat, and made her sit down by me.

"What's this great news that's making you cry?"

She dabbed at her eyes with soft tissue paper which she pulled out of a containing box on the low table. She took her time, evidently to compose herself, before she could trust herself to speak.

"Things are beginning to fall into place for poor dad," she said, her voice still tremulous with emotion. She looked into my eyes, and added: "I don't even know how to begin to tell you about it. It's just – you know – huge."

"I don't understand," I said. "How can news that's good for your dad be difficult to share with me? A minute ago, you made me the happiest man in the world. That means only one thing –"

I stopped because of the way she was staring at me. Her eyes were blank. I was not even sure they were focused on me. Soon, as I watched her, tears began to flow from her eyes. Her mouth was all aquiver, as if she was struggling to say something. But no words came.

"Okay, girl," I said soothingly, "let's take this slowly. My first guess is that this good news has nothing to do with him finding a better job than the one he has in the accounting firm – what's the name?"

Chizube found her voice, and a faint smile. "*Onyeama and Ani*? No, it hasn't."

"Then it must be something to do with his status in the country – you know what I mean – the Green card and that sort of stuff?"

Chizube threw her head forward so it came to rest in the cup of her hands, on her lap. Her whole body trembled with the powerful emotions that overwhelmed her. So I decided to press her no further. Instead I made her sit upright, and encircled her with my arms, and held her close. We stayed like that for perhaps a minute or two, her head resting on my chest, her tears now uncontrolled and flowing freely down her cheeks.

At length, her quivering abated, and then stopped. I pulled some more tissue paper out of the box, and wiped her tears away. Slowly, she raised her head and looked at me with eyes of surpassing tenderness. Her voice, when she spoke, was steady.

"I love you, Bola. And you're right about sharing news that's just absolutely wonderful. This must be one of the happiest days for my dad. For mum too, and me. You just proposed to me, didn't you?"

"And you accepted, remember?"

"I did, didn't I?" The smile on her face now went from ear to ear; a smile of pure contentment. "But, about the good news. You remember the letter I've mentioned to you – you know – a few times?"

"About a hundred times, actually. Yes, of course, I remember. That's the one his friend –"

"Mr. Bernard Ekwekwe was no friend of dad's."

"Of course," I quickly agreed. "But what happened to the letter?"

"As we speak, dad has that letter in his possession!"

"No!"

"Oh, yes he has! Can you believe it?"

"How did he – I mean, who gave it to him?"

"You won't believe this," she said. "The letter was found by Mrs. Joy Udozo."

"Joy Udozo," I mused. "That's the wife of –"

"Obi Udozo. That's the friend to whom Mr. Ekwekwe wrote the letter."

"The same letter both denied ever existed, right?"

"Yes, and as a result, sent my poor dad to prison, for a crime he never committed. Can you believe it?"

"There's a God in heaven, after all," I said. "That's all I can say. But what happened? How did the letter finally resurface? Did Obi Udozo suddenly become a born-again Christian, and confessed – ?"

"Mr. Udozo died several years ago. Cancer, or something. I must have told you about it –"

"If you did, I forgot. So, how did his wife find the letter?"

"That's what I'd like to know," Chizube said. "Dad didn't want to tell me over the phone, and asked if I can come right away."

"So what's keeping you?"

"You!" said Chizube, smiling. "What a day it's been! What are the odds that on the same day you propose to me, my dad gets hold of the letter that has given him nightmares for – I don't know how many years?"

"Your entire lifetime, actually," I suggested.

"That's absolutely correct – my entire lifetime. That's nineteen years. Nineteen long years! And dad has suffered and agonized, over that letter, every slow hour – what am I saying – *every slow minute*, of those nineteen years. I don't know what happened, but now I know miracles still happen."

"Is it okay for me to come with you to see your parents?" I asked. "You must have told your dad on the phone that I am here, visiting."

"I did."

"Did you tell him – ?"

"You think I'm crazy?" she asked, looking at me with wild, very crazy, eyes.

"Meaning, you didn't. But still I can come with you, I hope."

She looked at me for a long moment, thoughtfully. I could tell she was struggling with herself, and let her take her time. At length, she nodded once, twice, then smiled and said: "Why not? I suppose it'll do no harm. And we might even consider whether to tell them about us."

"Okay!" I said, getting up. "Let's go."

Chizube pulled me back down into my seat beside her. "Not so fast, buddy boy," she said. "You haven't answered my question."

"What question? I thought I was the one asking the questions."

"You've forgotten? But we're going nowhere, you and me, until you answer the question. I asked you, Bola, if you told your mum about what you just did."

Truthfully, I had not forgotten; I only hoped that *she* had. The telephone call from her dad, at the very moment she had asked the question, had – as it turned out – evidently not saved me from fashioning some kind of an answer. Worse, it had not given me even the luxury of the time to *think* about my answer. The startling news from her dad had been so momentous, I think I can be forgiven for hoping it would have wiped all else from her thoughts.

"Did you?" Chizube persisted.

"It really depends on how you look at it –"

"Meaning – ?"

"Meaning that she knew I would."

"I see," said Chizube. "You just didn't tell her it's today you were going to propose – ?"

"You could put it that way, I suppose."

"And what did she say?"

"Does it matter what she said? Sorry, I take that back. It does matter what she said. She said to wait; that you and me, we're still too young to know what we're getting ourselves into."

That was a bare-faced lie. But I had little or no choice in the matter. I could not sit there, side by side with the girl who had become my world, and tell her the bitter truth: that my mum knew about her dad's imprisonment, and did not approve of her son marrying the daughter of a convicted felon. I was well aware that Chizube herself already had a sense that my mum did not approve, and probably thought the Igbo-Yoruba dichotomy might be the reason. If, eventually, the truth should come out, there would be time enough to think up a hundred and one explanations. This was definitely a bridge I would rather not cross till I got to it.

"Do you think we are?"

"What?" I asked.

"Too young – you know – what your mum said."

"Do *you* think we are?"

"That's not fair, Bola. *I* asked you first. Are we?"

I pondered the question for the briefest moment, and said: "Perhaps we are. But it isn't as if we're thinking of getting married tomorrow."

"I sure hope not. And there's another thing. I take back what I said about our telling my parents –"

"I agree," I said. "That would have been crazy. I know our people well enough to know that's no way to go about something like this. When the time comes to ask your dad for your hand in marriage, it's got to be done nice and proper."

Which set me wondering how, in the world, I was ever going to do what needed to be done, *nice and proper!* Ideally, my father, were he around, would be the leader of my delegation to Chizube's parents' home. But I did not know my father. Therefore I did not know his relatives, or even his town or village in Nigeria. For all I knew, there might well be hordes of his relatives somewhere or the other in these United States. For my purpose, any adult male relative of my dad's could have substituted for him. Just about the only thing I had was this gut feeling that my dad must be Igbo.

"You're day-dreaming, Bola? Let's go."

I snapped out of my reverie, thankful that we still had a long way to go before I would need my father for this most important venture into the Jideofo family.

*   *   *

END OF BOOK II

BOOK III

CYRIL JIDEOFO'S AGONY

Chapter XIX

EDITH BREEZED INTO the office of the Senior Partner, Chikezie Onyeama, as if the office door was merely a decorative fixture.

"You didn't knock," Okechukwu Ani, the Junior Partner, observed with a smile.

"She hardly ever does," said Mr. Onyeama, "unless she wants to ask a favor."

"Why even bother to waste your breath?" I asked. "It's like ranting and raving at the leopard. That's in fact all you can do: rant and rave. The leopard doesn't give a damn."

"Isn't that also why she's called – what's that name – *Akwaa-okwulu?*" asked Mr. Onyeama.

The object of our collective reproach stood, arms folded across her heaving chest, a tired, tolerant smile on her lips, her expression, one of total resignation. It was a familiar scene to her. And to us. I knew, as did my two senior partners, that Edith was the cog on which the wheels of the office turned. She knew it; knew, too, that she had the freedom of the entire office. We had all grown accustomed to her ways, accustomed to her manner of breezing into any one of our offices, quite often without knocking on the door. She usually did this when she had a message of some importance for us. And she had learnt to accept our good-natured ribbing for what it was: a gentle tease.

Edith looked pointedly at me. "There's a phone call for you, Sir."

Edith seldom wasted her use of the word, sir. She almost always used that form of address as a hint to us that she was in no mood to counter our playful tease with hers. Over the years, I had developed a healthy respect for her dark, brooding melancholy, whenever that humor was on her because, though the partners only teased, her riposte tended to be sharp.

Oh, yes, I was now a partner in the accounting firm of *ONYEAMA AND ANI, CPAs*. Chikezie Onyeama and Okechukwu Ani conferred that honor on me, though I was not a Certified Public Accountant, and had little or no hope of ever getting my CPA. On account, of course, of my status as a convicted felon, who had done time! It was their way of telling me that they shared my sense of the colossal injustice done to me, and that my work for the firm was sterling.

I was happy with my work at the firm. My promotion to a partner in late October 1997, the fifth anniversary of my assumption of duties, was the crowning moment of my working life. My family life was serene and happy. Chizube had grown up into a very fine young lady. She was a loving daughter too, an honor student in Rutgers University and, to boot, an athlete with Olympic potential, though I say it who perhaps shouldn't. Ndubisi, her brother, though on occasion given to a little wildness – it was not for nothing that she named him *the little devil* – was nevertheless a good, loving child. Their mother, my wife Rosemary was, quite simply, my life.

But there was always that Red Sea in my life that I could never quite ford: the fact and reality that I was a convicted felon. Lacking a Moses to strike that sea and part it, so I could walk through it on dry land, I lived my life, in my most private moments, like *a man shut out*. My only hope had been Obi Udozo; and the hope was that in the last several weeks and months of his terminal disease, he would produce *the letter*.

"Where?" I asked Edith. "And who's on the line?"

"In your office of course. From Joy."

At that point in my life, a phone call from Joy – that is, Joy Udozo – was one of the things I seemed to live for. I think I mean that literally. Ever since her husband, Obi, passed away about six years earlier, in February 1994, I had kept in touch with her and her children. And like a despairing swimmer, buffeted by a stormy sea, I had clung to the hope, day after day after day, that sooner or later, she would throw me a lifeline.

Obi spoke to me about the letter, lying in his hospital bed, in the Robert Wood Johnson Hospital, in downtown New Brunswick. He might have experienced an epiphany. Or, he was just deeply grateful for the role Rosemary and I had played when his wife Joy rather unexpectedly went into labor, and gave birth to their fourth child and second daughter, Chioma, in May 1993. That was ten long years after their third child! Not quite two weeks after Chioma's birth, Obi had written a touching letter to me from Nigeria, where he had gone on some sort of a business trip. I was also moved by the fact that he had written that thank-you letter so soon after the birth of the child.

Rosemary and I were regular visitors to his hospital bed. A relationship had developed between our two families: a relationship that was at once cordial and – for me, especially – awkward. I never could get over the feeling, whenever I stood by Obi's bedside, that he had the key that could spring the lock that would liberate me from my manacles; and that would bring glorious summer to my seemingly unending winter of discontent.

On one such visit – I remember that his condition was visibly deteriorating, and even he knew it – he took my hand and squeezed it harder than he was wont, in his feeble condition, to do. I was alone with him in his half of the room. Our eyes met, and held, for a long moment.

"Cyril," he said, "you must not think I've forgotten –"

"About what?" I asked, as he paused.

"Well, you know, about the promise I made to you in my letter, that we'll talk."

"What letter?" I asked, though I had a pretty good idea to what letter he referred.

"You know the letter I'm talking about. The one I wrote to you from Nigeria soon after Chioma was born."

"Oh, that one."

"I'm sorry to raise the matter now, lying like this in a hospital bed. But I must, because time is – who knows – running –"

"Don't say it," I said. "We must hope for the best, as long as there is a God in heaven."

"I'm not really afraid to return to Him, when He calls," said Obi, smiling faintly, and struggling to raise his body to a less recumbent position.

The effort evidently sapped his strength, and he went into a fit of coughing. When he quieted down, he motioned to me to come closer still.

"Cyril," he said softly, "I don't know why you are so good to me and Joy. After what I did to you, so many years ago, you have every reason to hate me."

He stopped for a moment or two, to take a sip of water from the cup that was always ready to hand, and to recover his strength. "I'm glad neither Joy nor Rosemary is here, because it is much easier for us to talk, just you and me. I never wanted to admit it to myself, but I realize now that for the past what – ten, twelve years – it has been a living hell for me. Look at me now, Cyril. I know this is God's punishment for all the wrong I've done to people, but especially to you. You know when I first thought about this?"

Obi paused again, looking steadily at me with eyes which seemed to be pleading for my understanding, or perhaps compassion. It was quite a moment; for him, as for me. I was hanging on every word he spoke, scarcely daring to breathe.

"You know about my first son, Uzoma? He was born in – let me see – in May 1980, a few months after you were – that is – what I'm trying to say –"

"Soon after I was sent to prison," I somehow found the strength to say.

"Soon after, yes. Uzoma was my first son. But God took him from us one day, suddenly. He was not sick, or anything like that. They said it was sudden-infant-death syndrome. Joy believed what the doctors said. Me, I had an idea that it was because of what I did to you."

"You shouldn't say things like that, you know," I said gently.

"Things like what?"

A fit of coughing seized him again, rocking his feeble frame so violently I feared he might pass out. But he did not and, gradually, he calmed down. He took another sip of water.

"I'm talking too much," he said. "That's why I'm coughing so much."

"You must take it easy," I urged.

"I can't. Do you hear what I'm saying, Cyril? I can't. I don't know how long this feeble attempt to hang on to life will last. Don't our people say that it is when we are desperately looking for the kitchen knife that we remember what we ate the previous night? I'm ashamed to confess that now I am pleading for God's forgiveness, and yours too, I remember all too clearly the great wrong I did to you."

He sipped some water, cleared his throat, and went on. "Cyril, you know, and I know, that I lied like sin when I told the court officials that Bernard Ekwekwe didn't write that letter that unfairly implicated you in his drug business. From that day to this, I've lived with the knowledge that my lie – that one horrific lie I told – sent you to prison for eight miserable years."

"But why – ?"

"Cyril, please let me finish what I'm telling you. Do you know what I did, Cyril? I mean, to Bernard's letter. I hid it. But that's not the worst part. I hid the darned letter so well I could not afterwards find it –"

"What!" I screamed. At least, it would have been a scream, had I not remembered, in the nick of time, where I was. I remembered too that Obi shared the room with a very old and very ill patient, who seemed in worse shape than himself, and had, for the past half-hour, been drifting in and out of sleep.

"Can't find it," said Obi, looking more crestfallen than I had hitherto seen him. "Joy and me, we searched high and low, but no luck. I was not looking for the letter because I was thinking of anybody but myself. I feared that if I revealed the truth, I would myself be in trouble with the law. I think I needed to find the letter only in order to be in some sort of control over the situation."

"What are you telling me, Obi?" I asked evenly, scarcely believing I could be in so much control over my feelings.

"What I'm telling you, Cyril, is that that letter is somewhere among my things. I'm as sure of that, as I am that I'm still alive and breathing. God has never let me forget what I did. I hid the letter from you and from the law, thinking how clever I was. But I should have remembered what we say, that when a man eats rats in the darkness of the night, though human eyes may not see him, the spirits do."

I slumped in my chair, by the bedside of my dying friend, and unashamedly wept tears, not for him, but for my miserable self. I wept because I could not cope with the thoughts that overwhelmed my mind at that moment. I could not believe that my destiny would bring me this close to what might have been the final, positive, solution to my misery and wretchedness, only to leave me groping in the dark. I covered my face so Obi would not see my tears.

"I'm sorry, Cyril. I'm really sorry. There's no way I can make this up to you, unless the letter is found. With my last breath, I'll be praying to God that Joy will find it one day. After all that has happened, I don't know that it'll do much good –"

"I need that letter," I said, "like I never needed anything in my life. Are you saying that you – I mean, that Joy is still looking for it?"

"Since I came back from Nigeria, I've kept her at it. And she's promised me she'll keep an eye out for it. Cyril," he said, reaching for my hand, and somehow lifting himself from off his pillows, "I ask for your forgiveness. I don't deserve it, but if it's humanly possible –"

He left the sentence hanging, and fell back wearily on to his pillows. I looked at his emaciated frame, and my heart totally went out to him.

"If you forgive me, Cyril, perhaps God, in His infinite mercies, will too. If you don't –"

"Obi, I forgive you," I heard myself say.

"You mean that?"

"How could I not forgive you. Somehow, by telling me all you've told me, you've lightened my burden. I'm deeply touched that you were willing to tell me everything. I leave the rest to God."

Obi again reached for my hand. "There's one last thing. I saw Bernard at home."

"You did?"

"Just once. In fact, he came to me, when I had given up all hope of ever seeing him –"

"In all these years," I heard myself ask, "you only ever saw him once?"

"Just once, this last visit home. He said he heard through some friends that Joy gave birth to our second girl. Who those friends were, I had no idea, and I didn't ask him."

With difficulty, I kept a tight rein on my feelings, conscious of the fact that I stood in the shadow of death, by the bedside of a repentant and dying friend.

"I only know this, and he told me so himself. Bernard has found a way to come back to the United States on – he said – two visits. He apologized for not making any contact with me; told me it wouldn't have been in my interest if he had contacted me!"

"A sudden attack of guilty conscience?" I asked. "Or just making sure no one would identify him?"

"Don't know, and didn't ask him."

"Bernard came back here?" I asked rhetorically. "But surely, that's impossible."

"He looked quite different this time," said Obi. "Not the same baby-faced Bernard you and I had known. He wears a monstrous mustache and a full beard. I'm not sure if a plastic surgeon worked some changes in his face, but I had to look really hard at him to recognize the Bernard of old. I have no doubt he uses a false name and passport. He was not eager, he told me, to contact old friends and acquaintances abroad, or even at home. Can you believe this, Cyril?"

That was a good question. I reached for a chair, drew it nearer me, and slumped into it. Did I believe any of this? After only a momentary hesitation, I decided that indeed I believed that Bernard could be so bold as to come back into a United States of America that had deported him, with a one-way-only ticket, to Nigeria. Bernard was one of the most fearless human beings I had ever known. No, he was absolutely the most fearless!

Nothing ever seemed to faze him. Not even the certainty that if the U.S. authorities caught up with him, he would be thrown into prison so fast he would not know what hit him. And the eight years I suffered needlessly, on his account, would be like nothing compared to what he would get. Especially if he was up to his old nefarious activities!

Bernard in the United States! I thought about it some more, and then it hit me. If indeed it was true, that was surely one more proof that there really is a God in heaven. A criminal was returning to the scene of his crime! Bernard, sooner or later, would make the slip that would doom him. The more I thought about that inevitability, God being God – the all-merciful and the ultimate dispenser of justice – that chink of light that I never thought to see at the end of my long – very long – dark tunnel of frustrated hope, shone so brightly it came near to blinding me. And as I sat by my dying friend's bedside, I silently prayed that God would spare me long enough to witness Bernard's discomfiture, when his unbelievable luck would have finally run out.

"Cyril," said Obi, reaching for my hand one more time, "I think I know what you're thinking."

"You do?"

"And, if I'm right, I cannot blame you."

"But, Obi, I'm not –"

"Cyril, please don't even try to deny your true feelings. I do not know what is happening to me but, lying here in my darkest hour, and in despair about my own life, I think I see more clearly what I never before bothered about: life, and what is, or is not, important."

"What are you saying?"

"Simply this, Cyril. Leave vengeance to God."

I withdrew my hand from his grasp determinedly, but as gently as I could manage in the circumstances.

"Obi, you don't know what you're –"

"Of course I do, Cyril. It is hard, I know –"

"Very hard," I said. "What you're asking of me is something I don't think I can do, as God is my witness."

"Which God is your witness?" Obi asked, feebly shaking his head from side to side. "Cyril, Cyril, you invoke the Lord's name, but it seems it is only to ask Him to harden your heart."

"If it sounds like that, I'm sorry," I said. "But I'm only human, Obi. I don't think I can ever find it in my heart to forgive Bernard for what he did to me."

Obi looked at me with eyes which seemed to have sunken further into their depths than ever before. He stared so hard and so long at me, his head and body motionless, that after a while I thought that life had drained out of him. Then suddenly he struggled to raise his head. But his strength failed him, and he let it fall back on his pillow. He then heaved a long sigh of exhaustion and despair.

That was the last time I saw Obi Udozo alive. Two days later, he died, mercifully, in his wife, Joy's arms.

Chapter XX

I MADE MY excuses to my partners, and was following Edith out of the Senior Partner's office, when Okechukwu Ani's voice called me back.

"You won't forget to call your friend, will you?" he asked. "We must make sure we land his client's retainer. We can use the fee."

"Are you telling me" I asked, and added, smiling, "but I hope you don't mind if I take Joy's call first."

He laughed, and waved me out of the office. He could laugh because it had been a good day for the firm. Thanks to an old friend of mine, Attorney Cornelius Okwu, we were about to secure the retainer of a significant African-American company that had fairly extensive businesses with three State governments in Nigeria.

"Are you coming, or not?" Edith called out to me impatiently. "Joy can't wait for ever."

I hurried after her, into my office. This was the office I had shared with Okey Ani. Now I had it entirely to myself. Just under two years after my promotion to Partner, in mid-September 1999, the firm acquired additional office space. Our office neighbor, a thriving Hispanic attorney, had himself been looking for additional space and, finding none in our office complex, decided to relocate. Okey Ani moved into the new office, which was marginally larger than the one we had shared. There was already a connecting door, always of course shut and locked, between the Hispanic attorney's office and our Senior Partner, Mr. Onyeama's office. The resultant set-up was that Mr. Onyeama had Mr. Ani's office to his left, and my office to his right, as he sat at his huge mahogany desk, now repositioned to face the entrance door.

I shut the connecting door to Mr. Onyeama's office and picked up my phone. "Hello, Joy," I spoke into the phone. "This is Cyril."

"Hello, Cyril." Joy's voice sounded buoyant. "How are you? And, Rosemary! Hope she's fine?"

"We're all fine. How are you yourself? We've not spoken for a long time. What's up?"

"What's up, Cyril, is that God has finally heard our prayer," she announced dramatically. "I can't –"

"What happened?"

"It's the letter we've been searching for –"

"You found it?" I screamed, unmindful of the continued presence, in my office, of Edith, who stood by the connecting door of our two offices, and was staring at me with a quizzical look. "For God's sake, Joy, did you find it?"

"Yes, yes, Cyril, I did. Can you believe it? I have it in my hands as I speak –"

"Joy, please stay where you are," I shouted into the mouthpiece. "I'm leaving the office right now, and I'll head your way. I take it you're at home? Good! So help me God, I'll be there within the hour, max."

I hung up, and turned and saw my two partners standing together by the connecting door between my office and Mr. Onyeama's. They both wore expressions of concern as they stared at me.

"Is everything okay?" Okey Ani asked.

"We could hear you through the closed door," said Mr. Onyeama. "What's up?"

For a moment or two, I stood as if transfixed, looking from one partner to the other, unable to answer their questions because, in my state of such unutterable excitement as I had seldom experienced before, I could not think straight.

"I'll tell you when I get back," I mumbled, and rushed out.

I was in my car, in the parking lot, and had turned the key in the ignition before it dawned on me that I had not so much as asked their leave, or told them where I was going. I took consolation, however, in the certainty that Edith would tell them what she had overheard of my conversation with Joy. I was about half-way to Princeton before it occurred to me that I should have called Rosemary to at least alert her about this sudden, and most welcome, development. A thousand thoughts crowded my disordered mind.

What a story it would be if – or rather, when – I finally got Bernard's letter in my hands! The only clear thought I could manage, in the confusion of my mind, was that God is a benevolent and merciful God, omnipotent and omniscient. I pinched myself once or twice, as I drove, just to satisfy myself that I was not in some dream land, or in a trance, from which I might wake up at any moment to the stark reality of that utterly lonely world of a never-ending shame in which I was stranded. And which I could not share with anyone, not even Rosemary!

I turned right into Huntley Avenue, off Route 27, in the heart of Princeton, at a junction dominated by an old and magnificent Roman Catholic Cathedral. Princeton is an old university town that has rather more than its share of the kind of noise and bustle usually associated with inner cities. I drove down Huntley Avenue for about a mile, to the apartment complex where Joy Udozo lived with her three children and her mother, *Amalachukwu*. Actually there were only two children now: her seventeen-year old son, Ndukaku, still in high school, and her seven-year old daughter, who was born on the day, in 1993, that I found, and reestablished contact with Joy. Joy's daughter, Uchenna, about twenty-one years old, was a junior in Georgian Court College, in Lakewood, NJ.

I parked my new 2000 Honda Accord in the first free parking space that presented itself. I remembered to lock my car, and secure the steering wheel with a club. Princeton might be a cut above other cities, being the seat of an Ivy-League university. But the crazies that steal cars have scant respect for universities, however prestigious.

I took the steps two at a time, thankful that there were only two fights of stairs to Joy's apartment, in a four-storied building. Joy opened the entrance door before I could knock, having obviously watched my arrival from the window of her apartment overlooking the parking lot. The envelope she clutched in her right hand was the white envelope that had burned itself into my memory from the day, in 1980, that I had taken it out of the black sac that Obi Udozo had handed to me.

Joy ran into my arms, which was a bit of a surprise, and hugged me with the warmth reserved for an old friend one had not seen in some time. Then wordlessly, she stepped back and away from our embrace, and placed the white envelope in my hand. It was then that I realized that my hand was shaking, on account, no doubt, of the extraordinariness of the moment. I closed my trembling fingers over the envelope, and carried it to my chest, and held it there for a long moment. Then, holding the envelope away from my chest, I stared at it fixedly. I had lost all sense of time and place.

Then the memories came flooding back. Twenty years had passed since the cataclysmic sequence of events began, that ultimately landed me in a prison to which I most assuredly did not belong, either under the laws of God, or of man. But now, holding Bernard's letter in my hand, I relived every minute of that sequence.

In my near state of trance, I could vividly see Obi Udozo reach out his hand to give me the black sac and the white envelope, as we stood in the living room of my cousin, Dr. Aloysius Jideofo's home in Bound Brook, NJ. I recalled Obi's words as he handed me the envelope. "It's from your friend, Bernard. The letter is mine, but you should read it." I remembered that Obi was extremely nervous about the sac and the letter, with my cousin's wife, Obiamaka, hovering around us. He had not expected her to be home when he came. I more fully understood the cause of that nervousness when I opened and read Bernard's letter. Twenty long years ago!

Joy's voice brought me out of my trance. "Cyril, are you all right?"

"I am, thank you," I said. "I suppose I can scarcely believe that any of this is actually happening. God! I've waited and prayed for this, for twenty years. Now I have the letter in my hands, and it doesn't seem real."

"Cyril, I'm really sorry about what happened –"

"Joy, please don't worry too much about it," I said earnestly. "You had nothing to with any of this –"

"Perhaps, but my husband had."

"And he was sorry. Me and him, we talked about the matter. And in the end, thank God, we made our peace before he passed. You should be proud of him."

"I am," said Joy. "He told me how you two talked. And until the day I held him in my arms, as he breathed his last, he kept hoping I would find the letter."

"God be praised! Miracles still happen."

"It took – what – six years since Obi died," said Joy, misty-eyed, "for us to stumble upon it."

"The important thing is, it's been found. Nothing else matters. Joy, please can I use your phone? I've got to call Rosemary about this."

"Please!" she said with a smile, gesturing toward the telephone, which was placed on a low pentagonal table set beside a medium-sized television set. The TV was not on, presumably because the children were not home from school, and Joy's mother was enjoying her siesta.

Rosemary was in her office. The moment she heard my voice, she must have sensed that this was an unusual call.

"What's it, C.Y.? Where are you?"

"I'm at Joy's –"

"Which Joy?"

"How many Joys d'you know"? I chuckled. "Ányway, please don't interrupt me –"

"This had better be good news," said my wife, completely disregarding my wish not to be interrupted.

"It is," I said, in my most gracious voice. "Listen, Rosemary, as I speak to you, I have *the letter* in my hand –"

"Which – what are you talking – ?" A pause. "Did you say the letter?"

"*The letter!*" I fairly screamed into the telephone.

"C.Y.! This is no time –"

"You're not listening, Rosemary. I have it in my hand as we talk."

"Joy – ?"

"Yes," I said. "She found it, and called me straightaway. I left my office as soon as I put down the phone and rushed over to her place."

"The same letter we've prayed for these past – what – twenty years?"

"I've looked it over," I said, with a wink at Joy, who had remained standing in the middle of the room, looking keenly at me. "The very same letter, yes!"

"This is the Lord's doing, C.Y. I'm coming right over. Probably take me less than ten minutes."

I heard the click, and knew she had hung up. I was on cloud nine. For a moment or two, I paced up and down the sitting-room. Then Joy pointed me to a chair, but I could not sit still. I must have taken the letter out of its white envelope a hundred times, and did nothing but stare at it, scarcely daring to believe that, finally, I had in my hands the document that would surely bring bright light into the dark despair of my life. Then, gradually coming out of the clouds of my elated wonderment, I remembered to ask the question that had been on my mind, and on the tip of my tongue, from the moment Joy announced the good news.

"What happened, Joy? Where – I mean how – did you find the letter?"

"It's just one of those things one can't explain," said Joy. "I found it in my bedroom, in a cabinet I must have ransacked a hundred times before. This time, I wasn't even looking for it. It was in a pile of old letters and whatnots in the cabinet. I can't remember exactly what I was looking for. But it – so to say – sort of leapt into my hands. I don't know, but there was just something about it that made me take a closer look. It was then that I saw Bernard's name in the sender's corner –"

"I don't recall seeing his name on the envelope," I said, my mind racing back twenty years, to the day I first saw, and held, the letter in my hands. I now looked again at the envelope. And there it was! The name 'Bernard Ekwekwe' was so lightly scrawled, in the top left corner that, in my excitement, I had not noticed it when Joy first handed the envelope to me.

"You're probably right," said Joy. "It wasn't Bernard that wrote his name on the envelope, but Obi. I know my husband's handwriting."

I looked again, and nodded in agreement. It was not Bernard's quite atrocious handwriting, which I thought I would have recognized. Besides, the name was written in pencil, and not in the dark blue ink in which Bernard wrote Obi's name on the envelope.

"So Obi must have written the name on the envelope, to help him identify it easily?"

"Perhaps," said Joy. "And yet we didn't see it, even though we repeatedly searched everywhere for it. You know, it's very likely that our move from our old place to this one may have somehow helped to put it where eventually we *had* to find it. But it sure took a long time –"

"God's time is best," I said.

"I'm glad you think so," said Joy, with a mild smile. "You *are* a patient man."

"It's not patience really," I said fervently. "I have prayed for this to happen over the last two decades. But there was nothing I could do about anything. I was not in control of the situation. There were times I thought I would go raving mad, in my desperation. It has been a long nightmare. Now, thank God, and thanks to you, I think I can begin to breathe again."

"So what, next?" asked Joy.

Before I could answer, the door bell rang.

"Must be Rosemary," I said, moving to open the door.

It was. Rosemary threw herself into my arms, burying her face in my chest. I had expected that. What I had not expected was the fierceness of her embrace. She squeezed me so hard I struggled to disengage her arms. I held her a little away from me, and then I saw that her face was tear-stained.

"Where's the – the – ?" she asked through her tears.

"Here," I said, offering her the envelope.

She took the envelope from me with one hand, even as she wiped her tears away with a soft tissue she took out of her purse. She cast a mere glance at the envelope, and then walked over to Joy. Silently they hugged each other twice, thrice, rapidly; and then they enfolded each other in a long and rocking embrace. After a momentary hesitation, I went to them, my arms held wide open, and was welcomed into their embrace. We remained like that for a long, long moment, with both women silently sobbing.

Rosemary suddenly broke into song, and was immediately joined by Joy. The hymn, sung to a beautiful and haunting tune, was one of Rosemary's all-time favorites. I loved it too, but did not have the same mastery of the words as she had. No matter! I hummed when the words eluded me, and joined full-heartedly when I could.

> *"When peace, like a river, attendeth my way,*
> *When sorrows like sea-billows roll,*
> *Whatever my lot, Thou hast taught me to say:*
> *It is well, it is well, with my soul."*

It was, indeed, well with my soul. After the long years of lost hopes and increasing despair, it was now well with my soul. I remembered too the words of the psalmist:

> *"I lift up my eyes to the hills;*
> *From whence cometh my help?*
> *My help cometh from the Lord*
> *Who made heaven and earth."*

Slowly, we disengaged from our long, triangular embrace. Rosemary took my hand, and made me sit with her on a two-seat sofa. She then took the letter out of the white envelope, unfolded it and spread it out on her lap, and gazed at it, like one mesmerized. Watching her, I could not tell if she actually read the contents. She seemed immensely satisfied to just look at it. When she finally raised her eyes from it, and looked sideways at me, her tears were flowing freely down her cheeks. She mumbled something to herself.

"What was that?" I asked.

"Nothing, really," she said. "I just can't believe that this is happening. So I was saying to myself that 'Jesus is alive.'"

"Amen!" I said.

"Joy, my sister, how did this happen?"

"I already asked her the same question," I said.

"And I don't mind telling the story a second time," said Joy, smiling from ear to ear, her face glowing. "It's not a long story anyway. Rosemary, all I did was idly flip through a pile of old letters, in a cabinet where I had looked for this same letter a hundred times before. Miraculously, something about it caught my eyes in a way it never did before –"

"You think it was there all the time?"

"I don't know what to think. It may very well have been – but I'm not sure of it. But it was somewhere in the house. I do not know in what corner it was buried. But when we packed up and moved to this place, something must have happened to place the letter where luck led me to find it."

"Wasn't luck," said Rosemary. "It was God's hand that led you to it."

"Same difference, as Americans say," I said. "God creates luck. The question now is: what do we do –"

"Aren't you forgetting somebody?" asked Joy.

"Chizube!" Rosemary shouted.

"The phone is there," said Joy, pointing.

"Hold it one moment!" I said, as Rosemary made to pick it up. "We'll call her when we get back home. I don't think I want her rushing down here –"

"You mean," said Rosemary, with incontrovertible logic, "as I just did?"

I caught the tone and tenor of her words. "I'm sorry. I didn't mean it that way. Of course *you* had to join me here as quickly as you could. Chizube is different. It's quite enough for her to come to the house. Come to think of it, I'll make whatever other calls I need to make, from home."

"Your partners?" suggested Rosemary.

"Of course," I said. "And Cornelius."

"Okwu?" asked Rosemary.

"The same."

"Cornelius Okwu?" asked Joy. "The name sounds familiar."

"A lawyer," Rosemary told her. "CY's friend from their Rutgers years. I doubt your paths have crossed."

"I'm not so sure," said Joy, brows wrinkled in thought. "I believe I know him – or at least have heard of him. Let me see. Is he not the lawyer – I believe he practices in DC or Baltimore, married to an *Akata* woman – ?"

"A what?" I asked, though I knew what she meant.

"Sorry, I should have said a Black American woman."

"And you'd still be wrong," I said, smiling. "His wife is as pure white – or pink – as they come."

"You know how our people think," said Rosemary. "When we hear that one of our own is married to an American, some of us automatically think Black. But anyway, Joy, you certainly know something about him. He lived in the DC area, and his wife is American."

"I thought so," said Joy triumphantly. "When you do business in our African traditional clothes, you get to meet more of our people than you may remember afterwards. People used to come to our store from as far away as Washington, DC and Boston."

"D'you ever regret closing your store?" I asked. "I really thought it was a shame you had to."

"I suppose I do – a little bit. But when you have little or no choice, what can you do? After Obi's death, I knew there was no way I could continue in the same line of business –"

"There are some who might disagree with you."

"Let them. We're not all made of the same stuff. I know I could never think of making the trips he made to Nigeria for the business."

"And now you're an R.N.," said Rosemary.

"And happy in what I do now, thank you!"

"Including the occasional night-shift?" asked Rosemary.

"Occasional or not, that's okay. It's a little tough, no doubt. But I'm adjusting to it. My mum is a great help."

"I can imagine," I said. "Couldn't have worked out better for you, I must say. And on top of that, she has her green card now."

"It's the Lord's doing," said Joy reverently. "Don't even ask me how we did it. All I know is that America is the most generous country in the world."

"You really think so?" I asked.

"This is a nation of immigrants," observed Rosemary, "except for the native Americans."

My mind was on my sense of the American system of justice that had me incarcerated for someone else's crime. Then I thought about the fact that I was *still* in this country. I thought about how I would have felt, had I been put on a plane bound for Nigeria, when I was released from prison, as I could so easily have been. And I shook my head in bewilderment at the contradictions and complexities of my life.

"You wouldn't happen to be on duty tonight, by any chance?" Rosemary asked.

"I am, but don't let that worry you. I had plenty of sleep earlier today. And, as if I knew this would happen, I prepared plenty of food, just before Cyril came."

"You're not thinking to ask us to stay and eat something?" I asked. "Because if you –"

"Of course I am, Cyril. With all the excitement of the letter, I didn't even think of offering you anything to drink or snack on. Please forgive –"

"Come on, Joy!" I said. "Just this letter I have in my hands is worth a million times more than any kolanut or whatever you could offer us. And as to staying longer, to eat, it would be inconsiderate of us to do so, knowing you're due on night duty in a few short hours. However, as Americans say, we'll take a rain check, if it's okay with you."

"There's nothing I can say to change your mind?"

"Nothing," I said, looking at Rosemary, who nodded emphatically. "And thank you so very much – in fact, words are totally inadequate to express how much we appreciate what you've just done for us. Like I said, I'll see Cornelius Okwu, and discuss matters touching on what to do with the letter –"

I stopped, because a thought suddenly occurred to me. "You know what, Joy? This letter is your property. But I hope you'll not mind my keeping it until I've spoken to Cornelius and some other persons. Perhaps I should make a copy, which you can keep, until I can return the original to you. How's that?"

Joy looked steadily at me for several moments, but the smile on her face was most reassuring. "Cyril, I know what this letter means to you. I'm only sorry it took so long for me to find it. For that, and for Obi's role in the whole sad situation, I ask your forgiveness, and God's. Please keep the letter as long as you need it. I don't even care if I never see it again."

Rosemary and I stood up, ready to leave. Joy came and stood before Rosemary, and they looked into each other's eyes for a long moment.

"Please Rosemary, forgive me. I just wish none of this ever happened."

Rosemary, too tearful to trust herself to speak, instead reached for Joy, and pulled her into another long embrace, at the end of which, they were both unashamedly shedding tears like – well – women. I stood by silently, the lump in my throat the size of golf balls. But my machismo would not let me shed a tear.

Chapter XXI

CORNELIUS AND ANN walked into our Mount of Olives apartment in West Brook, NJ, within an hour of my phone call to him. He, not I, had insisted that he come to my home to talk about the letter.

"I'm the client," I had pointed out, modestly.

"Yes," he replied, "and we're friends. You need your friends to rally round you. I wouldn't dream of pulling you away from your home at this particular time. Don't worry, Cyril. There'll be no extra charge for my calling on you. Just make sure Rose has my favorite snack out of the fridge. You know I don't like it too cold. By the way, I hope Rose is home. I'm coming with Ann."

He always called her Rose. "Rosemary's too long," he had said the first day he met her – some twenty years earlier. That was in Washington, DC, shortly after Rosemary first arrived in the United States. I remember that day as if it was yesterday. Rosemary and I were dining in a Chinese restaurant – then, my idea of introducing my newly-arrived girl-friend to the gastronomic delights the country offered. And I had chosen well because, in all the years I had lived in Enugu, Nigeria – where Rosemary also grew up – there simply were no Chinese restaurants. She fell in love right away with Chinese food.

Cornelius Okwu had walked into the restaurant with a statuesque white girl. That was no surprise – I mean, the white girl. As a fellow student at Rutgers in the nineteen-seventies, Cornelius had exhibited a noted partiality for our pink-skinned sisters. He and I, and a bunch of other African students, had regularly hung out together, at restaurants and movies. He took his law degree in my junior year, and then lived and worked for a law firm in Washington, DC. We immediately re-established contact. Indeed we remained connected, even after he relocated to Atlanta, Georgia, in the second year of my imprisonment. He did not visit me in prison, which was all right, because *I* discouraged him from doing so. Instead, he called me on the phone periodically, to ask how I was doing; and he would sometimes repeat his request to come in person. But I did not want visitors who were not family. I did not think I could bear the shame and humiliation of receiving my friends in the morose and utterly melancholy environment in which I found myself.

In 1995, Cornelius once again relocated; this time, to New Jersey, in the city of East Orange, in the very heart of the county of Essex. There, he set up his own, private, law practice. He was attracted, he told me, by the concentration of our Igbo people in the county. Besides, it had been, for him, something of a home-coming. As a student at Rutgers, he had lived in Irvington town which, with a cluster of little towns of indeterminate boundaries, form one great conurbation with the Oranges. He had made many friends in and out of the county.

It paid off handsomely for him, I believe, because he interacted extensively with the Nigerian community, and made his presence felt in many community activities. He quickly became the President of the *Mbanaodum* Patriotic Association, New Jersey, Inc. *Mbanaodum*, his home village in Nigeria, had many sons and daughters resident in New Jersey. Without wishing it, he also – in quick time – found himself the General Secretary of the Patriotic Association of *Mbanaodum*, USA, Inc. (PAMUSA), the national umbrella organization of the association. The Secretaryship was more or less thrust upon him, when he badly timed his arrival at an afternoon session of the 1999 national convention meeting, held in Atlanta, Georgia. The general body had been scratching its collective head, in frustration, because no member seemed willing to accept nomination for the office, which was a rather thankless job – all work, little play, and no appreciation from the membership.

Cornelius arrived late – not unusual for him. As he strolled into the meeting hall, unusually without his wife, Ann, he drew undue attention to himself from the entrance door when he began to shake hands with everybody in his path, and doing so rather loudly. Suddenly there was a cry from a corner of the hall: "Here comes our new General Secretary! Chief Okwu for Secretary of PAMUSA!""

The cry was taken up by more than a dozen voices simultaneously, and reverberated around the hall: "Chief Okwu for Secretary of PAMUSA!"

Before the dazed and befuddled Cornelius realized what was happening, he had been nominated, the nomination was quickly seconded, and a rapid-fire voice vote made him the General Secretary of the Patriotic Association of Mbanaodum, USA, Inc. And all this – from nomination to acclamation – had lasted just thirty seconds. Cornelius – as he later recounted to me – briefly thought about declining the honor, in spite of that loud acclamatory vote, if for no other reason, at least on account of the fact that he was not a chief, and that therefore it was not *really* him that had been nominated. But he knew better than to offer that fact as a serious reason for declining the position. He knew, as did whoever it was that first screamed his nomination, that the word Chief had been used so loosely within the American Igbo community, it had inevitably lost some of its luster. His main regret was that Ann was not with him to help stiffen his resistance to the totally unexpected development. However, his sense of duty to his community finally turned his reluctance into a grudging acquiescence, and ultimately a whole-hearted service as the General Secretary of the Association.

Ann looked most fetching. In the twenty odd years since I first set eyes on her, she never lost that sleekness of form that often turns a slim woman into a smashingly feline beauty. Her somewhat close-fitting, flowery, knee-length dress accentuated the gentle curvatures of her body. Her hair was pulled back – not too severely – and gathered at the nape in an elaborate coiffure.

She was that rare American sister that somehow found a way to combine an air of sophistication with total comfort in the company of her husband's Igbo people. She glided with seemingly effortless ease into the Mbanaodum Association of New Jersey, was a regular at their monthly meetings and, from all accounts, joined enthusiastically in the traditional kolanut breaking and eating. She seemed to enjoy the peppery *okwo-ose*, a peanut-based condiment that goes very agreeably with the bitter taste of the nut. She certainly enjoyed the sobriquet of 'First Lady' of the association, as the wife of the New Jersey association's President.

Cornelius was wrong about Ann not being with him, at the election meeting of the national association's convention in Atlanta. I know, because Ann herself privately told me, when I posed the question to her, that she regarded service to the Mbanaodum community, at both the state and the national levels, as an obligation that should be readily accepted whenever the call came. So far from stiffening the back of Cornelius's objection to the vote that made him Secretary, Ann swore she would have joined in the acclamation, had she been present.

"Hello, First Lady!" I greeted her, though I was not a member of PAMUSA, as I held the entrance door open to let her and Cornelius in. "As always, you look regal."

"Thanks, Cyril," she beamed, her wide smile God's gift to the male of the species. "But what's this I hear? The famous letter has resurfaced?"

"It has, Ann. It has. Glory be!"

"Amen!" said Cornelius. He and I touched the backs of our right hands three times before clasping hands, in the traditional – though relatively infrequent – Igbo greeting between men. Except, of course that Cornelius was Cornelius, and had no use for the gentle touch! So, though I merely touched, he *hit*. Three really hard hits, and then a lively hand grasp. He was nothing if not enthusiastic, even exuberant, in his greetings with me. "I've waited for this day for ever. Cyril, this has the potential to change everything."

Potential! What did he mean by 'potential'? The letter I had in my hand – well, in my trouser pocket – the *original* thing itself, not a copy; *the letter* written by Bernard Ekwekwe to Obi Udozo in 1980, that dragged me willy-nilly into his (Bernard's) nefarious trade; the letter that implored me simply to take a bag containing eight thousand dollars to an old primary school mate, in payment for stuff he was doing – or whatever – for Bernard; the letter I could not produce, when I most needed it, to prove my innocence to the court of my eternal damnation; the letter was *dynamite*! It did not just have the potential to change things. It *changed* everything. It was – it *had* to be – the rod in the hands of Moses that would part my Red Sea, and let me walk, on dry land, over to the other bank. I knew what awaited me on that other bank: a full and free life, without the shame that clung to me everywhere I went, every day of my life, no matter whether I was in my home, or in the offices of *Onyeama & Ani, CPAs*.

I knew, within my soul, that there would be a Garden of Eden on the other side of my Red Sea. I could already smell the fragrance of its wild flowers, the aroma of its plants and trees. I knew now that the spirits of my forebears – the saints, if you will, in our Igbo pantheon – were watching over me. And that my *Chi* – that eternal flame of divinity that is in every one of us, and that guides us and is reflective of our whole life – had me in its protective cover, even in the darkest period of my life.

But what was keeping Chizube? I had called her more than an hour before I called Cornelius, because I needed to talk to her and her mum first, about the letter, before other persons, including even my lawyer-friend, got involved in the discussions. I picked up the telephone and dialed her number. When the answering machine came on, I hung up, because I knew she was on her way.

She came with her boyfriend. I must confess I was taken aback. I had not expected that on this one, very momentous day in my life as her father, when I needed only those persons very close to me and the family, she would come with her boyfriend.

I shrugged, and said: "Hello, Jacob!"

"Da-a-a-ad!" Chizube cried out harshly, but softly. "It's Bola."

"I'm sorry," I said. "Hello, Bola!"

"Jacob's all right too," said the young man, smiling.

"But you heard Chizube," I said. "Next time, I'll try to remember. How're you doing?"

"Fine, Sir. Thank you."

Ndubisi, who assuredly had the acute sense of smell of a bloodhound, came bounding out of his room, and rushed past me, and into his sister's arms.

"Chi-Chi," he said to her, "I knew it was you."

He then saw Bola, looked up at him with a smile, and extended his hand. "You came with your boyfriend," he observed to Chizube.

Chizube lifted Ndubisi off his feet, while he still had his hand in Bola's. "Hi, little brother!" said Chizube, beaming. "You remembered Bola."

"Hi, little devil!" Bola said to Ndubisi, gently and affectionately rubbing the crown of Ndubisi's head.

Ann and Cornelius, who had watched the exchanges with some interest, now got off the love-seat, and came forward to hug Chizube and to be introduced to Bola Akande.

"I don't believe you've met Bola," Chizube said to them. "Bola, meet auntie Ann and uncle Cornelius."

Bola bowed slightly to them, and said: "How are you?"

"Hi!" Cornelius said to Bola. "We haven't met. But we've heard of you."

"You have?" asked Chizube, turning and looking at me with accusation writ large in her eyes. "By the way, where is mum?" She drew closer to me and added, "And where's the letter?"

"All in good time, my dear," I replied, patting her on the head.

A key turned in the lock of the entrance door, and Rosemary stepped into the sitting room, lugging two Shoprite grocery bags. Bola quickly moved to her side, relieved her of her burden, and carried the bags to the kitchen.

"Bless you, Jacob,' said Rosemary gratefully, exhaling noisily.

"You mean Bola," I quickly corrected her, causing Chizube and Bola – from the kitchen door – to smile and look at me.

Rosemary smiled too. "I know, but I never seem to remember."

She gestured to Ann and Cornelius. "I didn't expect you'd be here so quickly. I rushed to the mall to pick up some snacks and what-not."

"You didn't need to go to all that trouble," said Ann to Rosemary, as they embraced.

"Speak for yourself," Cornelius said to his wife, hugging Rosemary in turn. "Let me guess, Rose. Carrots and dip, no?"

"Right. You'd never have forgiven me if I didn't – "

"You got that right, Rose. What's his name – Bola – I hope he hasn't put the stuff away in the fridge."

"I didn't, sir," said Bola, emerging from the kitchen.

"You might as well just bring out the carrots and dip here, so we'll fall to, as we talk." Cornelius stopped, and looked at me. "Unless our host has any objections?"

It was a question that was really no question. He said what he said out of politesse, so he would not seem to be an overbearing guest. For as our people say, a visitor should not be overbearing to his host, so that when he departs, his back may not become humped. It was a saying that I had occasionally thrown at him, but always playfully. We laugh about it, and I have never known Cornelius to take too seriously the implied admonition in that Igbo aphorism. He can sometimes be so relaxed, in speech and demeanor, that some persons, meeting him for the first time, had been moved to comment – behind his back – that he came on a little strongly. But Cornelius was a friend of inestimable value, and he could take as well as he gave.

So, though his question was meant to be rhetorical, I was ready with my answer. "Sorry, Cornelius," I said, beaming on him, "I have. I object. Today, everything is different. Normalcy is out! I want your undivided attention, at least for a little while. Let's all sit down –"

"That's if there are enough seats for this crowd," said Cornelius dramatically, looking from side to side, and around the room.

"There are," I said. "But if you don't want to share the love seat with Ann, you can always pull up a chair from the dining table."

"Can't we munch as we talk?" Cornelius again!

"Nope!" I said. "The carrot makes too much noise."

He took the love-seat with his wife; Rosemary shared the long settee with Chizube and Ndubisi; Bola, with a becoming show of delicacy, drew up a dining chair and sat by himself near the TV set, facing the rest of us.

I sat in the king's chair, my special chair, set at the angle of the L-shaped arrangement formed by the love-seat and the long settee. I took out the white envelope, and held it up for all to see.

"This is the letter –"

"The famous letter," said Cornelius.

"Yeah, Cornelius! It is indeed the famous letter –"

"Hold it there one second!" shouted Rosemary.

I looked at her, and she gestured with a flick of her head to her left, clearly indicating Ndubisi. When she gently shook her head from side to side, I caught her meaning. Chizube, who had also quickly caught on to her mother's gentle gestures, immediately rose from the settee, pulling Ndubisi up with her.

"Come, little brother," she said. "There's something I want to tell you."

"Where're we going?" asked Ndubisi, looking over his shoulder at his mum.

"To your bedroom," said Chizube, smiling at him reassuringly.

"But what letter is dad –"

"Not for your ears," said Chizube, pulling him along. "Little boys shouldn't –" The door of the corridor closed behind them.

"That's better," said Rosemary, and turned to me. "You were saying –"

I took the letter out of the envelope, opened it out, and held it with both hands, at a reading distance from my eyes. "Let me read it to you all."

The letter and envelope almost dropped out of my hand, but were quickly snatched from me by Cornelius, who sat closest to me.

"Your hands are trembling," said he. "Perhaps I should give it to Rose, no?"

"No! You go ahead, Cornelius," I said. "You're the lawyer. Please read it, and tell me – tell us – what it means."

I sat back in my chair, raised my arms, and intertwined my fingers at the back of my neck. I sat like that, immobile, as Cornelius prepared to read Bernard Ekwekwe's letter. My head was filled with sharp memories of that momentous day in early January, 1980, the day that presaged the long nightmare of my life, a day that had begun with arctic frigidity and ended with warm thoughts of Rosemary, who was due, in a matter of hours, for a rare visit to me from Washington, DC. In my mind's eye, I saw Obi Udozo once again, sporting a dark brown worsted jacket, as he stamped his feet repeatedly on the door rug, to shake off the snow from his shoes. I recalled, with sharp clarity, the black plastic bag he clutched in one hand, and the white long envelope that stuck out like a sore thumb from a pocket of his brown jacket. He had come to see me in my Bound Brook residence, which was actually my cousin, Dr. Aloysius Jideofo's house. Having, just a few days earlier, landed my first accounting job with the DC firm of Gable, Kline and Stevens, Inc., those were days filled with hopes and dreams of the bright future that beckoned.

Chizube came back into the living room, and resumed her seat by her mother, on the settee. "He's okay," she said. "He promised to stay in his room until I come for him."

"He's a good lad," said Ann, "and obviously listens to his big sister."

Chizube smiled modestly. "I'm not so sure, but he and I get along."

Cornelius cleared his throat noisily, but only to get our attention. He had the air of someone who knew that what he was about to do was truly significant, and that the piece of paper he held in his hand was no ordinary document. He looked about him and, seemingly satisfied that we were a receptive audience, raised the letter to his eye-level.

He cleared his throat again, waving the letter to and fro. "This letter is dated 4 January, 1980," he announced by way of introduction, "and is addressed to Obi – that's Obi Udozo. Now listen carefully.

"*Dear Obi,*

"*Greetings from the Coal City. Business is going great. I just returned to Enugu from Onitsha yesterday, and my little store room here is filled to capacity with beautifully embroidered jumpers and blouses that will surely sell like hot cakes in America, although I must say that some of my business contacts in Onitsha want to reap where they did not sow. But that is not what I want to write about now.*

"*Please deliver to my friend Cyril Jideofo the enclosed eight thousand dollars, which he should keep until an old friend and primary school classmate of ours, Sam Anolue, arrives in the United States. Cyril should remember Sam well, and will easily recognize him the moment he sees Sam, the 'Short Man Bogey' as we used to call him, because he was the shortest boy in our class. Sam may have added some three or four inches in height since then, but his face is still the same.*

"*As I write this, on the 4th of January, 1980, Sam should be arriving New York within about two to three weeks. He is carrying some merchandise from me, but neither you nor Cyril should be concerned about that. He has detailed instructions about where and to whom he should deliver the merchandise. When he comes, Sam will explain more to you about all of this.*

"*Please explain to Cyril that I am really very sorry to drag him into this matter. I could have asked you to deliver the money to Sam Anolue, but the trouble is that you do not know the man, and I am anxious to avoid any mistakes in this transaction. Mutual recognition is vital. But even if Cyril has forgotten him, Sam is sure he will have no problem recognizing Cyril. His boast is that he can pick out Cyril's face in a crowd, however large the crowd is. His only worry is that American hamburgers and doughnuts might have done their usual havoc on Cyril's body. But I told him that Cyril, from the last time I saw him, is still the same as he was.*

"*Sam has traveled to the U.S. several times, and knows some areas quite well. He will likely fly to Houston, and when he gets there, he will call Cyril. I will ask him to do so as soon as possible after reaching Houston, to avoid unnecessary delay.*

Cyril should be patient until Sam calls him. Sam will then fly to New Jersey to meet with him, on whatever day both agree to meet.

"Tell Cyril to hand over all the money to Sam, for my business associates. That's all he needs to do, and I promise never again to ask him to do me this kind of favor.

"My next trip to America, I hope, will be in March, if not earlier. Till then, God bless and keep you both.

"Yours ever,
"Bernard.

"P.S. I suggest it would be best if you give this letter to Cyril to read for himself. That way, it will be direct from me to him."

For what seemed like a full minute after Cornelius came to the end of the letter, no one spoke. In the total silence that prevailed, Cornelius refolded the letter, and stuffed it back in the white envelope. Then he raised his eyes, and stared at me intently. Our eyes held for a moment or two, and then he nodded emphatically, several times, like a person satisfied with something or the other.

Someone began to sob. I heard the sound, turned and saw Chizube and Rosemary clasping each other. Chizube's body shook with the sobs that racked her frame. I looked across at her young man, sitting by himself on a dining chair. Our eyes met and, on the prompting conveyed by the merest flicker of my head towards Chizube, he promptly got up, and went and sat next to her, on the long settee she shared with her mother. Chizube turned immediately to him, and fell into his arms, which he had held wide open to welcome her.

Ann exhaled loudly. "Incredible!" she said to her husband.

"What's incredible?"

"That there was this evidence – this powerful evidence – that Cyril's friend –"

"He was no friend," Cornelius said through tightly clenched teeth.

"I know," said Ann, this time looking at me. "What I'm saying is that it is unbelievable that there was this wonderful evidence that – what's his name – Bernard literally dragged you, willy-nilly, into his dark business, and you could not produce it. I can't believe Obi Udozo, or anybody else, would have had the heart to do this to you."

"You mean in not producing the letter at my trial?" I asked. "The poor fellow, I suppose, was only trying to save his own skin. Had he produced the letter, I dare say he might have had several uncomfortable questions to answer, about his connections to Bernard's drug business."

Bola coughed loudly, clearly to gain my attention. "Sir," he said gently, still clasping my daughter to his chest, "I don't think I've met many people like you. I know if it was me, I would go raving mad – at Obi Udozo, almost as much as at Mr. Ekwekwe – that's his name, I believe?"

"Yes, Bernard Ekwekwe," I answered. "I had plenty of time – seven years – to rant and rave, to my heart's content. And I did. Plus I've prayed and prayed to lay my hands on this letter. I never quite gave up. The good Lord has now seen fit to reward my patience, and I thank Him. What's the use now of being angry with Obi? He's been dead these – what – six or seven years. And he made his peace with God and – I might add – with me, over this letter. With his dying breath, he wished his wife would find the letter for me."

"Still and all –" said Bola, leaving his sentence suspended.

He did not need to finish the sentence, because the expression on his face said it all. And the way he shook his head from side to side. I saw fire in his eyes or – if it was not fire – a slow-burning hostility toward whoever did what they did to me and, through me, to the girl he held in his arms. Because of her, young Bola seemed poised to make my fight his fight. It was clear to me that he had become very comfortable with us.

Rosemary did something she had probably only done two or three times in all the years I had known her; certainly in the eight years of our marriage. She came to me, and sat on my lap, and leaned endearingly into me, holding me close. She had no use for words.

"Okay, folks!" It was Cornelius. When I looked at him, he was calmly looking from side to side, and his gaze took us all in. "We've all had the time to digest the content of this letter. The question now, is: where do we go from here? Cyril –"

"You're the lawyer," his wife interrupted him. "Perhaps you can best suggest what Cyril can do with the letter."

Cornelius turned to her. "You and I talked about this as we were coming here, what the possibilities might be, depending on exactly what the letter says. Cyril, you remember what I said earlier about the letter – ?"

"I remember. Something about the letter having the potential to change things?"

"Forget about potential!" said Cornelius with conviction. "It *changes* everything. My thinking is that with this letter, you can ask that your case be re-opened. There's no court in this land that –"

He paused, an uncertain look coming into his eyes. "Well, at least any court that is willing to review the entire case against you, back in 1980, cannot fail to clear your name."

"But you seem to foresee a problem?" I asked.

"I believe it will all work out well in the end," Cornelius said. "But there could be a question about the authenticity of the letter, I imagine. If that arises –" He paused.

"How do we solve that problem?" I asked.

"To put it very simply, we might need to produce one or two of the principal characters in the story –"

"Meaning, like Bernard himself?" I asked, alarmed.

"Or the other fellow," said Cornelius. "The one to whom you delivered the money in the hotel – in Newark, I believe –"

"Sam Anolue? But I have no idea where he is, other than that he has probably served his time, and been repatriated to Nigeria, like Bernard – if he was ever put in prison here."

"Oh, he must have been," said Rosemary, still cuddled up with me. "They found the stuff on him, and I think I heard that the Judge sentenced him to a long, long stretch in prison."

"Unless he was given a life sentence," said Cornelius, "Cyril might be right that he's probably served his term. Don't forget, all this happened in 1980, twenty years ago."

"You all seem to have forgotten about Mrs. Udozo," said Chizube. She was no longer sobbing, though Bola still had a protective arm around her shoulder. "She's the widow of the man to whom the letter was written."

"Meaning – ?"

"She's right," said Cornelius. "If we were to reopen your case, I believe her testimony about the authenticity of the letter would be crucial. I'm not sure I know her –"

"She thinks she knows you," Rosemary said.

"She does? Anyway, no matter. From your story of your meeting with her today, it sounds as if she would be very forthcoming about all of this mess. Her husband is dead, and so, whether or not he was involved with Bernard in his drug trade –"

"No way!" I said. "I am absolutely certain he was not."

"That's good," said Cornelius, though his eyes seemed to be asking questions. "Anyway, as I was about to say, Joy has nothing to worry about on that score. But I also think we should keep our ears close to the ground. You never know, one of us might get wind of Bernard's being in this country."

"He's too slippery –"

"Nobody's perfect, Cyril. He might slip up one of these days, and we should be ready to pounce when he does." He paused and, looking pointedly at Rosemary, asked: "Can we now have the carrots and things?"

Rosemary smiled, and jumped off my lap. "But of course," she said. "And not just the carrots and dip, but Chinese food as well."

"You know how to cook Chinese?" asked Ann.

"I don't have to know anything," Rosemary answered from the kitchen door. "Don't you know there are Chinese take-aways?"

*   *   *

Later, after Cornelius and Ann had left, and Rosemary was closeted with Chizube in one of the rooms, having their mother-to-daughter chat no doubt, Bola came and sat close to me.

"Sir," he said, his voice solemn and earnest, "about the letter and all that, if there's anything I can do to help in any way, please let me know. Your daughter means the world to me, and I cannot sit idle and see her agonize over the past, and not do anything. Now that the letter has been found –"

"Thank you, Bola," I said, putting a hand on his hand, which was on the hand-rest of his chair. "But I don't think I should drag you into this matter. Nor do I think there's really anything you can do to –"

"Sir, there's something I *can* do. I have friends at home, in Enugu. I can ask them to make discreet enquiries about this man, Bernard."

"Thank you at least for not calling him my friend."

In a voice full of suppressed anger, he said: "What kind of friend would do what he did to you? As I was saying, enquiries – discreet enquiries – can be made about his movements, especially his travels. That way, we might get to know if and when he leaves Nigeria. Is there any question but that if he leaves Nigeria, he is most likely to travel to the U.S.? And if that happens, we'll be ready and waiting for him. He might well be a snake, but if we are careful, we can take care of his venom."

I stared at the young man, for a long moment totally bereft of the words to convey the depth of my gratitude to him. Gratitude for the words he had just spoken to me. Gratitude for his willingness to take on a Bernard Ekwekwe he did not know. But my gratitude was tinged with some concern. Concern that because of his love for my daughter, this very young man seemed poised to make my enemies his enemies! Bernard Ekwekwe, I had no doubt, could be as dangerous a foe as he was slick and slippery as a friend. I did not think I wanted Bola to take any undue risks on my account, or on Chizube's, for that matter.

"Bola," I finally said to him, looking directly into his eyes, "you do not fully understand what we have here. But we'll talk again."

Chapter XXII

O N A BRIGHT late afternoon in mid-July 2000, about six weeks after the miracle of the finding of Bernard's letter, young Bola Akande came by. He was, mostly, now at ease with Rosemary and me, though I was not altogether sure what *my* attitude to him should be. We had, I supposed, pretty much accepted him as a boy-friend to our daughter, Chizube. But if I seemed hesitant, not so Rosemary. "Chi-Chi could have done worse than him for a boy-friend," was one way she put it. And when I still would not swing completely to her point of view, she would remind me about the old saying: "what can't be helped must be endured." But she did not need to teach me that lesson. The last twenty years of my life had been one long period of enduring what I could not help – first, my long incarceration for a crime I did not commit and, since my release, more than a dozen years of living through the agony of frustration about whether or not Bernard's letter would ever resurface.

The letter had now finally resurfaced – almost the best thing that had happened to me in all that time, except of course Rosemary, Chizube and Ndubisi. So why was I still feeling despondent? It might have been because, like the fictional character, "that damned elusive Pimpernel", Bernard was no where in sight.

Chizube, who was home on her second summer vacation, had told me earlier in the day that Bola would be visiting, and was anxious that I put on my most welcoming face.

"For me, dad," she had pleaded, with that patented smile to which I always seemed incapable of offering meaningful resistance.

"It's okay, Chi-Chi," I assured her. "You know he's always welcome."

"With you, dad," she said, head deferentially tilted to one side, "I'm never sure. Bola says to tell you it's important."

"What's important?"

"What he's coming to see you about," said Chizube.

"Oh! So it's me he's coming to see?"

"Of course," said she, rather illogically. "It's to do with the letter – I mean your friend's –"

"Bernard?"

"Yes, dad – sorry, I shouldn't have called him your friend."

Anyone coming to see me about Bernard, I said to myself, was welcome, any time of the day or night. Particularly if they were bearers of good news! Good news, for me at that particular period of my life, was news about Bernard's movements, especially any movements that might bring him into these United States. But I was under no illusion on that subject. I was not holding my breath that, any time soon, he would fall into our hands. I knew my Bernard – or at least I thought I did. But what did I truly know about a friend who was really only masquerading as a friend, who smiled while he sold me to the devil, dissembling his wickedness with false warm-heartedness?

One thing, however, I knew, and had always known. Bernard was a clever son of a bitch, very cunning and wise. He could sense danger well before danger got uncomfortably close to him. That instinct served him well, at least by his own account, during the Biafra-Nigeria civil war. Then a mere lad in his teens, he found himself in many tight situations in the bushes and wetlands of Biafra, and against Nigerian foes many times better armed than he and his ragtag companions were. His keen instinct for danger served him well – as he recounted to me – when, in the closing stages of the thirty-month civil war, he led sorties against the same foes with little or no assurance of back-up troops. And, of course it served him well – in a manner of speaking – when he warded off supreme danger to himself by treacherously cooperating with agents of the F.B.I. against me, in the darkest period of my trial and cruel sentence for a crime he, not I, had committed.

"Does your young man have good news for me?" I asked. "You said it's about Bernard's letter."

"My young man?" Chizube asked, eyebrows raised in mild disapproval.

"Isn't he?"

"He's not my –" She stopped, smiled and shook her head slowly. "Let's not talk about him and me now. He didn't tell me much, only that he's heard from a friend at home, about the matter."

"Sounds good to me. Did he say what time?"

"I think he said five o'clock."

"How's he doing?" I asked, going off at a tangent.

"Great. He's been accepted for Medicine by Columbia."

"Not surprising," I said, "after his magna-cum-laude performance in his Bachelor degree. He's good."

A beatific smile spread across Chizube's face. "He is, isn't he? Only problem now is finance."

"To me, he never looks as if he has financial problems. But there are scholarships, or he could take a loan. He's got his Green card, I believe?"

"He has. And he's applied to Columbia for financial aid. He's optimistic."

"He should be," I said. "He's a great young man. But don't misunderstand me, Chi-Chi. I simply mean –"

"Dad, I know what you mean. Don't worry. We haven't quite yet come to that."

"Haven't *quite yet*? What's that supposed to mean?"

My daughter looked at me steadily for a moment or two, a faint smile curling up a corner of her lips. Then she shook her head slowly. "Dad, I love you. You know I do. And I'll tell you anything you want to know about me. But this thing isn't about me only, is it? So, all I can say for now is: whatever you think I'm referring to, we're not yet quite there."

I was sitting in my chair, in the living room, while Chizube stood in front of me, as we talked. I now rose from the chair, reached for her, and drew her into my arms. I cuddled her in my arms for a long moment, in silence. Then I held her a little away from me.

"You're my little girl, Chi-Chi. There isn't anything in the world I wouldn't do for you, because your happiness means a lot to me, and to your mum too. You know what I mean, no? By the way, where's your mum? The last time I looked –"

"She was on her way out, with Ndubisi," Chizube reminded me. "She said they were going to K-Mart, to return a dress she bought last month –"

"Last month!" I cried out loud before I could stop myself. "Women! I wonder if the store will take back anything bought that long ago? In fact I hope they don't. Teach your mum –"

"That's why mum doesn't like going to the stores with you. You simply have no patience when it comes to things like that."

"I don't have. I know it. But that's not important now. Did Jacob – Bola – tell you what his friend in Enugu found out about Bernard?"

"As I said, he didn't. And I didn't press him to tell me, since I knew he'll be here at about five."

And he was. Perhaps I have a suspicious mind, but I think young Bola Akande must have sat in his car, somewhere in the neighborhood, and waited until the hour was about to strike. At one minute of five, he rang the door bell. And when Chizube let him in, he stood by the door for a fraction of a second, and looked at his watch, then at me, and back again at his watch.

I understood his body language. "I'm impressed," I said. "I see you're a punctual young man."

"Thank you, sir," he said with a satisfied smile, even as he embraced my daughter. "I try to keep to schedule."

"You mean, unlike the rest of us, no?" I teased.

"Not at all, sir. That's not what –"

"It's all right, Bola," said Chizube. "Dad's just trying to needle you."

"That's true, Bola, though in all conscience our people tend to think punctuality is a dirty word. But enough of that! You're welcome, Bola. Chizube tells me you have news for me. Please sit down – anywhere –"

"Except of course Dad's king's chair!" my daughter shouted.

The smile they exchanged looked suspicious to me. It was a knowing smile about something, probably to do with my king's chair, and the fuss I tended to make whenever I caught a young visitor sitting in it. Chizube made Bola sit with her on the love seat. He hesitated ever so slightly, then shrugged his shoulders, and yielded to her quiet insistence. I was very eager to hear his news, but decided to play it cool. I sat in my chair, and my idle fingers picked up a small photo-album that lay on the center table, and began to leaf through it as I spoke.

"So – er – Bola, I hear you've been accepted by your university for your medical studies. Congratulations!"

"Thank you, sir," he replied, eyes modestly cast down, but smiling from ear to ear. "I'm just very lucky."

"You're too modest, I think."

"He is," said Chizube. "Go on, Bola! Tell dad about the news from home."

Bola came straight to the point. "If my information is correct, your – I mean – Mr. Ekwekwe should be arriving in this country in just about two weeks from today."

The small photo-album fell from my hands. I hastily picked it up, and put it back on the center table.

"He is – who told you – I mean, how did you know about this?"

"As I told you, sir, I have friends in Enugu."

"And these friends know Mr. Ekwekwe?" I asked, my head still reeling from the startling piece of news.

"Sir, let me explain. I have this friend, actually an old classmate in my high school in Enugu. He's now a police officer in Enugu. It appears your Mr. Ekwekwe keeps a very low profile, and doesn't move around as much as people say he used to do. My friend –"

"The policeman?" Chizube asked.

"Yes, the officer. He told me when I spoke with him by phone yesterday – which is why I'm here today – that Mr. Ekwekwe has changed his appearance quite a bit, by growing a full beard and mustache –"

"That's what Obi Udozo told me," I said, "when I used to visit him in the hospital."

"My friend said people who knew him well are not fooled by his attempts to disguise his face."

"Tell me something," I said. "Do people know about his – you know – trafficking, and all that?"

"Sir, you mean about drugs? Of course. That's what my friend – Nnoli's his name – that's what he said. Word got around about Mr. Ekwekwe, and people are saying that one of these days, the man will surely get what's coming to him. Nnoli also said Mr. Ekwekwe has been known to change his travel plans, so no one can be absolutely certain where he might be at any given moment or date."

"I sometimes think I believe in nemesis," I said. "In fact we have a saying that if an adult feasts on rats in the darkness of the night, human eyes may not see him, but the spirits do."

Chizube laughed softly. "And, dad, you believe the spirits will –"

"They do sometimes. Now we have information that he is coming to America – something I think no one knew when he secretly came here in the recent past. We can now take steps to do what we need to do. If that's not the spirits – or God – working for us, I don't know what it is."

"There's something I don't understand in all this," Chizube said. "How can Mr. Ekwekwe go through any U.S. immigration without his picture popping up on their computers – or however they check for people like him?"

"You mean, because his name must surely be on the INS list of undesirable aliens. Especially one who was bundled back to Nigeria after serving his sentence –"

"For drug-dealing, for crying out loud!" said Chizube, none-too-gently.

"Didn't you ever hear about false passports, and such things?" asked Bola.

"I agree," I said. "I don't think Bernard would dare come into this country with the same passport he used in the past –"

"Or even the same name," added Bola.

"You mean – ?"

"Yes, Chizube," said Bola. "He almost certainly not only changed his face, with his new-grown beard and mustache, but his name as well."

"Plus," I added, "he may have obtained what one might call a genuine passport issued by the Passport office in Nigeria."

"That's impossible!" said Chizube.

"Nothing," I said, "is impossible in our country. You've heard people from home talk about *IMM*, no?"

"That's *i-ma-mmadu*," said Bola. "IMM. Knowing the right persons, or having the connections with people who can get you what you want."

"Right. You really know your country."

"Meaning *I* don't?" asked Chizube, with a face.

Bola sprang to my defense. "You know that's not what he meant," he said earnestly, smiling at my daughter.

"On whose side are you?"

"Yours of course," said poor Bola. "But please forgive me. I ought to know better than to get in between father and daughter."

"That's right, Bola," said Chizube smiling. "Probably the wisest thing you've said all day. But seriously –"

"Seriously," I said, "new face, new name, a real passport – what else does anyone need to get the better of the immigration officers, even in the US of A? My late friend, Obi Udozo, told me he heard that Bernard somehow came into this country on probably two occasions. My only question is, what's he looking for here? He wouldn't be so crazy as to indulge in his old trafficking business? Bernard's a smart fellow, too smart to even think he'd get away with it. He'd know, if he was caught a second time, he'd be put away for twenty or more years."

"What about his clothing business?" Chizube asked. "Maybe that's what he does now."

In the lull that followed, I thought about that possibility. Bernard himself had told me that his main business in the United States was in men's clothes – Nigerian men's clothes. That was almost a quarter century earlier, when we first met and talked, in the house of my cousin, Aloysius Jideofo, in Bound Brook, NJ. He had said it with a straight face, though he was well aware that I was, even then, very suspicious of his activities. He had probably been engaged in the two businesses: Drug trafficking and men's clothes. If he was now engaged solely in the clothing business, did that mean he had had a true change of heart, and was going legit, as they say? But try as I did, I could not bring myself to believe that the man had it in him to turn away from the nefarious activity that netted him thousands of easy – but illegal – dollars per trip, to embrace one where the profits came from honest endeavor, and accumulated at a relatively niggardly pace. I could not imagine how a person who showed a marked penchant, from quite early on, for reaping where he did not sow, could now – all of a sudden – become a model citizen. In those early years, in the seventies, he unashamedly took bribes from those who came to his little corner in the Enugu Land Office, seeking plots of government land. He was then a lowly clerk. But persons in search of real estate, who wanted to see his boss, had to *"see"* him first. And he made it his devilish business to frustrate such persons unless and until they gave him his own share of what they brought for his boss. Whenever I dared to challenge him on the issue, he resorted to the worn-out excuse – *"you chop, I chop"* – Nigeria's peculiar phrase encapsulating the odious notion that if my boss takes "a little something" in order to grant a favor, so can I, though I might be at the bottom of the pecking order.

"Daddy, where are you?"

I came out of my reverie. "I'm here, my little girl. Why?"

"You wandered off –"

"As usual?" I asked, as I looked into her eyes that were full of love and compassion; compassion for me, and for my tendency periodically to be caught up in a trance-like contemplation of my yesteryears, years long gone and buried, but whose memories tore at my heart. "You were saying – about Bernard –"

"That he might still be engaged in the clothing business?"

"He might well be," I said, "but I doubt it. Not the Bernard I knew! Too – how to say it – too dull for him. Too much fire in his belly to be satisfied with that kind of thing as his major business! No! Bernard's up to something if he keeps coming back to the US."

"So – ?" she asked, looking intently at me.

Bola answered her question before I could get a word out. "This time, when he arrives at JFK airport, it will not be business as usual."

"You got that right, Bola," I said. "If the Gods are with us, we should be able to bring matters to a head. I have prayed for this moment every minute of the past twenty and more years. I'll call Cornelius. We should be filing our papers in readiness."

Chapter XXIII

WE RECEIVED CORNELIUS Okwu almost like royalty. We always did that, particularly if we knew he was coming to the office. Our Senior Partner, Chikezie Onyeama, would insist that the partners put all business aside, to receive Cornelius, and to give him our undivided attention. He was *that* important to us.

His value to us derived, quite simply, from the fact that he brought us more company clients than any other person, and we could certainly use the retainer fees. These included a trio of quite significant American companies, two of them African-American companies that did business in Nigeria. Moreover, with his deep involvement in the social and cultural life of our Nigerian – especially Igbo – communities, he was a natural magnet for clients in his own legal practice, several of whom were attracted to us because we did business with him.

Our association with him was doubtless mutually beneficial, except that we needed him much more than he needed us. We did his tax returns for him, and might have drawn a handful of our clients to his legal practice. But whatever we did for him paled into insignificance compared to the riches he brought us.

I think I can claim that I had something to do with all of this. Cornelius was a personal friend whom I invited to the offices of Onyeama & Ani, CPAs, and introduced to my employers. My elevation to a partnership almost certainly had something to do with our profitable association with him, though neither partner told me so or even hinted at it. But I have learnt to thank God for whatever good fortune comes my way, however it comes.

I had called Cornelius, as I had promised Chizube and Bola. I updated him on the developments relating to Bernard, and the likelihood that he might be visiting the US in another fortnight or so. His reaction was exactly as I had expected.

"The man must be stark raving mad," Cornelius shouted. "But it is just as we say, that when a dog gets suicidal, it loses its ability to smell excrement. It's to our advantage, anyway."

"That's why I think now's the time to file our papers. Bernard's letter –"

"Bernard's letter," Cornelius interrupted me, "all by itself, was sufficient for us to have started proceedings, at least a month ago, to clear your name of a crime you did not commit, but for which you did time. But I suppose I've always known that you're a patient man."

"The time I did," I said, "taught me patience. And I have prayed that what Obi Udozo told me about Bernard would happen sooner or later –"

"You mean about him coming back here?"

"What else? And now my prayers have been answered."

"That's if the man is stupid enough to do so," Cornelius said. "I grant you if he actually comes, you could kill two birds with one stone."

"Or as we used to say back home, 'one blow, two *akpus*.'"

Cornelius laughed at the old joke, and then said: "It really would be great if the fellow could get what's coming to him, in full measure, at the same time that you cleared your name. That would be sweet justice. You deserve no less. Neither does Bernard – if you see what I mean."

"So now, Cornelius, what's the next step?"

"You know what? I'm due at your office in two days time, on Wednesday. I have a lunch date with your Senior Partner. And if you're a good boy, you might get invited to come along. Okey Ani too! When I last spoke with Okey, he said you'd mentioned about the famous letter being found, and that both he and Chikezie have talked about it, and would like to give as much help in the matter as they can."

"I know. They've been very understanding. Told me I could take as much time as I would need, when we go to court. Of course everyone seems to assume that the court proceedings will be a cakewalk for me. We'll soon see, won't we?"

"A cakewalk?" Cornelius asked. "That's a neat way to put it. But I think that's just about right. I don't anticipate any problems. In fact I think I'll call Chikezie and suggest we all meet in his office, and talk about your matter, and what we need to do. And if you serve your usual refreshments, there might not be any need to go out for lunch. Anyway, I'll see you all on Wednesday. Say hello to your partners for me."

* * *

Chikezie Onyeama's rendezvous with Cornelius was at 11 o'clock. Edith ushered him into the Senior Partner's office at exactly a quarter of eleven. I did not wait to be summoned to the Senior Partner's office. Edith, as she walked by my office, poked her head through the door, and pointed a finger over her shoulder in the direction of Chikezie Onyeama's office.

"He's here," she said.

"Already?" I exclaimed, rising from my chair, and glancing at my watch.

"And you don't have to remind me about anything," said Edith. "Coffee, tea and the usual will be served in the next ten to fifteen minutes. I've added a little surprise, but don't ask me what it is. You'll know when I bring it in."

Okey was already in Chikezie's office, shaking hands with Cornelius as I walked in. "You're early," I said, as he and I touched hands, back to back, three times, before we shook hands. And of course Cornelius being Cornelius, even in the formal atmosphere of an accounting office, both his hand-touch and his handshake were vigorous and painful.

"One of these days, you'll break my hand or something," I said, touching my right hand tenderly.

In some kind of response to my tired protest, Cornelius merely smiled and slapped me on the shoulder. "You enjoy it when I do what I do, no?"

"He does," said Okey Ani. "He's been heard to say that the day your handshake gets soft, that day he'll know you're losing it – or words to that effect. But he's right, you're kind of early."

"Which is surprising," said Chikezie Onyeama. "In the community, you're known for – you know – ?

"But that's only to our social gatherings," said Cornelius, looking at me with a smile and a wink. "But this is serious business. I don't joke with my office appointments, things like that."

"I've sometimes wondered," I teased, "if you are one of those persons who deliberately come late, in order to – so to say – make a grand entrance."

"Wasn't that how you got elected to an office you did'nt want?" Okey asked, laughing. "What was it now? Secretary-General of your town association, if I remember rightly."

"Please don't remind me about it," said Cornelius, shaking his head. But he laughed with us at the memory of that experience. "Anyway, let's get down to business."

With her exquisite sense of timing, Edith just then walked into the office, closely and dutifully followed by Dan Ofokandu, her clerical assistant. Dan was actually a Seton Hall University Economics Student, doing a summer vacation job with our firm. He needed the money, and we needed additional staff, but did not as yet want a full-time addition to Edith. They walked in with two trays laden with a shining aluminum pot of coffee, one of tea, four cups, and an assortment of cakes, cookies, cheeses and crackers. Her 'little' surprise, surprises actually, turned out to be sixteen Chinese egg and spring rolls, eight of each, and soy sauce for condiment. Evidently someone had decided we would not be going out to lunch after all; which was okay with me. This thing between me and Bernard naturally came before all else. They placed the trays on the conference table, around which we sat, and a cup in front of each of us.

"Anything else?" asked Edith, the sweep of her eyes taking us all in.

Okey Ani, who never missed an opportunity to taunt and tease poor Edith, looked up at her, and pointed to his cup. "How about you pour me a cup of coffee – no, tea?"

"*Ochiora!*" Edith fired back, addressing Okey by his praise-name, "we say that one can only respect a king so far, before giving him a piece of one's mind. If you're looking for –"

"*Akwa-okwulu,*" I jumped in, using her own praise-name, and eager to pour oil on troubled waters. "You know he's not serious."

"I don't know that," Edith snapped back, eyes still flashing with mock ferocity. "He should know that I am the water that says you cannot use me to wash your hands –"

"Or to scrub the floor of his house, as you always say," Chikezie Onyeama chipped in, a tolerant smile playing at the corners of his lips.

Dan Ofokandu saved the situation by reaching for Edith's hand, and gently leading her out of the office. At the door, as he let her go ahead of him, he turned and gave us a knowing and fleeting smile, a smile that said he was now familiar with the nature of the ragging that went on in the office.

Cornelius turned to Okey. "You seem to enjoy pulling her leg," he observed. "But are you sure you're not playing with fire?"

"Not at all," said Okey. "She enjoys the teasing."

"Generally, yes," I said. "But do you remember the day she kind-of got pissed off, and accused you of ordering her around because of your position?"

"I'll not likely ever forget how she put it," said Okey, "because that was the first time I heard that *Igbo* saying; something about the hair oil that flows down the head only in the direction in which the head is inclined."

"I never heard that expression before," said Cornelius.

"So you've heard it now," said Okey, laughing. "But, enough of Edith!"

"Right," said Chikezie Onyeama. "We actually have two things to talk about. But, if it's okay with you all, I suggest we concentrate on Cyril's situation, and take up the business of our realtor client after we've seen our way forward about Mr. Bernard – what's his last name – ?"

"Ekwekwe," said Okey. "Very odd name, if you ask me. Cyril, is the man as stubborn as his name seems to imply?"

"Oh, he's stubborn all right," I said, "though I doubt that has anything to do with his name. His father certainly wasn't like him in that regard. Bernard's just a natural born pigheaded human being. He doesn't shift easily once he gets an idea he likes into his head. Of course I'm talking about the Bernard I knew."

Chikezie coughed lightly, to gain our attention. "As I was about to say, about Mr. Ekwekwe, we need to be ready for him, should he actually be brazen enough to set foot in these United States."

"Rumor has it he's been here at least twice since he was repatriated," I said.

"Let's hope his luck will finally run out this third time, Cyril. That's my hope, and I know it's yours, and everybody's here. We need to organize a welcoming party for him. Question is, Cornelius, how do we set about it?"

"The matter is really not too complicated," said Cornelius. "It should be a two-pronged strategy. One is to immediately start the process for the courts to reopen

Cyril's case, so he can clear his name. For that action, I am confident that Bernard's letter should prove quite adequate."

"And the second?" asked Okey, as Cornelius paused.

"Quite simply, we notify the Police, give them all the information we have about the possibility that Bernard might return to this country, and then work with them. We don't have anything specific as to date, time or airline. But the police must know what to do. They might probably need Cyril to identify the man –"

"I'm sure they will." said Okey. "The fellow will very likely travel under a false name and passport –"

"Not to talk of his disguise – you know – beard and mustaches and all that," I said.

"Let me add – and this is something I've mentioned to Cyril," said Cornelius. "The two things don't have to go together. It may be that they can, since our information is that Mr. Ekwekwe might arrive here in just a matter of two weeks or less. And it would be nice if he himself could be *persuaded*, in court, to admit that *he* wrote the letter."

"And then of course," said Chikezie, rubbing his palms together gleefully, "the judge throws the book at him."

Cornelius nodded his agreement. "But of course!"

As we talked, we ate the Chinese rolls and the snacks Edith and Dan Ofokandu had served us. As the discussion went on, I found myself occasionally drifting off into my habitual daydreaming. I could not stop my mind from working over the likely scenarios at the John F. Kennedy airport on the day of Bernard's arrival in New York. Or from the contemplation of the day that would finally see my Red Sea parted; the day that would surely bring glorious sunshine into the darkness in which I had been lurching and groping my way, uncertainly, into what future I might yet have. Up until then, I had not been sure if I truly had a future that would fulfill my potential as a husband, as a father of two of the most wonderful children anyone could have wished for and, not least, as a fulfilled professional. Suddenly, or so it seemed to me, I could taste the deliciousness of the opportunity to sit and pass the examination that would add the coveted acronym – CPA – to my name that had been starved of that style of address. I could see myself holding my head high, and walking with the untrammeled dignity that is the divine birthright of our human condition; able to look even the most severe interlocutor straight in the eye, eyeball to eyeball, unflinchingly, and as calmly – or as aggressively – as the circumstances might dictate. I could sense total freedom – *my* freedom – from the fetters that so unfairly shackled my mind and spirit because of my long stretch in the pen. Freedom to laugh with family and friends, without wondering, always wondering, if any might be laughing *at* me and the eight long years of my degradation and melancholy.

Okey touched me on the shoulder, and I came quickly awake. "Cornelius was asking you a question," he said.

"I'm sorry. Please excuse me. What was the question?"

"I was only wondering," said Cornelius, "how you want to proceed. Do you want to start action immediately for a retrial, based on Bernard's letter? Or wait for his arrival in the country, and then take it from there? My advice is that we go with the letter now. When your friend – I mean, Bernard – comes, we'll welcome him. But that would really be more a police matter than yours. It's your call, Cyril."

"Let's do as you've suggested," said Okey.

"I think so too," said Chikezie Onyeama. "Start the retrial now. Mr. Ekwekwe is master of his own time. He could change his schedule as he likes, and not arrive here at the time we are expecting him. He could even cancel his trip, we don't know."

Three pairs of eyes riveted on me. I looked at my companions in turn, and then settled my gaze on Cornelius. "I think I need to consult just one more person," I said.

"Rose?" asked Cornelius.

"Rosemary, of course," said Okey.

"Actually," I said, "you're both wrong. I was thinking about young Bola Akande."

Okey grinned from ear to ear. "That's your daughter's – how to say –"

"Yes, boyfriend," I interrupted him. "How did you know about him?"

"Do you need to ask?" asked Chikezie. "Our entire community knows your daughter. She's done all of us proud, as an exceptional athlete. Everyone now knows who she hangs out with. I've known about him for quite some time. If you ask me, they make a great pair."

"Oh?" I said, not knowing what else to say, but happy for my daughter that she was so well regarded in our community.

"The fellow is devilishly handsome," said Cornelius. "The day we met him at Cyril's, Ann said to me privately that she didn't think she'd ever met anyone handsomer. So I asked her what about me? And she –"

"I don't think we want to know what she said," said Okey, holding up an arm to stop Cornelius.

"Speak for yourself." I said. "Go on Cornelius, tell us."

"Sorry to disappoint you, Okey," said Cornelius, with a smile. "She said nothing about my face which, I'm sure, is what you're thinking – although I don't believe there's anything wrong with it. Anyway, isn't it said that men don't have to be good-looking –"

"You're just going round and round," said Okey. "If you don't want to tell us, we'll understand."

Cornelius laughed. "There's nothing to understand –"

At that moment, there was a light rat-a-tat, Edith's signature knock, on the office door. She opened the door, and signaled to me to follow her. "Your daughter's on the line."

"You could have told her I'm in a meeting," I protested without much conviction, as I walked past her out of Mr. Onyeama's office.

"I said it's your daughter," Edith said, shutting the door after me. She pointed to my desk telephone. "You've forgotten? You always said to call you, no matter –"

But I was no longer listening to her. I quickly picked up the receiver, and said: "Hello, my little girl –"

"Sorry, sir," said a voice that was not my daughter's. "It's me, Bola. Good morning, sir – or is it afternoon?"

"It's not quite yet noon," I said. "So, good morning to you too! What's up, Bola?"

I listened intently to him for some thirty seconds, and then slowly put down the receiver, my mind in a whirl. Edith was still standing by the door to Mr. Onyeama's office. I did not know why she was still standing there. But she opened and held the door for me, her eyes fixed intently on mine, as I went silently by her. I stood in the middle of Chikezie's office and, for a second or two, stared at my two partners and Cornelius.

Cornelius slowly rose from his chair. "What's the matter – ?"

"Bernard's plane," I blurted out, "is due to touch down in another hour or so."

"That's impossible!" said Okey.

"What happened?" asked Onyeama.

"Did your daughter – ?"

"It wasn't Chizube," I said. "She was there, but it was Bola who gave me the news."

"Your friend – I mean Bernard – was supposed to be arriving in ten days or so," said Cornelius.

Chikezie shook his head slowly, and said: "Didn't I just say that the man could change – ?"

"But not like this," said Cornelius. "By the way, is it still JFK – ?"

"Wrong! It's Newark International airport."

"Wow!" Cornelius exclaimed. "This turns everything on its head. Listen folks. This changes everything. There's no time to waste. We must notify the police right away."

"There's no time for that," I said.

"You can't be serious," said Okey. "What do you plan to do? Arrest the man all by yourself? A citizen's arrest, or what?"

"You know, Cyril," said Cornelius, "there's still time to call the police. Takes only two or three minutes –"

"You may be right," I said. "But suddenly I have this crazy idea to just stand there as he walks out of the immigration and customs hall. I want to look right into his eyes at the very moment he sees me, and realizes that his disguise, whatever it is, has done him little or no good; that his nemesis, however long it has taken, has finally caught up with him. Arrest him by myself? Of course not! But this meeting, face to face with my old friend, will be sweeter by far, than the sight of the police clamping their handcuffs on him. Suddenly it seems this meeting is what my soul has yearned for, above everything else, these many years. I want him to stand there right in front of me. I want him to look into my eyes and my soul, and see for himself the anguish I have endured these past two decades; the hatred buried deep in my heart for the grievous wrong he has done to me, and – yes – to our friendship. After that, what will be, will be. There are police officers at the airport, and perhaps Cornelius knows what to do to involve them."

I stopped because I was well and truly winded, and had nothing more to say. My three friends were staring at me, eyes glazed in total surprise.

"Wow!" said Okey and Cornelius together.

"I never heard you talk like that, Cyril," Chikezie said.

"What I said is exactly how I feel. If it's okay with you all, I think it's time to leave for the airport."

"Who else is coming?" Cornelius asked, looking from Okey to Chikezie.

"I imagine both of us want to go with you," said Chikezie. "But I think one of us had better stay behind." He turned to Okey: "*Ochiora*, you go."

Okey looked uncertainly at the Senior Partner for a moment or two. "Is this an order? Are you sure you don't –"

"I think I'm sure," said Chikezie, serious of countenance. "But if you'd rather not –"

"Who said I'd rather not," Okey interrupted him, laughing. "Just try and stop me."

"I won't," said Chikezie. "I know you too well to deny you an opportunity like this. By the way, Cyril, I hope your young man – Bola – I hope he's sure about all this."

"I believe so. It seems Bernard was up to his old tricks, deliberately misleading even his closest associates as to the date of his travel. Word came from a police friend of Bola's in Enugu. The story is that Bernard snuck out of Enugu two or three days ago. But apparently one of those associates, with some kind of a grudge against Bernard, caught on to the deception, and did not care whom he told about it. The police officer made contacts in Lagos, and Bernard was actually seen in the waiting hall for passengers boarding the British Airways flight out of Muritala Mohammed airport last night. Oh, my God! Rosemary!" I looked at Chikezie. "Please excuse me one moment. I've got to call her."

"You can use my telephone," he offered.

But I was already close to the connecting door to my office. "Thanks," I said to him over my shoulder. "But it's okay."

More by force of habit, acquired as a defense mechanism against especially Edith's omni-directional ears, than any real need for confidentiality on this particular occasion, I preferred to talk to Rosemary from my office. I dialed her office number, and when the answering machine came on, I put down the receiver and dialed her cell phone number.

"Cyril?" her voice came on promptly. "Don't tell me you're still in your office?"

"Where are you?"

"On my way to the airport," she said breathlessly. "I was out on a field assignment when Chi-Chi called and told me about Bernard. I'm close to the airport, maybe another three or four miles only."

"I'm setting out right away –" I started to tell her.

"Remember, CY," she interrupted. "It's Terminal B. Don't go wondering all over the airport. You're always confused about the terminals."

I wanted to protest that I was not *always* confused about the terminals, but I knew it would be pointless. So I smiled to myself, because I had to admit that *sometimes*, I was indeed confused. I was still smiling as I walked back into Chikezie's office.

Okey pounced on me. "Still very much in love with her," he observed. "After these many years, she can still make you smile like *that* just from talking to her? I envy you."

"Don't mind him," said Chikezie.

"I don't," I said, still smiling. "Okey must be Okey! Cornelius, Okey, if you're ready, let's go."

"You told her?" Cornelius asked.

"As we talk, she's probably only a mile or two from the airport."

"So, what's keeping us?" asked Okey. "We'll all go in my car. How's that?"

"Thanks for the offer, but –"

"You know what, Cyril?" Chikezie said, "I really don't think you should drive. Not to the airport, the way you look to me. And maybe especially not *from* the airport! Who knows what'll happen there, and in what shape you'll be after the encounter?"

I looked hard at him. "But Rosemary is driving herself –"

"Rose," said Cornelius, joining the opposition, "is Rose. You are Cyril. There's a world of difference there. Stop arguing, man. Let's go. By the way, I think I'll follow in *my* car. That'll give me some flexibility, just in case."

They really gave me no reason why it was okay for Rosemary to drive herself, but not for me. But it occurred to me that I could drive Rosemary's car back to the office, or wherever else the turn of events would take us. So I threw up my arms in a show of resignation, and followed Okey and Cornelius out of the office.

As we drove to the airport, Okey suddenly asked: "Who else are you expecting to be there?"

"You mean apart from Rosemary? Bola will be there; my daughter also."

"Chizube? She's coming too? What about your son, Ndubisi? Who's minding him?"

"Ndubisi is away to a summer camp. He's not due back for another three days."

For several moments, we fell silent, each of us occupied with his own thoughts. Then Okey shook his head several times, and whistled softly under his breath. He reached for my hand with his right hand, and gave it a light squeeze.

"Man!" he said, "that'll be quite a welcoming party for your – I mean – Mr. Ekwekwe."

I looked sideways at him, even as my face broke in a smile of deep satisfaction.

Chapter XXIV

THE BRITISH AIRWAYS plane had already landed, some fifteen minutes earlier than scheduled, when the trio of Okey Ani, Cornelius Okwu and I walked into a very crowded International Arrivals Hall. Rosemary had linked up with Chizube and Bola, and the latter was already well launched into his story of how the news reached him about Bernard's sudden change of plans.

Chizube ran into my arms and held me in a fierce embrace. Her eyes were tear-stained, as she looked into my eyes, and her voice was tremulous with the strong emotions that filled her heart.

"Dad, I love you, and I have so looked forward to a day like this –"

"That's if he really shows up," I said.

"He will," said Bola, shaking hands with me, "unless – but God forbid – he decided to stop in London for a day or two."

"God will not let that happen," said Rosemary, giving me a peck on the cheek, and then linking arms with me.

"Amen!" said Chizube, still holding me tightly.

"Hi, Rose!" Cornelius pulled her into a warm embrace. "Still as radiantly beautiful as the day we first met, back in D.C. – what – twenty-something years ago."

"And you're still the same flatterer –"

"How're you Rosemary?" asked Okey Ani.

"Fine – especially today."

"But please, Rose," said Cornelius, "remember, it's possible, Bernard might not be on this –"

Rosemary shook her head vigorously. "I don't believe," she said, "that the same God who miraculously let us into the secret of Bernard's movements can let us suffer such a disappointment. God meant for this to happen, exactly as it is happening. I believe that."

"The same God, is it not," I whispered in her ear, "that let me suffer eight years of prison hell for something I did not do?"

She looked at me reproachfully, and whispered back: "Stop talking like that, CY. Don't you know He's a mysterious God, and we'll never fully know His ways?"

Chizube, who had clearly heard our whispered exchange, actually laughed out loud. "Mum, can't you see dad's not serious?" She searched my face for a moment or two. "Dad, you didn't really mean – ?"

"Of course I didn't, my little girl! I thought your mum knew me better than that."

Conversation ebbed and flowed, as we huddled together, and watched arriving passengers filter out of the immigration and customs enclosure, and walk past us toward the exits, or into the welcoming arms of relatives and friends. And I said to myself that when Bernard emerged from the same enclosure, an altogether different reception awaited him. Would it be easy to recognize him? Did our friendship and close association, over many years, guarantee that I could spot him, and strip his beard and mustache, or perhaps a false nose, from off his handsome face?

In designing the waiting area, the airport authorities clearly underestimated the seating that would be required on an almost daily basis. What seats there were, barely sat a third of the crowd that thronged the hall. Bola managed to find an empty seat for Rosemary, but that was it. The rest of us stood and waited, or walked around to ease aching feet.

I had little option but to stand and wait. Even when, as at the beginning of our watch, we knew it was too early for the passengers on Bernard's British Airways flight to have completed their immigration and customs formalities, I stood where I was and closely observed each arriving passenger walk by. I paid attention only to the men, because I did not think that even Bernard would try to disguise himself as a woman.

We might have been waiting for about half an hour when I spotted a passenger whose luggage had labels that I recognized as British Airways tags. Discreetly, though it was something I hated to do, I leaned towards the man, and asked: "British Airways?" He nodded, and moved on.

It would be futile to try to describe the feelings that overwhelmed me at that moment. Just the thought that Bernard might soon emerge from the customs area, and walk towards me, set my heart aflutter. What would he look like? My Bernard – the Bernard who was my friend in my primary and high school years – was one of the handsomest persons I knew. With a beard and a mustache, and who knew what else he had changed in his physiognomy, would I recognize him? He might be falsely stooped in his gait, or wear a hat pulled down over much of his face. He could have blackened two or three front teeth, which would doubtless give him a hideous appearance.

I would not let my mind dwell too long on the halcyon years of our friendship. It had been a good ride, with him as my friend, though – and this was something I was admitting to myself for perhaps the first time – for many of those years of friendship,

I had played second fiddle to him. Especially when he made his regular forays into his favorite girls' school in Enugu – the Federal Technical College – to chat up the girls! I merely tagged along. He certainly had his way with some of the girls. But I was not like him. I had neither the fire in the belly nor, to be truthful, the strong desire to defy my father's moral edicts relating to girls, to follow Bernard's example.

I was still reminiscing when someone tapped me on the shoulder. I turned, and there was Joy Udozo, smiling, her eyes kindly and compassionate. I remember the first thought that rushed into my head was that she was absolutely at the right place, at the right time. And for the best reason in the world! *She* had found Bernard's lost letter, when I had practically given up all hopes of such a miracle.

"What are you doing here?" I asked nevertheless, mechanically, as we embraced.

"Same thing you're doing, Cyril," she replied, spreading her arms wide.

"How – who told you – ?"

"Your wife, Rosemary," she said, looking around her. "Where's she?"

"There!" I pointed to Rosemary where she sat, as it were, perched at the end of a bench seating some dozen or so persons. Joy made a beeline for her, with me in tow. Rosemary instinctively turned, saw us approaching, and rose to meet Joy.

"I thought you should know," said Rosemary as the two embraced warmly, "though I didn't mean for you to trouble yourself –"

"No trouble at all, Rose. This is a day we've all prayed for. I wouldn't have missed it –"

"What about your work?" I asked, concerned she was perhaps putting her job on the line, just to show support for me.

"I'm on night shift today," Joy said. "But even if I was at work when Rose called, I would have managed somehow to be here." She paused and looked at me. "I'm glad for you, Cyril. When Rose called, and told me everything about Bernard's surprise arrival today, I was like – this is God's work –"

"You mean you knew Bernard's original travel plans?" I asked.

Rosemary and Joy exchanged glances, and then Rosemary said: "I thought it was the only fair thing to do."

I nodded firmly. "Of course, you're right," I said. "Joy, I'm sorry I didn't think of telling you myself. I feel bad about it now, but I hope you'll forgive me."

"C'mon, Cyril, you didn't have to do anything like that –"

"It's kind of you to say that, Joy, but –"

"Okay, Cyril, if it makes you feel better, I forgive you."

"Thank you, Joy. It does. Please come with me. I want to introduce you to my friends."

Rosemary left her seat, and went with us. I did the introductions. But when it came to his turn, Okey Ani smilingly waved me aside.

"You don't have to introduce us," he said, drawing Joy into a swaying, laughter-filled embrace. "How are the kids?" he asked Joy, as they swayed from side to side.

"They're fine, Ochiora," said Joy. "How's Charity?"

"Still shopping!" said Okey. "She's sorry you closed your store."

"I know," said Joy. "D'you know she called me one day – that's quite a while ago – and told me she's never forgiven me for that."

Joy seemed quite captivated by Bola, when I introduced them. At one point, she said privately to Rosemary and me: "I wish my daughter, Uchenna, would find such a tall, good-looking young man. But there's still time –"

"How old is she?" Rosemary asked.

"Oh, I don't know," said Joy, vaguely. "She's twenty or twenty-one, something like that."

I continued to scrutinize the faces of the arriving passengers as they walked by. My mind was in a whirl, as conflicting emotions surged and ebbed in my overcharged brains. It was a strange situation because, though everyone in our group, like me, seemed to also search the faces of the passengers, only Joy and I had a realistic shot at recognizing Bernard. Perhaps Rosemary too, who had only met him once, in Enugu, when I brought the two together, and introduced Bernard to her. Rosemary had not even been in the court – thank God – on the day Bernard gave the damning evidence that sealed my fate, and sent me to prison for a crime *he* committed.

I moved slightly away from the group. I tried – I really tried – not to think too much about the past. But my mind would not let me. It stubbornly recalled almost everyday of the dozen or so years of my friendship with Bernard: the fun times, the sad times, the turbulent years of the Nigeria-Biafra civil war, the adventures we shared, and our separation when – in 1971 – he went up to the University of Ibadan for his undergraduate studies. I was left behind in Enugu, and needed to take a second shot at the university entrance examination a year – in fact two years – later.

I recalled the day I proudly showed off Rosemary to him, at the Sports Club in Enugu, during his second long vacation from the university. As we feasted on *ngwo-ngwo* and *suyah*, two Nigerian delicacies, I let a strangely taciturn Bernard engage in a slow conversation with my shy girl-friend, contenting myself with a brief interjection from time to time. And at the end, Bernard had pronounced Rosemary perfect, and had gone on to wonder aloud: "how in the world did you do it?" As if I lacked the necessities and wherewithal to win the love of a beautiful girl!

My mind relentlessly recalled my first meeting with my friend, in these United States, on the dance floor of the inaugural festivities of the Enyimba Union of New Jersey, the first Igbo association in the State of New Jersey. Bernard's totally unexpected donation of three hundred dollars to the Enyimba Union had set off alarm bells in my head, and I began to ask myself – and him – about the true nature of his business trips to America. And I kept asking that question until the day my friend stood in the witness box, in the court of my eternal damnation, and testified falsely that I was a member of his drug-trafficking ring in the United States of America.

An agonized sigh – more actually like the strangled cry of a drowning man – escaped my parched throat. In my heightened state of confusion about everything, of anger against my friend who was really my deadliest foe, and of sadness about the contradictions of my life experiences with the same friend, my head – held between my hands – fell forward of its own volition.

Then I heard Joy Udozo's solicitous voice. "What's the matter, Cyril?"

I turned to her and, instinctively, took a step back. Her eyes, at once tender and challenging, held mine with such intensity that I quickly lowered my eyes. When I looked up again, she was still staring at me. But now a soft smile played on her lips.

"If this works out for you, Cyril," she said gently, "maybe Obi's soul will finally rest in peace, and maybe you'll find it in your heart to forgive us."

The mention of her late husband's name was like a dagger driven deep into my heart. I immediately felt a strange sensation overwhelm me. And I heard a solemn voice call out my name twice: "Cyril! Cyril! Remember?" From whence the voice came, I was not sure. For just a brief moment, I thought it might have been Joy. I looked again at her, and somehow knew *she* had not called my name. But her eyes shone with a light that sparkled, and did not waver, as they continued to gaze at me. Then, suddenly, with another strangled cry, I remembered; and I knew that the voice was Obi's, calling out to me from beyond the Great Divide.

The voice again asked: "Remember?"

I remembered. I remembered what Obi Udozo, gasping for breath on his hospital bed, had said to me on the day of my last visit to him. And remembering, I knew what I had to do.

I pulled Rosemary and Chizube aside. I held both in an encompassing embrace, and then spoke the words I never thought – in the last twenty years of my life – that I would ever utter.

"I cannot go through with this," I told them in a voice that was strangely calm and measured.

"Go through with what?" Rosemary asked me, backing away from my embrace, an edge of alarm evident in her voice.

"Bernard," I said simply.

"I don't understand," said Chizube.

"I – think – I – do," said her mother, slowly, drawing out her words. "But, CY, what you're saying is impossible. We're here. And any moment now, Bernard will emerge from the customs area. We have no other option but to challenge him –"

"Dad, what's the matter?" Chizube asked. "Are you saying – ?"

"We'll show ourselves to him," I said. "No question about that. But I cannot – *I will not* – call the police or anything like that. I cannot do it."

"Why?" Chizube was looking at me with wild eyes. "What happened? What about your friends – Uncle Okey and Uncle Cornelius? Do they know?"

"When did you decide – ?" Rosemary asked.

"Only a moment ago," I said truthfully.

"But why? What happened?"

"What's going on there?" Cornelius asked, as he and Okey, and the others, came towards us. "A family caucus, or what?"

"Please tell them," Rosemary said to me. She turned to Cornelius. "He says he'll not go through –"

I drew her to me once more, and held her close, as I told my friends about my decision. "I would much rather concentrate on clearing my name with the help of Bernard's letter," I said, and proceeded to tell them about my last conversation with Obi Udozo, as he lay on his death bed. I repeated to them the words Obi had spoken to me, which have rung in my head ceaselessly, from that day on, in spite of my determined effort to shut it out: "Leave vengeance to God," Obi had pleaded. I looked keenly at Joy as I ended my story, and said to her, almost as in an aside: "I decided to let the soul of a departed friend rest in peace."

Okey and Cornelius stared at me in shock and disbelief.

Joy, very deeply affected, covered her face with trembling hands. She said: "I don't know what to say, Cyril." Then turning to Rosemary, she added: "Please Rose –"

"It's all right, Joy," Rosemary said quickly, coming up to her, arms open. They embraced, and held on for a long moment.

Bola, eyes as wide as I had ever seen them, came up to me. "Sir," he said, "you are an extraordinary man."

Joy, disengaging from Rosemary's embrace, separated herself from the group, and went and stood by herself, as sobs shook her slender frame.

Rosemary shook her head slowly, but not in anger. "If anyone had told me you would do this –"

That was as far as she got when I heard Joy let out a soft scream, as she pointed towards the customs enclosure. "Cyril!"

I knew right away that she had spotted Bernard. I rushed to her side, and immediately, I too saw him. Totally fascinated, I watched as he approached us. I turned to Cornelius and Okey, and signaled to them to come closer. The first to rush to my side was Bola. He pointed, and asked: "Is that him?"

I looked at him, and silently nodded. Bernard wore a two-inch beard, and a luxuriant, well-groomed mustache. Other than those two adornments, the Bernard who walked purposefully towards us, with a strong and very erect gait, was the same Bernard I had known, though perhaps a little leaner in the face than of yore. I was surprised that he had not made a greater effort to disguise himself. But then it occurred to me that he had no notion that there would be a welcoming group for him, a group that would include *me*. Bernard had just one suit-case, on a roller, and an overnight bag slung across his shoulder.

"I'll be damned!" Okey Ani softly exploded.

"Phew!" Cornelius whistled.

I was the leader of my group but, as Bernard got nearer and nearer to us, a strange force held me rooted to the spot where I stood. I wanted to go forward and be the first to meet him, but my feet would not move. The next thing I saw were Bola and Chizube as, hand in hand, they strode forward and stood in the path of the approaching Bernard.

His sixth sense must have told Bernard that the two young persons quite deliberately stood in his way. He paused, and stared at them, and then a strange light came into his eyes. From where I stood, not quite ten paces from him, I saw his eyes light up.

At that moment, from somewhere behind us, a woman's voice called out: "Bola! What are you doing?"

We all turned in the direction of the voice, and I saw a woman running towards us, an arm stretched out in Bola's direction. She was out of breath, and her chest heaved with the effort.

"Mum!" exclaimed Bola. "What are *you* doing here?"

"What are you doing?" she asked again, but did not pause as she literally ran towards Bernard, and threw herself into his arms.

Bola and Chizube, visibly transfixed with horror and astonishment, their senses seemingly paralyzed, could only stand and stare.

"Mum," Bola found his voice, "do you know this – ?"

"This man," said Bola's mum, "is your dad."

It was an indescribable and extraordinary moment. I felt the power literally drain out of my legs and the life blood out of my faculties. I might have stumbled – I certainly felt my knees give – because the next I knew, Okey Ani had an arm around my shoulders. Cornelius, who also stood next to me, kept muttering, over and over again: "I don't – I can't – believe this!"

Neither could I! A woman I had never met in my life, stood there – not quite five yards in front of me – arm in arm with the man that had blighted my life, desperately proclaiming that she and the blighter – no pun intended – were mum and dad to the young man Rosemary and I had virtually accepted into our family as somewhat more than just a boyfriend to our daughter.

But I had to believe what my eyes were seeing, what my ears had heard. Else, I had gone into one of my trance-like states. But this was no trance. The Bernard, at whom I was looking, had substance. His arms held Bola's mother, but his eyes now found and held my eyes. For a moment or two, I could not take my eyes off him. A beatific smile had spread across his face, but the smile was not for me, or it would have been the very devil of a smile. The smile was clearly for Bola, his son, on whom he now focused his gaze.

Bola and my daughter had not moved since Bola's mother's momentous declaration. They stood, hand in hand, alternately looking at Bernard and at each other. Then they both turned to me. At that moment, the strength mysteriously returned to my legs, and I stepped forward, and stood in front of them.

I pointed. "This is Bola's mother?" I asked Bernard, looking him straight in the eye.

Bernard's smile widened. "Cyril," he said softly, "it's good to see you again. Yes, Hannah is Bola's mum."

I could not believe his sang-froid, but then he was always the consummate dissembler. He knew – at least he must have sensed – the great danger in which he stood at that moment. He surely knew that his nemesis had finally caught up with him. I did not need to be a Solomon to see that his smiling demeanor – how beguiling soever it was – was merely an act of bravado, put on with intent to deceive, to make me think that, for him, this was just another day at the arrivals hall of the Newark International Airport.

Bernard, an arm around the waist of the woman I now knew to be Bola's mum, looked past me at his son. He was still smiling, and the strange light I had seen in his eyes still shone brilliantly. I do not know what impelled me, but when he made a move to go to his son, I stepped aside to let him pass. Bola, still obviously in shock, watched silently as Bernard came up to him and reached for, and took his free hand. Chizube, no less in shock, poor girl, clung to Bola's other hand.

Fascinated, I watched father and son. Letting go of Bola's hand, Bernard placed a hand on Bola's shoulder. But Bola stepped back and away from him.

"Don't touch me!"

"Bola," said Bernard gently, "I'm sorry you had to find out this way. I'm truly sorry."

They were two of a kind. Both were tall, with Bola – at about six feet four inches – some two or so inches the taller of the two. Bola had his mother's light complexion, and the cast of her face: the somewhat aquiline nose, the full lips. But, in a strange way, it was easy to see that Bola's facial expression, the dimple when he smiled, the shape and cut of his ears, were Bernard's too. And now I remembered that something about the younger man had struck me on the day my daughter first brought him to our home, though I had not then thought about any resemblance to Bernard.

Bernard looked around, and his eyes soon settled on Rosemary and Joy, as they stood close to each other staring, as we all were doing, at him. He looked at both intently for a brief moment, and his smile broadened. "That's Rosemary, and – let me see – yes! Joy Udozo. It's been a very long time, but I remember both of you. Rosemary, I believe we only met once –"

"I remember you too," Rosemary said coldly. "You are the devil himself."

"Easy now, Rosemary," I appealed to her.

Cornelius came to me, and whispered in my ear: "What do we do now?"

"The exact same question I was going to ask," said Okey Ani, coming up to us.

I looked at both with as much calmness as I could muster in the circumstances. "Nothing," I said. "Something terribly important is unraveling before our eyes. On a scale of one to ten, ten being of the utmost importance, I'd give this a ten, and my old desire for vengeance, a two. Let's give some space to Bola and his dad and mum, and then see where we go from there."

At that moment, an airport official – at least he looked like one – came up to us. "Do you mind moving to one side? You're blocking the way for other passengers."

We moved as a group to an area not clustered with passengers and their families and friends, close to an exit door. Bola came and stood in front of his mother, his eyes ablaze with stark hostility. He stared at her for a moment or two, and then moved to confront Bernard. Bernard again made to reach for Bola's hand, but his son's eyes gave him pause.

"You can have no idea how much I've looked forward to this day," Bola said to him, "ever since I knew what was what. But now, I'm sorry I met you. You are not my –"

"Bola!" his mother shouted, "Don't say that! I'm sorry –"

"You should be!" said Bola. "I'm sorry too. I'm sorry that what I have to say now, I'm compelled to say."

He paused for a moment, looking Bernard straight in the eye. When he next spoke, his voice was clearly still charged with passion, but it was modulated to a pitch that made the words even more biting.

"It takes more than biology to be a father," he said. "As far as I'm concerned, you are *not* my father. I have no father! Mr. Jideofo may forgive you, but I can't. On top of everything else, you've just about destroyed any meaningful relationship I had with him and his family."

He turned to Chizube. "I'm sorry –" he began, but I would not let him go any further. Quickly moving to his side, I took hold of his and Chizube's hands, and held them firmly for a second or two.

"Bola," I said, "please hold it just one moment." I let go of Bola's hand, and turned to Bernard. "Do you know who this young lady is? She's my daughter. Her name is Chizube. She and Bola have been – well – friends for some time now. Your son Bola has been almost like a part of my family. Do you understand the strange twist of fate that brings *your* son and *my* daughter together? I hope you do, because I don't. Of all the improbable things that can happen, this must surely rank as one of the most bizarre. You heard what he said just now?"

Bernard was staring at me with wild eyes. "About you forgiving me? I can't believe it, after everything that happened. You don't know how much I've regretted –"

"Have you, really? But it is of little consequence to me now. I finally reached an accommodation with my God, and with your friend Obi Udozo – you remember him? Almost with his dying breath, he asked me to leave vengeance to God. He was truly sorry for his role in my story. His wife Joy, here, has been an angel to me and my family. Without her, I doubt I would be standing here this moment."

I paused, and looked around me. Six pairs of eyes were staring at me steadily. Not a person among them moved so much as a muscle. I beckoned to Joy, and she stepped up to me. I put my free arm around her shoulder, and made her stand by my side, only a hand-reach away from Bernard.

"Bernard, do you know why it was easy for me to forgive you? Joy found your letter –"

Bernard looked up sharply, even as one of his hands flew to his mouth. "You are surprised? She found your letter, when I had almost given up hope it would ever be found. I don't need to ask you if you know the letter I'm talking about. The same letter you and Obi – God rest his soul – denied you ever wrote. As I said, Obi made his peace with me. I know God has forgiven him. And I have no further need for the anger and the hatred that have burned in my heart against you, and what you did to me and to our friendship.

"Your son loves my daughter. For both their sakes, I will pray that Bola will one day find it in his heart to give you a second chance to be the dad he never had –"

'I can't –' Bola said under his breath, but in a tone of suppressed intensity.

"You can, my boy," I said reassuringly. "It depends of course on him –"

"Mr. Bernard Ek-we-k-we, you are under arrest for entering the country with a false passport."

Two airport police officers had materialized out of thin air. They stood, as the police always seem to stand – with an air of great imperturbability – when they need to project the seriousness of what they are about to do to an unsuspecting civilian.

I looked quickly at Cornelius. "What happened?"

Cornelius stared back at me. "Beats me," he said earnestly, spreading his arms wide. "I had nothing to do with this."

One of the police officers allowed the ghost of a smile to curl up his lips. "A tip-off from Nigeria, moments ago," he said, and turned to Bernard. "Come on! We don't have all afternoon for this –"

"But he just passed through the immigration –" I began to say.

"I don't have to explain this shit to you," the same officer said, with a sneer on his face. "But if you want to know, the tip-off came just a little too late for that. But we finally caught up with him – is all that matters. Come on, Mr. Ek-wek-we, you know your rights. Anything you say can be used in evidence against you. If you don't have a lawyer, the court will appoint one for you. So, say goodbye to your friends. And let's go!"

For just a fraction of a second, Bernard seemed on the point of challenging his arrest. Then he looked, first at Bola, then at Bola's mum Hannah, who had stood by his side all the time. And, suddenly, his spirit went out of him, and he hung his head in surrender. Slowly, he extended his arms towards the officers for the inevitable handcuffs.

Softly – so softly I had some difficulty hearing him clearly – he said to me: "C.Y. I'm awfully sorry about everything. You were a good friend; the best anyone could have wished for. I know I do not deserve your forgiveness. Nor yours, Bola! Your mum and I had thought it best that you do not know me, until the fullness of time. But God, in His infinite wisdom, chose this moment to bring things to a head. It is a long story, and your mum will explain things more fully to you in due course. Bola, please do not blame your mum for any of this. She did what she did because I persuaded her that it was for the best."

Bernard had spoken in Igbo, because of the police officers, and more earnestly than I had ever known him speak. The change in him was startling. The Bernard of yore – the Bernard who had been my best friend in the world – *that* Bernard was a prince of dissemblers, a man who seemed to have steel in his spine, a charmer par excellence and, without question, one of God's gifts to the female of the species. The Bernard who now stood before me, and before his son Bola, was a broken man. His eyes suddenly seemed sunken – hollow and haunted.

The police officer who had done all the talking, and seemed the senior of the two, tapped Bernard on the shoulder. "Let's go!"

Bernard turned to him. "Just one more second, please. C.Y. Please do not let what happened between you and me, stand in the way of your daughter – what's her name – Chizube – and my son. Let it be for them as God wills. I don't care anymore what happens to me. I deserve whatever it is, and more."

He looked around him one more time, and his eyes took us all in. "This was quite a welcoming party, C.Y. I didn't expect it, but that's all right. I don't know your two friends there, but this is no time for introductions. Bola, my son, I love you. I know in time you'll learn to forgive me. Officer!"

His back stiffened once again by that spark of vitality which he seemed to possess in superabundance, and with Bola's mum in tears, but clinging desperately to his arm, Bernard let the police officers march him away. He did not once look back at us.

Bola's knees gave, and he sank to the floor. Chizube went down with him, and held his head to her chest.

*   *   *

"Was that a whirlwind, or what!" Cornelius said.

"What happened just now?" Okey Ani asked, moving his head vigorously from side to side, his arms spread out.

"An old friend got his just deserts," I said. "That's all. But I must confess I did not expect to be the least bit affected by any of it."

"Meaning you were?" asked Cornelius. "You have a soft heart, my friend. That's the trouble with you."

"He *was* my friend," I said. "Bola! Chizube! Let's go. Joy, would you like to come to the house? There's a lot to talk about, and you're very much a part of all this; especially because of the letter. Cornelius will file papers to have my conviction overturned –"

"It'll be a piece of cake! Trust me. And with Bernard the way he looks now, I'd imagine even he would not stand in your way."

"*Ochiora*," I called to Okey by his praise-name. "I hope there'll be no problem if I do not return to the office? And I trust you'll tell our senior partner what happened here?""

"No problem at all," said he. "I'll fill Chikezie in on our very strange encounter with your – I mean – Bernard Ekwekwe. But what about your car?"

"I'll pick it up later in the day, or tomorrow. I'm going straight home from here."

Rosemary took my hand in hers, and gently led me out of the International Arrivals Hall of Newark's Liberty International Airport.

"Free at last!" I said softly to myself, echoing the unforgettable and immortal words of Martin Luther King, Jnr. *"Free at last! Thank God Almighty, I am free at last."*

Epilogue

M Y MOTHER MADE me sit down by her, and listen to her and my father Bernard Ekwekwe's story. I mostly let her tell her story, because it was the most important story of my life. There was very little I could do about anything. I did not choose my parents. For better or for worse, Bernard Ekwekwe was my father – more biological than real, to be sure, but my father nevertheless. If Chizube's dad could not figure out what strange twist of fate brought Chizube and me together, neither could I. If I had a choice now, I would renounce my father. But even if I renounced him, I could not blot out the stain he had left on me, and perhaps on my mum, by his nefarious activities. As the Igbo say, if one finger touches oil, the oil quickly spreads to the other fingers.

Perhaps I listened patiently to my mum's story because I had not recovered from the staggering developments of the day. How could I recover from a shock so earth-shattering for me that I just plain assumed that I had lost Chizube? My father was the notorious Bernard Ekwekwe – notorious, that is, within the family of the Jideofos, the family that was on the point of becoming my family too, when Chizube and I did what was inevitable by reason of the fact that she had become my world, and I, hers.

"It is important that you know," she said, "so you can understand why we did what we felt we had to do to protect you."

"Protect me from knowing who my dad is?" I asked.

"Yes," she said emphatically. "The story goes way back to 1975. That was the year your father graduated from the University of Ibadan. That was also the year we met, and fell in love. We practically got engaged, but my parents would not let us marry, because Bernard is Ibo. We went to see my parents in Surulere, Lagos. But it was useless. I argued that I had grown up practically an Ibo girl. I wasn't born in Enugu,

261

but the family lived there from my childhood till my dad retired from the Railway Corporation, and returned to Lagos. During the Biafran war, I was in Lagos with my parents, but I returned to Enugu almost as soon as the war was over. I was in the Enugu campus of the University of Nigeria when your dad and I met."

"So you did not marry –"

"We didn't. But we were very much in love, and in 1977 you were born."

"When did your parents know about me?"

"As soon as you were born. *They* insisted that you be given our family name –"

"And my father did not object?"

My mum laughed. "Very few Ibo men –"

I could not take it any longer. "Mum, you know it's *Igbo*, not Ibo."

"I suppose I know," she said, "but how many of the people themselves pronounce it 'Igbo'? Any way, I'll try. As I was saying, very few – er – Igbo men will come forward and claim their child, *born out of wedlock*, if they can avoid it. It suited Bernard also, for reasons which became clearer to me as time went by. He was always on the move, traveling to Europe and America, on business."

"Did you know what his business was – ?"

"I didn't, at first. But I got suspicious the day I found a wad of hundred dollar bills – and I mean United States dollar bills – in his traveling bag. He was reluctant to tell me anything, until I threatened to leave him. Even then he would only admit to being an errand boy for some highly-placed, and very powerful, individuals in the country. He made it sound as if they – the powerful persons – held a gun to his head. He said it was either that he did what he was told to do, or he would pay with his life.

"I'll confess one thing to you right away Bola. Little by little, I got sucked in. The money was good, and your father was a supremely confident man, who never believed he would get caught. I was not thinking clearly enough at the time. But although I allowed myself – as I said – to get sucked in by your father's cocky confidence, I was always appealing to him to get out of the drug trafficking thing."

"You should have left him," I said gently.

"I know I should have," she lamented, "and taken you with me. My father wanted me to return to Lagos, with you –"

"*He's* a good one, your dad," I said. "He didn't want his daughter married to an Igbo, but he did not mind my taking his family name, and would have taken me into his family if you had left my father. I don't understand."

"There's nothing to understand. When you were born, and I took you into my arms the first time, you were such a beautiful baby the midwives had to literally tear you away from my hands. I found, soon after, that you had the same effect on everyone. Your father said you were the jewel of his heart – or words to that effect. My father, who visited us soon after your birth, when he knew Bernard was away on one of his trips, fell in love with you. He said you were a reincarnation of his grandfather, Adetowun, who was reputed to be the handsomest man in our town and several of the surrounding towns."

"Did he know the nature of my father's business?"

"He didn't, and we made it an article of faith that he would never know. That was when all this effort at secrecy began. Your father, who knew well that his business was bad business, was determined to shield our two families from knowledge of what he did. He told me that you must never know. Not only that you should not know about his business, but that his identity – meaning his relationship to *you* – had to be kept secret –"

"Until when?" I asked, exasperated.

"Perhaps until *thy kingdom come*, who knows," said my mum. "He never told me clearly when everything would be revealed. All I can say for certain is that he was very much aware that his business stank to the high heavens, and he did not want his son to be a part of it, by association, should word about it get out."

"I imagine he helped you take advantage of your green card lottery win, to come and settle here, in America?" I asked.

"He did. And we set up an elaborate system of communication between us that did not involve letter-writing –"

"I can believe that," I said. "His famous letter put Chizube's father in prison for a crime he never committed."

"Don't you think I know that?" my mum wailed. "What was it Chizube's dad said at the airport, that he could not understand what brought you and Chizube together? I know what did – or, at least I thought I knew. I saw the devil's hand in it. The day you brought her here, and I realized who she was, I had to try anything I could think of, to throw a spanner in the works –"

"Sorry, mum, but you failed. Thank God!"

"Chizube's a great girl," said my mum. "Now that everything's in the open, I can wholeheartedly wish you both all the luck in the world. Her dad did what no man or woman I know, could have done. He said he had forgiven your dad. And the strange thing is – don't you see – I believe him. I really do. I looked into his eyes when he said it. And what I saw convinced me that he was telling the truth. Your dad's extremely penitent about everything, but of course he understands that Cyril's forgiveness has no weight in law."

"It's rather late in the day to be repentant about the evil thing he did to his best friend –"

"In the eyes of God, it is never too late to repent," said my mum. "It is never too late to try to make amends even in the most hopeless of circumstances. God knows – and so does your father – that had Cyril not showed up at the airport, it would have been business as usual. But I'm proud to tell you that the business we are now talking about is strictly legit. Men's Nigerian attires! That's all. And that's all it's been these – what – ten, twelve years or so. Ever since he resumed his trade travels to America. Believe me, Bola, your dad's a changed man. Except that he knew he could no longer come into this country under his real names. They'd never have given him the visa for the trips."

"So now," I asked, "is my father ready to – ?"

"Your dad knows, or expects, that the judge will – how do they say it – throw the book at him. I offered to stand trial with him –"

"You did what?"

"I offered to stand trial with him. But he would not hear of it. I still went ahead and told the police officers interrogating him that I was just as guilty as he was, but your dad told them he didn't know what I was talking about. That I was hallucinating, as usual! The last thing your dad said to me before he was taken away to jail – what's the time now – eight p.m. – some three hours ago, was that I should do everything in my power –"

The phone rang, and I rushed to pick it up. I had been expecting the call. "Hi!" I spoke into the phone.

The response came from the sweetest voice in the world: "Hi, Bola! It's me."

"I know it's you. What's the word?"

"My parents say they'll be happy for you to come see them about the matter. But only as a tiny part of the first step, if you know what I mean! In the fullness of time, things have to be done properly."

"Thank you, Chizube. That's all I need. I love you."

"I love you too. Please say hi to your mum."

My mum was waiting impatiently when I returned to my seat by her side. "Chizube said to say hi to you. What was it you were saying – about what my father said to you?"

"That he'll never be able to forgive himself if his misdeeds become an obstacle to you and Chizube, and that I should do all in my power to support you. Bola, you have my blessing if you and Chizube wish to take your relationship to its logical conclusion."

"And *his* blessing?"

"Yes, of course! Your dad's only worry was that you might throw his blessing back in his face; that you might even think of it more as a bad than a good omen."

"Nothing more need be said," I said, rising from my seat, and pulling my mum up with me. "I must go to bed now, though it's a little early. The events of the day have left me sapped of all energy. But this I know: God is great! I know now that nothing stands in the way of my making Chizube my wife. I also know that if my father is genuinely penitent of his criminal activities in the past, somehow God will shed His light on him."

THE END

About the Author

CHIKE MOMAH (Nnabuenyi): A Short Bio

CHRISTIAN CHIKE MOMAH was born on October 20, 1930 to Sidney and Grace Momah, of Obiuno, Otolo, Nnewi, Nigeria. He was educated at the St. Michael's (C.M.S.) School, Aba; the Government College, Umuahia; and the University College, Ibadan, where he earned a Bachelor's degree in History, English and Religious Studies in 1953. In 1959, he obtained the Associateship of the Library Association from the University College, London.

He was the first Nigerian graduate Land Officer (1954-1956) in the Public Service of the Eastern Nigerian government. Then he worked as a librarian in the University College, Ibadan (1956-1962); the University of Lagos (1962-1965); and the United Nations, first in Geneva, Switzerland (1966-1978), and then in New York (from 1978 till his retirement in1990).

He has four published novels: (1). FRIENDS AND DREAMS (1997); (2). TITI: BIAFRAN MAID IN GENEVA (1999); (3). THE SHINING ONES (2003); (4). THE STREAM NEVER DRIES UP (2008). He has written several articles on Nigeria and on the United States of America.

Chike Momah has been married to Ethel, nee Obi, since 1959. The couple has two sons (Chukwudi and Azuka) and one daughter (Adaora), and has been blessed with seven grandchildren, and counting.

He is an involved member of the Nigerian community in the U.S.A.:

- 1994 to 1995: one of the two Vice-Presidents of IGBO-USA, NJ, Inc., the umbrella Igbo organization in New Jersey, founded in 1994;
- 1995 to 2001: the first Executive Director of Songhai Charities, Inc., a Nigerian community-based charitable organization incorporated in New Jersey, USA;
- 1996-2000: the first President of the NNEWI UNION, New York Tri-state, Inc.
- 2000 to date: Patron, Nnewi Union, N.Y. Tri-State, Inc.;
- 2001 to date: Patron, Government College Umuahia Old Boys Association, USA, Inc. (GCUOBA, Inc.);
- 2003 to date: the first Chairman of the Board of Directors, GCUOBA, Inc.;

He has been honored with awards recognizing his involvement in the above associations and organizations, including the first meritorious awards given by Songhai Charities, Inc., and by the GCUOBA Inc., both in 2003.

In 2003, he was honored with a chieftaincy title *(Nnabuenyi-Nnewi)* by HRH Kenneth Orizu, Igwe Nnewi.

Arlington, TX 76012   August 21, 2008

Edwards Brothers,Inc!
Thorofare, NJ 08086
19 January, 2011
BA2011019